ALSO

Careful-ish
Daughter of Careful-ish
Bride of Careful-ish
Billion-Dollar Branding
Lightning Branding

To Michelle,
Remember, fangs are a last resort.
Cheers,

V-LIFE

SO IT BEGINS

HONEY PARKER

SLOW BURN MARKETING LLC

V-Life: So It Begins by Honey Parker

Published by Slow Burn Marketing LLC, PO Box 982521, Park City UT 84098

© 2024 by Honey Parker

All rights reserved. No portion of this book may be reproduced in any form without permission from the publisher, except as permitted by U.S. copyright law. This book is a work of fiction. The characters in this book and their stories are the product of the author's imagination or are used fictitiously. Any names and resemblance to actual persons, living or dead, is entirely coincidental.

For permissions, contact:

hp@slowburnmarketing.com

Cover by: Slow Burn Marketing LLC

ISBN 979-8-986205 1-4-4 Ebook

ISBN 979-8-986205 1-3-7 Paperback

CONTENTS

Prologue	1
1. Seriously?!	3
2. Company in a Leopard Coat	6
3. Sleep Well	11
4. Beware of Invitations in the Night	16
5. Call of the Wild	23
6. Testing, Testing...	29
7. Who Can You Trust?	37
8. Outed	48
9. Catch and Release	55
10. Jam Bands and Tech Talks	60
11. Circle of Friends	68
12. Smoke With Me	81
13. That's Snow Fun	87
14. A Loud Silence	96
15. The Surprise Inside	100
16. Down the Drain	108
17. The People in Your Neighborhood	113
18. Life Is Change. So Is This	124
19. Where You Been?	131
20. Comes the Fall	141
21. Messages from Friends	145
22. Say Goodnight, Gracie	150
23. Go West, Young Lady	155
24. Red Rocks and High Times	161
25. The Trouble with Grooming	169
26. A Day of Pampering	175
27. Retreat!	185
28. Go East, Young Lady	192
29. Down Time	201
30. Any Questions	212
31. Outta Here	218
32. By the Light of the Moonglow	221

33. Show Yourself	228
34. So Damn Close	235
35. One Day More	241
36. Good Night Moon	245
37. Good Morning. Or Not	254
38. Welcome to New Jersey	256
39. The Drop	261
40. Walk of Shame	265
41. Ladies' Night	268
42. There's No Place Like Home	274
43. Mazel Tov!	282
44. The Reception's the Best Part	295
45. Party in the Back	301
46. On the Road, Again	307
THANK YOU	311
Acknowledgments	313

To Melissa Jones for showing me how to be steely when it's all on you.

PROLOGUE

Clayton Junior landed on the windowsill, not excited to deliver his news. But she would sense his arrival, so there was no putting it off. Holding back his broad shoulders for maximum effect, he walked the ornate hall. Crystal sconces shook with each of his purposeful footsteps. He was about to enter the grand dining room when, from beyond the door, came a scream. This was nothing new. Clayton waited for silence to return before sliding open the heavy pocket doors. There, seated around the long mahogany table, were half a dozen young men. Dining. Feeding on some nameless woman who likely would be missed by no one.

At the head of the table, in a black satin cocktail dress with a full hood straight from the pages of *Vogue*, sat his maker. Alexandria. She'd made him. She'd made all of them at the table, and they gave their allegiance willingly. There was blood on her lips, but she was done feeding. She always drank first, then left the rest to her minions. She eyed Clayton as he strode towards her, then said his name as if it were a threat.

"C.J. Tell me."

"She's one of us."

Alexandria pushed back her hood, revealing her chiseled features. She was strikingly beautiful. "That's bad news."

"What do you want me to do?"

"Find her. Fuck with her. I'm not yet sure how I want to dispose of her."

"Yes, ma'am."

She snapped. "Don't call me ma'am. It makes me feel so old." He stood silent as she calmed. "Go. Dine. Before your friends finish it all."

"Thank you. But I grabbed a bite outside a convenience store."

Alexandria smiled a devilish smile. "You always were a sucker for snack food."

1

SERIOUSLY?!

A Jew, a vampire and a busload of regret walk into a bar...

Sadly, Sugar Bernstein already knew the punchline to that one. Sitting in the dark next to her flat tire, she told herself, *Be steely. But seriously, this blows out loud.* She thought, *What else will go wrong?* Then she thought, *Wait, no. Questions like that only invite more trouble.* And she'd already had enough trouble for ten lifetimes. Which, sadly, she might be around to watch play out.

There were no streetlights on this spit of road in the middle of 'who the hell knew where.' No one around. It was like a scene from a horror film where the ingénue is too blond to realize a hatchet-wielding killer is right behind her. *Should I look behind me? Screw it. Let's be surprised.* Just then, some nocturnal raptor began shrieking in the distance. Sugar always had an exaggerated startle response. The slightest sound could send her ducking under a desk, or a bed, or a barstool. But now, she was too bogged down by incredulity to flinch. After a long, dramatic breath that begged the question, "How the hell did I get here?" she pushed herself up from the curb, because she already knew the punchline to that one, too.

"Suck it up, buttercup."

She shook her head at the irony of the word, suck. Then, *Crap. Was that curb damp?* Wondering what lovely, new stain she might be wearing across her ass, she said, "That'll teach me to wear white denim." But she knew it wouldn't. She'd always loved the look of winter white. But that wasn't important right now, either. *Focus on the task at hand. How the crap do you change a tire on a Mercedes Sprinter van?*

In a former life, Curtis would have done it. He did all of it. The mechanical, the electrical, the plumb-ical. *That was the before-times. It's not going to help me now, is it?* Again, she reminded herself of Curtis's patented two-word phrase: "Be steely." *Fine. Where did they hide the spare on this thing, and how do I know it'll involve crawling under something?*

After she'd sold her Manhattan condo wanting/needing to get the hell out of Dodge and avoid all people, Sugar bought the converted Sprinter van. New, of course. She wasn't about to drive some stranger's old smells or, God forbid, their solids all over the country. The vehicle's length did take some getting used to. She'd almost taken out a gas pump on her first night on the road. But "almost" meant that she didn't. No harm, no foul. Just a story to tell and no one to tell it to.

Still, nothing on the damn thing was obvious. She'd endured one fumble session after another. Water lines, batteries, air conditioning. So not her skill set. Choosing the right throw pillows, making interesting lunch plans, negotiating a better price on a hotel room, those were more her strengths. After a long moment, Sugar told herself to stop procrastinating (another one of her strengths).

Her next thought, *When in doubt, YouTube it out.* YouTube had already gotten her out of oh-so-many jams. After five or six viewings of a video on how to release a tire from its cage beneath the back of the van behind the bumper, Sugar made it so.

Feeling only slightly accomplished, she was ready to move to the next step, jacking up the van to make the switch from flat to full. She wondered, *Dead to live? No. Stop that.* Sweat was rolling down her neck and strands of dark, curly hair stuck to her forehead as she got on the ground. Sliding on her belly, she did her best to position the jack below the rear axle. Feeling the wet earth seeping through her shirt she thought, *Swell, now my top matches my pants.* Loosening the lug nuts was surprisingly easy. She gave ten or so good pumps to the jack handle, and saw the van begin to rise from the ground. But before she could pull the tire off, the jack lost its footing in the mud. The van dropped to the wet earth with a heavy, decisive bounce.

"Mother of..." *What? Not God. Clearly not God.* "Mother of pearl? Shit, shit, shit! I can't even curse like I used to."

Right before completely losing whatever scrap of cool she had left, Sugar again thought back to Curtis. Handsome, kind, capable. He could always talk her off the ledge. *Be steely. Be steely. Okay. Deep breath in. Deep breath out.*

"I'm steely."

Crouching back down, Sugar got under the van and repositioned the jack. Again, she cranked the van up off the ground. *A little more. A little more. Done.* A feeling of "Look how mature I am" swept over her. But pride cometh before a fall. A baby blue minivan with a bumper sticker that read, 'Honk if you love puppies' sped past, throwing a wave of mud across Sugar's face and whatever was still winter white. And...snap!

In a flash of super-human strength, Sugar got up, grabbed the bottom of her van, and with one hand, hoisted the vehicle clear off the ground. Then, with her free hand, she grabbed the dead tire hurling it down the road at the puppy lovers. It flew through the air until, BAM!

The blue van swerved, missing the heavy projectile and continued down the road. The anemic honk of its horn echoing as it faded into the darkness. Still holding her home in the air, Sugar reached for the spare tire with her now free hand and muscled it into place.

Once it was on and the van was back on the ground, she looked at her hands. Seeing what havoc the events had wreaked upon her manicure, she called into the night, "I hate everyone. And puppies!"

2

COMPANY IN A LEOPARD COAT

As dusk fell, Sugar drove across Iowa on a secondary road at a moderate rate of speed. No need to attract attention. Against the darkening sky, the van appeared smoky gray, its blue tones fading with the light.

Driving, Sugar wondered if she should name her RV, or if that would be too cute a move for her. A moment later, a Bengal kitten with markings similar to a leopard, jumped up on her lap. Absently petting her new van-mate's head she said, "You're right. I should name you first."

Looking up at Sugar, the kitten gave a small cry. "Meeeeow-ah."

"I said you're right. Don't push it." Having the cat there made her feel like speaking aloud was okay. And the sound of her voice made the place feel less empty. Less lonely.

The cat made multiple small circles on Sugar's lap and when things were just right, came to rest in a ball. Sugar almost smiled to herself, thinking, *That's the nicest thing I've felt in some time.* Her right hand ventured back to stroke the kitten's fur. *Has there ever been a cat this silky?*

Since the flat tire incident, she'd felt bad about her hating-puppies remark. She thought, *Maybe I should get a dog.* A dog would be good company. And honestly, it would be nice to have the extra protection. *Do I still need protection? Yes. Things haven't changed that much.* But, of course, they had. It seemed that canines were no longer into her. She'd met with snarls from the two dogs she'd tried to adopt, and then, ultimately, from the people selling them. *Fine,* she thought. *Who needs a dog? If you don't want me, I don't want you.* Which had also been her motto with men. Clean breaks. She never understood when a girlfriend would say, "I'm having him over for dinner so I can tell him we're done." *Why would you want to choke down a meal before dropping that boom? Or worse, dropping the boom and* then *choking down a meal. No.* She'd told Curtis on their second date, "If this ever stops working for you, a phone call will suffice." He, of course, laughed it off. Right from the start, Curtis knew how to manage her crazy.

But just when Sugar thought she'd be forever pet-less, she came across a squat, older woman at a gas station holding a small box. Both the woman and the box looked like they'd seen better days. As she passed, Sugar peered inside the box, seeing one tiny kitten. It was a light gold color with dark brown spots and large ears that made it look like a mini wild cat.

The squat woman croaked, "Want her? She's yours."

"How much?"

The woman shrugged. "A pack of Marlboro Light, 100s? Menthol."

"Seriously?"

"I can't give this thing away. Everyone around here thinks she's some fuckin' baby mountain lion. Gonna grow up and rip their throats out. Fuckin' idiots. You want her? Take her. I just wanna go home, nuke a pot pie and watch *Real Housewives of Bullshit County*. Get me my smokes and I'll take out my throat the old-fashioned way, with cancer."

Slowly reaching her hand to the cat, Sugar wondered if she'd once again be rejected by an animal. But the kitten leaned its warm body against the back of Sugar's hand, closed its eyes, and began purring softly. *Fine. Dogs don't want me, I'll go cat.* Still staring at the spotted feline, she agreed to the terms. "Done."

Sugar bought the woman three packs of mentholated cancer for her troubles and drove away with a new, furry van-mate. She had no fear of the tiny beast ripping her throat out and no delusion that it would protect her from, well, anything. Just company. Life is compromise. And so was whatever it was she was currently living.

"My pet should have a name."

Sugar wondered, *Spot?* She liked the in-your-face-to-dogs nature of it, but would others find it too obvious? Spotted cat. Spot? Then she thought, *What others?*

"What say you? Do you like Spot?"

The kitten had no visible reaction to the question.

"Fine. Be that way. I didn't like it either."

The more Sugar drove, the more she felt the distance grow between herself and her former life. She'd gone from a driven advertising creative director with a full social calendar to a lone wolf with zero attachments or obligations. Just one horrible task to accomplish, if that's what you'd call it. Just thinking about doing it made her feel crazy. But she had to try. She owed Curtis at least that much.

She looked to the kitten. "Yes, cat. I've sunk to revenge. Don't judge. Now, ask me if I have a plan."

She had none. And there was no timetable for her revenge, just a need.

Her mind drifted. In her "new now" she realized she missed no one from her office. Considering her extensive circle of friends, she realized she didn't miss any of them, either. *How can that be? I had real friends. Good friends. People I cared about, shared things with, went out of my way for. But how could any of them relate to me now?* In a flash, they had nothing but their past in common. In truth, she no longer felt like she deserved their friendship.

After several more hours of driving, she was beginning to tire and pulled into a Walmart parking lot. She'd quickly learned that most

Walmarts allow RVers to park overnight for free. The thinking was probably that these travelers will eventually end up coming into the store to make a purchase. Beer, crispy-shaped corn products, baby wipes. Like many people living on the road with limited space for water storage, Sugar found baby wipes to be one of the smartest things to keep in supply. *In this world, there is always something to wipe.*

Parking as far from the huge, boxy building as possible, Sugar cut the engine and rubbed her eyes. *How long till dawn? At least a couple of hours.*

As much as she wanted to stretch out and think about nothing, she should play into Walmart's genius plan and go buy a few items. Top of the list was cat food and litter. Braving the harsh lighting inside the store, Sugar made zero eye contact as she wove her way past the other shoppers. But her hearing now felt sharper, and strangers' personal conversations were seeping into her brain.

Passing a fifty-ish husband and wife, both rail-thin, she could hear them arguing over pants.

"I need more room in the seat. I like room."

"Jack, they're too big. You look like you're wearin' a goddamn diaper."

"Someday, I will wear a goddamn a diaper. Now I'll have room."

"And some day, I'll leave you for a man who doesn't shit his pants."

In her old life, Sugar would be loving that little nugget of banter. But now, she just wanted everyone out of her head.

Reaching the pet section, she stood in front of her options. Having worked on the Happy Cat Cat Litter campaign the previous year, she thought, *Why not support my work?* She grabbed a large box, then impulse grabbed a small mouse toy.

"I'm a sucker."

Next, food. Even thinking about the smell of wet cat food made her feel queasy. She wondered if her sense of smell was now more acute or if it was just her imagination. Narrowing down to the bags of dry food meant there were still too many options. So, she grabbed an orange bag with a picture of a calico kitten.

"Why not?"

At checkout, the lanky tattooed dude at the register told her why not. "That stuff's no good."

"What stuff?"

"That food. It's shit. Filled with cereal."

"I like cereal." She wasn't lying. Sugar used to feel like a bowl of cereal with ice cold milk was a brilliant late-night treat.

"Cereal sucks for cats. Cats need meat. You should go back and get the wet stuff. In the cans."

"You should ring me up."

Lanky Tattooed Dude squinted at her, clearly struggling to keep his thoughts to himself. He rang her up and bagged her bad choices. As with all of Sugar's small financial interactions now, she paid in cash. She'd seen too many movies where someone was tracked down by their charge card and she didn't want to be found.

Sugar was almost out the door, some fifty yards away from Lanky Tattooed Dude, when he whispered under his breath, "Some people shouldn't be pet owners."

Without looking back, she called out, "And some people should work the night shift at Walmart."

3
SLEEP WELL

Back in the van, Sugar stretched out on her bunk and poured a few bits of cat food into her hand. She counted eight. The nameless kitten had no problem with the dry bounty. The crunching made Sugar think, *Another reason to get the dry stuff.* Misophonia, a condition where people have strong reactions to certain mouth sounds, had plagued her since she was a kid. Just thinking of this kitten smacking up wet food made her squirm. "I made the right choice."

Next, Sugar pulled her tablet from its charging station on the narrow shelf by her bed. The plan was to do research until she fell asleep. Instead, she started assessing her home's interior. *What does it need? A plant?* The wood-slat ceiling gave the space a warm feel, but it was all still generic. Almost nothing personal. She'd been unable to make herself put up pictures of family or friends, thinking *I can't bring them with me on this journey.* She'd slipped a photo of Curtis under the mattress when she first hit the road, but had yet to find the strength to look at it.

The only unique item visible was a blue and green afghan her grandmother had made. She wondered, *Was it disrespectful to bring it?* Sugar considered her grandmother, Esther. A feisty dame in her time. A hatmaker who enjoyed hard work, a clean house, and straight vodka. *Maybe she'd be okay with it. Although, she'd no doubt have more than a few choice words of advice. Choice, yet practical. Like, "You can't only shop at night. You'll never get the good cold cuts." Or, "Eat carrots and you won't look so pale. If anyone asks why your skin looks orange, tell them you're pre-tanning for a trip to Boca."*

Enjoying the thought, Sugar finally settled into her reading. In an attempt to learn something, anything about her *condition*, she'd taken to reading whatever she could find on the topic. Of course, there was no such thing as a textbook. No how-to pamphlets. It was all novels, novellas, ancient myths, and folklore. Her Kindle was now filled with relevant titles. Starting with the obvious, she'd taken on Bram Stoker. *Why not?* His was a pivotal work and as she now knew, the basis for so many current beliefs, like no sunlight and no reflections. Both of those she now knew were mostly accurate. She could make out her muddled reflection, but it was more shapes than anything. And there were things she hadn't known, like requiring an invitation to enter a home. Although she'd yet to test that one. While the book was only somewhat informative, she'd enjoyed the read. Or, the first half of it, where Jonathan Flynn Harker travels to the Count. It was all so dark and suspense-filled, its details carefully teased out. Discovering the Count's surprising skills alongside Jonathan made her intrigued as to what she herself might be able to pull off. But when the story moved to London, the assumed female frailties o' the day filled Sugar with frustration and she'd huffed her way through to the end, rooting for the villain.

From there she moved to something more current. The *Twilight* series. But, perhaps trying to break into the popular tales via the movies was a bad choice. It was all high school angst, red juicy boy-lips, and endless shots of teen-girl brooding. The final nail in the coffin, a sentiment which was the only thing about the first movie that made Sugar laugh, was the baseball game.

She'd jokingly ranted, "Who picks baseball as a break in the tension? Why not something even slower? Fancy a game of cricket? How about a few rounds of Mahjong before the next bloodletting?"

Learning nothing concrete from the films, she ventured back to the beginning: a text by John William Polidori written in 1819, which was the oldest related story she could find in print. It had been a challenge to get used to the language. And the portrait of people being so weak that upsetting situations could throw them into such devastation they simply died was, well, hard to swallow.

The book she was now reading, *Varney the Vampire*, was set in the English countryside in the mid-1800s. Two brothers, almost positive their new neighbor was the mysterious figure who'd visited their sister's bedroom the night before, argue over whether or not to confront the man. What if they were wrong? The social misstep would be inexcusable! Sugar couldn't believe these two fools were too trapped in polite etiquette to confront this evil and save their sister. "Schmucks."

Several slow blinks let her know she had reached her limit. Frustration and fatigue were winning. She laid her head back.

"This is such bullshit, cat."

Dropping the antique tale of the naïve verses the un-dead on her chest, she slipped into sleep. The book had done at least part of its job. But while her sleep was deep, it was far from restful. That was her new normal. Since the change, Sugar's dreams were more like journeys. She was traveling back to places in her life and experiencing them with an echoey realness. This time, Sugar was jumping from one challenging moment of her life to another. A stream of seemingly minor events where she'd regretted not sticking up for herself. Having been a strong person, these lapses stung. Yet, here they all were and she was powerless to change them.

Nine-year-old Sugar was in grade-school English. Her twin brother David sat behind her. The teacher, Miss Whitsett, a large, smug woman wearing a large bland print, was trying to shame Sugar for not doing her homework.

"I see Sugar didn't feel the need do her homework. I suppose she thinks she's better than the rest of you."

The truth was Sugar had done her work but was afraid to turn it in. She was aware she couldn't spell as well as the other kids. Current-day Sugar knew she was dyslexic, and not stupid, but nine-year-old Sugar hadn't learned that yet.

The teacher continued, "Do the rest of you think Sugar is better than you?"

Young Sugar was holding back angry tears.

Current Sugar whispered in her younger ear, "Don't pay any attention to that cow. You're smart. You'll do great. Better than her. Miss Whitsett keeps a bottle of Seagram's in her desk drawer and in two years she'll get picked up for shoplifting a blouse from Banana Republic that wasn't even her size. She'll lose her job and grow old and bitter writing content for a vitamin website from her dump in Hackensack."

When Sugar looked up, the classroom was gone. She was seventeen and working her summer job in her father's family's department store. She'd loved working with all the clothes. Women's and men's. But this day found her in the shoe section. God, she hated the shoe section. All those feet. And there *she* was. Her. The ample, angry woman who became a store legend and turned Sugar into the butt of endless jokes. Current-day Sugar cringed watching herself try to help the woman cram her enormous foot into the tiny shoe.

As nicely as she could, seventeen-year-old Sugar suggested, "Why don't you let me grab you the next size?" knowing the woman actually needed to go up at least two sizes.

The woman barked, "You're just not pushing hard enough. I've always been an eight. You think I don't know my own shoe size?"

Saying nothing, young Sugar returned to pushing. As the woman grunted, people in the store were starting to pay attention to the struggle, including Sugar's father and two uncles. Three men with the same face.

Current-day Sugar wanted to look away, knowing what was coming. She called to herself, "Get out of there!"

But young Sugar was trapped. She pushed again. And the woman pushed harder. Then Sugar. Then the woman. Finally, the woman pushed so hard she lost all bodily control and broke wind right in Sugar's face. Current day Sugar was surprised to see that the expulsion didn't actually blow her hair back as it had in all the subsequent retellings of the story. And there would be many retellings.

Through tears of laughter, her father would say to his brothers, "Watch. Dollars to donuts, she'll buy those damn shoes."

His brother Sal, still laughing said, "I should be as sure of goin' to heaven."

Sugar knew it to be true. The woman bought the tiny shoes. *Maybe she'd put them on a keychain.*

Before Sugar could tell her younger self to roll with it, she was flashed forward to her New York apartment. There she was, cradling Curtis' limp body. He was dead in her arms. She looked up at the woman who'd caused them both unfathomable pain.

Devastated all over again, current Sugar thought, *How did I allow myself to be drawn in by her? By evil? How could I have committed such a transgression? I'm a savvy person. I should have seen it Why didn't I see it?*

But instead of leaping at the woman and fighting to the death, New York Sugar simply stared as tears rolled down her face.

Current-day Sugar had had time to process. To hate. She looked at Curtis, her love. Then, ready to unleash the full force of her venom, dove for Alex's throat.

But all she grabbed was her own bedding.

At Sugar's abrupt movement, the nameless cat jumped straight up in the air.

It was midday. Fortunately, the sun outside was unable to penetrate the dark tinted windows of the van. She scooped up the kitten, holding her close and wondering what the hell she was doing.

She whispered, "Should I just stop? End this now? What chance do I have of paying Alex back for Curtis? Do I even deserve a chance after what I did?"

4

BEWARE OF INVITATIONS IN THE NIGHT

Parked under an oak tree on a suburban Illinois street, Sugar was experiencing one of the benefits of her RV choice. It let her be stealth. She could park without flagging to the world that anyone was inside. No slide-outs or pop-ups that had to be employed before stretching out. She had no bikes, kayaks, or off-road strollers hanging from a sports rack. Just a simple parked van that said to the world, 'Move along. Nothing to see here.'

But she wasn't sleeping. In the dim light above her fold-up desk, Sugar sat reviewing her chart. All the notes she'd been keeping from her research, including personal trial and error, now went onto the chart. She'd marked down what books had mentioned what rules. How folklore changed from region to region. What years saw shifts in common beliefs. Few traits were constant across the board. Even the ability to walk in daylight was challenged in several stories. In her own short-lived experience, daylight was a non-starter. The first time she ventured into sunshine, she started blistering in seconds. And not those sexy blisters the boys like so much. The best she could do now was slather on SPF 80, put on a hat, sunglasses, make a mad dash, and hope. Although, she was definitely a faster runner now, and getting faster.

"Is that my lemonade from lemons, cat? Can I be an Olympic miler? No. They run that during the day. And, right back to lemons."

Sugar heard the kitten purring as she crunched down her food.

"Bitch."

God, I want cereal. A little Special K.

The cat was eating crunchy bits, so Sugar wanted crunchy bits. She had always been crazy suggestible when it came to food. If someone was eating a donut, she wanted a plain cruller. If she walked past a steakhouse, she pined for a New York strip, rare. If she saw an ad for Doritos, she wanted a bag. And she didn't even like Doritos.

How long has it been since I enjoyed food?

She flashed back to the first time she tried to eat after the "incident." Curtis had made her a small lemon tart to cheer her up. As if.

He sat down next to her on the edge of their fireplace and handed her the treat. "There's nothing a little tart can't fix."

"That's what she said."

They both laughed at what may have been their last joke together. But the tart fixed nothing. It actually made things worse. After only a few minutes, the retching began. The tart itself must have been about two ounces, but Sugar threw up at least twice as much.

Curtis attempted to make light of it. "Want me to hold your hair?"

"For eternity?"

We didn't get eternity, did we, baby?

It seemed both like yesterday and forever ago. Sugar chided herself, *Stop it. Solve the problem at hand.*

She'd found over time that she could eat a tiny bit without turning completely inside out. But she had to go slowly, chewing for a long time before swallowing. Plus, she didn't seem to benefit from it, strength-wise. So, Sugar was now going long stretches without eating and was noticeably dropping those extra pounds. Something she'd always struggled to accomplish was now simply happening. But she was running out of extra pounds.

Sugar wondered if she could monetize this. Turn it into a diet book. *If I somehow live through all of this, I'll need an ongoing source of income.* She muttered, "What would I call my book?"

Her advertising brain ran through the possibilities. She mused aloud, "Dying to Be Thin? Suck Away the Pounds? The Midnight Diet?"

Remembering there already was a book, *Eat Right for Your Blood Type*, she wondered about getting into affiliate sales.

Finally, in a flash of ironic inspiration, a tough-love title came to mind. "'Lose Some Bloody Weight!' Kitten, we could make a splash in the UK market. Lose Some Bloody Weight. What do you think?"

Kitten let out a long, slow, "Mee-yooooow-ah."

"Fine. But it's good."

"Meow-ah."

"Who's in advertising, you or me?" Kitten just stared and Sugar got off her high horse. "You're right. Neither of us."

Having won the argument, the feline climbed onto the bunk, bounced several times, fought with the air, then pawed herself a nest, and settled in. Sugar envied her peace.

A moment later, the sound of her new burner phone broke the peace. Having cut off all other ties, the only person she'd given the number to was her brother. She probably should have cut him off as well, but they were twins and had been each other's special person since day one. She thought, *I'm weak.*

After the fifth ring, Sugar picked up the call and took it to her bed, careful to not disturb her bunkmate. "Yeah?"

"Great to hear you, too."

Her brother's voice hit her like a warm blanket she wasn't allowed to curl up in. She even missed his snark.

"Sorry."

"Bad timing?"

Sugar let out a slight laugh. All their natural lives, David, or "D," as she called him, had the uncanny ability to phone at the absolute least opportune moments. As she was running out the door for work. As she was sitting down to dinner. As she was lying down to sex. But there was now no such thing as a good time.

"No. It's fine."

"So, where in the world is Sugar Bernstein?"

"On the road."

"Can you be less specific."

"I'll try harder next time."

David let out a heavy breath, then began again. "I miss you, Shug."

"Yeah, I miss you too, D." Absently, Sugar pet the kitten.

"But not enough to come stay with us."

"Let's not do this again."

"We have that huge guest room with a private bath. Or, I could convert the garage. Amy would love the company. And you'd get to watch Sarah grow—"

"I appreciate it. I do. But I can't be with people right now."

"Not even the bestest brother in the world?" No response. "Fine. But I don't think Curtis would have wanted you to go on like this. I know I can't imagine how sad you are. But you still have a lot of life to live."

More silence from Sugar's end as she thought, *So much more life to live than you know.* How could she expect him to understand? She couldn't. Not even the "bestest" brother could. And D. was the bestest. A good guy. A great friend. He lived on a nice suburban cul-de-sac and worked a nice suburban job at a company that did background checks. Honestly, she had no idea what he actually did. In her mind, D. sat in his office and moved the stack of papers from the right side of the desk over to the left. Then he moved the stack on the left over to the right.

The kitten strolled up Sugar's arm and cried at her face. "Meow-ah."

"Do I hear a cat?"

"A kitten."

"You got a kitten?"

"Don't sound so surprised."

"No. Sorry. I think it's great. I love that you have some company out there. It borders on...optimistic."

"Let's not get carried away."

"Well, I'm glad. What's its name?"

"I haven't gotten that far."

More silence. She just didn't know what to say to him. She wanted to spill her guts out onto his lap like she did when they were kids. But how could she burden him with this? And, she had to admit, the truth would only make her sound crazy.

She thought, *Wouldn't that be nice, if I was just crazy and none of this was real?* "Listen, thanks for the call..."

"I know what, 'listen' means. But you don't get off that easy. Amy and I want a confirmation that you'll be at Sarah's *bat-mitzvah*. I gave you tons of warning so you can't say you have other plans. April 17th, noon. Promise me you'll be there."

Wow, that's a lot of real-life right between the eyes. Then she did the math. "Noon?"

"Saturday, April 17th."

"What about a Friday night? Wouldn't a Friday night feel more special? With the candles and everything." Hearing herself, she wondered why she was arguing this. *Yes, a night event would be easier for my condition, but there's just no way I could endure an evening of relatives and their endless interrogation. And facing the folks would be...What would it be? I can't even.*

Not knowing what was in Sugar's head, D. pressed on. "Have you priced a bat-mitzvah lately? A night event is almost double. Oh, and I know Sarah's going to ask you to do an aliyah."

Sugar's head was spinning. *How can I stand up on the bema in synagogue? Will the place go up in flames or simply explode?* It was all too much. But then she thought, *Calm down. The event is months away. Maybe I'll be done being undead by then and just be dead dead.* She wondered, *Is getting out of a bat-mitzvah invite by killing myself a new low? Probably. But a girl can dream.*

Not wanting to feel so self-absorbed, she started, "D., If you need help with the cost..."

"I told Amy you'd probably offer. No. But thanks. We're good. Tight but good." He laughed a bit. "Hey, we could take a page from cousin Mitzy's bar-mitzvah for Jeffrey and just serve dried-out, day-old coffee cake."

Suddenly, as if nothing had changed in her life, Sugar was thrown back to the before-times. Just hearing her cousin Mitzy's name triggered her standard impersonation of her mother, and every other woman in the family. In her best Philly accent, Sugar whined, "We drove over an hour for that kid and all we got was one lousy piece of coffee cake. I could have just as easily stayed home and had an Entenmann's."

David laughed. "Poor Jeffery will forever be That Kid. You know he's a podiatrist now."

"That plus a piece of old coffee cake and he's a total swipe-right."

David laughed again. Finally, after another lapse into silence that said this chat has come to its end, he added, "But seriously, Sarah's counting on you being there. I'm gonna tell Mom and Dad we spoke."

"Don't."

"They should know you're okay."

What does okay mean anymore? "Just leave it."

"You're putting me in a spot."

"I'm sorry."

"Fine. I won't say anything. For now."

"Thanks."

"Drive safe, and don't be a stranger."

"Just strange."

"Go with a strength. Love you."

"You, too." Clicking off the call, she thought, *I should never have tried to stay connected to D. It's too damn hard. And selfish. And dangerous.*

Her stomach made a loud gurgling sound. "Damn, I want that Entenmann's."

5
CALL OF THE WILD

The pain of not eating was becoming unbearable. For several nights, Sugar had stayed parked in eastern Kansas. She'd pushed through Missouri because Missouri sounded too much like misery. *Too redundant.* The van was now parked in the middle of a stand of trees, away from any civilized life. Sugar was making a serious go at her new plan of starving well before the bat-mitzvah. Curled up in her bunk, she wondered how long it took to starve. Then her thoughts ventured to Curtis and how she would never get to avenge him. She had failed. When she'd first left New York, Sugar thought she had one task to accomplish before expiring: Find Alex and make her hurt. But now, that seemed an impossible achievement. She was weak, ill-informed and in pain. Her guilt rivaled her hunger. The purring of the kitten helped relax Sugar's mind and she finally fell asleep. Or did she pass out?

Over the last few days, there'd been someone lurking in her dreams. A man. An interloper in her memories. He seemed to be studying the scenes from Sugar's life. She wanted him gone and decided that in her next dream, she'd try to maintain the presence of mind to confront him.

Today's dream had her in her parent's house in suburban New Jersey. She and David were high school age and sitting at the dinner table. The family always ate dinner together. It was nice, even when it got loud. The room was decorated in classic, early upper-middle-class suburban with too many collectables. Or as her father called them, dustables. Where was her older brother, Barry? *He must have been in college by then.*

Seeing herself, she thought, *Look how big my hair was. I have better product now.*

The sound of her parents arguing out in the kitchen was wonderfully familiar. Not angry arguing. Just the arguing that Jewish people do instead of listening.

She heard her father say, "Faye, Faye, Faye, would you stop and hear me out?"

Her mother quipped in her usual way—the way a psychologist who never works on herself does. "Why should I hear you out? Perhaps, just perhaps you should hear me out."

"I've heard you out."

"No, you have not."

"Fine. Let's hear it."

"Forget it."

"What?"

"Just forget it."

"I'm telling you to say what's on your mind."

"No. I'm done. There's nothing on my mind."

"Jesus, Faye!"

Sugar's mother entered the dining room carrying a platter of spaghetti and meatballs. Except for Friday night brisket, Italian cooking was Faye's thing. She was mid-size in every way. Not tall. Not short. Not fat. Not thin. David favored her. He nudged Sugar under the table, signaling he was about to make a play.

"Hey Mom, I'm curious. What's on your mind?"

Faye looked back at her husband, "Don't be a jerk."

"What? That was your son. Not me." Henry, the parent whom

Sugar favored, was coming to join his sitcom family at the dinner table.

Winking at Sugar as she served, Faye said, "No. Tonight, he's *your* son. I'll take Sugar." And just like that, the tension was broken and they were back to being a laughing, loving family enjoying their sarcastic ways.

Sugar asked, "D., didn't you have a test today?" She knew he did and that he'd done well. But as David started sharing his accomplishments in calculus, Sugar noticed movement behind him. Someone was there, trying to sniff him.

Who the hell are you?

Determined to get back some control of her existence, she thought, *Take action!*

Current Sugar got up, leaving her high-school self sitting at the table to support her brother's calc results. Approaching the space behind D., she saw the trails of someone moving towards the kitchen, like colored streaks left in their wake. Picking up her pace, Sugar seemed to glide over the floor as she closed in on the interloper. She could now make out that the man was cloaked in a long, ornate emerald-green jacket. Just as Sugar reached out to grab the stranger's shoulder, the uninvited dinner guest turned.

His face was now inches from Sugar's as he hissed, "She has a message for you, Sugar." Then his eyes went wide as he bared his fangs.

Sugar recoiled, "No!"

Snapping out of the dream, Sugar sat up bolt-straight in her bunk, causing the kitten to leap up, causing Sugar to grab her chest and cry, "Shit, cat!" The kitten leapt up several more times.

Sugar listened to the sound of her own heavy breathing. She'd failed, again. This was all too much. She wanted to go home. To her back-in-time home where everything was sarcastic and loving and possible.

Ready to forgive the outburst, the kitten cautiously approached Sugar and settled on her legs. Returning to a semi-calm state, Sugar could no longer escape her wrenching stomach pain. It was like the lining of her gut was being scraped with knives.

"It's time." She gently lifted the kitten and placed her on a pillow. "Sorry kiddo. I have to go pick up dinner."

She stood and lowered her jeans without unzipping them. "How much weight have I lost, cat?"

There was no way to know. When she was twenty, okay twenty-five pounds overweight, there was no such thing as getting on a scale. Even on her five foot, nine frame, it was too much extra weight and who would want to confront that? Pulling her jeans back up, she looked at the baggy ass of her pants in the bathroom mirror.

"Damn. I have room for a diaper."

Her stomach squealed with a sound she hadn't heard before and Sugar winced from a fresh shot of pain. *Press on.*

She mused, "What should I wear?" then thought, *Who cares? No. Be smart. Athleisure wear will keep movement unencumbered. Am I really going to do this? Stop. Don't think about it.* Her father had always said, "If you're going to do something, don't think about it. Do it." She was pretty sure this wasn't what Henry had in mind when he'd said it, but it was still sound advice. Her father always had good advice, even if he didn't take it himself. She pulled on a jog bra, the black leggings with the green marbling, and a matching green marbled swing top.

Catching her reflection she asked, "Cat, why did I need this madness to look good in gym clothes? There is no justice."

Pulling open the van's sliding side door, she peered into the night then called behind her, "Guard the place while I'm gone." There was no response.

Stepping out into the darkness, Sugar had no real plan other than putting an end to the intense stabbing in her gut. *Will I actually do it this time?* She had stood in the dark several times before, ready-ish, only to stop herself and skulk back to her bunk, a failure. It all seemed too ridiculous. But that was part of the struggle. She was afraid of being a success. *So much conflict.*

Another sharp stab caused her to double over. She thought, *Somehow, this ends tonight.* For a long moment, she stood stone-still listening, waiting for a sound to tell her where to go. But it wasn't a sound that finally caught her attention. It was a smell.

What is that? It's gamey, yet light. Rabbit?

The smell was so complex and multi-layered, she could virtually see the animal. Its white and tan fur. The notch in one of its ears. The slight twitching of its nose. She felt her eye teeth begin to reach out. A moment later, she was moving forward. Crossing a field, then dodging trees. She was closing in. At the last second, she saw the adorable little bunny turn to her, wide-eyed. One swift moment later, Sugar was on the ground with the creature's blood running down her chin. The feeling was dizzying, yet the world was coming into sharper focus. Energy was slowly returning to her as her pain was subsiding. Sugar held the dead animal against her face, half mourning, half savoring.

She'd done it: crossed a threshold she could never walk back through. At least her pain was finally gone. Not knowing what to do next, Sugar decided to dig a small hole and bury the rabbit's carcass.

Am I burying the evidence? No.

She wanted to show respect to the animal that, for the moment, had ended her suffering and saved her non-life.

Trying to remember the details of the event, she wondered how swift the kill was. *Could it have been considered kosher?* In the Jewish religion, the laws of kosher govern how an animal should be slaughtered. The idea is to do the deed quickly, slicing the animal's jugular, so it would be insensitive to pain. It was meant to be humane. Of course, she knew what she just did was not kosher in any way, but she liked the idea of being as humane as possible, given the inhumane circumstances. It was a way to rationalize away the guilt. Sugar had been raised to cultivate guilt like a crop and she was now a professional farmer.

Sometime later, she slid open the door to the van, thinking about her stash of wipes.

Would blood-wipes be something I could monetize? Tagline, It gets the red out. Then she remembered that Visine already owned that one.

Before she got to wipe away the remaining evidence, she spotted the fluffy kitten drinking water from the slow drops coming out of the kitchenette faucet. The feline looked up at Sugar's blood-stained face with its sweet eyes. In that moment, Sugar was sure her kitten was the cutest thing on the planet. She stepped inside, scooped up her roommate and the two laid down on the bunk.

Sugar whispered her confession. "I just killed Thumper."

Then she wondered what or who would be next.

6

TESTING, TESTING...

Dusk cast no shadow on Sugar as she sat outside the Sprinter van in her one and only folding chair. She'd seen no reason to buy a set. From under the canopy, she looked to the distant mountains, considering her choice to head west. She had no real connection to anyone out here and little knowledge of the region beyond her few ski trips with friends. Maybe she'd headed west because driving south would be too much like old family road trips to visit relatives in Miami. The pattern was always the same: argument, lunch break, argument, dinner break, argument, sleep break, rinse and repeat as they drove the miles to the Sunshine State. That was enough to send her in another direction.

Out here she hit patches, like this one, of almost complete emptiness. Just breathtaking landscapes and few people to enjoy them. There truly was a purple mountain's majesty out here. She wondered, *Do I deserve to enjoy something so majestic? How many members of the Bambi universe can I take out before my heart turns completely black?*

Not reading her book, she wrapped her arms around herself,

bracing against the slight chill. The kitten's head popped out of the front of Sugar's puffy jacket like a gopher from its hole.

"You warm in there, kiddo?"

"Meow-ah."

"You're welcome. Want me to read to you?"

Sugar lifted her tablet. She'd put down her last book. Too plodding. This book was from the early 1900s. But, to her disappointment, it too was bogged down by a blanket of slow-moving melodrama. These were a people not used to action. They clearly had no ESPN or Instagram Reels and overthought everything. "Ready, cat?"

The kitten purred.

"Okay." Sugar read, "'Barnaby'...that's our hero, cat. 'Barnaby took several long strides across the garden to the spot where Lavinia had stood, sick that he may have given her location away. The creature seemed able to read his every thought. Quite sure he was standing in the very spot where the beast had flown away with Lavinia frozen in horror, he found nothing. Surely there would be some evidence. Some sign of struggle. Yet, upon his arrival, he saw nothing. Had the creature vanished with Lavinia so completely? Flown into the night with her in its horrid grasp? Barnaby questioned his own sanity. These things, these visons, if real meant his beloved was in the possession of a horror beyond reason. If only he were simply going mad and Lavinia was safe somewhere and free to love another. He could live with that.'"

"Meow-ah."

"I know, cat. Pretty sappy stuff."

Although, she herself had wished she was simply going crazy. So, not completely off base. Sugar thought about the powers of this 'creature.' *A skill for mind reading. But maybe that's just heightened intelligence. Intelligence has been pretty much a standard trait. Am I smarter now than before?*

"Cat, ask me a question. Anything. Math. Science. State capitals." But, the cat was unwilling to test her.

Not being able to recall a time in her past when she could deadlift a van, she knew she was stronger than before. And faster, for sure. And since her meal, or meals, her stamina was up. She could run for several miles without feeling winded. This book was the earliest she'd come across that clearly had mind reading as a skill. *Do I have that one? Can I read minds?*

Not being around people, she had no idea how to test herself. *Wait! Brainstorm!* Reaching into her jacket and gently pulling out the kitten, she held the feline so its tiny head was against her own forehead.

She whispered, "Cat, I'm going to tell you what you're thinking."

Sugar concentrated, trying to feel her pet's thoughts. Thinking of Obi Wan in *Star Wars*, she told herself, *Reach out with your feelings.* So, she reached out, but after several attempts found she was just making things up. Obvious things. "Feed me." "I love you." "Why haven't you named me yet?" "Have you lost weight?" Laughing at her own ridiculousness, she put kitten back in her jacket, her temples burning from the effort.

"Maybe mind reading is just another myth, cat."

Still, that flying thing, that would be nice. Not as safe to test as mind reading. Do I dare? Sugar considered ways to test flying that wouldn't get her entered on *America's Funniest Home Videos*. A running leap to see if she was able to long jump farther than in highschool? It seemed safe-ish, and she was up for something that wasn't sitting and reading.

After putting the kitten in the van, Sugar looked out towards the now-dark horizon, noting that her night vision was crisp and clear. Focusing in on her surroundings, she saw a small stream to her left. *How wide is it from bank to bank? Nine feet, ten maybe?* That would be her first test. Getting into a low stance that emulated an athlete on a sprinter's starting blocks, she pulled in a determined breath, and took off running. Approaching the water, she felt confident. *I can do this.* Pushing off from her left foot, she leaped easily over the span. Success.

Sugar looked back across the small divide. *Was that something I could have done before? Did it feel like I'd flown? Maybe a bit of a glide. Or maybe I'm pretending, like mind reading the cat. Hard to say. Next test?*

Farther upstream, the divide was wider. If she had to guess, she'd give it about twenty-five feet. There would be no question as to whether she could have done that before. She couldn't have. Getting back into her runner's stance, she told herself, *I can fly,* and took off. As she sped closer to the near bank, she spotted a grassy area on the far side and mentally marked it as her landing zone. *Eye on the prize. Failure is not an option. Well...* Again, using her left foot for takeoff, Sugar leapt across the water feeling herself almost running through the air in slow motion as she crossed the expanse. She landed on the grass as planned, but the lush ground cover was hiding a gopher hole. Defeat was snatched from victory as she rolled her ankle and smeared wet grass stains along her pants.

"Son of a...!" Pain shot up her leg as she grabbed her ankle. "Crap, crap, crap!"

After letting the initial shock of pain pass, she tried getting up, but a new wave of pain filled her leg, dropping her back to the ground.

Without thinking she cried out in frustration. "Shit, Curtis!"

Then came the emptiness that always followed knowing he was no longer there to answer her. She was utterly on her own.

Assessing the situation, she tried to guess how long it would take to crawl back to the van. Sugar sat on the grass gripping her ankle thinking, *I can do more now but I'm just as big a klutz.*

Feeling sorry for herself, she let her imagination drift to what she wished for in this moment. Her fantasy was clear and had dimension, as if it were a hologram. She could see him.

Curtis came up behind her. "Get up, you idiot."

Gazing up at him with a look of self-deprecation, she reached her hand towards his. "Save me, fine sir."

"Don't I always?" He pulled her up and placed her arm over his shoulder. Leaning into him, she breathed in his scent. A mix of outdoors and man products. *I could dine out on that smell for a week. Yes. I will definitely let him have his way with me later.* Her head swirled and her fantasy moved to a session of making love to Curtis in the comfort of their bed. The best version of their sessions, where it started slow. Almost too slow. Making her crave him even more, if that was possible. As they went, they seemed to breathe as one. She could almost feel his pelvis pushing against hers as the heat built inside her. It was intoxicating. As they were about to hit what promised to be a climax for the records, Curtis whispered in her ear, "You should really name that cat."

Snap. The spell was broken. She was alone.

"Goddamn you, Curtis."

If she'd had any tears in her at all, she would have used them right then. *I miss you so fucking much.* The loss was almost too immense to bear. "Fuck everyone."

Sugar sat in her self-pity until she was finally ready to cowgirl up. Wiping her brow, she forced her lip to stop quivering and thought, *Be steely*. On inspection, she realized her ankle no longer seemed to hurt. Not really. Maybe a lingering discomfort. *Should I try to stand? Why not?* Getting back to her feet, she tested putting weight on her bad leg. No pain. *Is quick healing a new skill or did I imagine it hurt more than it did?* At the moment, she didn't care. With her eyes focused on the contours of the ground, she cautiously walked back to the van, waiting for pain that never came.

But as she got closer, she noticed the van's door was slightly ajar. *Did I leave the door open? No. No way.* Sugar picked up her pace. Her one and only thought was the kitten. *Did she get out? Shit.* She was about to call to the cat then thought, *What if I'm not alone?*

As quietly as possible, she moved to the far side of the van and tried peering into the window. It was hard to make out anything through the tinted glass. All she could tell was there was no movement. It felt empty, but she didn't want to take any chances. She looked around. Spotting a branch on the ground, Sugar devised a plan. With one smooth motion, she tossed the branch onto the roof of the van. It landed with a loud thud. The branch must have been heavier than she'd realized. But as the sound echoed into the night, there was only stillness. She was ready to take the chance that whoever had been there was now gone.

Thinking that if someone was indeed still inside, she should try to startle them, she thrust herself into the van. "Hey!"

No one. The van was empty.

Quietly she asked, "Kitten? Kitten, are you here?" There was no response.

Sugar looked around. On the bunk. No cat. Under the bunk. No cat. She thought about how the kitten sometimes got under her feet when she drove and went up front to look around the floor of the cab. No cat. Back in her living quarters, she noticed something wasn't as she'd left it. *What?* She chided herself. *Think. Concentrate.* She stopped moving and stared at her work space. Then she closed her eyes. She whispered, "The chart." Her chart that housed her research was folded neatly in the webbing above her drop-down desk. But she had folded the chart twice over the long way. Now it was only folded once. *What the hell? Who the fuck was in here?* She looked out into the night. Nothing.

Then, *Do I smell anything?* Trying to stop all other thought, Sugar concentrated on the smells around her. There was something new. Musky. *What is it? Or, more accurately, who is it?* Whoever it was, she could tell they'd been all through her home.

Then came a man's echoing hiss. "She's watching you. Watching, waiting."

"Who are you?!"

There was no answer. A chill went up Sugar's spine. Then came the blow to the back of her legs. Down she went. The van fell silent. Fear was front and center. What was she supposed to do? To her man she admitted, "Curtis, I'm so fucking scared."

I have to get out of here. Don't pack. Just get the hell behind the wheel and drive. Now! And she was about to do just that when she remembered: *Kitten.*

Sugar stepped outside the van and dropped to the ground hoping she might be able to pick up the kitten's scent. *Did that man, whoever he was, take her cat?*

"I'll kill the son of a bitch."

At that moment, she realized how much the little cat meant to her. She was Sugar's one link to feeling human. To feeling like she might still be worthy of love, if only from a cat. And if she let the cat get taken, well...

Time passed and her hunt led nowhere. The sun would be up soon. *How many hours have I been searching? If I don't find her, I'll have to take shelter and try again at dusk. Who knows how far she could be by then?* No. She was not about to let this go that long.

With her hands on her head, Sugar stood spinning slowly as she racked her brain for a solution. She muttered to herself, "What? What? What?"

Then, a plan flashed into her mind. Without questioning herself, she took off running into the threat of dawn. After about a mile and a half, the grass gave way to a single-lane dirt road. In another mile, it became a small, two-lane street. In the distance, Sugar saw the light from an old wooden building that leaned ever so slightly, and ran for it. It was a small gas station with a grocery store. Making her way past the pumps and into the weathered, wood-sided building, she grabbed what she came for. On her way out, Sugar left a five on the counter in front of the old attendant who was slumped in his chair, snoring.

Soon, she was back at work in the van. Next, she stepped outside. The sun was starting to come up over the mountains. Its heat almost felt good until it felt awful. It hadn't occurred to her to apply sun screen. No time.

Putting an open can of wet cat food on the ground, Sugar didn't know which made her feel worse, the sun or the stink of Ocean Medley.

Holding back nausea, she called out, "Kitten! Food! Kitten! Look what mommy got for you." Hearing herself, Sugar felt like an idiot, then thought, *Screw it. I'm going to get my goddamn cat back!* "Kitten! Food! The good stuff. Don't make mommy grovel."

Sugar had thought for sure this would work. She called again, "Come on cat. Kitten!"

The sun was rising and Sugar felt the burning starting under her skin. She thought, *Maybe I should just sit down and boil to death.*

Then, *Was that a meow-ah?*

Suddenly, Sugar spotted the kitten. *Where had she come from?* Sugar didn't care. The small, not-really-a-leopard cat bounded through the grass towards the van and stopped at the open can, licking her lips. Sugar scooped her up, grabbed the tin of food, took them both inside, slammed the sliding door closed, and with relief, puked into the sink.

Wiping her mouth, she looked at the cat, "Mother-may-I get us the fuck away from here now?" But was there any place far enough away?

7

WHO CAN YOU TRUST?

Sugar drove across lower Nebraska with the kitten resting on her left shoulder as if she had one furry epaulet. As miles of flatness passed, she thought about the break-in. She was pretty sure it was the same voice as the interloper in her dream. *Is the "she" he spoke of Alex? Who else would it be? Should I use him to get to her? Am I ready for that?* The answer was a clear, *Hell no! Should I just drive off a cliff and stop this whole thing right now?*

"Kitten, find me a cliff."

But Kitten wasn't much of a navigator. After her scare, Sugar decided the cat's official name was Kitten. Clean. Simple. Not too cute. It seemed to work for both of them.

After another hour of watching the lines on the road, Sugar was ready for a distraction. She was about to play a book on tape. Her current audiobook was a 21st Century take on the situation. Very hip. Very gritty. Over-stylized. Already not in the best mood, a book about the grimier side of the dark underworld would only serve to further annoy her.

Maybe music. Music? Wow. It felt like a thought from someone else's life. Sugar hadn't listened to music since she'd hit the road. *It seems so cheery. But maybe that's what I need.*

"Kitten, what would you like to listen to?"

"Meow-ah. Meow-ah."

"Show tunes? Really? I would have pegged you more as punk rock, but okay."

Scrolling Pandora, she found the Broadway channel. The song "Memories" from *Cats* began playing. Scratching Kitten's head she said, "Well, that's appropriate."

After a minute, Betty Buckley finished the maudlin, yet hopeful tune. Next up, from *La Cage Aux Folles*, "I Am What I Am." As the song started, Sugar absently began humming along. Her parents had gone to New York whenever they got the chance, and show tunes were like part of their home decor. Like growing up in a house with two languages, Sugar didn't have to think about the words. They were there for her. Once the chorus hit, she was singing along. Hearing herself, she realized how bizarrely apropos this tune was. *Wait. Is my tone truer now? Must be wishful thinking.* But she liked the thought.

Sitting up straighter, she enjoyed the new-ish sound of her voice. With one hand on the wheel and the other on Kitten, she felt something new. *Pride? No. Acceptance? Definitely not. Maybe it's just defiance.* Knowing that whatever this positive feeling was likely wouldn't last, Sugar let herself indulge in a moment of "In your face, world. Deal with me as I am."

As the final chorus started, she was in full voice. By the time she hit the last line, she was belting it out in her best Patti LuPone. She was about to take a mental bow when...

BAM!

The Sprinter bounced off something, then seemed to swerve on its own. Sugar struggled to keep her home from rolling off the road and into a ditch. Kitten's claws were digging deep into her flesh as the animal tried to not fly out a window. "Crap! Do I turn into the swerve or out of it? Stop. Don't think. Just do."

After regaining control, she slowed the van. "What the hell did we hit?"

Sugar pulled to the side of the road as safely as possible to assess the situation. But before she could do anything, she had to detach the cat from her chest. "Come on you pussy. That's right. I went there."

After a cursory walk around the van checking for damage, she saw nothing obviously wrong. *Maybe we avoided trouble.* Looking at the ditch next to the van, she thought of her mother's words. Whenever Sugar came home late, Faye would be waiting up and say, "Where were you? I imagined you lying in a ditch somewhere." Sugar's standard response was, "What ditch? Where are all of these ditches I keep lying in?" Now she knew. Nebraska.

Looking around for the culprit, Sugar spotted a large object in the road about thirty yards behind her. *What the hell is that?* At about ten yards away, it appeared to be a large box of some sort. *An equipment box?* She scanned the area to make sure she was alone. She was. *I guess no one's going out for milk or cigarettes in Nebraska at this hour.* Venturing closer, Sugar bent down to inspect the box's contents. Suddenly, there was the squeal of tires.

"Damn. Company." Then she saw it. "What the hell is that?"

An old ambulance, the box-truck style, closed in behind her and came to an abrupt stop just feet away. Sugar stood, but before she could think about fleeing, the ambulance door flew open. A blond with more curls than head came bounding from the vehicle, making a beeline for the box. Her clothing was sporty-shabby. There was something instantly appealing about the woman. As if Sugar wasn't there, the blond called behind her, "I told you it wasn't on tight."

A man exited the passenger side of the vehicle rubbing his eyes as if he'd just woken up. He was medium build, toned, had short hair, and was equally appealing. "If it wasn't on tight, it's because you didn't tighten it."

"You were the last one to put it on."

"Bullshit. You were."

"If I'd put it on, it would have stayed on."

"Like the time you were so sure you tied down the bikes and we had to drive back an entire day to find them?"

The blond put her hands on her hips. "I can't be held accountable for bad bungies."

"They weren't bad. They were brand new."

"Well, I didn't like them."

"You didn't like—What does that even mean?"

Sugar took a few steps back, wondering if she could make a quiet exit from this domestic scene. These two strangers didn't seem to pose a threat. Still, she didn't care to linger. When Sugar moved, the curly-haired blond's attention shifted, her energy turning on a dime from annoyed married woman to bubbly gal pal. With a confident familiarity, she thrust a hand towards Sugar. "Hey. I'm Maddie. This is Matt."

The capable looking man stepped forward and put out a hand. "Hey. Matt."

Suddenly, talking to other people felt like the most awkward thing on Earth. "Hey."

Reassuringly, Maddie said, "We're not really mad at each other. When you spend as much time together as we do, you just have to yell sometimes. I think arguing is good for a relationship. Don't you?"

Before Sugar could answer, Matt jumped in. "Is that your Sprinter up there?"

"Yeah."

"Nice. What do you get to the gallon, eleven, twelve?"

"Uh, I think I'm getting about thirteen."

"Thirteen? That's pretty sweet." He thrust a thumb back in the direction of the ambulance. "We're getting fourteen on the flats."

Sugar was confused. "Is that an RV?"

Maddie jumped in. "We call it the Blood-Mergency Vehicle." She beamed with pride.

Matt offered, "Wanna check it out?"

Morbid curiosity got the best of her and Sugar followed them to their homemade home.

As she opened the door, Maddie switched into tour-guide mode. "Come on inside. Come on. Okay..."

Sugar followed her inside, with Matt bringing up the rear.

Maddie gestured to an unmade bed at the back of the living space. "...Here, back here, is our bunk that turns into a sofa."

"But someone's usually too lazy to do that."

Looking at Matt, she added, "Over here we have: Shut up." Gesturing to all of the cabinets that had previously been used for first-aid supplies, she said, "Check out all this storage. It came with all this. We put our toiletries here. Clothes over here. This is our RV heater. It looks like a cute little wood stove, right? We made it out of a boat heater."

Matt ribbed, "We?"

"Whatever."

As the two pretended to argue, Sugar thought about domesticity with Curtis. Yet, instead of it making her sad, she merely enjoyed the rhythm of it all. She missed normal, pointless conversations.

While Sugar was still lost in her head, Matt had taken over the tour. "Out here is what we really love about this thing. All the equipment storage." Walking around the outside of the converted ambulance, Matt began opening and closing compartment doors. "We keep skis and ski poles in this one. Hiking packs and trekking poles over here. Helmets go in here. And more skis back here."

Maddie turned to Sugar with a look of childlike excitement. Or was that how she always was? "Do you ski?"

"Ah. I have skied."

"Cool."

Not having any more to add, Sugar was ready to make her exit. "Well, I really should—"

Matt interrupted. "Where are you parking tonight?"

"I, ah, I figured I'd just drive for a while."

"We're heading to Moonglow RV Park. Know it?"

Sugar couldn't explain why, but the question seemed to have more behind it than the obvious. *Should I know it?* "No."

Maddie urged, "You should come. They have a pool. It's super fun."

"It's a little cold for swimming."

"No. We skate on it."

Again, calling his wife on her shit, Matt asked, "We?"

She ignored him. "Do you skate?"

"I'm afraid I don't. I'm also not much of an RV park person. I should get rolling."

Maddie's bubbly veneer lost a few of its bubbles as she leaned into Sugar. "I really think you should come."

Feeling the shift, Sugar thought, *It's time to detach myself.* "Thanks for the offer, but—"

Matt gently put a hand on her shoulder, and let the warmth of his intensely blue eyes seal the deal. "I think you'll want to come see it."

What's happening here? Should I go with these two magnetic but pushy strangers who for some reason seem to want to adopt me? Should I be scared? What's my intuition telling me? I don't know. My intuition sucks.

Sugar looked at them both trying to sense if they were good, evil, or just pleasantly crazy. *What do I feel? Whatever it is, it doesn't feel evil. But what's evil? Am I evil? The line has moved. Screw it. Make a choice.* Ready to feel less vulnerable, she said, "Fine."

Maddie clapped her hands in delight. "You'll come? Yay! Matt, you can put the box back on and drive the BMV." Hooking her arm around Sugar's like they'd been besties since the womb, she said, "I wanna ride with...Hey, we don't know your name."

"It's Sugar." *Crap. Why didn't I make up a name? How much do I suck at being stealth? So much!*

"Sugar? Seriously? OMG. I love that. I think I need a better name."

For a second time, Matt shook Sugar's hand. "Great name. Nice to meet you, Sugar. Now you drive safe with my wife. That's precious cargo you got there." With that, Matt winked and turned for his ambulance, leaving Sugar standing in the road, arm-in-arm with her new BFF.

Seated in the cab of the Sprinter, Maddie's head seemed to be on a swivel. From the passenger seat, she looked all around the interior. "This is so nice. New?"

"New-ish."

"It's so clean. Oh, we're gonna drive straight on this road for another twenty miles."

"Got it." Turning the engine over, Sugar started them towards their home for the night.

After taking in a deep breath and letting it out, Maddie noted, "It smells so clean in here. Try traveling with that guy. Your whole rig'd smell like ass. His digestive tract, I swear." Maddie giggled to herself and confessed "Well, I do produce my own share of methane."

Sugar raised an eyebrow, remembering how she'd dated Curtis for a full year before she let him hear her do that. What total freedom it was to not have to hide that truth about herself anymore. *Not hiding. Nice.* "We're only human."

Maddie bounced in her seat. "I don't know about that. You look kinda..."

"Kinda, what?"

Before Sugar could find out what "kind" she looked like, Maddie pointed at the large pickup pulling a trailer headed in the other direction. "Anal Adventure!"

"Excuse me?"

"Anal Adventure!"

"I'll pass, thanks."

"No. It's a road game. You don't know it? Whenever you pass an RV, you put the word "anal" before the name of the rig. The model of that RV was "Adventure," so "Anal Adventure!" My personal favorite at the moment is Anal Leprechaun. I can just picture him with his little pointy green hat."

"And matching assless chaps?"

Maddie laughed. It was nice to make someone laugh again. Sugar was still picturing the randy little man in green with his cheeks out when a double "meow-ah" came from over her left shoulder. Kitten climbed out from behind her hair, as if parting a theater curtain to check on the crowd. She leaned, craning her neck towards Maddie. "Meow-ah."

Sugar made the intro. "This is Maddie, Kitten. Say hello."

"Meow-ah."

Maddie looked like her heart was about to explode with joy. "Oh! Oh, a kitten. Oh. Is she nice? Look at that little leopard kitty cat! Do you want to come sit with Aunt Maddie?" To Sugar she asked, "Can I?"

"She's a free agent."

Maddie reached her hands toward Kitten. "Come here, you cutie. You little tiger leopard." Kitten obliged, allowing herself to be picked up by the enthusiastic stranger. Holding the cat to her cheek, Kitten sniffed Maddie's face, then leaned in pressing her silky fur against Maddie's skin. "Oh, my God. She's so soft. I love this kitten cat so much!"

"She's a sweetie."

"See? Matt says we can't have a pet. But you have one."

Sugar wasn't sure what one had to do with the other, but she didn't ask. She followed Maddie's directions to the RV park while Kitten received the petting session of her lifetime. Making the final turn, Sugar could see a green and yellow neon sign reading, "Moonglow RV Park - Park it like you mean it." *Not a great tagline.* Sugar wondered who did their marketing.

Maddie pointed to a parking spot by the office. Sugar obliged, and a moment later Matt pulled up next to them. Rolling down his window, he called out, "I'm parking in our regular spot. You can get her settled, right?"

Maddie held up the kitten. "Look Matt. She has a kitten. I told you we could have one." Matt shook his head as if he'd heard this plea a million times, then drove away.

Not defeated, Maddie turned to Sugar. "I'll wear him down. I'm getting a cat. Come on, I'll introduce you."

Leaving Kitten to guard the place, the two women got out of the van and climbed the three steps to the covered porch wrapping around the RV office. Sitting in a rocker was a boho-looking woman in her mid-forties with a sweet, round face. Her brown hair was threaded with a subtle mix of color. Even while seated, her clothing seemed to flow.

Opening her arms wide, Maddie smiled at the woman. "Hey, Mary Helen. Miss me?"

"Baby, you know I did." Mary Helen got up and the two embraced like old friends.

"Mary Helen, this is my shiny-new best friend, Sugar."

Sugar put out her hand, but Mary Helen was having none of it, giving her the same hug she'd given Maddie. There was something so comforting about her embrace. Sugar felt quietly accepted. *So strange.*

With a Southern swing in her voice, Mary Helen said, "Sugar? Welcome. Great name. I've had all types here." Mary Helen put extra emphasis on all. "But I never had a Sugar."

"I can't take credit."

"You lookin' for a place to park that sleek rig?"

"I am."

"You're in the right spot. How long you stayin'?"

"Probably just a night."

Cutting in, Maddie added in a sing-songy voice, "But you never know. You always want to leave the door open for opportunity."

"I like to leave the door closed and then crack it for opportunity."

Mary Helen laughed. "Well, we're happy to have you here for however long. There's a spot two over from Maddie. Number nine. Just pull around past the large elm and those nice folks arguin' over the washin' machine. It's a good spot. I was always partial to the number nine." She winked. "Three threes, you know."

Maddie agreed. "That is a good spot. You'll like it. Want me to show you?"

"I think I can take it from here, but thanks. Oh, wait." Looking back at Mary Helen, "How much? And do you take cash?"

"It's as good as money, honey. Twenty-five a night. You can get me tomorrow. I know where you live." Mary Helen gave one more warm parting wink and sat back down.

Maneuvering the van towards space number nine, Sugar's short drive took her past two dozen or so expensive, A-class rigs—big, bus-sized vehicles with multiple slide outs and blue under-lighting. For sheer living space, most New-York apartment dwellers would be envious. As she rolled her dwarfed, B-class van closer to her spot, the rigs became less expensive and more "interesting." Less vacation-home and more "home" home. Pulling between a tree and a converted shuttle bus, Sugar turned off the engine. Exhausted, she looked to her copilot. "Well Kitten, we're home. Want to go around and hook up the water lines for me?" Kitten jumped off the passenger seat and disappeared into the back of the van. "Freeloader."

Sugar went out behind the van and pulled an array of hoses from their storage locker. She squatted down and did her best to keep straight which hoses went to which connections. *Graywater. Black-water. Drinking water. Which is which? And why can I never remember?* It was like a mental block, and she knew why. She resented having to do all of this for herself. Resented her new existence without her lover slash handyman. About to get her phone out and YouTube an answer yet again, she thought, *Screw it. Does it really matter if I'm going to be moving on tomorrow? Fresh water. That's the only line that really matters. Be steely.* Sugar tried turning off everything else in her brain and getting the city waterline connected to the faucet.

Back in the van, Kitten was now perched on top of the wipes like a princess. Sugar lifted the cat, grabbed a wipe and replaced her lay-about van mate. "You're no help."

With the sun about to rise, Sugar pulled the cover over the front windshield. Then she looked out a tinted rear window, scoping her temporary neighborhood. Not much life out there. Just a rather pale, slim gentleman wearing vintage slacks and jacket with no shirt. He was adding seed to a small bird feeder that hung from his awning. When he finished, he stood back, arms folded. In short order, a small bird flew up, looked round, then started pecking quickly at the food. Suddenly, in a move so swift it was barely visible, the man snatched the bird and seemed to eat it.

"Holy shit! Holy—Holy shit!" *Did Mr. Skin & Bones just eat a fucking bird?* She was pretty sure he did. The man then looked up to the sky, down to the ground and, apparently sated, turned up his collar, and stepped inside a trailer as vintage-looking as his clothing. The door slammed behind him, ending all visible signs of life in Moonglow RV park.

"Where the hell are we?"

8

OUTED

So many questions. The most pedestrian of them was, *What state is this? Colorado? Does it matter? Not really.* The question that mattered was, is it safe here? She didn't have that answer. Sugar climbed on her bunk to read.

"Scoot, Kitten."

Kitten moved to a pillow and waited for Sugar to get in place.

Sugar whispered, "I promise I'll never eat you. Can I count on you to return the favor?" Kitten twitched her nose but said nothing. "I thought we were friends."

Wanting a break from her dark reading, she found a book on personal finance. The first question it asked was, 'At what age do you plan to retire?' A flood of thoughts swept through her brain. *How long will I need my money to last? How long do I want to need it? I'll need millions if I'm going to live untold years.* While her salary in the before-times was good, it wasn't millions. In the stories she'd read, where characters lived well beyond human years, having money seemed so easy. As if it was a simple fact of eternal life. No end in sight? No problem! And, many stories featured characters that came from generations of wealth.

But she didn't come from generations of wealth. Her father co-owned a one-off department store with his two brothers. Henry had struggled all his life to make his siblings "Keep their fingers out of my cookie jar." While there was love, there was also the territorial struggles that come with a family business. Each brother had kids and each one felt that when they retired, their progeny should take over. Henry was the oldest and his eldest son, Sugar's brother Barry, worked alongside him. Faye was always on Henry to put his foot down with his brothers, but Henry could never bring himself to deny family much of anything.

Sugar and D. had dubbed their mother The Strip-Mall Psychologist. Faye was part-time now. More a hobby than a career. She maintained her small strip-mall practice with a handful of patients who kept her rich only in tales she should never tell—but, of course, did. They'd get dropped into conversations like little fables from The Brothers Grimmstein. If Sugar said something negative about a cousin, she'd be told, "H.M., no names, once told her cousin his pants were too short. Now he's dead. She still cries when she passes a men's store." Or if Sugar went to the mall with friends, she might hear, "You know, a certain J.B., no names, overspent every year on Hanukah. Such excess. What happened? He had to sell the BMWs and move the family to Camden."

Sugar's bottom line was there was no big Bernstein fortune to build from. She marveled at stories like *The Highlander*, where a man who lived for centuries became a wealthy antiques dealer.

To Kitten she ranted, "It's all so, but-of-course. I want details. They never share the nuts and bolts of the business. Where did he find his clients? What was his business model? Where are the P&Ls? Did he have branches? Franchises? Did he change associates after a decade so no one noticed he wasn't aging?" She wanted a clear guide to creating and sustaining a fortune over centuries. "Is this another book idea, Kitten? *Financial Freedom Always and Forever: The Undeads' Guide to Personal Finance*. It would help if I learned how to do it for myself first. With all the shit that's happened, how is money still one of my biggest issues? Madness."

As the financial book got technical, it became laborious. After several long blinks, sleep came. Sugar's dreams flew by in rapid succession with no theme. She was drifting from one time in her life to the next. Birthday parties, business meetings, ladies' nights, family gatherings. She was younger and older and younger again. Then came order. She flashed to her first kiss. She was nine. Edwin, the boy she'd had a crush on, was kissing her backstage after the school play. While the kiss was more of a peck, she was delighted to know she was in a two-way crush.

Flash forward. She was in a college dorm room kissing Gregg Somebody. This was less delightful. Gregg turned out to be not much of a kisser. More of a groper who pressed his mouth against hers as his hands traveled. She politely waited for him to finish.

But then the kissing got much better. When she pulled back, she was in a New York bar with a stranger. Just a guy in a bar with firm lips and a skilled tongue. *Thank you, sir. May I have another?*

Flash. She was getting another. From Curtis. They were in a corner at her friend Tess's birthday party. To be heard above the music, Curtis leaned into her ear. "Can I kiss you again?"

Trying to pretend she wasn't dying to be re-kissed, she said, "I don't know, can you?"

He could. He really could. She hoped she was giving as good as she got.

Flash and she was in a dark club sitting across from Alex. The scene was black on black with little definition except a slight glint of light on Alex's red lips. Sugar felt Alex's hand sliding into her hair as she whispered, "So soft." Heat rose in Sugar's body and a moment later they were kissing like they would die if they stopped. Not wanting to let the scene play out, Sugar battled to wake. *I don't want to be here! Stop!*

BANG, BANG!

Sugar's eyes snapped open at the banging on her van door. She gasped. Once again, Kitten leapt to the ceiling. The cat then jumped straight up three more times before assuming an attack stance on the blue and green afghan. Another bang was followed by, "Tweedle-tweet. Hello! It's Maddie. Tweedle-tweet."

Trying to focus on the present, Sugar could still taste the kiss on her lips. "Give me a sec."

"Okay."

Shake it off. You have company. Company? She got up trying her best to pack her memories into a trunk, lock them up, weight them down with a boulder, and sink them somewhere deep inside her.

"What does my hair look like, Kitten?"

Bed head is never forgiving to someone with curls. Straight hair would have been better. But she hadn't had the drive to straighten it in months. She told herself there was defiance in going native. *Screw it.* She slid open the side door and there was Maddie, all waving and blond curls. Apparently, she was going native as well.

"Tweedle-tweet?"

Maddie laughed. "I never learned how to whistle. How'd ya sleep? Hope you don't mind visitors. Can I pet your cat?"

"Do you care what order I answer in?"

Bounding into the van, Maddie went straight for Kitten. Sugar guessed that her answers were irrelevant and kept them to herself. With zero objections, Kitten accepted the outpouring of love from her shiny, new friend.

Holding the fur baby up to her face, Maddie spoke for Kitten. "Mommy, I love this lady so much. If you die, can I live with her?"

"Do you know something I don't?"

Laughing it off, Maddie hugged Kitten. "Just playing. But I think she really likes me."

"I'm sure she does. Hey, I have a question. What's up with Mr. Skin & Bones in the vintage trailer over there?"

"Jasper?"

"You tell me. I think I saw him eat a bird from his feeder."

"Yeah. That's Jasper. He's harmless."

"Not if you're a bird."

"I heard a bug flew into his ear years ago. Now he eats birds so they'll go kill the bug."

"That's nuts."

"I know, right? So sad. But Mary Helen has such a big heart. She lets him stay in our section. He won't bug you. Get it? Bug?"

"I got it."

Maddie laughed at her own joke but added no more intel to her "our section" comment. Without invitation, she headed for Sugar's closet and peered behind the door. "Nice clothes. They look expensive."

"Some."

"My stuff's so old. I hate shopping, but I love having new things, don't you?"

Sugar'd been born into a shopping culture. Her Aunt Selma would say, "Your shoes, bag, and belt should always match." And there was, of course, her father's store. Then there were the impromptu outings with her mother. Every so often when Sugar was a kid, Faye would come to Sugar's bedroom door and ask, "Do you want to go to school today, or shopping and a movie?" Sugar liked questions with easy answers. Then in her late teens, weekly trips to the mall with girlfriends, and as a professional, lunchbreaks with coworkers. Thinking back to her favorite New York clothing haunts, Sugar got wistful. "I do love shopping. Anything but bathing suits."

"Why? You're so thin."

Sugar'd been called many things over the years, but never thin. She wasn't fat, *per se*. Just thick, which in New York, made her feel heavy. *Enough self-indulgence and body dysmorphia. Deflect.* "Well, you have a nice figure."

Still scanning Sugar's clothes, "It's the big plus of our lifestyle, am I right?"

What does she mean? "Van life?"

Maddie giggled. "Our life. You know. *The* life. V-Life."

What am I being told? "No. I don't know."

Turning and staring directly at Sugar, Maddie said flatly, "I think you do." After a thick slice of silence, she added, "It's okay. We're safe together. We can just be us here."

"We?"

Without looking away, Maddie hopped backwards, up on the bunk. "Us. Vampires. It's cool."

WHAM! Sugar couldn't believe what she had just heard. Maddie had used the V word. It was like cold water to the face. A wake up to the world around her. Like a supercomputer, her mind started clicking off the clues she'd noticed, but didn't. All the odd feelings and signals she was getting. *Is this possible?* But of course, more was possible than she'd been aware of just weeks earlier. *Am I actually in the presence of a...Damn.* Just thinking the word made her feel exposed. She yelled at herself. *Just think it. Think it! A vampire.*

Her next thought was *How obvious am I?* Carefully, she asked, "How did you know?"

"All your tells."

"I have tells?"

"We all do. You know, the red flecks in the pupils, the pale, slightly translucent skin the..." Off Sugar's confused look Maddie finally did her own math. "You don't know this stuff, do you?"

Leaning back against the counter of her kitchenette, Sugar admitted, "No. I don't know anything."

"Damn. How new are you?"

"A few weeks. Four. Six. More. I'm losing track."

Maddie picked up Kitten, gently petting her head. "Weren't you given any mentoring?"

"From who?"

"Your maker."

Feeling only hate towards that person—no, that creature who'd shattered her world forever, she scoffed. "No. No guidance." Just like that, everything Sugar had packed away rose back to the surface. But now, in addition to her hate issues, she suddenly got to enjoy abandonment issues. *How twisted is that? How many therapy sessions will this little revelation require?* And because she couldn't hire her mother, it would cost a bloody fortune.

"I'm so sorry."

Trying to re-sink her feelings, Sugar simply offered, "Yeah. Well."

Maddie got up and, still cradling Kitten, wrapped her free arm around Sugar. "Well, you have us now."

Two hugs in as many days. What's happening? "It's okay. I'm good."

"You mean you want me to stop hugging you?"

"Well..."

"Nope. We're not done. 26, 27, 28, 29, 30. There." Releasing Sugar, Maddie stepped back to the bunk. "You need to hug for at least thirty seconds to get the full healing effect."

"Got it."

"I bet you have a lot of questions."

"A few."

"Ask me anything. Tips. Rules. My blood type." Maddie laughed at her own joke.

What to ask first? "Is Matt?"

"Is Matt a vampire? Sure. He made me. That was, oh shit, next year will be our forty-fifth anniversary." Maddie started on one of her tangents. "I wonder what I should get him. He has so many skis. What color is forty-five? Silver? I think it's silver? I like silver. Anything sparkly, really. Oh, wait. I got it. I could surprise him and paint the blood-mergency vehicle silver. Pink and silver? What do you think?"

Sugar kept what she really thought to herself. "I don't think forty-five is silver."

"Bummer." Maddie suddenly put a hand over her mouth. "I'm sorry. I kinda made this about me. Go ahead. Ask me a question."

Sugar felt a slight pain in her chest. It had been days. "What's for dinner?"

9

CATCH AND RELEASE

By the light of a half-moon, Matt, Maddie, and Sugar stalked across the open land. Sugar had so many questions for her new acquaintances and they seemed completely willing to answer them. At least to a point. Does V-Life make you smarter? In a way. They're mentally faster. Which often makes them seem smarter. But your baseline intelligence is where you start from. So, if you were a bag of rocks before well, too bad, too sad. Any skill is like that. If you were already good at something, now you're better. Heightened sensitivity? Yes, in all areas. Sunlight? Just don't. But she knew that. Is food ever a good idea? She'll get no real nutritional value from it and too much or too fast would lead to complete body rejection, aka toilet hugging. Yet sometimes, fiber for women isn't a bad idea. "You know, to stay regular." Bug-like wall climbing? Maddie could do it better than Matt. It was apparently a sore spot. Flying? Yes. Like any sport, some are better at it than others. But most can at least travel short distances. It takes nerve and a lot of dedication to get good, but totally worth it.

Then Sugar asked, "What about mind reading and manipulation?"

Matt explained, "Don't sweat that one yet. Mind reading is a really tough skill. Not everyone can do it. Most of us end up trying too hard. And if you force it, it'll hurt. Really. You'll feel it burning in your temples. You have to stay loose and let it happen naturally or you'll just end up with a headache and hearing your own thoughts screaming back at you." With a small laugh he added, "One time, oh shit, it was like 1977 and *Star Wars* had just come out. I really loved that movie."

Sugar raised a hand. "Me, too."

"The best. So, we were in Wyoming and I was trying to get this liftie to let me on a ski lift without a pass. I was all, 'Read his mind. Read his mind. Tell him what to say.' But *Star Wars* was all I could think about. I hold up my driver's license instead of a ski pass, wanting him to say, 'that's a ski pass,' right? Nope. I was so *Star Wars*-y, he looks at my license and goes, 'That's no moon.'" With that, Matt laughed his goofy, Muppet-like laugh and Maddie joined in.

Having Matt talking so openly and matter-of-factly about their experiences, and laughing at things, made all of this seem almost normal. "Next question. How many of us are there?"

As they were walking, Maddie took Sugar's hand and started swinging it as if they were grade-school classmates. "Do you mean on the road or in general?"

"I'm not sure. Either. Both."

Matt mused, "Hard to say how many at large. On the road in the U.S. I'd guess, what, fifty? More?"

Maddie shook her head. "Way more. Think about that time at Burning Man."

"Shit. You're right. The RV-Lifestyle is so perfect for us. I'm kind of surprised more don't do it. All the moving around keeps us seen but not seen. You know?"

Sugar agreed. "That was my thinking. That, and I didn't know how to face anyone from the before-times."

Maddie squeezed her hand in support. "The 'before-times.' I'm stealing that."

V-Life

"Be my guest."

Looking away, Maddie said, "It was so long ago for me. I mean, people I knew have moved, or died. I still see one or two of them skiing. But it's not like I can be all, 'Hey, remember me? I bet you do. I look exactly the fucking same. But you sure look like aged cheese.'" Her face grew wistful. "Bummer."

Sugar could feel Maddie pining for someone from her past. But not seeming like one who dwells on the unpleasant, Maddie quickly shifted the topic. "I love your kitty. I want a pet. But it's so hard to find animals that like us. I had a pig once. We called him Sir Francis Bacon, after the—"

"I get it."

"He was the best little piggy. And pigs are handy because they eat anything. You know. Anything."

Sugar knew that Maddie meant. Evidence.

Maddie continued, "But when we decided to live on the road, we found out Sir Francis had an inner ear problem that made him get car sick on S turns."

Sugar laughed at the ridiculousness of it, and Matt and Maddie joined her. She was enjoying this casual conversation about topics from the taboo to the absurd. They were just friends on an outing. A dark, evil, something's-about-to-die outing.

Then, without speaking, Maddie pointed to their destination: a pile of boulders about a hundred yards in the distance. Instinctively, they all got quiet and crouched down. After sniffing at the air, the three moved forward. Their strides seemed slow, but they were crossing the expanse quickly. Then Matt and Maddie each took one of Sugar's hands. The next thing she knew, her feet were off the ground. This was flying. She was so excited, she almost forgot about her hunger. The feeling was utterly freeing. Up ahead, between two of the rocks, Sugar saw multiple pairs of green glowing eyes, peering out. Matt let go of her hand, and Sugar went to the ground. He swooped in with an unexpected grace that sliced the air. In a split-second Matt was draining the life from a fox. A second after that,

Maddie had her own trophy. But the commotion alerted the other foxes and they were off and running. *Damn it.* Sugar'd missed her chance. Then, the smallest snapping sound caused her head to tick up to the right. A hawk was perched up in a cottonwood tree. A moment later, it had company. Sugar barely felt herself touch the branches as she scaled the trunk and quickly bagged her prey.

Sitting on the ground below the tree with her prize, Sugar felt energy slowly flowing through her body. She could literally track the life-giving force as it surged from her chest, past her shoulders and hips, down her arms and legs, and out to her fingers and toes. It was as if each digit was getting fractionally longer as it tried containing the power. Yet, as she felt her strength increase, there was that feeling of guilt at what she'd done. *But God, I needed that. But the guilt. But the energy. I hate myself. I wondered how I'd feel if I'd been born Episcopalian.*

Matt and Maddie strolled up, hand in hand. *How lucky are they? Even if luck isn't exactly the word for their existence, they're going through this V-Life together. Apparently, that's more than I can ask for. Correction, than I should have asked for.*

Matt pointed up to the tree. "You scaled that thing like a beast. Pretty sweet."

"Did I?"

"Thirty feet-ish."

"How 'bout that."

"Oh here." Matt reached into his back pocket and pulled out a handkerchief. "Never be caught without. Old habit." He licked the cloth, then wiped something from Sugar's cheek. "Piece of hawk."

"I'm sure Martha Stewart would frown on that." She gave a wry smile.

"Hey, real food doesn't come in cellophane-wrapped trays on aisle five."

"Profound."

When Sugar stood, the dead hawk dropped from her lap. Seeing

the carcass hit the ground, Maddie immediately bent forward, pu
her hands on her knees and threw up just a little.

Matt laughed. "She was never good with birds. Even back in the
day, or—"nodding to Sugar—"the before-times."

Wiping her mouth, Maddie frowned. "It's not funny. Birds are
disgusting."

Sugar quipped, "Too *fowl*?"

On the heels of the pun, Matt and Maddie started back towards
Moonglow but Sugar kneeled to the ground. "Hold on." The two
turned to see Sugar giving the hawk a small burial. When she
finished, she got up to join them.

Maddie seemed surprised. "You do that every time?"

"Guilty." After she'd said it, Sugar wondered whether she meant
she does it every time or that she feels guilty. She wasn't sure.

Heading back, Matt put his arm around Sugar. "I knew I liked
you."

Maddie scooted up and wedged herself between them. "But you
like me more."

He gave his wife a squeeze then turned to Sugar. "Piece of
advice?"

"Sure."

"You need to be careful about caring too much about your kills."

She shrugged, "Only human."

Bluntly he said, "We're not."

Sugar walked contemplating the gravity of not being human.

10

JAM BANDS AND TECH TALKS

After her best sleep in weeks, Sugar wasn't ready to hit the road. Not just yet. She now had people she didn't have to hide from. Plus, she was learning things that might help her take down Alex. While Sugar had no interest in revealing her plan for revenge, she could dig around for insight without tipping her hand. So, she tenuously unpacked more of her things while trying to pack away her fear and hate.

"Kitten, I think Moonglow is as good a place as any for us right now."

Even though Sugar didn't see Kitten at that moment, knowing there was another life in the van made her feel like speaking aloud was okay. And the sound of her voice made the place feel less empty. Less lonely.

In the near distance, she heard a low, rhythmic beat. "Is that live music?"

After some light tidying, she got herself together and followed the sound. The pleasant rhythm pulling her in. Wandering past the fancier A-class RVs, she felt dwarfed. They now seemed much bigger than when she'd driven past them on the road. She thought *These* shiny, bus-length homes with all their slides could house entire families. Including the members no one likes. In her head, she started playing Maddie's anal name game. Then she let her ad-gal mind plus it by adding taglines after each name.

Anal Raptor—Careful with those talons. No. *Anal Raptor—For tearing up the back roads.* Better.

Anal Thunder—Run!

Anal Prospector—Oh, the things you'll find.

Anal Montana? Now, that sounds more like a new state motto lying in wait in case Montana ever goes all Freddy Mercury.

Sitting in folding chairs outside the Anal Montana were two older couples in color-coordinated puffy jackets. Their look was a mash-up of retirement-money meets box-of-crayons. Flanking a campfire, they spoke over their empty dinner plates. Sugar stopped to listen.

The woman in the bright red jacket was explaining, "No, no, no. I never drive it."

Bright Blue Jacket Lady was in alliance. "Oh, no. I told him, 'If you want that thing, you'll have to drive it.'"

Bright Blue Jacket Man looked at Bright Red Jacket Man and pointed a thumb to his wife as if to say, "Women." To his wife, he asked. "What are you making for dinner tomorrow?"

"I don't know. We just finished eating. I have leftover burgers. I can re-heat them."

"Please God, no. They were dry the first time."

"Then you try working with that cooktop."

Bright Red Jacket Man asked, "Why don't you use your grill? We're camping." He spread his arms wide. "We're supposed to grill in the great outdoors, am I right?"

Bright Blue Jacket Woman shook her head and with a small laugh said, "Oh, no. Until my eyebrows grow back, he can grill. Am I ri—" She stopped when she noticed Sugar standing there. Clearly about to get snippy with her eavesdropper, something about Sugar seemed to make her rethink it. In a polite tone that didn't quite mask her annoyance, she asked, "Can we help you?"

Sugar shrugged, "I doubt it." then continued on her way.

Once in the center of the park, she found a small crowd gathered around the main office, listening to four people playing acoustic instruments on the porch. Mary Helen was there, sitting off to the side and working a tambourine with perhaps more flair than was called for. Sugar came up behind Matt, who was sitting on a folding camp stool. "Does this kind of thing happen a lot?"

He smiled his warm smile. "Hey, Sugar. Mostly weekends."

Maddie looked up. "But we can never keep track of weekends. Hey, wanna go skiing with us?"

"Ahh, I don't know about that."

"You totally should."

Sugar wondered if Maddie and Matt's speech pattern and slang had evolved over the decades. *I suppose, to blend, you can't follow the time-honored path and turn into a crabby old person blowing off "those kids with their new-fangled words."*

After finishing their song, the musicians launched into a new, more upbeat number. With no warning, Maddie got up, hurrying in the direction of the ambulance, leaving Matt to explain. "She's going to get her ukulele."

"Is she any good?"

"No. But don't tell her I said that. She's been playing ever since she saw Tiny Tim on *Laugh-In*. It makes her happy."

Sugar smiled. "Not a word."

Minutes later, Maddie came gliding past with her instrument and bounded onto the porch to join the band. No one seemed to mind. Perhaps they'd done this dance before. Matt offered his wife's folding chair to Sugar. She sat, becoming part of Maddie's audience.

After getting lost in several numbers, Sugar was confronted with an unpleasant sound. Someone was chewing gum. *Fuck!* Her misophonia kicked in hard. She tried willing the chewer to stop. It didn't work. But it did provide her with a lovely little headache. Sugar was sure her mouth noise issues had gotten worse. Even brushing her teeth was now a balancing act. Could she brush fast enough to get rid of any tartar build up before hurling? Thinking about her teeth made her suddenly concerned at the prospect of maintaining stellar dental care for decades. *How long does enamel last? Is that something that will regenerate?* She made a note on her phone in the "Ask Maddie" file. "Tooth enamel longevity?"

Sugar scanned the rest of those gathered, assessing them. *Can I tell who's living the V-Life and who's just seeing the country?* At first, everyone seemed like everyone. Anyone. People happy to be out of the house or the office. Perhaps a bit dustier than most, but normal. *What should I be looking for?* She thought of what Maddie had said they had noticed in her. The red flecks in her iris. But Sugar couldn't see into most people's eyes from where she was sitting. Also, her skin had a slight translucence. She focused on people's skin tone, and there it was. Subtle, for sure, but the two gentlemen with matching baseball hats to her right seemed to have the telling cast to their skin, and the slightest extra something. She wasn't sure what it was she was seeing, just that she was seeing it. The two looked foreign and attractive. Not in a classic way. And not from the same country. But they had a gravity. *Who else?* There was a slight, fit Asian man in a long puffy coat sitting by himself, quietly enjoying his evening alone in a crowd. She felt it from him as well. It was exciting to feel like she had peers. Exciting and daunting. *Am I really like them?* Then she did a tally of her kills, stopping herself before things got too dark. Remembering Mr. Skin & Bones, Sugar looked around. *Is he here? Yes, up near the porch. Is he one of us?* After intense squinting, the verdict was, no. Just a wounded bird. Still, she was happy to not have him as a member of her new tribe.

Her next thought was unsettling. *Who out here is pegging me as one of them?* Without moving her head, she did her best to see if anyone was staring at her. While she couldn't make out anyone looking her way, she suddenly felt exposed. Maybe it was time to call it a wrap. But then she sensed someone was indeed staring at her. Up on the porch. Mary Helen. The pleasant woman was looking right at her. *Does she have the red flecks in her eyes?* Sugar hadn't thought to check her out before. *No. She didn't and her skin is ruddy, not translucent in any way. Still, there's something. What is it? And why is she staring?* Sugar could almost feel the woman inviting her to come sit beside her and talk. She thought, *I will not be pushed around. If that's what you're doing.*

As quietly as possible, Sugar got up and made a slow, silent retreat. A Dutch goodbye. Something she'd perfected at many an office soirée. Walking home to her van, Dutch goodbye nostalgia crept in and she reflected on her last company holiday party. At this particular event, she'd been talking to Brooke, a twenty-something gal from research with short, dyed blond hair and chunky, black-framed glasses. But when Brooke had to make a bathroom run, Sugar was left to focus on a 40-something guy from Media wearing a sweater that couldn't contain his girth and a constitution that could not contain his alcohol. As a rule, she never had more than one drink at those events. Too dangerous. This guy clearly did not have the same rule. He was trying to cozy up to the boss. Sugar felt her feet tightening in her red pumps as she waited for the entertainment to begin. She didn't have to wait long.

He babbled, "Who are they kidding? It's not a fucking holiday party. It's a goddamn Christmas party. A tree, a Santa, elves. For Christ's sake, why doesn't HR let us call a spade a spade? Am I right?"

Beyond the non-PC issue of "Christmas" versus "holiday," the man from Media had overlooked the use of the word "spade" in front of his Black employer. Sugar had not overlooked that, and folded her arms preparing for the fallout from her boss—a woman who clearly hadn't overlooked it, either.

The boss, wearing her most tasteful office-holiday-party garb, shifted her weight. "Charles, are you quite sure that's the verbiage you'd like to stick with?"

The man was oblivious to his blunder. "You have a problem with me callin' 'em like I see 'em?"

"I do not."

"Well?"

Politely she responded, "You have a nice Christmas party, Charles." With that, the woman turned, made a small nod to Sugar and disappeared into the party. Charles was left to stumble around looking for his next "for Christ's sake" victim. Sugar had been to enough of these events to know that things would only devolve from here. She made her Dutch goodbye thinking, *Goodbye, Charlie.*

Back in the present, the memory could still make Sugar laugh. But there would be no more office parties for her. She was pining for her old life and listening to her feet crunch along the gravel road when...

"Welcome home."

"What that F—!?" Taking a page from Kitten, Sugar was ready to shoot straight up in the air.

Mary Helen put a hand over her heart, stepping back. "My, what a big startle response you have."

"The better to freak out with."

Mary Helen laughed. Sugar laughed along with her, but she didn't mean it. *How the hell had this woman gotten here so fast? Did I meander more slowly than I realized? Ugh. Use your words.* "Can I help you with something? I'd offer you a chair, but I only have one."

"Oh, baby. You're so sweet. Actually, I was wondering if I could help you."

Sugar tried pegging the Southern swing in Mary Helen's speech, but while she could tell exactly which New York borough someone called home, she had no skills with the South. "Um. I'm good?"

"Well, I thought you might like to download my app." As Mary Helen pulled out her phone, Sugar wondered if she was about to be sold Mary H. Cosmetics.

Holding her phone so both she and Sugar could see the screen, Mary Helen explained, "Here we go. Moon...Glow...RV. All one word." She laughed. "I hate when I do that. All one word. I sound like someone's mother. But this is it. You can find all the Moonglow parks across this great land of ours. It's super simple. Oh, and here's the fun stuff. This red counter tells you how many of y'all are currently in residence in the V lot, and the green one tells you how many residents are in gen-pop."

"Gen-pop?"

"You know. General population. It's prison vernacular. Not that I've been." Mary Helen thrust an easy elbow. "I just ain't been caught yet." More giggles. "But each park has an area just for y'all."

"Y'all who?"

"Y'all. You. Vampires. I try to not have more than a half-dozen at a time. Don't want to be too conspicuous."

Sugar felt like she'd just been outed. "So, you know?"

"Oh my gosh, Shug. It's as plain as the jelly donut stain on my shirt."

Sugar thought, *Mm, Boston cream. No. Stop. Not now.* "I'm not sure what to say."

Mary Helen waved her hand. "Baby, it ain't nothin' but a thing. You can get it at the app store. It's free. Just download it, easy peasy, lemon squeezy. Click on the upper right. There, see? The Lifetime Membership. When I see it's you, I'll accept you and you'll be able to see it all. Locations, amenities, rules. Just don't tell anyone in gen-pop."

"I won't. But how do you stop them from wanting to join?"

"Look at the price."

Sugar saw that a lifetime membership was a hundred grand and turned to Mary Helen.

"Don't you worry. That's just momma's little gatekeeper. For you, it's free. Well, if you ever need anything, even an ear, I'm always up."

Mary Helen winked, then moved past Sugar and started back towards the office. Stopping, she looked back. "I'm curious. How'd you get that name, Sugar? Are your parents hippies?"

Just the thought of Henry and Faye as hippies lightened her mood. "It's a long story."

"I love a good story. You'll come over some time and tell me." Mary Helen turned and left.

Inside the van, Sugar stood watching the thoughts swirling in her head. It had been a full couple of days. Or, nights. When the dust in her mind settled, she drifted to thoughts of her "maker." *Hello hate. It always comes back to you, doesn't it?* She considered what she might learn from her new friends that could help. There was so much she didn't know. Still, she didn't like the thought of using these people. She genuinely liked them. *It's such a relief to be out of the closet. Or coffin.* She immediately chided herself for the mental Dad Joke.

Looking at the phone in her hand, she decided to download Mary Helen's app. It opened with a slight, electrical crackling sound, as the neon sign flickered. To Sugar's surprise, the app was quite professional looking. Clean and easy to navigate. As instructed, she clicked on the Lifetime Membership and a moment later was accepted. *Was Mary Helen just waiting for me to jump on?* Scanning the app, she found an impressive number of Moonglow Resorts. There was at least one in every state out West. Fewer states in the Northeast had a location. Sugar assumed it was because those states are smaller. More tightly packed. The amenities varied from park to park. All had laundry and showers. Some had pools and hot tubs. A few had shuffleboard. One even had mini-golf.

"Hey Kitten, this one has tennis and bocce."

She imagined becoming a tennis hustler to make money. *There'd be virtually no ball I couldn't return and my serve would be like lightning.* Just the ridiculousness of the idea made her smile.

Many of the parks featured music on weekends as well as movie nights. She wondered if they dared show *Interview with a Vampire*. "Kitten, what do you think? Too much chance for the audience to point out the inaccuracies. How about *Lost Boys*? We could all root for Kiefer Sutherland."

Moving on, she clicked on the app's rules tab. There was only one. It read, 'Please, Don't Feed on the Guests.'

"At least she said, 'Please.'"

11

CIRCLE OF FRIENDS

Sugar's phone rang. For the second time in a week, she was forcibly woken from a dream state. Not that she minded. Like most of her dreams now, it would end poorly. This one had started as a less vivid, more dream-like dream. She and Curtis were entertaining her parents. That in itself was odd because Henry and Faye never did get to enjoy that pleasure in real life. Sugar had dragged her feet on the intros because of Curtis's complete and utter lack of any gene that could be misconstrued as Jewish. But Sugar had been single long enough that her parents were starting to wonder if she was gay. Not that they'd have had a big problem if the woman in Sugar's life was a member of the tribe. Then she and her "friend" would be able to adopt a child and raise it with Hanukah, Passover, and Purim, and be relatively confident they wouldn't have to learn the words to *Oh, Holy Night*. But Sugar waited too long and the meeting never happened. It became another log on the fire called "Sugar's Massive Pile of Regrets." But certainly, not the biggest log.

Yet in the dream, here they all were, together and as happy as she could expect her parents to be. Faye was asking Curtis about his work, and not understanding how he made ends meet in New York City on handyman's money.

Curtis took it all in good stride. "I'm not actually a handyman, Mrs. Bernstein. I'm a carpenter."

Almost to himself, Henry said, "Like Jesus."

Ignoring or not hearing her husband, it was hard to tell, Faye pressed on. "Please, call me Faye."

Curtis nodded politely, "Okay, Faye."

"So, what's the difference?"

Sugar to the rescue. "He's a highly sought-after craftsman, Mom. He does high-end woodwork in some of the spendiest apartments in town, for CEOs and CFOs…"

Henry cut her off. "But you pay your bills?"

"I do. And on time."

"Good enough."

Curtis leaned to Sugar. "It's cute, you sticking up for me."

She whispered back, "I *am* cute."

About to kiss her in front of her parents, Sugar pulled back. But Henry was on Curtis's side. "Go ahead. Then we'll know she likes men."

Faye added, "The J.'s daughter, no names, she was married for ten, no, eleven years before she said she was a lesbian. It happens, you know."

Formally, Sugar said "Fascinating."

Faye rolled her eyes. "Don't be a jerk."

Playfully, Henry hugged his wife. "No. That's my job."

In his best Cary Grant, Curtis said, "Kiss me, you fool."

But when Sugar turned to break the seal on public displays of affection, it wasn't Curtis leaning into her. It was Alex, her maker. As Sugar recoiled in a mix of horror and fear, Alex sneered, "Go ahead. Kiss me again you fool."

Before Sugar could run, or scream, or fight, or explain to her parents that it wasn't what it looked like, that Curtis wasn't in drag or trans (not that there's anything wrong with that), or that she was sure the J.'s daughter was a fine person who loves her parents, before getting out all or any of that, her phone rang and she was pulled from the sitcom-turned-horror movie.

Sugar's heart seemed to be beating louder than her phone was ringing. "Goddamn you Alex! I mean it. May God damn you."

The disturbing thought Sugar had been holding at bay was now front and center. *Is Alex just in my dreams, or is she actually following me around?*

By the time the dream-fog had lifted and she was completely in the present, the phone stopped ringing. Sugar figured D. would just call back later. She was right. Her phone started ringing again. *That was fast.* She picked up. "That was fast."

"Impressed?"

"No. You okay?"

"Yeah. You?"

"Then why the immediate callback?"

In his best Downton Abbey, D. explained, "Thought you might have been in the East Wing and weren't able to get to the phone in a timely fashion. And clearly, I was correct."

Trying to shake off the scene with her parents that didn't really happen, Sugar *Downton-Abbey*'ed him back. "Clearly."

"Where you at?"

"Some RV Park. I think this is Colorado."

"Wow."

"Wow, what?"

"That was like an actual answer."

"Just trying to keep you on your toes."

"I thank you." David changed course. "My turn to need an ear. Not that you actually share anything. You just should. Anyway. Sorry. Do you have a sec so I can vent about my wife and then go back to not hating on her?"

After her crap dream, Sugar was happy for the normalcy of her brother's life. "Hit me."

"You know I mostly don't hate her."

"Most-ly."

The word "mostly" was part of the twin-banter they'd cultivated over the years. It was from the movie *Aliens*. In speaking about the monsters, the little girl in the film, Newt, was found alone on the mining planet. She warned Ripley, "They mostly come out at night. Most-ly." There was something about her strange, enunciated delivery of "most-ly" that Sugar and D. honed in on. Now they never let the word slip by without repeating it, Newt style. And sure enough...

"*Most-ly.*" D. let the word have its moment. "Sarah wants to invite this boy she has a crush on to the *bat-mitzvah* and Amy is completely raining on her parade. She's telling Sarah that she shouldn't. That she probably won't even like this kid by then."

"That's a bit harsh. Not to be judgy."

"You're not. Well, a little, but I opened the judgy door."

"What's her real reason?"

"See. I knew you'd get it. It's not the kid at all. The real reason is the kid's mother, who is a complete douche. Seriously. She's been keeping track of what every parent of this *bar-mitzvah* class is spending on their event and getting all, 'Well, I suppose if that's as much as you're willing to put into making your child's day special, it's up to you. Priorities, am I right?'"

"Oh, damn. She *is* a douche."

"Oh, and she's the synagogue treasurer, so she's privy to everything everyone's planning."

"Let me guess. Her kid is having an array of Disney ice sculptures and a command performance by Harry Styles."

"Probably just an ice sculpture *of* Harry Styles, but you get it. And Amy's got her panties in a bunch. I can't get her to let it go. I mean, the woman *is* horrible. She is. But Amy's making the rest of us pay for it. I wish she'd just tell the bitch off."

"When in doubt, laugh it out. Tell Amy, the next time this *lovely woman* starts in, laugh right in her face. It's like telling someone they're a clown. There's no comeback for it."

D. was quiet for a beat, then: "I like it. Thank you for *most-ly* saving my marriage."

"Most-ly. I'll send you a bill."

"Just don't name names. Initials only." They both laughed at the Faye callback. "So, what's new with you?"

"Mmm."

"Still have a cat?"

"I do." Sugar looked around for her bunkmate. Where was she? "Kitten? Kitten?" Nowhere in sight. "She seems to be hiding at the moment. I think I scared her. But for the most part, we're good. She's letting me share her van, rent-free."

"How very cat of her. Shug, you sound, okay."

"Comes and goes. I'm alright."

"I won't press."

"Smart."

"But maybe try being with people a little. Not just a cat."

"You may be surprised to know that I sat out and listened to live music last night. With actual people. Or near them, anyway."

"Really?"

"And, I've had an invitation to go skiing."

"What the what?! Oh, my God. Are you going?"

Before Sugar could answer, not that she had an answer ready, there was a knock on her sliding door followed by a "Tweedle-tweet!"

Walking D., via cell phone, to her door, Sugar slid it open for Maddie. Holding up a finger she said, "One sec, I'm finishing with my brother."

Instantly delighted, Maddie reached for the phone. "Oh. Let me. I wanna talk to Sugar's brother." Before Sugar could stop her, Maddie had the phone in her cold little hands. "Hi. I'm Maddie. So, you're Sugar's brother. What's your name? No, wait. I wanna guess. Basil?"

Sugar tried grabbing the phone. No luck. She could hear her brother stammer a "No" to this new voice on the phone.

Sugar nudged Maddie. "At least put it on speaker."

That much Maddie obliged as she continued her inquisition. "Buckwheat? Buck? Wheaton?"

"Sorry to disappoint. Nothing fun. Just David."

"Oh, that's so sad. Where are you? On the road? Are you in a van, too?"

"Nope. Prepare for more sadness. I'm in New Jersey."

"Oh. I am sorry." Looking at Sugar, "Your brother's kind of depressing."

"I know."

Sounding offended, D. said, "Hey. I'm still here."

Maddie gave Sugar back her phone. "I thought that would be more fun than it was."

Sugar took David off speaker. "Listen D., I'm gonna go."

"While I still have some dignity?"

"Yeah."

"Love you."

Quietly, as if she didn't want Maddie to hear her caring about someone, she said, "Love you, too." Then clicked off the call.

But Maddie was only half listening at that point. She'd found Kitten in a corner of the bunk and was engaging in major petting. "Oh, you love me so much."

"Meow-ah."

Sugar smirked. "She said she'd love you more if you had a pocket full of tuna."

"You disappeared early last night."

"Tired."

"You should join the music tonight. Matt said you sing."

"I don't remember telling him I sing."

"He said you sang along last night. He said you're good."

"Did I? Hm. But no. I'm strictly audience."

"My mother always said you shouldn't hide your light under a bushel."

Happy for an opportunity to learn more about Maddie, Sugar

asked, "I don't know *anything* about you. Were you and your mother close?"

"No." With that bubble-free response, it was clear Sugar wasn't going to learn any more. Not tonight. Maddie kissed Kitten's head and placed her on the bunk. "Come on. Lance and Willie want to meet you."

"What if I don't want to meet them?"

"They're sarcastic like you."

"I hate sarcasm."

"See? Come on."

Moments later, Sugar was standing in front of Lance and Willie, the two men in ballcaps she'd spotted the night before. Lance had her hand in his. "*Enchanté*, m'lady."

Her first thought was to wonder how old Lance was. Her guess was that he had walked the Earth much longer than Willie. Than any of them. Something about him said old, old world. Something about Willie read mid-fifties modern. Lance was as fair as Willie was swarthy. She assumed he was even swarthier in the before-times when he still had all his melanin.

Maddie filled the dead air. "Sugar's from New Jersey. Isn't that awful?"

Lance put his other hand on top of the one already cradling Sugar's and in a French accent, which had been watered down over the decades or even centuries said, "I am so very sorry for you." She was about to give a snappy retort, but his wink let her know he wasn't trying to start off on the wrong foot. Quite the contrary.

Still, she wanted to give back as good as she got. With a wink of her own, she said. "And I'm sorry about the Treaty of Paris and losing Canada."

Willie laughed. He had a thick Spanish accent. "Hmm. Smell her."

Lance said, "Well, I was never a fan of ze accent, anyway. Ay?" Lance released Sugar's hand and turned to Matt. "I like zis one."

Lance and Willie had quite a set up. Under the awning of their shiny, silver Airstream trailer sat six high-end folding chairs draped in matching furs. The chairs were all neatly arranged on a grass mat with a geometric two-toned blue pattern. Helping to make their outdoor space feel homey were several well-placed potted plants and a cherub statue in a small fountain. They also had a chiminea going that was sending the scent of mesquite smoke into the night air. Through their open front door, Sugar could see that the interior of their trailer was equally welcoming, though more antique, even lush.

Willie offered, "Come. Sit. Maddie has been telling us about jou. Now it's jour turn. Jou tell us about jou."

Sugar enjoyed Willie's accent. Trying to sound nonchalant as she took a seat, she replied, "Oh, let's not."

Willie whispered loudly, "Come on. One juicy tidbit."

Lance flashed his best flirty look. It was pretty good. In that moment, it hit her just how attractive all these people were. Even if they weren't classically good-looking, they were all somehow visually appealing. *Is that a thing? Am I more attractive now?* She'd always considered herself average. Not a head turner, but not a stomach turner. *Stop it! You're being self-absorbed. Focus. What is Willie saying?*

"...Please. Jou can make it short. Just give us jour dating app description."

Now it was a game. She considered how she might tease her life. The advertising woman kicked in. "Okay. Nice Jewish ad gal with a love of musicals. Hates cleaning. Appreciates a personal shopper, a seat in first class, and a well-timed throat punch."

Lance politely bowed his head to her. "You may stay."

"I thank you. Now, I showed you mine..."

Lance took Willie's hand. "Okay. I was ze primary and brought Willie into ze life. I myself was born into ze life, mere centuries ago."

Willie smiled at him as if to say, you're not so old. "But jou don't look the day over a hundred."

"Thank you. I was born thirty kilometers outside of Paris so, born in Paris. Yes?" He laughed at his own small joke. "I have lived in homes grand and small. Some of zem mine. Some not. My likes are interior decorating, subtle cologne, and a well-kept secret. I have made and lost fortunes, survived wars, sexual and vampirical persecution, and through it all, managed to keep my boyish good looks and rapier-like wit."

Willie applauded his partner's small speech.

Sugar clapped as well. "I'd love to chat about that 'making fortunes' part some time."

Maddie added, "And you never lost your accent."

"Why would I want to when I sound zis lovely? Zis not American?"

In his own thicker accent, Willie said, "Now, me. I will go. I was born William Marco Louis Hildago Hernandez. When my parents move to this country from Cuba, that was Batista's first term, they change their name to Handle to sound more American. I am officially, Mr. Willie Handle. I sound like a porn star, no?" Sugar laughed as Willie continued. "Then, I meet this lovely creature at a bar in Miami Beach."

Sugar asked, but not really, "Across a crowded room?"

"No. A back alley. I made a smile at the wrong fellow. It was a different time. And, long beating short, the *gentleman* and his *friends* left me in the alley. I would have died there. I know that for sure. But this one, he saved me." Willie leaned on Lance.

Moved, Sugar said, "I'm so sorry."

Willie smiled, "It's okay. Really. Everything works out. Yes?"

Seeing the affection between the two men had Sugar thinking of Curtis.

Lance took her hand and looked in her eyes. "You miss him. I can tell."

Willie chided him. "Don't read her thoughts. It's no nice."

Sugar remembered what Matt had said about mind reading. It's hard. Not everyone can do it. She made a mental note to not underestimate Lance, no matter how charming and matter-of-fact he seemed.

"I'm sorry. I shouldn't pry. But you seem so sad."

Maddie clapped her hands. "So, let's be happy. Someone say something happy." She raised a hand. "I'm someone. I'll go first. I'm happy for Sugar and her cat, Kitten."

Matt went next. "I know something happy." He turned to his wife. "I fixed our ladder."

Sugar smirked. "So, it can no longer have little ladders?"

Two, three... Everyone started laughing until they laughed even harder. The deep sadness was gone, at least for the moment. In the welcoming warmth of these strangers, things felt safe and Sugar was able to admit, "I do miss him. So much."

Willie took the opening. "Can I ask how he died?"

Without looking at anyone, Sugar flatly stated, "Vampire."

And, silence. They glanced from one to the other. It's not like the news was a shock. A scenario they'd never heard before. But still.

Feeling bad for bringing the party right back down, Sugar said, "I'm sorry. What's our game? Say something fun? Okay. I'll go. I have one. Curtis and I were invited to this very uptight Christmas party at one of his clients. Picture lots of money. Men in holiday vests. At one point, it becomes clear, I'm *the* Jew in the room."

Willie made a mock gasp. "No!"

Sugar played along. "*Jes*. And this woman in a crisp white blouse and crushed velvet red skirt says, 'We just took our grandchildren to that lovely Holocaust museum. Sugar, I'm sure you've been.' She literally said, that *lovely* Holocaust museum, like it was a New York boutique. So, I said, 'No. They won't let me in.'"

Lance laughed immediately. "You did not."

"I did. It was a complete needle-scratch on the record moment. Total silence. Except for Curtis. He quickly thanked our host, we left as fast as we could, then laughed our asses off. We went out for Thai and spent the night thinking of inappropriate taglines for businesses that don't exist. Wait. What did we come up with? Oh, Mama Cass's Deli. Would a sandwich kill you? And, Jesus Brand Furniture: Christ, that's good wood."

The laughter was starting to become contagious. Matt raised his hand. "I have one. Vote for Taft. A tub full of fun."

Matt laughed at his line, but Willie looked confused. "I don't get that."

"Taft. Fattest U.S. president. He got stuck in his bathtub."

"That's so sad. What if someone else was dirty?"

Maddie was now laughing so hard she was doubled over. "Oh my God! Oh my God! I might throw up." True to her word, Maddie retched and threw up a little.

With an extravagant hand gesture that didn't go with his normal, get-it-done-guy demeanor, Matt added, "Ladies and gentlemen, my wife."

With laughter continuing, the slight Asian man from the other night walked past. His face gave the look of someone who had just smelled rotten eggs. "Perhaps you all could be a bit louder. Hmm?"

Lance called out, "We could certainly try."

Willie stood up. "Oh Happy. Why do jou have to be such a Mr. Scrooge? Come join the party."

"Piss off, Willie. And the name is Harry." Harry continued on his curmudgeonly way without breaking stride.

Lance leaned to Sugar explaining, "Well, you just met Harry. Or as we like to call him, Happy Harry. Or, Happy, for short. Because, he is not."

Willie clarified, "*Not* happy. He *is* short."

Maddie snorted.

Sugar said, "Seems a shame to separate yourself from what's already a small group."

Taking both Matt and Willie's hands and swinging them, Maddie smiled, "Don't be fooled. He loves us."

After a moment, they all shook their heads and in unison said, "No, he doesn't." More laughing.

Sugar asked, "How many of *us* are at this park?"

Matt replied. "The five of us, Liz and Vickie just left, and Harry. So, six."

That brought up a new question. "And is everyone friendly? I mean besides Harry. But does everyone... Do they leave each other... Are vampires nice to each other?"

Willie laughed. "We are like anyone. All kinds."

"So, no. They're not all nice."

Matt shrugged, "Some good. Some bad. For the most part, all of us on the road seem to get along."

With the wisdom of several lifetimes, Lance added, "And like anyone else, we all get more into our, shall we say, patterns ze longer we are here. Zat means, for our kind zere is much more time to dwell and fester. To get good and shitty."

But Sugar's real question hadn't been answered. She pressed on. "How bad are the bad ones? 'Steal your lunch from the office fridge' bad, or 'Kill your cat' bad?"

Bluntly, Matt said, "We're talking 'Kill your cat, suck its kittens dry, and leave the carcasses in the office fridge' bad."

"Do any of the bad ones ever stay at Moonglow?"

Lance shook his head. "Fortunately, zey find us too *pedestrian* for zeir liking."

Willie raised his chin. "Well, la-de-dah."

Matt added, "They're bullies. Nasty little fuckers. I could tell you a story that—"

Lance put his hand on Matt's shoulder. "We should stop. I zink we're upsetting ze lady."

"It's okay. I was raised to believe I was always seconds away from being upset about something."

"Still..."

There was a long, worried pause. Then Maddie abruptly stood. "Who wants to see me do a double back flip?"

All hands shot into the air.

Maddie turned her back to the group. She stood on her toes with her arms thrust out in front of her, like she was a diver at the end of a diving board. Then she made several readying arm swings, crouched and quickly shot both arms behind her back, flipping everyone the bird with both hands.

Putting his hands behind his head, and as if he was an Olympic judge, Lance said, "Ze French judge gives an eight and a half. Nice execution, but ze toes were not pointed."

When he stopped laughing long enough to speak, Matt turned to his wife. "You're so *pedestrian*."

"And you love it."

"All night long."

Sugar sat on what felt like the outside edge of this bizarre circle and smiled. She was a fan of all of them. The laughter continued for hours. It was like a protective bubble and she tried desperately to not think of its inevitable burst.

12

SMOKE WITH ME

The dusk sky was washed in dramatic pinks and purples. Walking to the RV office, Sugar mused, *The colors out West are so much more spectacular than in New York.*

It was time to pay for her extended stay. Who knew she'd be able to relax in one place this long? But her new acquaintances seemed to be exactly what she needed and the nights passed quickly. Yet, Mary Helen made her feel both comfortable and uncomfortable, so she'd been putting off the visit. She was another unknown. Someone who ran a rest-stop for wayward vampires. Still, Sugar didn't like being negligent. Almost before tapping on the doorframe, she heard, "Come on in, baby."

There was Mary Helen, behind her cluttered counter, lighting a pipe with a wooden match. After taking several drags to get the thing going, she let out a long, thin plume of smoke. The office smelled faintly of cherry. When the smoke dissipated, she turned to Sugar. "All my life. Can you believe it? I've lived all my days without ever smokin' a pipe. Well look at me, tryin' somethin' new."

"And?"

"I'm not mad at it." Mary Helen struck a pose like a 1950s magazine ad for pipe tobacco. "Somebody left these here. How do I look?"

Sugar assessed the scene. Between Mary Helen's gauzy white blouse with purple ribbons, the wood pipe fashioned to look like the head of an old English sea captain, and the robotic pose out of a 1950s magazine, all Sugar could come up with was, "Incongruous?"

Mary Helen laughed out a small puff of smoke. "I like that. Incongruity. One of my life's pursuits. How can I help you, Shug?"

"I have something for you." Sugar pulled cash from her back pocket. "How much do I owe you?"

"Depends. How long you stayin'?"

"Honestly, I'm not sure. But I'd like to pay for my time so far and maybe a little extra for the unknown."

Mary Helen giggled. "I'm always happy to take money." With her new fashion accessory clenched in her teeth, she opened a battered ledger covered in stickers and flipped through it. "Let's see. Well, you certainly passed your original plan. What was it you said? Probably just one night?"

"What can I say? The place grew on me."

"We're like a fungus." More warm giggling. "Well, we like havin' ya here. How about you give me a couple hundred for now?"

From her wad of bills, Sugar thumbed out the cash and handed it over. As she did so, her hand lightly touched Mary Helen's. In that moment, a serious wave seemed to wash over the light-hearted innkeeper. She looked up pointedly. "I'm so sorry for your loss."

"Excuse me?"

"My bad, Shug. I don't mean to pry. Well, not to your face. It just happens." She smiled in a way that said she was trying to be a friend.

"*What* happens?"

"I see things. Really, I feel them. Kinda' crazy, right? Used to make my momma uncomfortable as hell. She'd say she was goin' out for cigarettes. She knew I knew she was really keepin' time with Mr. Barret up the road. But I echo The Lady Ga-gah." With relish, Mary

Helen put extra emphasis on the second syllable of "Gaga." "Baby, I was born this way."

Sugar didn't question Mary Helen's claim. The woman likely did feel things. The world is a strange place. *Does that explain the uncomfortable feeling I get from her, or is there more? Hard to know.* Sugar started stepping backwards. "So, we're good?"

"Are you leavin' me?"

This was the exact same question Faye would ask whenever Sugar was heading out the door. Any door. It was meant to be playful, but not completely. There was always that little dig of Jewish guilt that had been handed down over generations like sourdough starter. "I figured, you had...things."

"Things? Look around. We're in the middle of bum-shit nowhere and my big plan for the day was smoking this pipe, which I've done. Maybe seeing if I could get Happy Harry to fix my heater. He's very handy, that one." She winked and added, "In more ways than one."

"Hmm." *Well, that was a surprise.*

"Don't judge. Still waters. He can knock boots with the best of 'em. One time—"

Sugar put her hands up, "I'm good."

Mary Helen laughed. "TMI? Yeah, I do that. Guess I'm just a sharer. So, tell me about you."

"I thought you could feel everything for yourself." Hearing her words, Sugar immediately regretted how abrupt they'd sounded. "Sorry. That came out wrong. I'm just...private."

"And I'm nosy. It's okay. Most of y'all only share up to a point." Mary Helen came out from behind the counter, hooked an arm with Sugar's, and escorted her to a back room. "Come visit for a little."

The back area was more home than office, and decorated with treasures from around the world. Not junk, but actual *objets d'art*. It was eclectic and inviting. Sugar spun around slowly, getting lost in studying the different pieces. There was everything from gilt reliquary boxes and golden idols to Buddhas and tribal fertility god carvings, even some Church of The Sub-Genius religious parody art.

Every item seemed to be somehow connected to spirituality, both mainstream and obscure. Light and dark. The only item that seemed out of place was the "What Would Dolly Do?" tea set.

Looking comfortable in the corner of an overstuffed antique sofa with carved wood trim, Mary Helen beckoned. "Come on. Sit with me."

Sugar obliged and sank into a jewel-green wing chair.

"Tell me how a nice Jewish girl from New Jersey gets the name Sugar."

"Oh, that. Well, it's simple. My parents wanted to use an S name. After my grandfather Sam, who'd just passed. They'd picked Suzan. But the day we were born..."

"We?"

"I'm a twin."

"That's fun."

"Sometimes. Usually. Anyway, the day we were born, my mother's best friend came to the hospital. She was holding me and asked my mother what they were naming me. Faye said, 'Suzan,' and her friend said, 'Sazan? That's my sister in-law's name. I hate that bitch. I'm just gonna call your child Sugar.' She handed me back to my mother and, as the legend goes, Faye started singing 'Sugar' by The Hollies. And bonus, it was an S name. That was it. From that moment on, I was Sugar."

Mary Helen let out a long, pleasing plume of smoke. "I love that story. Hey. You wanna try a pipe?"

"No, I—"

"Don't be a pipey-pooper. Life is long. You might as well try somethin' new."

"I'd lie for mystique and say I'd been a pipe smoker for years, but I'm afraid you'd see right through it."

"It's a blessing and a curse."

After getting Sugar set up with her own pipe which was carved to look like a ship's figure head, the two women smoked in silence, enjoying the odd civility of the act and the cherry-scented tobacco.

Sugar noted it was interesting how some smells and tastes were so objectionable now, but that smoking felt utterly satisfying. *Hey, maybe I could die of lung cancer. Or would my cancerous cells repair themselves before things got too far? That would be just my luck.*

"I like your bracelet"

"Oh. Thanks. I'm a jewelry gal."

"You make jewelry?"

"No, no. My career was in advertising. I just like jewelry, and clothes, and shoes. My father's family has a department store. Lots of clothes. Lots of family."

"You miss them?"

Sugar felt that it was more a statement than a question. And of course, it was true. She missed them all. The whole "being in everyone's business" thing used to be a source of constant arguments, but she'd give everything to have it back. "Yeah."

"Tell me a family story. Something that lets me know your people."

Feeling more comfortable with Mary Helen, Sugar didn't mind sharing a bit more of herself. But there were so many stories. *Which one?* "Okay. Wait. I have a my-crazy-family story. It was my grandparents' anniversary. 50? No, had to be 60. Faye and Henry threw the party in the department store. All the family parties are in the store. They roll back the racks and bring out the big round folding tables. And magic, it's a party. The whole family was there. The whole *mischpoke*, as it were. The women cooked enough for five parties. Side note: Avoid anything that Aunt Gert cooks. So, the party's going. The band's playing. And my father and his brothers take D. aside. D., that's my brother, David. D. So, they take D. aside and say, this is such a great party. It'd be a shame to waste it. Why don't you announce your engagement tonight?"

Mary Hellen was absorbed in the tale. "Was he planning to announce his engagement?"

"No. That's the my-crazy-family part. He'd been dating Amy for over a year. She was a nice Jewish girl. They knew her family from synagogue. And all on their own, my family figured it was time. They never consulted D. I don't think he'd even talked to Amy about it yet."

"What happened?"

Sugar laughed, remembering her brother trapped in the Hebrew headlights. "D. tried to worm out of it saying he didn't even have a ring. A really dumb reason when you're standing in the middle of a department store. Uncle Lou, he handles the jewelry department. Lou goes away and comes back with a ring and tells my father, "You can owe me." And that was it. D. caved and a minute later Henry and Faye are raising glasses to their son's impending marriage. D. caught a fair amount of shit that night from Amy, but she said yes. So, that is my family. And scene."

Mary Helen applauded, seemingly delighted by the story. Sugar enjoyed being able to tell it.

Then, with a caring look, Mary Helen leaned forward, saying quietly, "That life is over, Shug. You know that, right? You can remember it. Smile about it. But don't try to hold on too tight or somethin' will get broke."

Well, that was a sobering punch. It seemed to come from a place of genuine caring, and had way too much gravity to be ignored. *What's she telling me? That I need to break ties with D.? Block his number? Ghost him completely?* Sugar took a deep drag from the pipe and held the smoke as if releasing it would be saying goodbye.

13

THAT'S SNOW FUN

Pulling on the pink ski pants she'd borrowed from Maddie, Sugar was still in disbelief. *How can I be going skiing? Should vampires get to ski? Aren't we too inherently dark for such a gen-pop activity? Should I feel guilty for taking a break from feeling guilty?* Yet, here she was, suiting up. Lance had said, "If you don't find something you take pleasure in, something to fill all ze nights to come, your existence will be, well, like Happy Harry's. Ze V-Life goes on too long to be maudlin. Maudlin can lead to bitterness, and bitterness can lead to darker feelings. Once you start giving in to zose, well, just don't." So, she let herself get talked into joining their outing.

Maddie's passion in life had been skiing and she saw no need to change her ways in her V-Life. Who knew how long Matt had been skiing or if he even predated the sport? Sugar felt like asking that would be rude. She thought, *Funny how in her previous life, being young was prized. Like it was an accomplishment or a choice. But in V-Life, longevity is the accomplishment. Something earned and respected.* Then she thought, *That's enough epiphanies for one day.*

Reaching over her desk and grabbing her gloves, she glanced down at Kitty who was sitting on her note pad. "Meow-ah."

"What?"

"Meow-ah. Meow-ah."

"I know. Pink was never my color. Come here." Picking up Kitten, Sugar kissed her head. Right in mid-snuggle, there was a loud bang outside. It startled the cat who flew out of Sugar's arms. As Kitten scrambled to get onto the bunk, she caught the edge of a piece of paper. It was the picture of Curtis Sugar had hidden under her mattress when she first hit the road. She'd been avoiding it, but the seal was now broken. Sugar took the photo and leaned on her kitchen counter, staring at it. *God, he's as handsome as I remembered.* She put the photo to her nose, hoping for some lingering scent. There was none, so she made it up. Pretending to breathe him in, she whispered, "I miss you so much."

Kitten leaned against her.

Without looking, she scooped up her van-mate and showed her the photo. "Look how handsome, Kitten?"

"Meow-ah."

"Don't be jealous."

Another loud Bang! Bang! was followed by, "Tweedle-tweet!"

Sugar kissed Curtis, slid him back where Kitten had found him, and called out "One sec!"

Matt's muffled voice called back. "We're burning moonlight!"

Grabbing a bedazzled gear bag along with the rest of her loaner equipment, Sugar collected herself and slid open the van door. There were Maddie, Matt, Lance, and Willie. All but Willie were dressed for the ski date. Sugar jumped down. Noting Willie's non-skiing attire, she asked, "You're not joining?"

"We don't ski in Cuba."

Maddie pointed out, "You're not in Cuba."

"Shame."

Lance quipped, "Is it?"

"No really. But snow. Ugh. It gets between jour little mittens and jour sleeves. And jou shiver. No thanks."

Matt was on top of his rig, locking the equipment box. "You don't know what you're missing."

"Jou can take a picture for me."

Sugar pulled at her pants a bit, trying to extend them. "Thanks, Maddie. The stuff is great. I fear the pants are a bit short."

Maddie, in purple camo ski gear waved her hand. "I say, if your ass is covered, you're good."

Sugar started closing the van door and called in, "Kitten, make yourself useful while I'm gone. Maybe do my taxes."

From inside the van came a rather loud and put-out, "Meow-ah."

Willie seemed intrigued. "Hold my phone. Do jou really have a cat?"

"I do."

"Truly?"

"I am many things, but I'm not a liar. I have a cat."

With his mouth agape, Willie turned to Lance and in an almost whisper said, "Sugar Lady has a real cat."

"I heard her."

"Wait. I'm Sugar Lady?"

Lance shook his head. "Willie loves a nickname."

"When you're named Sugar, you don't expect many nicknames. Not good ones. In grade school, I was Sugar Pops. In high school, I was Sugar Lips. And in the office, people were afraid to utter my name at all, fearing a nasty visit from HR."

Willie was now a highly-intrigued vampire. "Do you think your kitten would like me to cat sit?"

Maddie bragged, "She *loves* me!"

In a bit of a beg, Willie said. "Oh, my God. I want to pet your kitten."

"That's the best offer I've had in some time." Sugar handed him the key to her mobile kingdom. "I'm sure Kitten will love the company."

Willie cupped the key like a jewel in his hands. "Jou people take as long as jou like. I have a date with a kitten."

Lance put his hand on Willie's shoulder. "Before you fall in love with her cat, kiss me good-bye."

"Jou first."

Lance rolled his eyes. "Fine." The partners bid farewell and the rest loaded into the ambulance.

Once all the night skiers were in, Matt sent heavy metal music through the speakers and grabbed the shifter. "Everyone have their seatbelts on?"

Clicking in Lance asked, "Why? You zink you might kill us...again?"

The older vampires shared a dark laugh. All Sugar could manage was an ironic snicker. *What a bizarre circle of friends I have now.* Still, spending the first weeks of V-Life by herself had been painfully lonely. *I prefer this.*

It took them just over two hours to reach their destination. Closing in, the brilliant white lights illuminating the three runs that were being used for night skiing seemed to declare, "Party ahead!" Matt pulled into the lot and parked between too beefy pickups. Turning back from the co-pilot seat, Maddie warned, "Sugar, people always stare when we get out of this thing. Don't worry about it. They're looking at the vehicle. Not us."

"Got it."

Matt added, "Still, boot up before you get out."

"Check."

"Here." Matt started handing out red ice cubes on toothpicks. "For energy."

"Oh Sugar, you'll love these." Maddie put the whole thing in her mouth at once, causing her cheek to swell in a cube shape.

"What is it?"

Matt explained, "Blood pops."

Through a full mouth Maddie corrected him, "Blood-sicles."

Matt rolled his eyes at the correction. "They're really handy for a little pick-me-up on the road."

Lance took his and smelled it before killing it in two crunching bites. "Mm, gopher. You two are so inventive."

Sugar followed Lance's lead. She had to admit, it was kind of genius. Her first V-Life hack. After they were fortified, the crew donned gear and went down a list to make sure they had everything. Looking around, Matt asked, "We all ready?"

Sugar declared, "Let's do this." though she was not at all sure that she should.

"Yay!" Maddie chanted, "Night ski! Night ski! Night ski!"

Grinning, Matt said, "My girl gets excited."

As they walked the hundred or so yards to the lift, Sugar couldn't get over how odd it was to be surrounded by normal people out doing normal people things. She eavesdropped on one couple in expensive ski clothes arguing with each other.

"We always ski the runs you want to ski. What about what I want to ski?"

"There are only three runs. We'll get to all of them."

"But in your order. Not in mine. Right?"

"Oh, my God!"

"Don't 'Oh my God' me!"

The dour duo tramped towards the ski lift, determined to not enjoy themselves.

To Sugar's right, a father chided his son who was dragging his skis and poles as if they weighed a hundred pounds. "Buddy, if you want to ski, you have to carry your own equipment. That's the rule. Now pick 'em up. Let's go." The boy made a show of lifting his oh-so heavy skis, but as he walked, he continued dragging his poles. Sugar thought, *Life is going on without me.* She supposed that was as it should be.

She caught up to her friends in the lift line and clicked into her skis, which were an old pair of Maddie's. As they all loaded onto the quad chair lift, Sugar admitted, "I've never gone night skiing."

Maddie giggled. "Watch out for zombies."

"What! You're not serious?"

Matt flashed a knowing smile. "That's what we call the knuckleheads who don't know what they're doing and stop in the middle of a run like some fuckin' zombie."

Feeling somewhat relieved and a touch foolish, Sugar said, "Oh." Then she hoped she wouldn't be one of them. *How many years has it been since my last ski trip?* She'd done a ladies' trip to Park City about three or four years earlier. But really, the trip was more about pampering than skiing—massages, dinners, champagne—the skiing was more of an excuse to have something sporty to talk about at the après-ski. Specialty bourbon drinks for all. They'd laughed about everything and nothing. *Good times.* Sugar looked down at her ski togs. Definitely not the spendy garb she'd worn with her ladies. *But these aren't my ladies, are they?* As the foursome reached the top of the lift, Sugar told herself, *Get over it and don't be a snob.* Putting aside concern about her wardrobe, she was free to focus on the dread of potentially sucking at this in front of her new friends.

Maddie waited for no one. The second her skis touched snow, she pushed off, heading down a run. Matt shrugged. "She gets excited." And then he was gone as well. In the brief moment before they disappeared from sight, Sugar could tell that they were both excellent skiers. *Well, they've certainly had time to get good.* Remembering that they'd told her V-Life makes you better at what you're already good at, she mused that Maddie was likely an excellent skier in her before-times as well.

Next was Lance. "See you at ze bottom, darling." His form was different from Matt and Maddie's. Less balls-to-the-wall. More refined. More European. He was a lovely skier.

The father and son from earlier passed her next, starting their way down the slope. "Keep up with me, buddy!" A moment later, son was passing father.

Knowing she couldn't stand there forever, Sugar reminded herself, "Be steely." As she started letting her skis run, she thought, *Curtis's catch-phrase is like the Swiss Army knife of advice.* After a few careful test turns, she began remembering the movement and allowed herself to gain more speed. And then more, until the feeling of the air rushing past her was thrilling. She couldn't believe she could still experience something this optimistic. This freeing. *Maybe I still get to have moments not cast in darkness. Maybe I can...* "Shit!"

A college age kid on a snowboard came to a stop directly in front of her and sat down smack in the middle of the run. Sugar swerved to avoid him—almost taking out a little girl skiing in front of her mother. The woman yelled, "Look the fuck out, asshole!"

Sugar was about to yell back but instead chose to use her energy to not hit a tree. "Crap! Shit! Crap!"

Finally, she managed to get herself back into a decent fall line and finished the run. Pulling up next to her companions, she dropped her head and took her first breath in what seemed like minutes. "Goddamn zombies!"

Matt laughed. "Told ya."

Maddie was already skiing away to the lift line. "Again!"

They all obliged and went back for more.

After almost two hours, Sugar had lost track of how many runs they'd made. Eight, nine? She figured this one would be her last. But she didn't dare declare it out loud. Remembering on her ladies' trip, her friend Bunny had said, "You never say out loud it's your last run or the gods will hear and make you pay." *Gods? How relevant is that now? Still, why risk it?* She stayed silent.

They'd all agreed they'd go back to the run named Botox Bonanza. It was longer than Devil's Pimple, and lacked the moguls of Crater Face, which were getting pretty iced up. One mogul had thrown Sugar into a split position so wide, she thought it might rip her in half. It didn't, but she now owed Maddie a new pair of ski pants.

Resigned to being nowhere near as good as her escorts, Sugar hoped to make this her personal best run of the night. Right from the start, her friends skied past her. Maddie's jubilance rang out as she disappeared down the hill. "Hoot! Hoot!"

Sugar called out in reply. "Hoot! Hoot!"

She didn't go flat out, but maintained a good speed and tight form, careful to keep an eye out for any rogue snowboarder who might randomly decide that one yard in front of her was the best seat in the house. *Fool me once.* As she angled towards the left side of the run, Sugar shifted her weight, prepared to make her next, easy turn.

Suddenly, two dark figures in long, emerald-green coats stepped out from behind a tree and stood arms akimbo like sentries at a gate to something sinister. At that moment, all sound disappeared. A chill shot up Sugar's spine causing her legs to lock and instead of turning, she was heading straight for them. *What the hell is happening?!* Fear filled her completely. In her head she yelled, *Turn! Turn! Turn!* But she couldn't. She was going to fly right into them. Now just yards away, the one on the right reached to open his jacket revealing a long, shiny blade. The other figure crossed his arms and pulled out two blades, one from each hip. He was bizarrely familiar. *Do I know you? Yes. He was the man from her dream.* But this wasn't a dream. Imagining his blade sliding into her heart, Sugar wondered, *Will it hurt? No!* She scolded herself for being weak mere seconds before her death. *God, why can't I turn!* Both men grinned at her. Dark, sinister grins inviting her to die. In the last moment, she chose to not cover her eyes. *This is my fate. Own it.*

As both figures took a deadly fighting stance, a snowboarder shot between Sugar and evil, plopping herself down for a break. In that instant, the spell, if that's what it was, broke. Sugar cut in her edges and turned from her impending demise, throwing a wave of white over the snowboarder slash savior. Only she could hear herself utter, "Best seat in the fucking house!"

Having to dare herself to look back over her shoulder, Sugar saw that the men were gone. "What the hell?! Who are you?" The only thing she did know was that they were vampires. And not the RVing pedestrian type.

Finally coming to a stop at the bottom of the slope, Sugar's heart was pounding in her chest. It took only a short time for the ambient sounds of the resort to return to her ears.

She was dizzy with exhaustion when Lance approached her. "Are you okay?"

"I don't know. Am I?"

"Do you know those *men*?"

Before she could answer, Matt and Maddie came over. Matt's head was turning right and left and right again as he scanned the area. "What the shit!? They're not supposed to be here. What the fuck, this is our territory."

Grabbing both of his hands, Maddie looked firmly into Matt's eyes. "It's okay. Calm down. It's okay."

Matt broke her hold. "Bullshit. What do they want? They want something. She-vil's thugs don't crawl out of their hole without a reason."

Lance couldn't argue. "He is right. Zey want somesing. Or someone."

They all started looking at each other, questioningly. Utterly confused, Sugar asked, "Who's She-vil?"

Matt answered, "The worst of us."

"She-vil? A woman? A vampire?"

Lowering his voice to prevent anyone nearby from hearing him, Lance quietly explained, "She-vil, aka Alexandria, is a shitty little vamp who lives on hate."

Alexandria? Sugar's heart got its next jolt. She feared Alexandria might be Alex. Her Alex. Dread and guilt filled her throat as if she'd just committed a horrible crime. It was almost too thick for her to swallow. Her mind was reeling. Thoughts tumbling over thoughts.

Lance was still talking. "She-vil does not send her henchmen out randomly. But we can tell you her nasty little tale later. We should get out of here. Now."

No one argued. Sugar thought, *Fuck. The gods heard me.*

14

A LOUD SILENCE

"Getting out now" proved more difficult than anticipated. The ambulance wasn't starting and Matt couldn't figure out why. Lance and Maddie offered suggestions. But knowing nothing about what to do under the hood except where to add the oil and the windshield washer fluid, and only on her own vehicle, Sugar could merely stand and watch.

Matt was playing shop teacher and talking as he worked. "Sugar, you need to know this stuff if you're going to live alone in an RV. You have to be self-sufficient." But when he finally figured out what was wrong, the explanation made little sense to her. Perhaps the information would have had a better chance of penetrating if she wasn't preoccupied thinking about Alex and how she almost just died again. *I never feared for my life in Advertising.*

Time ticked by. Knowing what the problem was and fixing it were two different things. After hours of tinkering, Matt lowered the hood. He put a hand on Sugar's shoulder as if he was her coach. "That make sense to you? Think you could do that?"

"Sure. Thanks." It was a fib, but Sugar felt that in that moment, fibbing was more expedient.

Maddie passed her whispering, "Liar."

After driving only an hour, dawn started breaking and they made the group decision to pull over and sleep. Or think, then sleep. Or just think.

Matt and Maddie's conversation in the cab of the vehicle was getting increasingly heated. It was hard to tell exactly what it was about. He said something and she said she didn't like how he said it. The argument was escalating.

Lance was sitting in the back of the ambulance, speaking quietly to Sugar. "She-vil is a vengeful creature. She has no heart. No remorse. And she overdresses for everything."

Sugar half smiled, appreciating Lance's willingness to attempt humor in the face of potential doom. "And you think she sent those...*men* to harm us."

"Why else?"

"I don't know. I don't know anything." Which wasn't totally true. She may know something about Alexandria, if she was indeed Alex. But what she meant was, she didn't know the rules of this life. As much as Sugar hated what she now was, she hated being so ill-informed at least as much. It made her feel foolish and vulnerable.

"She-vil is mad at ze world. She believes zat ze horrible first life she lived entitles her to a glorious V-Life."

The thought that this could be her Alex made her feel sick. *But is it her? Maybe not. But if it is her, am I putting my friends in danger?*

Lance continued, "Honestly. It's been centuries. You would think she could have gotten some therapy by now." Sugar laughed a nervous laugh. "She is not to be taken lightly. She is true evil. You don't want her mad at you. Sugar, I am serious. You do not want her zinking about you at all. Our kind, we do not die easily. It hurts."

Great. Something new to fear. Pain. She added it to an ever-growing list.

"Look me in the eyes. Do you have any reason to zink you could be her target?"

Yes, Sugar had a reason to believe that. But she also had a reason to hide it. She wasn't yet willing to share her shame. Shame at what she'd done. At what she invited into her world, and maybe now theirs. Remembering that Lance may be trying to read her thoughts, she knew she couldn't lie.

SLAM!

Before she got to be evasive with Lance, Matt slammed his fist on the dash and stormed out of the cab, away from his wife and into the back of the ambulance. The couple was deep into something marital that was the opposite of bliss and more intense than a spat.

Matt was flailing his arms and yelling. In the small space, Sugar and Lance had no choice but to eavesdrop on their friends' private life.

"I've told you everything. I don't have secrets. That's your jam."

"My jam? I'm not a secret keeper." Maddie flailed in response. Sugar waited for someone to break something.

"Bullshit. Two words: Targhee Festival."

Maddie was suddenly flustered. "Well, that's, no. Who? James. That doesn't count."

Matt threw his head back in exasperation. "Everything counts!"

"He was going to let me pet his llama."

Making violent air quotes Matt said, "Pet his *llama*? Is *that* what he called it?"

"You're being a child."

"Am I? Fine. Then I'm going to my room." Quickly slathering on thick sun lotion, Matt grabbed a wide-brimmed hat and wrap-around sunglasses, and stormed out.

Surprised and concerned by his exit into the growing daylight, Sugar asked, "Where's he going?"

Still angry, Maddie folded her arms. "To his room." The ambulance rocked and Matt's footsteps could be heard on the roof. "After we fight, he sleeps in the equipment box." Then she corrected herself. "Sorry. After we have a 'discussion.'" She added air-quotes to emphasize the word.

Sugar remembered her parents' loud *discussions*. One time, she had a friend over and Faye and Henry were going at it over how much caraway seed on rye bread was too much caraway seed. Her friend, whose ethnicity was Wonder Bread, asked if she should leave. When Sugar asked why, the girl said, "Because your parents are fighting." Sugar just shrugged, "That's not fighting. That's how they talk. Want a snack?"

Being the coolest head in the RV, Lance said, "Let's get some sleep. We'll wake up and start fresh. No?"

Although it didn't seem any of them thought they'd get a fresh start, Maddie agreed and Sugar was happy to not have to discuss Shevil any further. Lance stared at her but asked no more questions. This ski trip that had started with such excitement had ended with a two-shots-of-dread and a domestic argument chaser.

15

THE SURPRISE INSIDE

Sugar had guessed her rest wouldn't be a peaceful one. She was right. But not-peaceful isn't always bad. She was first treated to flashbacks she could entitle, *Bedtime for Curtis*. All the places they'd made love. His bed, her bed, their bed. The sofa. Her friend Terri's closet. Then she was back on her camping trip with Curtis. It was all so real. She could smell the mix of pine forest and campfire. Why had she let him talk her into camping? Once her people were done wandering the desert, they never looked back. Roughing it for her family meant having to cross the street to get to the beach.

In the dream, as had happened in her life, Sugar and Curtis were sitting in folding chairs by their tent. A campfire was burning, and all the fancy groceries she'd picked up at Zabar's were in the Yeti. With everything she'd bought, they could have hosted a lovely cocktail party for eight right there. As the fire crackled and the sounds of nature sounded so very natural, Curtis leaned to her, "See. It's fun, right?"

Dryly she said, "So much."

"Come on. You like it. You got to buy new hiking boots."

Sugar admired her feet. "Admittedly, my weakness is footwear."

Jokingly, she hung her head in mock shame, then leaned back onto Curtis, letting the campfire ignite all their senses. Curtis kissed her neck and she knew she was about to try out sex on an air mattress.

Inside the tent, things started less on the romantic side of things and more on the comedic side. The air mattress was under-inflated courtesy of a slow leak. They kept sinking to the ground and laughing at the ridiculousness of their Twister-like moves. But after a while, his touch started stirring her and she stopped laughing. God, she loved his neck. And his abs. And those notches just inside his hip bones. And he knew exactly how to get her going. What it does to her when he kissed between her breasts. Every part of her was alive. With each touch, grab, and stroke, they dove into the utter fulfillment enjoyed when being with someone who knew you so completely. They hadn't been shy about telling each other what they liked and they were now benefitting from their honesty.

"Yes. God, that's so...Yes." Sugar believed in reinforcing good behavior.

They shuddered together, then held each other tight. He whispered, "But wait. There's more."

He traveled down her body. Her fingers reached deep in his thick hair as he worked his magic below. Slowly, then more intensely. The feeling was amazing. She loved this man so much.

When it was over, they laid on top of the sleeping bags, naked and satisfied. But, as too often happened, Sugar woke having to pee. First, as she usually did, she laid there hoping the feeling would pass. Thinking, *This is the best position ever. I'll never be able to replicate it Don't make me break the spell.* But the feeling didn't pass, and after minutes of hoping, reality set in and she got up. Trying not to wake Curtis, Sugar quietly slipped on sweat pants, a T-shirt, and a headlamp. She unzipped the door and ventured into the night.

Not wanting to go far from the tent to complete the operation, she walked just far enough to not be unsanitary. Nervous out in the dark, she pulled down her sweats, squatted and was thankful for strong thigh muscles. She thought, *Come on. Pee, already. I want to go back to the protection of my nylon tent. Nylon will save me.* Her plea was answered, but just as relief came, she felt something else: Hot breath on the back of her head. "What the fuck?!"

Without pulling up her pants, she leapt, diving through the air for the tent opening. Landing with a thud a few feet away, she quickly scrambled for the entrance. Once safely in the protective nylon shell, she looked back to the night. Nothing. All was quiet, inside and out. Somehow Curtis was still asleep. Every nerve in her body was on high alert. She was sure she had pee on her sweats.

In a low panicked voice designed to wake Curtis while not alerting anyone who may be lurking, she shook her man. "Curtis. Curtis, get up. Curtis." But he didn't stir. She was now shoving him. "Oh, my, God. Curtis. Something's out there. Curtis. I think it's a chupacabra." More sleeping. Sugar had no more patience for gentle persuasion and started forcefully rocking him back and forth. "Are you seriously going to sleep through this? Wake up and save me."

Curtis started to stir. With sleep in his voice he asked the world, "What?"

"Curtis. There's something out there."

"It's probably just an animal."

"Yes. I think it's an animal!"

"It's okay. There are animals out here. They live here."

"And you brought me to mingle with them? No. This was big. It was breathing on my head. My literal head."

Confused, Curtis looked around. "There's nothing in here."

"No, out there." Sugar thrust a finger towards the door. "I was peeing and this chupacabra came up behind me. We need to get the hell out of here. Now."

"Baby. Calm down. Let's go see what it was."

"No. We could get eaten."

"We won't." He took her hand. "Come on. We'll stare this chupacabra down together. Be steely."

Readying herself to confront the beast, Sugar slowly repeated, "Be steely."

First, they listened. Hearing nothing, they carefully stepped into the night. Curtis passed a flashlight over the immediate area. Sure enough, a pair of eyes was glowing back at them from the near distance. Sugar tried to flee, but Curtis grabbed her hand. "Wait."

"No."

"Yes." He moved towards the glowing eyes, dragging Sugar. As they got closer, they heard a clank. The sound was hollow and familiar. "That's a cowbell. Baby, it's just a cow." Sure enough, the flashlight revealed a light brown heifer, nonplussed, standing a few feet away.

"A cow! Are you serious?" Sugar shook her head at the cow, herself, her man, her peed-on pants, and the ridiculousness of it all. They both started laughing.

"You were almost taken out by a killer cow."

"Hey, that's a big animal. What if it stepped on me? We wouldn't be laughing then."

"Yes, we would."

"You're right. We would."

They both laughed as Curtis pulled her close for a hug. "Come on. Clean up and I'll let you back on the horse."

"You're aroused after that?"

"What can I say? I'm a man of peculiar appetites."

They returned to the tent, but once they entered it was no longer their tent. It was their New York apartment. Curtis was sitting on the sofa looking contrite. Sugar remembered that look and she knew exactly what night it was. It was *that* night. Sugar was standing and he was reaching for her hand.

"I'm so sorry. I can't explain it."

His hand hung in the air, unmet. She was working up a head of steam. "You could try. You could fucking try."

"She was...I don't know...It was like she..."

"God, Curtis. Use your goddamn words!"

"I'm sorry. I love you. She's nothing to me. I just..."

"I can't do this. I won't." Sugar grabbed a jacket and stormed for the door.

"Let me explain. I need you."

Her world was crashing down. It was all too much. "I need air." Without looking back, she walked out, letting the door slam hard behind her. With a head of steam, Sugar bounded down the hall. When she turned the corner, she was suddenly looking into Alex's face. Sugar had turned right into her. She gasped.

Mockingly, Alex said, "I'm hurt. You haven't called. You haven't written."

Horrified, Sugar saw Alex bare her teeth. She felt Alex's fangs piercing her neck, then biting down hard. "Curtis! Help!"

As she felt her life fading away, she heard Alex whisper, "You don't get to have Curtis. No one does. It should have been you."

A new voice spoke. "It's okay. It's okay, ma petite. Sugar."

When Sugar opened her eyes, she was struggling with Lance who was holding her shoulders. Finally, she remembered where she was. *Crap. What did I say? What did he hear?*

"You're with friends."

Still frightened and now embarrassed, Sugar replied. "I'm alright. Bad dream."

"Hmm." He seemed to know more than he said, but immediately changed topics. "We need to move. Someone stole Matt."

"What?"

Dressed and ready for action, Maddie looked back from the driver's seat. Her voice a mix of panic and determination. "The equipment box is gone. We searched the area. Motherfuckers. Hold on!"

With that, Maddie punched the gas and Sugar and Lance rocked backwards.

Turning to Lance, Sugar asked, "How does she know where to go?"

"Maddie saw tire marks in ze snow, heading east. So, we're heading east. I called Willie. He's coming in from ze other direction.

With any luck, we'll cut ze culprits off." In an un-Lance like moment, he added, "Fuckers."

Lance and Sugar moved forward to see out the windshield as Maddie drove. It was well past dusk and getting darker by the minute. They came to a fork in the road. Which way? Maddie pulled over and climbed out of the cab. Lance and Sugar joined her roadside. After silently smelling the air, Sugar pointed left. "That way."

Maddie looked surprised, but didn't question Sugar's instinct.

Back in the ambulance, they barreled down the dark road. Time ticked away silently as they went speeding through the night. What would they find? Their answer was just ahead. Willie was standing to the side of the road waving his arms over his head, his truck parked just beyond, as was an unfamiliar truck. From the rapidly closing distance, Sugar tried to read him.

The ambulance skidded to a stop on the dirt shoulder. In a small field, they saw the open equipment box. Matt stood over three motionless men with his hands on his knees. His stance said he'd just finished a hard run. His bloody face said he'd been engaged in something much darker. As Maddie raced over to him, one of the men on the ground began moaning, and grabbed at her leg. Snap! Fangs out! In a split second, Matt sunk his teeth into the already dying man's neck and ripped out his throat. Maddie was unfazed. It was like her man had just killed a bug. Wrapping her arms around him she said, "You're such an asshole. Why do you fight with me?"

"I missed you, too."

Kissing the blood on Matt's face, Maddie licked her lips. "Mmm. Vegetarian?"

Exhausted, he joked, "They *are* the tastiest."

She again hugged the man she loved. The one she'd still get to fight with.

In a hushed tone, Willie explained to Lance and Sugar, "By the time I got here, he did no need my help. I suppose we should remove those *persons*." Letting Matt and Maddie have their moment, the three went to the work of cleaning up after their friend. They each grabbed lifeless limbs and pulled the carcasses into the woods.

About thirty yards in Lance declared, "Zis is as fitting a spot as any for zis road scum."

Sugar watched Lance and Willie begin removing things from the strangers. Watches, wallets, keys. Off her look of displeasure, Willie explained, "We have to make them not identifiable. Coyotes will do most of the hard work. But no evidence."

Sugar understood and began helping them with the morbid task. In one man's shirt pocket, she found a receipt from a gas station and grabbed it. Then she removed his class ring.

When they finished, Lance and Willie stood over the bodies and peed on them, as if they'd performed the ritual a million times.

"Seriously?"

Once his bladder was empty, Willie explained like a game-show host, "We like to leave a fabulous parting gift. And it helps alert hungry bears."

"You couldn't have just, say, left them bleeding?"

Willie shrugged. "This works best. And we like peeing on them. If jou were a man, jou'd understand."

"Let me make a note. Peeing on the corpse. Guy thing. Got it."

Lance didn't seem up for banter. "Children, can we do zis another time? Let's finish ze job and move on."

That was the end of the sarcasm session. They covered the bodies with leaves and turned to rejoin Matt and Maddie. But before they did, Willie looked back and spit on the pile.

Hands on her hips, Sugar asked, "Sure you don't want to cop a squat on them before we go?"

"If I had anything cooking, I would."

"Come on, you two."

When the trio got back to the roadside, Matt was on top of the ambulance and Maddie was lifting the equipment box up to him. He called down with a laugh, "Guess I'm like Cracker Jack. There's always the surprise inside."

Willie pointed at him. "No, jou are like a stripper in the birthday cake."

Clearly liking that thought, Matt stood and did his version of a seductive dance, letting his ripped t-shirt drop down off his shoulder. He was a man without rhythm, but plenty of charm. "Someone put a dollar in my pants!"

Lance snarked, "You'll have to dance better zan zat, mister."

"No. Then everyone will want my fella."

Willie cooed. "Jes, he is one shoulder-roll away from sexiest man not alive."

Sugar was glad Matt was okay, but this was the first time she was confronted with the savage killing of another human being. Now that the immediate danger had passed, it was sinking in. Rabbits and birds were one thing. And even that took time to process. But this was so much heavier. So much more sinister. Her friend Matt, this fun, capable guy, just killed three men and they were all okay with it. Joking about it. *Am I okay with it? Did these strangers deserve what they got? Are we really the not-evil ones? And by we, I mean me. I'm an accomplice after the fact.* She knew her verdict wouldn't come down in a court of law. And her sentence would be much harsher.

16

DOWN THE DRAIN

Sugar opted for riding back to Moonglow with Willie and Lance, leaving Matt and Maddie privacy and time to make up. It seemed right. That, and she wasn't sure what to say to Matt after his triple murder. But she had questions. Would it be impolite to ask? Hell, they'd all just laughed over fresh roadkill. The line for politeness was now a moving target.

With no tee-up, she asked, "How many people have you killed?"

Lance and Willie looked at each other and laughed. Willie finally said. "Sugar, we don't count. We all end up killing peoples sometimes. It is no avoidable."

"You didn't really zink you'd never kill someone, did you, darling?"

She knew the answer. "No."

"Okay zen. Zese are just ze facts of us. We know zem and we move on. Yes?"

She nodded. "Yes."

Lance's tone changed as he smiled at her in the rearview mirror. "I know another fun fact about us."

She could see him winking at Willie and the two shared knowing and devious grins. "Oh, jes. That is a fun fact."

"What?"

Playfully Willie said, "I think we should let her find out for herself, don't jou?"

Sugar hated not knowing a secret, but she hated admitting that even more. "That's fine. Keep your secrets. I don't need to know."

With a sing-song delivery, Willie added, "I hope jou like surprises."

What could they mean? Fuck it. I'm not going to ask. Willie's poking only made her resolve stronger. She'd always had a strong polarity response. And now, like everything else she was good at, it was stronger.

When they arrived back at Moonglow, Mary Helen was standing on the front porch, listening to an argument between neighbors, but staring questioningly at the returning party. Willie lowered the windows to eavesdrop more clearly. An older man wearing a cap that let people know he'd served in the armed forces was pointing at Happy Harry. "This guy was sniffin' around my rig and I don't like it."

"I was not sniffing."

"Then what do you call it, sir?"

"I was listening in on you and your wife fighting over who ate the last piece of peach pie. Personally, I think it was you."

At that admission, Mr. Ex-military seemed to levitate. "What?" He pointed at Mary Helen. "Did you hear that?" Then he pointed back at Harry. "You have no shame."

"Shame is wasted on the shameful."

"What does that...are you implying...I fought in the war."

Harry shrugged. "I fought in them all."

The sound of the argument faded behind them as Willie drove his truck back to its spot in front of their Airstream.

Sugar got out, looking around. "Guess we beat them back."

Willie continued his needling. "That's because they already know the fun fact."

With that, Sugar was ready to be alone. She wasn't mad. But the voices in her head were enough noise for her right now. She didn't need Willie's. She smiled and raised a parting hand. "Gentlemen, it's been a real slice of peach pie."

Willie came up and hugged her. "Hand shake, schmand shake, Sugar Lady. Hug me."

From within his embrace she asked, "Did I have a choice?" But she enjoyed his genuine affection.

When he released her Lance added, "*Ciao*, darling."

"Ciao."

Purposefully shutting out the many sounds of domestic life from the world around her, Sugar was back at her RV in short order. She unlocked the door, an act that made her think about the time she'd found it ajar, and of course, the echoing threat that she was being watched. *Was it one of the men from the ski slope?* She was sure it was. Pretty sure. Mostly sure. Without D. there to play with the word, mostly. she called out for feline friendship. "Honey, I'm home."

Kitten greeted her not with friendship, but with an RV-load of chiding. "Meow-ah! Meow-ah! Meow-ah! Meow-ah! Meow-ah!"

Scooping up Kitten, Sugar glanced around the space. "You took fine care of the joint. Mommy's little security guard."

"Meow-ah! Meow-ah! Meow-ah!"

"What? I just praised you."

"Meow-ah!"

Then it dawned on Sugar what the problem was. "Oh, shit. I'm such a bad mom." She quickly filled Kitten's bowl. But not quickly enough. Kibble rained down on the cat's head as she scarfed up the cat chow. The cat ate faster than Sugar could count the little star-shaped pieces. *Why do I always want to count them?* She didn't know. She just did. She was half tempted to stop the cat from getting her first meal in over a day so she could play Rain Man. Sugar forced herself to look away, then filled the water bowl, and walked both containers onto the bunk so Kitten could indulge by her side.

Lying there, she mulled over a challenging thought. *Friends are complications.* She tried balancing the pros and cons of getting close to other vampires. There were plenty of cons, and she tried rationalizing them away. *How good of a rationalizer am I?* She'd been better before she'd realized Alex was gunning for her.

Her phone rang. *Did D. sense I was just thinking about him? No.* "Hey."

"Hope you don't mind. Couldn't sleep."

Thinking back to her last dream, Sugar said, "Sleep is overrated."

"Only if you can't."

"What's on your mind?"

"Well, I have this sister, and she's so great, and I love her, and I'm getting a feeling she might be in trouble, but she won't let me help her. And..."

"Feelings are overrated, too. I'm fine." Sugar reconsidered just how strong their twin bond really was. As kids, they often felt they knew when the other was having strong emotions about something. *Was it real or the wishful thinking of children? Move on.* "You help me by being there for me."

"You never reach out."

"No. But you do. And that works for me."

"Does it?"

Sugar answered honestly. "It does."

"Your friend Tess called looking for you. She's worried too."

Shit. "What did you tell her?"

"I said exactly what you told me to say. I don't know anything."

"Thanks."

"You don't have to be alone. A lot of us care about you."

She knew he was right. She also knew she'd been wrong. She should be pushing him away. He can't be part of her new existence. This world on the wrong side of right. *What would he say if I told him about my ski trip? The dark figures, my friend being stolen, and of course, the murders I helped cover up? At least I didn't pee on anyone.* It was cold comfort. She decided to rip the Band-Aid. "Listen, I don't know if I'm going to make Sarah's..."

"Don't say it."

"But I can't..."

Getting angry, he cut her off. "No! I call, bullshit! You can do whatever you want to do. Don't do this to me."

"What are you now? Mom?" She imitated Faye. "Don't do this to me?" Back in her own voice she said, "Isn't that her line?"

"Are you *trying* to piss me off!?"

She didn't answer. From D.'s side of the line, Sugar could hear Amy. "Honey, who are you talking to?"

To his wife, David whispered. "It's no one. Go back to bed."

Sleepily Amy said, "Don't stay up too late talking to no one." Then, louder, "Good night, Shug."

"'Night, Amy."

D. returned to the call, still assertive, but more thoughtful. "You *are*, aren't you? You're trying to make me mad. Well, fuck you if you think you can push me away that easily. We've been through too much. I can take it. I'm stronger than you think. I'm not leaving you. And I won't let you leave me."

Mocking him, she got sappy. "I just can't quit you."

"God you're trying hard to end us. Well, try harder! See you at the *bat mitzvah*. I'll be the asshole putting up with your shit."

D. clicked off.

Sugar looked at Kitten and scratched her head. Quietly she whispered, "I just can't quit you." She played the events of the last days in her head ending with purposefully being shitty to D., who she loved to the end of the Earth.

"Fuck Alex, and fuck revenge, and fuck skiing."

17

THE PEOPLE IN YOUR NEIGHBORHOOD

Sugar spent the next few nights alone. She privately tested her hunting skills, speed, strength, agility. Everything had continued to increase. She could now take down multiple targets at a time. Her goal was to get comfortable with her new abilities. Hone them and own them. *What good is a skill you can't count on? What hope do I have of getting in even the smallest amount of payback if I don't improve my current level of ability?* She knew the answer and it wasn't comforting.

But Sugar still couldn't fly on her own. Not well. There was no obvious take-off position. She'd run and jump and land. All great efforts if she wanted to be an Olympic long jumper. *But again: daytime events. So, no Olympics.* Putting her better judgment on the shelf, she was ready for a new approach and headed out into the night. As she climbed a tree, Sugar could hear her mother's voice in her head: "Are you completely *meshugganah*? If your friend jumped off a bridge, would you?" She thought, *No, but a tree...*

Up in the oak, staring down at the world from about 40 feet, she urged herself, "Come on kid. Be steely." Sugar spread her arms then lowered them. "Crap." She repeated that motion three times, then finally, "Just do it." She leapt out of a tree. Mad flailing was followed by a hard landing and a mouth full of mud and bugs. Spitting out the insects, Sugar was cured of wanting to make any further attempts that night. *Faye was right. Nike was wrong. Just don't do it.*

Sugar sat on the ground feeling like a fool, and waiting for her bones to mend, again. By now she knew it would take about ten minutes and feel like there were gears grinding below her skin.

Walking home, dried leaves stuck in her hair, she thought about the non-physical skill she wanted to get a handle on: Mind reading. It could be key to knowing what was in Alex's head. Alex, who seemed to have no problem getting in and out of Sugar's thoughts.

As she reentered the park, she tried focusing on three men sitting around a fire pit by an older RV. All had on flannel, held beer, and had nothing to say. *What are you boys thinking?* But as much as she tried to read them, all she came up with was, *Mm, Beer. Maybe they're just vapid. What did Matt say? Don't try so hard or you'll only read your own thoughts.* He also said it would hurt. She rubbed her temples. He was right on both counts.

Sugar passed the rest of her alone time reading and having short discussions with Kitten about what she'd learned. Kitten was easy company, but shared no usable insights. It was more a book club of one. Staring at a book she'd kept coming back to, she once again began stewing over the title: *Varney the Vampire*. It was one of the older books she'd come across. The laborious pace of the text made turning pages a plodding affair. Plus, it contained several side stories that seemed to meander and go nowhere. This was a harder nut to crack, and she frequently found herself musing about how stupid the title was.

"*Varney the Vampire*, really? Possibly the worst book title ever. It sounds like a children's book that should go between *Ernie the Elephant* and *Barry the Bosc Pear*. It would never sell today. But apparently it was the rage in 1895. A different time." Sugar chose to infer Kitten's lack of response as silent assent.

Still, she found a few items of interest and made notes to be added to her chart later. One passage that made her stop was, "If any accident should befall them, such as being shot, or otherwise killed or wounded, they can recover by lying down someplace where the full moon's rays will fall upon them."

Sugar wondered, *Is it true and, if so, what does this mean for me? If I get shot, will I only rise back and rejoin the undead if I get touched by a full moon's light? And after how long? Could I be dragged into moon light after a year, two years, ten, and just get up, dust off and go shopping?* "God, I hope not."

On the fourth sunset after the ill-fated ski trip, there was knocking on the side of Sugar's van, followed by a "Tweedle-tweet!"

She lifted her head an inch from the pillow. She'd been lost in a dream about after-work cocktails with Bunny and Tess. A fine dream that had yet to be destroyed by her dark party crasher. The three were laughing over Manhattans and sharing tales of their respective partners—the kinds of tales their partners would rather they not share. And it was so much fun. *Can I get it back?* Sugar tried to rejoin the dream and her New York pals. *Focus on their words.* Bunny had been talking about Jackson's Johnson, or Jack John as they called it. *What was she saying? Something about bending to the right. What was it?* But as hard as Sugar tried to grab hold of Jackson's Johnson, it slipped from her fingers. She was awake.

The call came again. "Tweedle-tweet!"

Groggy and annoyed at the fact that she could no longer enjoy her friends or cocktails, Sugar moaned, "Let yourself in. Take whatever you want. Just don't talk to me."

The soft light of the RV park spilled into the van as Maddie did as told, but not really. "Cool. I'm taking Kitten."

"The fuck you are."

Sugar wrapped her arm around Kitten and cradled her in close on the off-chance Maddie wasn't joking and whispered, "You wouldn't leave me for someone who can't whistle, would you?"

Kitten purred and buried her head in the hug.

Maddie hopped onto Sugar's bunk and made herself comfortable. "Nice bedhead."

"Thanks. I've been working on it for days."

"Looks like it. We haven't seen you in a few. Not that Matt and I noticed for a night or two." Giving a girl-talk wink she explained, "We were deep into making up. I swear, he's extra good when he's sorry. I lost count after twelve. He likes to play The Count. You know, from *Sesame Street*?" Maddie did her best Transylvanian accent, which was marginal at best. "Nine! Nine orgasms! Ah! Ah! Ah! Ten! Ten orgasms! Ah! Ah! Ah!"

"I get the picture." *Shit. Is Maddie serious? Did Matt really get up to bat over a dozen times?* She wasn't going to ask. Yet, Maddie's face didn't read exaggeration.

Reaching for Kitten, Maddie purred, "Come here, baby. Be with Auntie Maddie." Kitten put up no fight, which made Sugar feel a bit slighted.

Maddie asked Kitten, "Is Mommy being a downer?"

Sugar answered on Kitten's behalf. "Yes."

"You need to come out tonight."

"Maybe."

"No, you have to. Willie and Lance are leaving tomorrow at the crack of dusk."

Wow. Sugar was surprised how bummed that news made her. *How many days had it been? Or weeks? Not that many. Not enough to feel like I'm about to lose dear friends, but I do. Am I being overdramatic? Needy? Human? No. Not that last one. Maddie's right. I have to go and say goodbye.*

"Come on. Get dressed. Kitten and I will wait."

Looking at her dwindling wardrobe, Sugar pulled out a pair of tan, straight-legged, heavy denim jeans and a cable-knit white sweater. *Yes, I still like winter white.* In her previous life, she might have thought twice about changing in front of Maddie, but such propriety no longer mattered to her. She slipped out of her sleepwear and into her clothes. The jeans were baggy enough that they needed a belt. The tight cinch on the too-large pants gave them a more grunge look than intended, but Sugar decided to roll with it. Turning to Maddie she asked, "Are we ready?"

"I don't think I'd go with white."

"Why not?" She wondered, *What does this person who's so happy in pink and sparkles possibly have to share with me, an ex-New Yorker, about fashion?*

"You don't have the skin tone for it. We're too pale. White just points it out."

Shit. Is she right? Probably. I can't see my reflection clearly enough to judge. But holding up her hands she thought, *Damn it. Fine.* Sugar pulled off the sweater, then grabbed another white top from her closet and dumped both in her trash can. "I loved that blouse." Mourning its loss, she reached for a sage top and pulled a plum colored, V-neck sweater over it. "Better?"

"Totally. Hey! Let's bring Kitten."

"Hey! Let's not."

Once Sugar was able to pry Kitten away from Maddie, they headed out and over toward the group gathered around Mary Helen's porch.

Music played as Sugar leaned over Willie's shoulder. "I understand you're leaving me."

He tilted his head back. "Only with great sadness, *mi amor*. Come. Sit."

Sugar and Maddie joined Lance, Willie and Matt, and enjoyed the music until it ended. When the musicians began packing up, Lance said, "Shall we adjourn to our place for a nightcap? For ze record, zat is not a question."

Surprised and hopeful, Sugar asked, "Seriously?"

"Of a sort."

A sort was enough for her. The five-some made their way to Lance and Willie's trailer. The fake plants, the fountain, and most of their other homey touches had already been packed away. Ever the host, Lance offered everyone a seat around their fire pit while he and Willie went inside to grab a few things.

Mary Helen walked up with a box of wine. She took Sugar's hand. "They come and they go, baby. No long faces."

Sugar wondered, *Was I wearing a long face? I have to work on better masking my emotions.*

Willie and Lance returned with a tray of glasses, each filled with what appeared to be dark red wine. *Is it possible? God, I miss wine.* Social media had become an endless tease. All those posts saying things like, "Corks are for quitters." And, "Drink wine. Because it's not good to keep things bottled up." Or, "Roses are red. Violets are Blue. Poems are hard. Wine." All so trite. All so shallow. All so off limits. But here came something promising. Sugar took the glass that was offered her. On closer inspection, it was clearly not wine. "Thank you?"

Once the glasses were distributed to all but Mary Helen, Lance made a toast. "Tonight, we drink to no flat tires, slow-moving vegetarians, and ze sassiest Vs on ze road. May our friendship be everlasting."

Everyone cheered their approval. Matt added, "Because being a dick in our circle can get you on the outs for decades." Laughter and more cheers.

Willie nodded. "To not being the dick."

They all repeated him. "To not being the dick!"

Mary Helen lifted her glass to her lips. "Mamma's home!"

Watching her V-friends drink without retching, Sugar thought, *Well, I don't want to be impolite. Who am I kidding? I want a goddamn glass of wine.* "Corks are for cowards."

She took a full sip and felt the cold liquid pass across her tongue. *Nope. Not wine. But wine-like. And not unpleasant.* As she felt a surge of energy, she knew she recognized the flavor.

Lance asked, "How do you like your—" He made his patented air quotes, "—foxed wine, my dear?" Off her look he explained, "Foxed. It is our little joke at boxed wine. Personally, I zink it drinks much better, don't you?"

Sugar raised an eyebrow. "If I say yes, I'm admitting to being an aficionada of boxed wine. *N'est-ce pas?*"

"Touché." The two raised their glasses to each other and drank.

Mary Helen raised her wine box. "Not me. I'm a gal who loves the box." Then, at the accidental joke, she began laughing. "Did y'all get that? A gal who loves the box. You know. Box?" It wasn't even that funny, but everyone enjoyed it in the familiar, easy way you do with good friends.

Mary Helen quickly killed her glass. "I just love drinkin'. Oh, sorry."

With nostalgia in her voice Sugar said, "It's okay. But I do miss it."

Lance shrugged. "You can't miss what you've never had." He and Matt clinked glasses.

Maddie laughed. "Well, I used to get *ham-mered.*"

Willie's hand went up. "Also guilty."

Raising her hand as well, Sugar said, "The last time I got drunk we were celebrating my friend leaving her shitty boyfriend. Actually, he dumped her, but we were trying to put a good spin on it. Shit, we must have hit every bar in Tribeca. I can't say for sure because I only remember the first hour. I call it my gap year."

They all laughed and Lance did an impression of a London subway announcer. "Please mind the gap."

Sugar shrugged, "Maybe next time."

Matt raised his glass. "Hey, I don't think I said it enough. Thanks again for coming to find me."

Willie nodded. "No need. Jou would have made it back just fine on jour own."

Maddie hugged up on Matt. "No, no. You helped save my man. To Willie!" More toasting.

The evening rolled along with a mix of reminiscing and laughter. Stories from the last week and eras gone by. Sugar drank it all in, enjoying the warm company and learning a few things from the different tales. She was surprised to find out that Willie came from an influential Cuban family in the 1940s. He was finishing telling the story of one of his first dates with Lance. "The sky was like purple crush velvet. So dreamy. Then Lance...Then I... Then Lance..." The tale sounded like it had been well-polished over the years. "...so then, this fellow, he holds up his garlic necklace like a shield and says, 'This is garlic and now jou will die!' Then I tell him, this garlic makes jou stink like a mojo marinade, and now jou will die."

Completely enthralled by the tale, Maddie leaned forward and listened with her chin on her hands. "Did you kill him?"

"No, I just took a little sip. Well, a big sip."

Sugar sat back. "So, garlic doesn't work?"

Matt laughed. "No. But it does stink, bad, so we don't go near it if we don't have to."

"Got it."

Lance leaned over to his partner. "It was very kind of you. Not killing zat very boring, scared, little man."

"I am the nice guy."

Maddie cooed. "You two are so sweet."

Jokingly, Matt took issue, "What? I was sweet 15 times the other night." Doing a better imitation of The Count he added, "Fifteen, fifteen times. Ah, ah, ah!"

Willie clapped, "Oh Matt, I have jour new nickname. Bat Man." Explaining what needed no explanation, Willie added, "Because jou swing jour bat so much and, jou know, bats."

Matt stood, arms akimbo, "I am Batman!"

Raising her hand, Maddie said, "Me next. What's my nickname?"

Lance and Willie mused for a moment, then in unison said, "Sparkles."

She pumped a fist. "Yes! Sparkles and Batman."

Waving an arm, Mary Helen tapped in. "Wait, wait. That reminds me of a good story."

Willie got excited. "I hope it contains a bat."

She smiled. "Just you wait, cowboy. There was this time I had all these giant, shiny A-class rigs come as a group. Happens sometimes. They had all the bells and whistles. Fancy. You know the kind. Anyway, all these folks were seventy if they were a day."

Lance interrupted, "Let's not get ageist."

Mary Helen giggled. "Well, one night I was up late, cause I live with all y'all, and I start seeing people sneakin' into this one A-class. And get this: They're dressed all sexy Goth. Leather, and studded chokers, whips, boobs out, butts out. I saw my share of wrinkled flesh that night, I tell ya.' But here's the real crazy part. It was a vampire party!"

Sugar shook her head. "I call cultural appropriation."

Playing at being offended, Willie put his hand over his heart. "I did no get an invite."

"Lucky you. 'Cuz after, I don't know, over a dozen of 'em stuffed in there, the thing starts rockn', hard. A' course, the whole V lot is watchin' this unfold like it's a TV show. But then a few couldn't help themselves and they join the party. Next thing you know, someone yells, 'Bud's havin' a heart attack! Bud's havin' a heart attack!' Sure enough, the EMTs come and Bud gets taken out on a stretcher in a leather jock strap with two holes in his neck."

Matt was loving it. "No shit"

"Yes shit. Bud's time playin' vampire was short. The authorities blamed the host of the party for getting too—" she made air quotes—"into character. But we all knew that wasn't it."

Willie leaned forward. "Who did it? Jou can tell us."

"I don't talk outa turn."

It was Sugar's turn to raise a hand. "I thought the one rule of Moonglow was don't feed on the guests."

Mary Helen giggled. "Why do you think I made that rule?"

As much as she didn't want to, Sugar laughed at the image of it all.

Lance snickered. "It's like waving meat to a lion and saying, 'No, no, mustn't touch.'"

Willie raised a glass, "To waving meat!"

Everyone toasted, "To waving meat."

Lance drank, then turned to Mary Helen and asked, "But what is ze connection to our friend Matt's prowess?"

"Oh shit. I forget."

That led to more laughter. When it finally died down, Sugar couldn't help herself. "Do you two really have to go?"

Lance and Willie seemed touched. "We do, love. It is as much for you as it is for us."

"I don't understand."

"We don't want to take a chance with ze She-vil One and her minions. She could be out looking for us. She's not ze biggest fan of yours truly." Trying to play off the darkness of it all, he added, "How anyone could feel zat way is beyond me, but zere you have it."

Sugar's guilt returned, squeezing at her throat. Not ready to voice her thoughts she pleaded, "But you don't know that it was you they were looking for."

"No. But why take chances? Plus, Willie and I usually start heading for ze beach zis time of year. I believe Hilton Head is calling our name."

Getting sing-songy, Maddie said, "You're gonna miss a lot of ski time. I saw that Montana is gonna get dumped on."

Willie put his hand over his heart, then over-enunciated each of his words. "I am no going to miss your reindeer games. I promise jou that."

There was laughter, then the conversation continued well past its normal tapering off time. Apparently, it wasn't only Sugar who didn't want the night to end. But they didn't get their way. Lance finally stood up. "Ladies and gentlemen, I fear zat my man and I are going to call it a night."

A collective "No!" rang out.

"Yes. All good zings, as zey say."

Sugar winked at her friend, trying to deny her guilty feelings. "Leave them wanting more?"

"Exactly."

She looked long and hard into Lance's eyes thinking, *It's me she wants.*

In her head she felt him say, *I know.*

And there it was. She'd read his mind. *Is it only because he wanted me to?* She had no idea. But, more importantly, she had fessed up. And while she hadn't confessed to everyone, it did relieve some of the pressure. She'd been truthful, if only to Lance.

After several rounds of hugging and an exchange of phone numbers, Willie and Lance stood with an arm around each other, waving as their friends reluctantly backed away. Willie called out, "Make the good choices."

They each knew they wouldn't.

18

LIFE IS CHANGE. SO IS THIS

With Willie and Lance gone, Sugar was left feeling like summer camp had just ended. She wondered what social activity she'd be enjoying at 8:00 pm on a weeknight in the before-times. *Wait. Is it a weeknight? Yes. It is. Who would I be out with now? Girlfriends.* When she felt like reenergizing by going out, Curtis often played the homebody card. It took a while for her to believe him when he'd say, "Go. I don't mind." In the language of her parents, "Go. I don't mind," would have meant, "You go. Have a great time with the people you'd rather be with. And until you're done having your fun and drag yourself home to be stuck with me, I'll just sit here in the dark, not unscrewing light bulbs." It would then be the job of the person on the receiving end of the sarcasm to decipher the message and defuse the situation with something like, "No. No. I'm happy to stay home. I thought you wanted to read. But let's stay home and watch something. What do you want to watch? Can I make you a snack? Rub your feet? Kiss your ass?" Sometimes it would work. Sometimes not. But Curtis only meant the words he actually said. "Go. I don't mind." It took some getting used to and she never did reach a point where she trusted it one hundred percent.

Not feeling like going back to Varney and his inept pursuers, she decided to thumb-type a new list of questions for Maddie into her phone. "Let's get some fresh intel, Kitten."

"Meow-ah."

"No. I'm not asking her that."

After rechecking her list, she added one last question, inspired by her advertising days. "What do I not know to ask that I should be asking?" *Smart.*

But stepping out of her van and looking over to where the ambulance was supposed to be, she saw it was gone. *No. Did they leave me, too?* Happy Harry passed and without pausing offered, "They went skiing...again."

Did he read my mind or my face? In her mind she said, "Get out of my head, Harry." He never broke stride. *Hmm.*

To her right, Mr. Skin & Bones was lurking by his feeder. God, he disgusted her. She chided herself. *Is that fair? He's a troubled man that Mary Helen took pity on. Give him a break.* Sugar heard a bird singing on a nearby branch. When it swooped overhead, she swore she could see Mr. Skin & Bones lick his lips. *Enough,* she thought. *Back off, birdman! Go inside, now!* A second later, Mr. Skin & Bones turned and went into his RV. *Did I do that?* Sugar looked right and left to see if anyone had witnessed her power. But there'd been nothing to notice. *Was it power? Or just coincidence?*

Now what? Already out, she decided to stroll. In the more moneyed section of the park with the big rigs, she watched couples and families enjoying the night, oblivious to the tiny world parked nearby. *Are they lucky?* Tonight, it felt that way. There was an older couple in folding chairs in front of a campfire. He was holding a forked stick, each tip of the fork capped with a marshmallow. When he deemed them ready, he nodded and his wife sandwiched the gooey white balls with chocolate-covered graham crackers. It was all so perfectly choreographed. Sugar wondered how many times the two had done that very move over their years together.

Across the way, a young couple was getting frisky in front of their fire. Sugar watched the woman climb onto her man's lounge chair, straddling him. The woman teased out kisses until the man couldn't take it and grabbed her to him. Their make-out session got hot and heavy until a woman from a neighboring site called out, "Get a room. I have kids here."

Playfully the young woman called back, "How do they think they got here?"

She and her man laughed, then got up and scurried, hand-in-hand into their high-end adventure camper. Watching them, Sugar stood with her arms folded. *I hope they have good leveling jacks or that thing's gonna start rockin', hard.* Apparently, they did. *Well, good for them.*

Now she was standing alone. But in truth, she was alone before they'd fled the scene. Just an outsider, observing people who were together and apart from her. She wondered if she should stop her pity party before it got out of hand. Then she thought, *Why? I'm entitled. I think losing everything I ever cared about is worth a tear. And since I no longer have tears, I'm going with the tried and true. Pity party, table of one.*

Indulging in her poor-me moment, she walked absently through the park. The sound of birds and insects was intense. So much so, she didn't hear the footsteps behind her. When an arm slid under hers, Sugar snapped around ready to pounce.

"Hold on there, Shug. We come in peace." Mary Helen mocked a defensive stance and giggled. To her left was a stranger who, at Sugar's abrupt response, had taken a step back.

Sugar relaxed her muscles. "Sorry. As we've established, I have an exaggerated startle response."

The stranger, a long, thin man with a mop of white-blond hair, stood tall. He was pale and had the telltale red flecks in his eyes. "Could come in handy one day."

Mary Helen hooked an arm back under Sugar's and hooked her other arm under the stranger's. Without a word, the three began walking.

Sugar's pulse was getting back to normal as Mary Helen made the introductions. "Shug, this is Werner. Werner, Shug."

He casually corrected her. "It's pronounced, 'Verner.'"

Mary Helen giggled, "You're so fancy."

Sugar asked, "German?"

"Would that be a problem?"

"Only with my parents."

"They're not here, I hope."

"You're in luck. They're in New Jersey."

"I'm so sorry. I'm also Austrian."

"I'm sorry, too."

"Why? Austria is beautiful. Have you ever been?"

"Have you ever been to Jersey?"

Mary Helen jumped in. "Shug, Werner, *Verner* here's just passin' through on his way to Napa."

"I have business."

"He has business. Isn't that interesting?"

"Fascinating."

"He owns wineries."

Momentarily forgetting her new self, Sugar pined, "Oh. I love a good California Cab."

"Do you?"

"I did." She noted that his skin tone was lighter than hers. The bits of red in his eyes almost sparkled. Odd how she never noticed these traits in the before-times. She wondered how many vampires, if any, she'd come across before entering The Life. Back when she enjoyed California Cabs. Wistfully, she corrected herself again. "I did."

"I see."

As the three continued on, Mary Helen threw out tidbits of information. "Shug here has a cat."

"Really. That's odd. Do all animals enjoy your company?"

"I'm not much of a dog person...anymore."

Werner laughed slightly at that. "Still, a cat. There must be something special about you."

"Hmm."

"Look Shug, that's Werner's RV. Sweet, huh?"

"It's a 1977 GMC. Ironically, I picked it because I liked the look of the windows. Of course, there are other things to like. I'm a sucker for mod."

Sugar had to admit, it was sweet. She liked mod as well and Werner's RV was the definition of the word. The clean lines, enormous windows, even the throw-back, white paint job with the thin orange and brown stripes. It was all well-balanced and appealing. Everything she liked about her own RV, but with '70s flare to burn. "Very nice."

"Care to get the tour?"

Mary Helen suddenly let go of their arms. "Would you look at that?"

Simultaneously, Sugar and Werner asked, "What?"

"It's almost time for the music to start. I have to get back and put out chairs." Before Sugar could point out that everyone brings their own chairs to music night, Mary Helen was gone. Sugar called after her. "Subtle!" Mary Helen and her giggle disappeared into the night.

Werner asked, "Well?"

"Well, what?"

"Would you like the tour?"

"Is that what we're calling it?"

The right corner of Werner's mouth raised ever so slightly and he took her hand. The moment he touched her, she felt the excitement of heat race through her body. The intensity was surprising. *What is this?* He started moving backwards with her hand in his, and she realized she was moving with him.

Without words, he opened the door to his home and politely invited her to enter before him. Inside, the RV looked as tasteful as it did on the outside. Despite the big windows, the inside was dark. She could see that he'd covered them with a dark window treatment that wasn't obvious from the outside. The interior space was open, yet warm. She looked down. *Is that a new shag carpet? Where does one find new shag? '70s Are Us'?* "It's very nice."

"Thank you. I like it. Would you like to see the bedroom?"

How can this be happening? I'm in mourning. She repeated Curtis's name in her head over and over. But the physical connection to Werner was strong. *Has he let go of my hand yet?* They moved the few feet to his bedroom. Dark and inviting. Violet lava lamps flanked the bed giving the space a seductive movement. Sugar could no longer pretend. *This is going to happen.* And at that moment, that's exactly what she wanted.

Werner whispered. "I'd like to undress you."

Sugar said nothing. He slipped her jacket off her shoulders, then reached under her sweater and lifted it slowly over her head. With her arms still in the air, he said, "Keep them up." He ran his fingers down her arms and torso. "Do you trust me?"

"No."

"Good."

He locked eyes with her and she felt him remove her bra. But he didn't touch her breasts. Instead, she felt the slight breeze from a small oscillating fan on her skin as he unzipped then lowered her jeans. He then hooked a finger around her panties. "I hope these aren't your favorite." And with a long fingernail, he sliced them off of her. She was aching for him to touch her, anywhere. But she was too stubborn to say so. He was teasing her. It was a game of sexual chicken.

She won. His tongue made circles around her nipples. The arousal was all consuming. But as he continued, he touched her nowhere else. So, the game was not over. She mentally begged him for more. She needed him to hear her. But he was at least as strong-willed as she was. Just as she was about to let her desire be voiced, he licked his fingers then lowered them to meet her. As he reached her, she could no longer contain herself. She moaned in delight.

He whispered, "It gets better," then lifted her onto the bed. In a split second he was naked. The next few moments—or was it hours—flew by in flashes of deep delight. She felt like he was touching places that had never been touched. Never even existed. They moved together with strength and excitement, putting off their climax as long as they dared. Finally, their bodies shuddered together and he deftly coaxed the last bit of ecstasy from her. She hoped this 1970s rolling pleasure palace was sound-proofed.

Who knew how much time had passed? She woke exhausted with Werner staring at her. She grinned. "It did get better."

"You didn't trust me. Smart lady."

"I have never... I may never walk again."

"You will. But you'll never forget your first."

Sugar let out a bit of a laugh. "You thought I was a virgin?"

"I'm your first V-sex. Yes?"

"Yes."

"Then I am your first."

Sugar wondered how she felt about that. Had he just taken something from her? No. She wanted it to happen and she was glad it did, although she knew that feeling would likely change when the guilt set in. But for now, she was where she wanted to be. "Then I will never forget you."

"And you shouldn't. I'm much deeper than a California Cab."

"And you have a longer cellar life."

He got a dark smile. "In this world, one never knows."

She thought, *No, one doesn't.*

19

WHERE YOU BEEN?

It was a crisp, clear evening. Sugar had never before taken the walk of shame at 6:03 pm. On one hand, the fact that people weren't glaring as they hustled passed on their way to the office, made her feel rather stealth. On the other, the guilt for being with someone who wasn't Curtis had already started setting in, and it was thick. *Yes, Curtis is gone, but shouldn't I have waited longer? How much longer? What's a respectable amount of time under these circumstances? If someone is dead and someone is un-dead, do the rules of respectability change? No.*

She thought, *Maybe I should write a guide book for rookie vampires.* Quick math told her that with what she was guessing was the average number of new vampires per year, the margin would have to be quite high to turn a profit. *Would a new vampire spend four figures for a book on being V? And can you market it on Amazon?* She backburnered the project. *Back to being a tennis hustler.* Then, she got down on herself for changing the topic in her head. *My focus should stay on the subject at hand. Guilt.* She wanted, almost needed, to feel it deeply. To engage in self-flagellation. Then she wondered if there was such a thing as a self-flagellating Jew. *Should I rename it?*

Gefilte guilt? I was always a sucker for alliteration. Then, she got back down on herself for leaving the topic again. *Guilt. Guilt. Guilt.*

As she stood still, lost in whatever it was she was calling it, Sugar suddenly felt her right knee being forced into a bend, from behind. When she turned, she saw Maddie wearing a smile. "Miss me?"

She did. "So much."

"We went skiing. Matt kinda figured you'd wanna sit this one out."

"He's a good figurer."

"Where we going?"

"You tell me."

"I saw you walking. So, where we going?"

"I was going home."

"From?"

"Aren't you a nosy Nellie?"

Maddie was not offended. "Yep. Let's go play with Kitten."

As they walked, they passed Mary Helen, who was speaking with a new arrival to the V section of the park, a slight woman with short red hair and a look that said, "Don't fuck with this one." Her rig was a converted school bus. Sugar had passed a few of those on the road. Some looked nice. Others looked rough, like they might stink of patchouli, which was likely stopping them from stinking of stink. This bus was one of the nice ones, painted sea-foam green with a white roof. The two women were laughing in a way that indicated they knew each other well. Mary Helen looked over, and Sugar wondered if they were laughing at her. She knew they weren't but felt like she was wearing a t-shirt that read, "Just got laid. You?"

Maddie and Sugar arrived at the Sprinter van and got greeted with a raft of shit from Kitten. "Meow! Meow-ah! Meow! Meow! Meow! Meow! Meow-ah!"

Sugar put her hands up in a self-defensive move. This time, she knew immediately what the problem was. "Yes, yes. She who must be fed. The chef is on it." As Sugar filled Kitten's bowl she added, "Have you never heard of the fasting diet?"

V-Life

She did her best to look away and not count kibble in front of company. But then Maddie said, "Twenty-eight."

"Excuse me?"

"Twenty-eight pieces."

"You count them, too?"

"We all count shit. We're vampires. We obsess."

Sugar laughed, somehow relieved. "I thought it was just me."

"Hell, no." Maddie got on the floor next to Kitten's bowl, not waiting for the cat's meal to end before the petting began. She glanced up at Sugar looking like she just swallowed a secret. "How long has Kitten been without food?"

Pretending to turn to something of interest above her bunk, Sugar shrugged. "Not sure." But she already knew Maddie well enough to know it wouldn't end there. And it didn't.

"Oh, I think you could figure it out." Sugar offered nothing, so Maddie continued. "A few hours? Five? Six? All day, maybe?"

"Meow-ah!"

Maddie looked at Kitten. "Really. That long?"

Why fight it? Sugar turned to confront both her friend and her roommate. "Eleven. I was gone eleven hours and change. Happy?"

Maddie spoke directly to Kitten. "Did you have to wait to eat because your mommy was out getting a dicking?"

"I hate that phrase."

"What phrase do you like?"

This time Sugar got the devilish smile. "Getting nailed to the wall."

Maddie clapped her hands in delight as she rocked back and forth. "Best sex ever, am I right? It's the funnest part of being a V-girl."

"V-girl? I like that." Sugar then thought beyond her new club name. "Wait. You're saying it wasn't just Werner. It's always like that?"

"Always. Your senses are heightened now. *All* of them."

Sugar considered a sex-filled future. *Didn't Lance say, "Find a hobby?" There are worse ways to pass the time.* But then she wondered how much time she deserved to enjoy. She was now a killer *and* a cheater. Before meeting her new V-friends, she'd planned on ending her own life after getting her revenge. *Do I still want to? Maybe not. Who am I fooling? If Alex is gunning for me... Just fuck it.*

Joining Maddie and Kitten on the floor, she said, "Then yes. So far, the sex is the best part."

"Right? I think Matt pisses me off on purpose just for the make-up sex."

"Can you blame him?"

"So, Werner. How was he?"

Sugar couldn't stop the smirk from taking over her face. "I don't climax all night and tell."

They shared a laugh. A V-girl laugh. Then reaching into a pocket, Maddie asked, "Wanna get high?"

Wow. Sugar hadn't considered whether vampires could get high or not. She knew she couldn't drink wine or bourbon and stopped there. "Is it okay?"

"I won't tell."

"I mean, will I get sick?"

"You might."

"So, why do it?"

"V-life is long. You'll have time to recover."

"I don't know. That heightened-senses thing."

"Yeah. It's a real money saver. One puff'll do it. Just don't take in too much or you'll be totally in the bag for like a week. One time I did three puffs." She went back to her bad Transylvanian accent. "Three! Three puffs! Ah, hah, hah! I woke up with tree branches and plastic cocktail monkeys in my hair."

Sugar laughed at the image. "Oh, you reminded me. I have questions for you. Like, how do you... How do *we* make enough money to keep going?" Then she thought, *Why am I still considering a long life? Hope must be hard to kill.*

Maddie smiled her "I ate a secret" smile and dangled a bag of weed from her fingers. "I'll tell you if you smoke with me."

An hour later, the two of them were on Sugar's bunk, laughing hard at things they would have deemed only mildly funny prior to puffing.

Maddie was saying, "That's so great that you and your mom were close."

"Yeah. *Most-ly*. Get it? *Most-ly*." Maddie didn't get it. Sugar didn't mind. "We had some fun. Oh, wait, wait, wait. I remember this one time we went to New York for the day. We lived in New Jersey. So, we'd drive to see shows pretty regularly. Musicals are a big thing with us."

"The Jews?"

If Sugar had been drinking, she would have done a spit-take. "No, you freak. My family. Anyway, Faye sees it's almost time for intermission, so she assumes the position." Imitating her mother, Sugar leaned forward and looked as if she was ready to spring to her feet at the sound of a starting gun. "The musical number finishes, and before the actors can take a step back, Faye is off and running to the ladies' room. This is her thing. It's all timing cause the line gets nuts. Faye had it down. First up. First in line. So, we're in the ladies' room and she's doing what she needs to do, and this woman comes in, takes a whiff and says, 'Ugh. Disgusting.' Without missing a beat Faye calls out from her stall, 'Lady, this isn't a flower shop.'"

At that, Maddie roared with laughter. Sugar joined in, thrilled to be able to share a memory from home.

"Okay, I shared. Your turn."

"Name it."

"How do you afford V-Life? You know? Where does the money come from to keep paying and paying for shit with no clear end?"

"Oh. I thought you were gonna ask me about sex."

"Sorry, Mom. I'm good."

Maddie chuckled and climbed back up on the bunk. Sugar sat

down at her desk, ready to take notes. Kitten paced back and forth between the two of them, as if she was in a quandary as to who she wanted to pet her. Finally, she opted for her mom then tried to grab at her pen as Sugar wrote on the top of a page, Financial Plan.

Maddie began, "First, it's not forever."

"No? Well, that's important intel."

"Oh no. It's long but no one goes forever. Something will eventually get all of us. Something nasty, like burning or getting your head sliced off. But most of us just end up starving to death."

"That's a pleasant thought."

"We just get tired and stop craving the hunt. There was this vampire, she was, I don't know, 480 or 490 years old. We met her in the desert, sitting on a rock. We were driving through the desert. There she was, on this rock, just staring at nothing. Matt pulled over. We could tell she was one of us. We asked if we could help her get anywhere. But she said she was fine. Just..." Maddie shrugged as she remembered the moment. "...done. She said she was done. She seemed so, I don't know, peaceful? We asked if she wanted company. You know? Someone to be with her at the end. But she just smiled and said no. She was ready for it."

"That's kind of sad, but maybe not."

"Yeah. Like Lance is really old. But I think Willie keeps him young. Don't you?"

"I hope so."

The two sat quietly for a moment as they thought about friends and futures. Then Maddie reached into her pocket and produced the bag of weed. She held it up and shook it like a maraca. "Time to recharge."

"Did we get too morose?"

"Kinda'."

"Fine." Sugar let Maddie light up for round two. This time they each took a bit more than they had in round one. "What did Willie say? Make good choices?"

"Fuck that!" Maddie put a hand in the air. "Come on. Don't leave a girl hangin'."

"I hate high fives." Sugar reluctantly high-fived her eager friend. "Yeah!"

As the effects started kicking in, Sugar looked at the pen still in her hand, and remembered how this started. She climbed onto the bunk next to Maddie and the two laid on their backs facing up. "You still haven't told me. How do you two support yourselves financially? You don't come from some damn dynasty, do you?"

Laughing Maddie said, "I come from the local radio dynasty of WMAI in Maine. Impressed? Dad announced the high school ballgames and did the news. Mom did weather and the fishing report. I think the station cost them more to run than they made. When I was little, I was gonna be a big singing star on the radio. But I had a little problem."

"What was that?"

"I can't sing for shit." They cracked up and couldn't stop laughing. Still snickering, Maddie sat up. "Wait, I'll prove it. Put on some music."

Sugar got to her feet and grabbed her phone from the desk. "What would you like? Pop, rock, show tunes?"

Maddie aimed a thumb at herself. "Classic rock for this bitch."

"Okay. Oh, I love this one. 'Beast of Burden.'"

"Great song. Stand back while I stab it in the heart."

The tune started, but it wasn't the Stones' version. It was Bette Midler's. Maddie looked around, grabbed Sugar's hair brush from a shelf and dove in.

As promised, she was awful.

The notes seemed irrelevant to her. With utter joy, she belted out the worst version of the song ever performed. When the second verse started, Maddie handed Sugar the brush and said, "Your turn. Take the mic."

The weed had removed all inhibition and Sugar obliged. By the second chorus she was in a voice that was as smooth as butterscotch.

"What the Whitney!?" Maddie made a big deal out of shaking her head in mock shock, blond curls swirling around her. "You would have been such a hit on WMAI."

Sugar took a bow. "I do like the singing."

"Me, too."

"Then I say, belt it out!"

Together, with the Divine Miss M, the two stoned friends finished the Stones song. Then Maddie clapped. "Another!"

For their next performance, they added small-space choreography to accompany their singing. They made their way through a half dozen more rock classics. Amid all the flailing, they knocked over only a headlamp and two books. Kitten sat out the set in the safety of the kitchen sink.

Exhausted from their private show, they flopped back onto the bunk holding hands. Maddie confided to her friend in a whisper, "Vampires don't like to talk about their money."

"Why?"

"It's an old-world thing. Lots of secrets. Like if someone knows where your money comes from, they'll try to hijack your revenue stream. Or just kill you for it."

"Does that happen?"

Maddie shrugged. "Sometimes." She turned her head to Sugar and admitted, "A lot. It's like the second most common way we die."

Damn. Vampires are avaricious. Yet another strike against the V-Life. "But Willie told me he had family money."

"He must trust you. Those guys are set for lives. Willie's family came from big pre-Castro cash. His parents got out before it could all be claimed by the new government. That happened a lot back then."

"Damn."

"Before Willie, Lance 'dabbled' in art." She made Lance-like air quotes. "And by 'dabbled', I mean he stole it."

"I thought he said something about family money."

"How do you think they got it? Stealing it from other people's families. Some high roller would die, and they'd break into the mansion. Stealing only from the dead. That was their *rule*. But I know they took out a few of their own. Then Lance took over the family *business*—" more air quotes—"He's an only child. We all do what we have to do and we make up rules to justify it, right?"

Sugar knew that to be true. "What rules did you break?"

Maddie laughed. "Whaaat? You don't think being ski bums pays the big bucks?" Sugar shrugged. "You're right. It doesn't. Matt's family is pretty bohemian for our kind. Living meal to meal. You know? He doesn't need much. We were pretty hand-to-mouth until bitcoin. At first, and this was in like 2009, Matt thought I was crazy. He didn't get the concept of decentralized digital currency or block chain or anything about an open-source system." Maddie began imitating her man, which was only slightly better than her imitating the *Sesame Street* Count. "Matt was all, 'But gold. Silver. Precious metal. Maddie, you can't change an established system.' Silly boy. So now he gets to be a ski bum."

Sugar said, "Look at you." Speaking like some people speak to pets or babies, she added, "Who's a little early adopter? Who's such an early adopter?"

As Maddie continued her tale of financial freedom, Sugar reassessed her friend. *Am I stoned or is a lot more going on under all those white-blond curls than I gave her credit for? Maybe that's how she likes it. Surprise them with your smarts.* But it didn't take much to figure out that this woman was set for a long life. And while that didn't solve Sugar's situation, she was happy for her friend.

Then Maddie turned the tables. "How much do you have?"

"Me? I dunno. Mid six figures? The sale of my apartment helped some. And I still get small checks from my parents' business. I'm a shareholder." Sugar's old friends would have been happy with an upper, mid-six figure savings at this point in their lives, but they were all still generating income and would be for years. If they invested well, they'd be fine.

"Bummer."

"One of so many."

"Don't worry. I have a motto. Wanna hear it?"

"Sure."

"Something will happen."

"That's it?"

"That's it. You don't have to worry that something might happen if you already know something will. It always does. Say it. You'll feel better."

Sugar gave it a go. "Something will happen."

"See? Now you never have to worry. You know, something will happen."

That's exactly what Sugar feared.

20

COMES THE FALL

After taking Maddie's Magical Mystery Tour, Sugar slept through the rest of the day, the entire night and into the next day. But now, after several failed attempts at getting back to sleep, Sugar gave up. Peering out into an overcast gray day she wondered, *Is it safe? Devil hates a coward.* Cautiously stepping outside, she stood waiting for pain. It didn't come. *Maybe I should do laundry.* Thinking about how much she dreaded that activity, she decided it might be a good day for hunting. She was hungry. Actually, very hungry. Munchies. Checking her weather app and seeing it should be like this most of the day, she thought, *Okay, then.* Knowing her friends would be sleeping, she ventured alone to the great outdoor pantry adjacent to the RV park.

This being the first time Sugar was hunting during the day, she didn't know what to expect. No eyes gleaming in the night. After finding a wooded area, she climbed a tree, hoping her perch on a branch would provide a good vantage point as well as cover. Slowing down her mind, she tuned in to the sounds and smells around her. The place was alive. There was scurrying everywhere. *I won't leave here hungry.* A deer walked slowly below her, then stopped to graze.

She could both hear and feel its heartbeat, but thought, *No. Bambi's too big. I don't need that much and I hate to waste.* Next, a skunk waddled past. *No. Not taking a chance on smelling like Flower.* Then she spotted her target. Rabbit, her favorite. *Waiter, I'll have the free-range Thumper off of the Disney menu.*

She readied herself to leap from the tree, swoop down and get breakfast. Maybe if she assumed success, the flying would simply work. *Don't think. Just Do. Is that my father's advice or Yoda's? Stop it. Focus.* She rocked a bit as she readied herself, emulating Kitten before a pounce. Then...

CRACK!

The limb she was on gave way and instead of flying or swooping or doing anything involving control, Sugar fell to the ground, taking out several branches on her way. She lay there with the wind knocked out of her for a full minute before realizing she'd broken her arm and ripped her jacket. "Fuck me!"

By now she knew the drill. *Suck up the pain and wait for my bone to mend.* Of course, her jacket would not mend itself. Knowing she was too pissed to try again, there was no reason to sit there and wallow. *But I am good at that. No. My arm can mend on the way back.* Sugar got up and headed home sore, hungry, and annoyed. "I should have done the damn laundry."

The low, soft rumble of dryers and cloying smell of fabric softener filled the dingy-white room. Rubbing her arm, Sugar had only her oversize sunglasses to shield her from the offensive florescent lighting. *Is there anything worse than having to use a public laundry facility?* Sugar knew the answer was yes. So much worse.

A nondescript woman from the gen-pop section of Moonglow came into the laundry room with an empty basket. Presumably, she was there to retrieve her things from a dryer, which was good, because Sugar had been waiting for one to free up. *Ah, the glamourous world of the undead.* As the woman slowly pulled each nondescript item from her machine, she held it up for inspection. What she was inspecting for, Sugar had no idea. The process was painfully laborious to watch. And then, things got worse. The woman pulled something from her pocket and popped it in her mouth. *Is that, gum? Mother of God!*

As the woman chopped, popped, cracked, and inspected, Sugar did everything in her power to not go mad, but her misophonia was kicking in hard. Annoyed and hangry, she slowly gathered her items from the washer then stood still, facing away from the offender. With each wet mouth noise Sugar squoze and resquoze the damp bundle in her arms. As her frustration slash anger increased, she felt her eye teeth lengthening. *This is it. This is fuckin' it. I'm gonna lose it. One more sound and I'm gonna have to kill her.*

POP!

Snap! Sugar pulled off her sunglasses and whipped around, just as the woman chimed, "All done."

Trying but failing to reel back her expression in time, Sugar watched the woman recoil in terror. Gripping her laundry basket in a way that would definitely leave dents, Mrs. Nondescript fled the scene, calling behind her, "Sorry! I'm sorry! It's only a dryer!"

Fuck! What did she see? What did I look like in that moment? Would I really have killed a total stranger over laundry? No. But gum chewing? Once her anger dissipated, it left room for fear. Mrs. Nondescript was not the only person she'd frightened. Experiencing this unexpected flash of rage, she'd scared the shit out of herself. Realizing her anger had increased right along with other skills. she wondered *What else might I do? What pain could I inflict? I need to learn control, fast.* Sugar stood amid the low thumping of the laundry room until, with no warning, a loud buzzer from a dryer rang out.

"Shit!"

Startled, Sugar sprang to the ceiling, where she stayed. Somehow, she was gripping the stucco ceiling of the laundry room thinking, *New skill?*

Heart racing, head spinning, she scanned the room from her new point of view. It all seemed empty and jaundiced. Looking down at her pile of damp clothes on the floor, a floor strangers had tracked all manner of who knew what on, Sugar knew there was no way she could pick them up and put them into Mrs. Nondescript's vacated dryer. She'd have to put them back into a washer and start over. It would give her plenty of time to contemplate the gravity of who and what she now was. And how much she hated public laundries.

21

MESSAGES FROM FRIENDS

After another two hours of laundry time that seemed so much longer, Sugar was finally on her way back to the Sprinter. Feeling her phone vibrating in her back pocket, she juggled it and her basket. It was a text from Willie. Seeing his name lifted her mood ever so slightly. She put down the basket and read his text.
 A little birdy told me you did the old bump & grind. [Wink emoji]
 She texted back, *A birdy?*
 Shook the sheets. [Bed emoji]
 Maddie is a blab.
 Baked the potato. [Potato emoji]
 Are you done?
 No. Did hot yoga. [Yogurt emoji]
 What the hell is that?
 Oops. My bad. Buttered the biscuit. [Butter emoji]
 If you must know, I slammed the ham. [Ham emoji]
 [Three laughing emojis] I'm so proud.
 That makes you proud? Then you'll [Heart emoji] *this. I almost killed a woman in the laundry for chewing her gum like she was slapping a wet rag on the floor.*

OMG, I hate that too much! You should have killed her.
Sugar was suddenly concerned. *Are you serious?*
Oops. Forgot. [Wink emoji]
She returned his wink emoji and added a *[laugh emoji].*
Remember, use a condom. Don't want to get pregnant. Ciao!

She suddenly thought, *What? Can I still get pregnant?* The range of horrors that sped through Sugar's head almost knocked her over. She made another 'Ask Maddie' note on her phone. 'V birth control?'

Picking up her basket, Sugar started back to her van. Suddenly out of nowhere, Mrs. Nondescript from the laundry room appeared in front of her. Actually, she was almost in front of her. Standing between her and the woman was a man, presumably her husband, Mr. Nondescript. He was thrusting a cross in Sugar's face. *What the hell?!* Quickly piecing the puzzle together, Sugar realized just how deeply she'd scared Mrs. Nondescript. This was the unhinged woman's way of warding off evil. In truth, Sugar felt a bit guilty for losing control the way she did. But this was ridiculous.

She stood looking at the fearful couple and their cross. Mr. Nondescript blurted, "The power of Christ compels you!"

What could she say? "Shalom."

They didn't move, so Sugar did. As she continued on her way, she heard one of them call out in a cracking voice, "Devil woman!" *Was that Mr. or Mrs. Nondescript? Does it matter? I'll be leaving shortly. They can have fun waving crosses at Mr. Skin & Bones.* She did make a note to herself, *Crosses? Nothing. Maybe they only work on gentile vampires.*

Back home with her laundry, Sugar hoped it would somehow fold itself. It didn't. "I am so not a day person." As night fell, she wondered if she should venture out or just stay home. With her current luck, home seemed safer. She folded her laundry neatly and carefully placed it and the basket in their proper places. After putting a few other odd objects in their assigned cubbies, she thought, *you have to keep a space this size beyond organized. Clutter is unforgiving in a small home. Hmm.* She wondered if she should start a blog for people who live in small spaces. "Kitten, what would I call it? How about, *Space Wars, Go Small/Live Big.* Or *Live Big/Go Small?* Which do you like?"

The sound of crinkling caused Sugar to look to the frolicking happening on her bunk. Kitten had a ball of crumpled paper and was batting it here and there and rolling over it in a game of solo-cat rugby. Ready to tag in, Sugar got on the bunk, snatched the paper ball, and flicked it towards Kitten. Kitten seemed delighted to have an opponent. The two flicked and kicked and pounced on the paper. Sugar loved when Kitten would hunker down, twitch her behind, then at just the right moment, leap and attack the ball from above. The match went on with no obvious goal and neither side scoring points. Just playing for the sake of playing. When Kitten noticed an insect so small Sugar could barely make it out, the match was over. Game called on account of bug.

Sugar smiled as she watched Kitten obsessing over invisible objects. Absently, she grabbed the paper ball to throw it out. *Can't have clutter in small spaces.* But before she tossed it in the trash, she unballed it to make sure it was nothing worth saving. A receipt she might need for her taxes. Laughing at the thought, she looked at the paper. Then she stopped laughing. Scrawled on it in red ink were the words, "I just made my move. Your turn." It was signed, "Kisses, A."

Sugar quickly looked around, as if the author of the note might be waiting right there, in her van. She wasn't. The dread that had become her on-again/off-again life partner was once again standing front and center. The thought of She-vil or those thugs in the van with Kitten allowed anger to join her dread. She felt violated...again.

Then came a sound so faint that Sugar wondered if she'd actually heard anything. *Did I?* She waited. There it was again. Her name. Someone was whispering her name. The now familiar voice was like an icy warning. *Where is it coming from?* Sugar let her instincts take over. She went out of her van and across the V-lot towards Werner's

GMC. The door was open and smeared with blood. Her dread carried her across the threshold and inside. There he was. Or part of him. Sugar gasped at the sight. In the sink was Werner's head half buried in white powdery crystals. His eyes were open, staring out and seeing nothing.

"It's sugar." Startled, Sugar turned to find the wiry little redhead Mary Helen had been talking to the other day. She was standing behind her and licking a finger. "He's buried in sugar." At that, Sugar bent over and wretched violently. Her mind whirled *Too much! Too much! Too much!*

With no emotions, the redhead said, "I guess there's no such thing as safe sex."

The words hit Sugar like a slap. "Excuse me?" Sugar stared down this stranger, but before she could demand an explanation, Mary Helen rushed in.

"Werner, no!" Harried, she turned to the two women. "Sugar, what happened?"

"I don't know."

"Angél?"

All the redhead aka Angél offered was, "Someone's in a bad mood."

Still trying to make sense of what she was seeing, Sugar's guilt burned like acid. She knew she had somehow brought this on. That this was, at least in part, her fault. *Werner. I'm so, so sorry.* She remembered what he'd said. *In this life you never know.*

Mary Helen seemed to be evaluating Angél. "Can ya' share anything else? Anything?"

"I'm not her keeper." With that, Angél turned to Werner. "Just the wrong place and time. You'll be missed." She didn't look at Sugar before she left.

What the hell? What does she know that she's not saying? Sugar looked back at Werner. Sadness. Anger. Fear. More anger. She wanted to be proactive like a good poker player, and reraise. But she didn't know how this game was played or, for that matter, where the other player was. But she knew a confrontation was coming. Mary Helen put an arm around her. It eased no pain.

Looking at Werner one last time she whispered, "I'll never forget you."

As she turned to leave the grisly scene, the only clear thought Sugar could formulate was, *I need to leave Moonglow. Now.*

22

SAY GOODNIGHT, GRACIE

Sugar prepped for travel stowing some things and strapping down others. Then she contemplated her next move. She'd considered employing her old friend, the Dutch goodbye, but felt she owed her new friends better than that. So, she walked over to Matt and Maddie's ambulance wondering what she'd tell them. *Should I come clean, or play it close to the vest? Close to the vest. They'll just worry.* She started concocting a story.

For a moment, Sugar just stood watching her first ever V-friends go about their business. Outside their ambulance, Matt was on a short ladder installing a new pink and white striped awning on their rig while Maddie gave unnecessary instructions from her chair.

"You have to make sure the sides are even."

Playfully sarcastic, Matt teased, "Even, you say? Did you read that in the manual?"

"I read it on your underwear."

"That doesn't even mean anything."

Sugar approached, but before she could tap Maddie on the shoulder, Maddie turned. "Mary Helen says you're leaving."

Matt looked over. "I'm so sorry, kid."

Realizing she'd have to tell the truth, Sugar threw away her excuse about a sick friend in New York. It was a good one, too. Lyme disease. The made-up friend had contracted it on a made-up ladies' trip to a winery. Not even a good winery. Yet, it had been an epic good time. The cops had to be called. No one went to jail but it went onto their records. And now, the made-up Lyme disease had progressed to the point where this once-vibrant young professional and wino needed help flossing. So very sad. *Oh, well.* Sugar put the made-up story in her back pocket for another time. "I gotta go."

Maddie stood. "You can't let anyone push you around. Not even She-vil. Stay. I'm not afraid of her."

The look on Matt's face said that she should be.

This was not going to be the easy goodbye to her friends Sugar'd wanted. *Why didn't I run with my first impulse and go Dutch?*

Matt came down from his ladder. "You're gonna miss us."

Maddie smiled. "Especially me. You think you should leave Kitten with us?"

"No, I do not."

"A girl can try."

With a sincere look, Matt said, "But if you run into trouble..."

"Thanks. I appreciate that. I do. But I think it's best to get away from anyone I actually care about."

Matt puffed up his chest. "Hey. What's got two thumbs and ain't afraid to joust?" He pointed both thumbs at himself. "This guy."

Despite the somberness of the moment, Sugar had to laugh at Matt's goofiness. She knew she'd have to speed this up, or she might cave. Wrapping her arms around Matt she whispered, "I'll miss this guy." She could feel the genuine affection when his strong arms hugged her back. Maddie then wrapped her arms around the both of them, and they all stayed that way for longer than most hugs get to enjoy.

Sugar counted out "28, 29, 30, 31." Finally, she untangled herself from her friends and forced a smile as she stepped backwards. "Till next we meet."

Maddie waved. "See you on the slopes."

Matt asked, "Which way you heading?"

"Rather not say."

Sugar turned away and started for her van. As clinical as she wanted to be in her new life, she felt like a parody of the Tin Woodman. She didn't need or even want a heart, but she still had one to break. *Damn it.* After a few steps, a force from behind almost knocked her to the ground. Maddie had run in for a final hug. "You're gonna miss me soooo much!"

"So much." Sugar couldn't look at her, but she put her hand over Maddie's hand.

Then, Maddie slipped something into Sugar's back pocket and whispered, "Just a little somethin' somethin'. Don't open it now."

Sugar walked forward, out of the hug.

Well, that sucked.

Back in her van, she scanned her belongings to make sure everything was secured in its proper place. She usually managed to miss something. Once, she'd left a bottle of shampoo on the kitchen counter. She forgot that she'd washed her hair at the sink and shampoo got everywhere, including in the stove burners. Not that she ever used them. But there were bubbles each time she wiped down the counter for over a week after.

Sugar spun around once more, and felt like this time, she'd gotten it all. "Kitten, what do you think? Are we good?"

Kitten looked up from the litter box. "Meow-ah."

Sugar assumed that was cat-speak for, "Some privacy would be nice."

But then, seeing Kitten in the litter triggered, "Crap, sewage. Thank you, Kitten."

Sugar had heard stories of people pulling away, forgetting their sewer line was still attached and creating a literal shit storm.

Working the lines, Sugar was surprised how capable she was becoming when forced to be. Sewage management skills were not part of how she was raised. Henry, although a great dad, was never handy. They'd always hired "a guy" to help with everything. The air conditioning went out? Get "a guy." A shelf fell down? Get "a guy." David's stuck in the fireplace? Get "a guy."

She had never dumped her tank, and it was time. Sugar began connecting hoses, including the bright orange sewer line, to the sewer connection in the ground. Then she went around the van to open the tank dump. After it emptied, she'd run water through the line to flush it. She opened the appropriate valves, and went back to check her progress.

But when she stepped around the van, Sugar found the giant orange hose flying around like one of those bright, "Look at me!" air dancer tube things you see in front of a car dealership—except you rarely see them spraying raw sewage out of the tops of their heads.

"Shit! Shit! Shit! Shit!"

Racing back around the rig, Sugar closed the valves. "Son of a bitch!" Returning to the scene of the crime, she thought, *This right here is why you don't poop in your rig.* Expecting someone to walk up at any moment and mock her incompetence, she packed up as quickly as possible. But no one came over. *Did anyone even see that?* She decided the responsible thing was to hose down the area.

Just when she thought she'd escape all shaming, Harry walked up. "Do all Sprinters come with that spectacular fountain feature?"

"I splurged for all the upgrades."

"Hm. Drive safe." Harry gave a small head nod and disappeared into the night.

"Thanks."

With all the unpleasant tasks done and the wipes deployed, Sugar got a plush blue towel and crafted it into a cat bed on the passenger seat. Then, she gently placed Kitten on the makeshift throne, took the con, and turned over the engine. Before backing up, she took a moment to soak in this mostly welcoming place that she was about to leave. She'd enjoyed her stay more than she'd thought she would. She'd been part of a community until...She thought again of Werner. *He deserved so much better.*

Backing out of her spot she saw no sign of Mr. Skin & Bones. That was fine with her. As Sugar maneuvered the van, she realized how much she'd enjoyed not rolling for a while. Driving past Mr. and Mrs. Nondescript's RV, she flashed a "let's make up" smile. But they just stood with fear in their eyes, watching her go by. Mrs. Nondescript held Baby Nondescript closer to her body. *Really?* Sugar pointed at the child and licked her lips. The Nondescripts ran inside.

She asked Kitten, "Too far?"

"Meow-ah."

"Yeah. Probably."

Driving past the office, Matt and a sad-looking Maddie stood hand in hand and waved goodbye. Then Maddie started retching and threw up a little. Matt laughed and hugged his wife. Angél was walking up the office steps and raised an eyebrow at Sugar, which made her wonder, *Should I back up and try to pump her for information? She clearly knows more than she said.* Instead, Sugar kept rolling.

Last was Mary Helen, who blew Sugar a kiss from her front porch. *What an odd woman. Sweet, but odd. Her story has to be fascinating. But aren't they all?* Sugar wondered if she'd ever see these people again. She hoped so. But not until after she took care of business. Or, the more likely scenario, it took care of her.

23

GO WEST, YOUNG LADY

The sign read, "Welcome to Utah - Life Elevated."

"How about that Kitten? You're in Utah!" Kitten didn't seem to care that she'd just entered the Beehive State. Having no real destination, Sugar wondered how much farther she'd drive. After a quick stop to look at the map, she decided to make the push for Moab. Curtis had talked about taking a hiking trip in Moab someday. They'd pored over pictures of Zion National Park, Delicate Arch, Goblin Valley, and all the red rocks. They'd even found a hotel with a winery that had rooms right on the Colorado River. While Sugar hadn't held out much hope for Utah wine, the idea of hiking and paddling through that dramatic landscape and ending the day on a private porch overlooking the river with a really great glass of wine (purchased elsewhere) seemed like a true getaway.

As she drove, she reminded herself that she wasn't on vacation. But Alex hadn't specified a meet-up location so Sugar assumed her job was to distance herself from any support, then Alex would come to her. So *why shouldn't I go to a gorgeous place? If the end is coming, wouldn't it be nicer to have it come in a place of natural beauty than in one of my mother's roadside ditches?* The answer was Yes. At least, it was tonight.

By the time she made the turn off of I-70 onto 191, she was starting to wonder if she might try to find a place to pull off and make the final push the next day. But it was less than an hour. She'd found lots of campgrounds online, although the Moonglow RV Park app showed that the Moab V lot was currently full. Fine by her. After Werner, she was reluctant to be around her own kind. *What to do? Suck it up. Just get there.*

"What do you think Kitten, time for show tunes?"

Kitten jumped down from her passenger-seat throne and onto the floor.

"That's not an answer."

Kitten looked up at her. "Meow-ah."

"Lizzo? Really? Okay, girlfriend. It's a party."

"About Damn Time" came on and Sugar let the upbeat music help release some of her stress. She bobbed her head and pointed at Kitten as she sang along with an appropriate amount of sass. But Kitten didn't take to being pointed at and ventured under Sugar's legs towards the brake pedal.

"No, no, no. Kitten, get out of there."

Kitten was not in a listening mood. Sugar reached down, trying to not lose sight of the road while grabbing for the cat before she caused Sugar to have an accident. "Kitten you little— I swear, if you don't... Goddamn it, cat!"

The van swerved onto the shoulder, the sound of the rumble strip only adding to Sugar's stress. "Mother of...Cat!"

There was no cooperation. Only swerving. And then, WOOP! WOOP!

The sound of a police siren felt equally surprising and inevitable. Blue swirling lights were now coloring Sugar's world. Checking her side-view mirror, she bitched, "Damn it, Kitten! We're being pulled over."

Careful not to step on her cat, Sugar slowly pressed down the brake pedal and pulled to the side of the highway. Looking down below her steering wheel at the fluffy trouble maker, she shook her finger. "Kitten, shut up and let me do the talking."

In her side mirror, Sugar saw the female trooper step out of her vehicle and approach the van. She thought, *A woman. Of course. I'd do so much better with a guy. Fine. Something will happen.*

Even watching the trooper approach, the KNOCK, KNOCK of her baton on the side window startled Sugar. Quickly trying to regain her composure, she rolled down the window. "Yes, Officer?"

"Trooper. Cut the engine." The stout woman in brown was wearing mirrored glasses. Sugar wondered how she could see in the dark. But she did as told. "Yes ma'am." The engine went off, taking Lizzo with it. "I know I was—"

"License and registration."

Crap. This woman is all business. Sugar pulled out her wallet, removed the requested items, and handed them to the trooper.

"You know you were swerving all over the road. Had a few drinks?"

"Not one."

"Hmm."

The trooper looked into Sugar's eyes. There was no looking away. *She seems suspicious. But isn't that her job? Does she know?*

Finally, the woman broke eye contact and looked at the license. "New York? You're a long way from home."

"I am."

Looking further at the license, the trooper seemed to be considering something. She looked off, deep in thought, then...

"Bernstein?"

"Present."

"Do you by any chance know a Mirrah Bernstein?"

"Mirrah Bernstein? Short, round woman?"

"Yes."

"In the high holiday choir for no reason related to tone or pitch?"

"That's her."

"That's my aunt."

Suddenly, the trooper's demeanor changed. A dose of New York slipped into her accent. "That's just crazy." She took off her glasses, revealing vibrant green eyes. "She was my Hebrew school teacher. I almost didn't ask because what are the chances, right?"

"Right." Sugar's shoulders relaxed a bit and for the first time, she noticed the trooper's nameplate, which said, "Goldberg."

"Such a crazy, small world," beamed Trooper Goldberg.

But Sugar, who a split second earlier was thrilled with this stroke of luck, was now worried about revealing too much to this out-of-place Jewess with connections to her past. In the before-times, she would have seen this door of opportunity and run through it, launching into a captivating tale of how at the high holidays, she used to sneak booze onto the *bema* in the cuffs of her choir robe as a favor to the older choir members. But now, less was more. She chose to merely echo Officer Goldberg's sentiment. "So crazy."

"God, what I won't give for great deli. It's like a damn kosher wasteland out here. When was the last time you had a proper deli sandwich?"

Now that's a good question. It had been a while, because even before "the incident," Sugar was hypervigilant about the carbs. Unless she'd been drinking, then all bets were off. "Damn. Wait, let me think. Okay, about a year ago I had a corned beef, coleslaw, and—"

Joining in, Trooper Goldberg completed the sentence with Sugar: "Russian dressing on rye!"

The previously tough trooper was now reveling in deli-food porn. "Oh, my G-dash-D! The best! Some people say the Reuben is the quintessential, but I'm a total corned-beef-and-coleslaw gal."

"Me, too."

"And a good knish. Not the crap in the vendor carts. The real-deal, deli-counter knish."

"Second Avenue Deli."

"Oh, five me, bitch!"

Again, Sugar did as instructed, high-fiving down to Trooper Goldberg out the window of the van.

"Great. Now I want a goddamn black and white cookie from Junior's." It took Trooper Goldberg some time to break from her food fantasies. Finally, with a curious smile, she asked, "What brings you all the way out here? You're not travelin' alone are you?"

"I am."

Trooper Goldberg shook her head. "You wouldn't catch me crossing this great land by myself. But I'm in law enforcement. I know too much. I guess ignorance is bliss."

"I guess."

"Until you pick up an axe murderer and end up dead on the side of the road in a ditch somewhere."

"My, you are Jewish."

Trooper Goldberg laughed. "It comes and it goes. Just when I think I got away from all that *meshugas* out here, some swerving bitch in a van hands me a New York driver's license and all that old shit sits down right in my lap."

"I am that bitch. So, what brought you out here?" Internally, Sugar commended herself for making it about the other person.

"Same old bullshit story. I followed some schmuck."

"Sorry."

"Don't be. I got a great kid, a pension, and I'm livin' like a queen in the goddamn desert."

"Good for you."

"Good for us. I'm gonna let you go on your shit drivin'. You're clearly not drunk."

"Nope. Just a shit driver. And there's no law against that."

Trooper Goldberg snapped back to her original all-business demeanor, "Actually there are hundreds of laws against that."

"Sorry. A joke too far."

"It's cool. Just watch yourself. And tell your aunt I said hey."

"Will do."

With that, Trooper Goldberg handed Sugar back her license and registration. "Here you go." As she headed back to her own vehicle, Sugar could hear her parting words echo into the night: "*Shalom, bitch!*"

Sugar wondered if she should pull away immediately, or give it a moment. *Which one would make me seem less guilty?* But then she remembered she hadn't really done anything except be a bad driver. And a vampire. She placed Kitten back on her throne, turned on the engine, and after carefully checking her side-view, pulled back onto the road.

"Kitten, that was some bat-ass crazy shit. And it was all your fault."

"Meow-ah."

"The hell it wasn't."

Seeing the cop car in her rearview, Sugar wondered how far Trooper Goldberg would follow her. She quietly prayed for a shit driver heading the other way.

24

RED ROCKS AND HIGH TIMES

After her run-in with the long, Jewish arm of the law, Sugar'd had enough of driving, and of people. No RV parks tonight. She didn't want to run the risk of waking up parked next to her old rabbi, or her mother's neighbor's cousin. The one with the chipped tooth which made her whistle when she used S-words. A simple, "Hello, sweetie!" would make dogs come running. So, she found a rutted dirt road and followed it up and away from the highway for almost five miles. She'd passed a few boondocking RVs parked to the side of the road, which was also her plan. But she wanted to be away from any other campers as well. She'd found an ideal spot. The van was now parked down in a dried-out wash, which made it hard to spot from the road. Not wanting to move, she'd leaned back in her seat and closed her eyes.

Kitten was ready to stir first. Sitting on Sugar's chest, the tiny beast forced cat breath into Sugar's face. Sugar wonder just how much of it she could take. After all of their time together, Sugar knew Kitten could outwait her. Kitten's chicken breath made Sugar think of Maddie. *No doubt she'd be throwing up by now.* The thought made her laugh to herself.

"Come here, you." Without opening her eyes, Sugar grabbed

Kitten and snuggled her in close. "I think you grew overnight, Kitten."

"Meow-ah."

"That wasn't a dig. What do we want to do with our night, Kitten? Research? No. Wait to be killed? No. Nothing? I like nothing. Hey, I got it. We could wallow in self-pity. Let's try it, shall we?"

"Meow-ah."

"Sit it out if you want. But I'm wallowing. Where do I want to start? Okay. Wait. I'm so pissed about being dealt this ridiculously shitty hand. God, I'm pissed. It is so unfair. I miss having a job. I was good at my job. It was nice to be good at something. Not like this. I suck at this. I miss staying out too late with my friends. I miss being honest with D. God, I hate being evasive with him. And I miss my man. I miss him so much." Sadness was taking over. Then she thought of her day with Werner. And then of finding him, that way. *No. Go back to wallowing.* "I miss...what else do I miss? Mom and Dad? I do. I miss you both and all your crazy, sitcommy ways. And great deli. And a good glass, no, a great bottle of wine." Again, she saw the image of Werner. The look on his disembodied face. "No. What else do I miss? Think. Oh shit, I miss a mani-pedi."

"Meow."

"What's that Kitten? You wanna do Mommy's feet?" No response from Kitten.

"I'm hungry. You?"

"Meow-ah."

"Oh, that question you'll answer. Fine."

Knowing she needed to care for her ward first, Sugar got up and poured food into Kitten's bowl. By now, she knew to look away as the bits tumbled out of the box. After talking with Maddie about vampire obsessions, it hadn't taken much research to discover the myth from Eastern Europe suggesting one could protect one's self from a vampire by surrounding one's house with seeds. A needle should be placed somewhere in the seeds and when a vampire came, they'd be compelled to count the seeds. When they pricked their finger on the needle, they'd have to start over, giving one time to run away. Sugar wondered how smart one would feel if the vampire didn't prick their finger, or remembered the count, or simply looked away. But the bottom line was, Sugar now knew the needing-to-count thing was real.

As the cat crunched down her indeterminate number of crunchy bits, Sugar thought about where her own meal would come from. Looking out the van window, she wondered if anything lived here. And if it did, could she put an end to that? "Don't get up cat. I'm just grabbing a bite." Kitten ignored her as she stepped into the night.

Walking the dry, scrubby terrain, Sugar's thoughts were more inward than outward. On how much more lonely she felt now that she had friends to leave. *Would it have been better to have never met them? No. Absolutely not. I should text Maddie. Tell her I got pulled over. She'd enjoy that.* As Sugar pulled her phone from her pocket, a small, pink envelope fell out. Looking at it on the ground, she remembered. Maddie had shoved something into her pocket as Sugar was leaving Moonglow. Sugar picked up the envelope, carefully opening it as if it might explode. It didn't. But glitter spilled out, sticking to her clothes. Inside the envelope was a tiny velvet pouch, a little bag of weed, and a note.

The note read, "The weed's from me, the jewel's from Angél. (She doesn't know I gave it to you.) Stay safe. Get high. Repeat."

Sugar opened the pouch. Sure enough, it contained a green jewel. *Is it an emerald? No. Too flat a finish.* While Sugar enjoyed both jewelry and jewelry shopping, she couldn't be sure what she was looking at. On closer inspection, she noted a vein of blue running through the stone. *So odd.* Sugar put everything except the glitter back in the envelope and the envelope back in her pocket. *I'll deal with it later. I'm hungry.*

Just then, she spotted movement on the ground to the right. Two large porcupines waddled out from around a rock. "No, thank you. I'm not that hungry." Suddenly the animals started chattering, showing their teeth, then turned, raised their quills and lashed their tails. Sugar threw her hands up. "Idiots."

Walking away from the chatter, Sugar searched for any other movement. There was none and all she smelled was rock. Looking up, she was suddenly struck by sky. Stars were out in force. Millions of them. Without any ambient light from a town or ballfield to dim their vibrancy, the vast sky seemed almost silver. It was truly awesome. *Wasn't this why Curtis had wanted to come here? Why not enjoy it?* Behind one of the few trees, which was more of a shrub, she found a grouping of rocks that seemed to have the right shape for lounging. Sugar settled into a comfy position and began stargazing. *Do I remember anything from science class? Not really. Just the stuff everyone knows. The Big Dipper, or is that the Little Dipper? There's Orion's belt. Can I find The Pleiades? No. Wait. There they are.* She was actually relaxing and doing it without Maddie's weed. The peace lasted about fifteen minutes.

Suddenly, there was music, the crunching of gravel, and the roar of an engine with a bad muffler. A rust-colored beater cargo van drove up with a cloud of dust in its wake. Or was that a cloud of rust? The driver-side front fender and hood were slightly caved in. Heavy metal was pumping over the sound of dirt and rocks crunching under its bald tires. It was hard to make out any lyrics through the heavy thud of bass on shitty speakers.

Not that anyone could hear her, Sugar said, "Really?" As she stood up, she gave herself a round of mental shit for not wandering even farther from the road.

The van stopped, sat idling for a moment, then the engine cut off, and the music with it. The sudden silence gave what had just been her refuge a new and threatening air. The van doors groaned open. Two scraggly guys climbed out, approaching her slowly. One of them was tall with shoulder length hair that would have benefitted greatly from shampoo. The other was only about five four, wearing a too-tight Slayer t-shirt with a rip on the sleeve. Both walked on their toes and seemed to almost bounce as they moved. They brought a stench that polluted the night.

The short one spoke through his gum chewing, "Saw your van. No one home, so we figured we better make sure the driver was okay. You okay?"

Something about how he asked seemed more hostile than concerned. And, of course, there was that damn gum chewing. She suddenly didn't feel okay.

"Me and Silent Jim here…" the little guy directed a thumb to his tall friend, "…We look out for campers who may be in need of a little assistance."

Sugar stood tall. "I'm all good. No assistance needed."

The greasy, little man pressed on. "Well, that's good. Care for a little company?"

"Nope. Not tonight." Sugar wondered if the tall guy would ever want a speaking part.

"Oh, hey, I didn't introduce myself. My bad. They call me Runt. You know, cause I'm so tall." Runt seemed pleased with the joke he'd likely worn down to the nub. He stepped closer, chomping away at his gum, and put out a hand.

Sugar didn't reach for it. "I don't mean to be rude, but I'm not up for meeting anyone tonight. I need some alone time."

Runt was undeterred. In a delivery Sugar had heard too many times in bars from guys saying things like, "Hey, what's wrong. Why don't you smile?" Runt said, "Hey, don't be like that. We're just trying to be friendly. Can't we be friends?"

"No, Runt. I don't think we can."

"Now you're just hurting my feelings." He turned to his lanky companion. "Silent Jim, did the nice lady hurt your feelings too?"

Jim didn't answer, and for a moment all she could hear was Runt's gum echoing through the desert.

Finally, "Yup." So apparently, Silent Jim could form words. Or at least syllables.

Runt kept moving closer. He was now only feet away and Jim

was right behind him. "Come on. Why don't you relax and tell us your name?"

"They call me, 'Back The Fuck Off.'"

Runt put up his hands. Almost in a laugh he said, "Woo. Wow. Where's all that hostility coming from? They say hostility is bad for your health."

"Really? Who says that?"

"You know what I think? I think we could help you release some of that anger."

"Trust me, you do not want me to release my anger." But Sugar knew right then that anger was about to be released.

A dirty little grin spread across Runt's face. His stained teeth hinted there might be tobacco in the gum he was now intermittently chewing and rolling over with his tongue. He reached out to touch Sugar's face and she batted his hand away. "Come on. Let's have some fun."

Feeling her fangs growing, she said, "I'm warning you. Get the hell out of here. Now."

"Hey, Jim. She's warning us. You wanna take that warning?"

"Nope."

With that, the two men closed in and tried to lay hands on Sugar. It likely wasn't their first mistake, but it was their last. Sugar whirled, whipping a leg around, catching Runt in the ear. He crumpled to the ground. Suddenly, Silent Jim was now lunging for her. Like a skilled martial artist, she leapt, kicking upwards, her boot catching him under the chin and sending him hurtling backwards. Jim's long body was completely stretched out as he went flying through the air. His head landed hard on a rock and his limp frame collapsed on the ground. Runt lifted his head in time to witness his friend's demise.

Whispering, almost as if to himself, Runt said, "I think you fuckin' killed him." He crawled to his friend and looked over the body. Putting a hand on Jim's heart, he lowered his ear, the one that wasn't bleeding, to Jim's mouth, presumably trying to hear breathing. There was nothing to hear. Still on his knees, Runt glared up at

Sugar. "What the fuck, bitch! We were just trying to have a little fun. You didn't have to kill him. Jim never hurt anybody."

"Based on tonight, I'm gonna guess that's not true."

"Bitch, you callin' me a fuckin' liar?" Runt somehow got to his feet. The little man was unstable; he looked crazy with rage. His head twitched and his fists were clenching and unclenching. Sugar knew crazy people were dangerous people. But he didn't come at her. Wide-eyed, he chomped his gum three times. His voice cracked as he cried out, "I'm gettin' the fuckin' cops! They're gonna lock your ass up. You're done. We got the death penalty here, ya know."

Runt turned for his van. Sugar felt she had no choice. Without worrying how to pull it off, she instinctively flew through the air at him. His face registered horror as he turned back in time to see her bare her fangs and swoop through the space between them. Runt was going to be her dinner.

Moments later, as Runt's warm blood fed hers, Sugar felt a strength that her Disney-creature diet couldn't provide. *This could be addictive.* She also felt like she had just ingested a six-pack and a pile of hot-wings. *Runt was not the healthiest man. This is likely why Matt likes vegetarians.* And there was something else. She'd flown. Without overthinking it, she'd flown to take down Runt. *Note to self: Don't think. Just do.*

Now, all she really wanted to do was resume her spot on the rocks. A decent meal and some star gazing. But if these two clowns found her here, so could someone else. *How best to handle this?* She considered staging the scene. Slicing and stabbing at Runt and leaving the knife in Jim's hand. But her footprints in the loose dirt would show that someone besides the two men had been present. And if she tried clearing away the prints, it would also be clear someone else had been there. Dead men can't cover their tracks. No. She found a sharp rock and, to get rid of her bite marks, she gouged at Runt's neck. Then she grabbed another rock, larger and more round, and bludgeoned him. She wondered, *Is it still considered a bludgeoning if the person is already dead?* Then she remembered Willie and Lance. "Take anything identifying." Sugar went through each man's pockets and grabbed wallets, a switchblade with the initials "J.W.," a wad of receipts, and a pack of ribbed He-Man Condoms that looked as dry as the desert. Size large. "Good for you, Runt."

Making her way back to her van, she dragged a scrub-oak branch behind her to hide her footprints. The scene wouldn't make any sense to the cops. But whatever they'd come up with as the likely course of events leading to this double murder wouldn't be anything close to what had actually happened here tonight. *How could it?*

No music played as Sugar drove slowly over and around the ruts on the way back to the highway. The soundtrack was just the crunch of tires. Each turn and dip felt ominous. In her head, Sugar replayed her run-in with Runt and Silent Jim. *What could I have done differently? Nothing. Be steely.* But if she wondered about being worthy of other people's love and kindness before, she certainly was unworthy now. She'd intentionally killed two people. And the curtain had been pulled back. She now understood the complete and utter, full-body satisfaction of feasting on human blood. *Is this what it feels like the first time people try heroin? The dragon you chase but can never catch?* She hadn't felt this strong since...she tried to block out the first time. But flashes of Curtis kept confronting her. "Stop it! Just stop it!" She looked at Kitten in the passenger seat. "We're never doing that again." Kitten slept through the declaration.

25

THE TROUBLE WITH GROOMING

With her hands gripping the wheel, the feeling of grime and death was distracting. She'd deployed a few baby wipes to do a quick cleaning before leaving. Her plan long game was to hit a pedestrian campground and once safely parked, do a complete clean up there. But as she came upon each campground, they were full up. One after the other, full. She'd have to find a place to park and deal with getting an actual camping spot the next day. "Where's a Walmart when you need one? Damn it."

She did find a Dollar General. *That'll have to do.* Once parked as far from the building as possible, she cut the engine and took a deep breath. Inspecting her hands, she saw a bit of blood still under the nail on her right index finger. "Kitten, this is why criminals get caught. Details. You always miss something."

No answer.

Sugar looked over and saw Kitten was no longer riding shotgun. She called to the back of the van. "If you make me talk to myself, people will think I'm crazy."

From deep in the Sprinter came a "Meow-ah."

"Thank you."

After she got undressed, she did a second round of wipes, climbed onto her bunk and looked at her phone. She'd missed two texts and a call from D. They must have come in while she was out of cell range, killing people.

The first read, *Mom and Dad really want to talk to you.*

That was both enough and too much. She chose to not read on. *Deal with it tomorrow. I need sleep.*

She considered trying a hit from Maddie's weed, but decided she probably didn't need it. And she was right. Sugar slept like the dead.

THUD! THUD! THUD!

Sugar strained to lift her head up.

THUD! THUD! THUD!

Once she'd fought her way out from a deep, meal-induced sleep, she realized someone was banging on the van door. And she was pretty sure it wasn't Maddie. She also realized it was mid-morning.

"Crap, crap, crap."

THUD! THUD! THUD!

"Coming!"

As quickly as possible, Sugar pulled on pants and a top, squoze a handful of sunblock into a palm and slathered it on her face. She donned sunglasses and ran her fingers though her hair figuring that the hair move was pure habit. *I have no reason to look nice for this door banger.*

Sliding the door open just a crack, she braced herself for the deadly rays of the desert sun. The door banger was a store clerk in a blue shirt and black vest. The older, foreign-looking man took an almost startled step back at seeing Sugar. The thick sunblock hadn't gotten rubbed in and she looked like she was wearing a Kabuki mask. Of course, she couldn't see it and had no idea what was happening other than she'd scared the man. *Does he know I'm a killer? No. I'll keep that to myself.*

The man finally regained his composure. "You can't camp here."

"Excuse me?" Her fear of the sun made it hard for her to focus.

But there was no sun. The sky looked like gray flannel, and it didn't hurt.

"You can't camp here."

"I'm sorry. I got into town late and…"

"You can't camp here."

"I just need to—"

"No camping."

"Okay, then. I'll leave now."

"You have to leave."

"I just said… Never mind. I'm going."

Having unpacked nothing, there was nothing to pack up. Sugar quickly hopped into the driver's seat. Pulling out of the lot, she heard the man call after her. "You can't camp here."

Back on the road, she called to Kitten. "Come look at this. It's daytime and we're out like actual people. People who kill people. Hey Kitten, think that's the lost verse from the song?" Sugar sang the song "People" from *Funny Girl*. "People! People who kill people! Are the deadliest people! In the world!"

"Meow-ah."

"Come on. It's good." She wondered if her meal improved her mood. *I hate to think that's what it takes. It's probably just a good night's sleep…from my meal. Hmm.*

The first two boondocking spots Sugar found were full up. As were the next two and the next four. Moab was more crowded than she'd expected. By multiples of three! The ninth time was the charm. Nine. She thought of Mary Helen. *You know, three threes.* She found a small RV park close to Moab's main drag, which she normally would have avoided. However, since it was a gray day, she'd be able to venture into gen-pop without fear of literally blistering to death. But first, a shower.

"Kitten, did you fill the tanks before we hit the road?"

Exploring a shelf, Kitten didn't look to her keeper.

"Oh, that's right. You didn't do shit." She grabbed her towel, looked at the tiny wet bath shower, and thought, *I'm covered in death. I'm taking a real shower.*

The campground's bunker-like bathroom facilities were modest. A cinderblock building with two of everything. Two toilets. Two metal sinks with cloudy old mirrors above each of them. Two shower stalls, each with a bench and an old, yellowed, plastic curtain. But the water pressure was good and the water temperature was hot. *Heaven.* Sugar considered her new, lower standards. How much had she loved a five-star hotel with fluffy towels and fluffier robes? Or a spa with all the different lotions? She'd sit in front of a mirror and slowly apply each, thinking they smelled like the perfect blend of relaxation and bliss. Anything felt possible in those moments. But now...

"You're using a lot of water."

Not knowing how long she'd been in her shower trance, Sugar responded to the voice from the public restroom. "Oh. Thank you."

"It's cool."

Shaking off her hot-water coma, Sugar finished her shower. As she was toweling off, the woman called back to her. "They have good showers here. Better than most."

"Mmm." Without rushing, Sugar got into her clothes and collected her few things. Opening her curtain, she saw her bathroom mate was a short, twenty-something woman. She was washing her face at a sink. Wanting to avoid even foggy mirrors, Sugar went to a counter on the opposite side of the bunker and started running a brush through her wet hair.

The young woman spoke easily, like she was talking to a girlfriend. "You hear about those guys in the desert?"

Shit. Already? "No."

"Yeah. Two guys found dead in the dirt. That's why we stay in an actual RV park. Too much can happen out there. Know what I mean?"

"I do."

The gal turned to Sugar with a hand out. "I'm Lili."

This time, Sugar took the invitation to shake a stranger's hand.

"Hey, Lili. Morgan." Sugar marveled at how easily the fake name popped out. She knew she wouldn't use her real name, but who's Morgan? Then she remembered. Morgan was the name on a wig she'd bought for a party she'd gone to with Curtis. The previous year, she'd made herself crazy looking for the perfect dress for the annual event and swore that the following year the only thing she'd buy would be a wig. And so, she did. A wig named The Morgan Wig.

"Hey, Morgan. You just get here?"

"Yeah."

"Bucky and I have been here a couple days. This is our regular Moab spot. I love a good shower."

"Me, too."

"Well, maybe we'll see you around."

"Maybe."

Lili turned and left with a smile. Sugar decided that she liked Lili. Then she wondered if she should leave town. Runt and Silent Jim had been found. *Could the authorities track their way to me? How?* But she'd watched enough true crime shows to know there was always something. Sugar decided that after this one gray day out in the world, she'd take off. She could head northwest towards Salt Lake. *Maybe Matt and Maddie will be skiing somewhere nearby. Dare I try again?* Then she reminded herself that she didn't want to be near her friends with She-vil on her tail. *No to Salt Lake. I'll figure out my next move after town.*

Back in the van, she considered what to wear for a daytime outing. She looked at her ever-dwindling selection and landed on her sage-colored jeans and a light, navy sweater with flecks of teal. Looking at her shape in the mirror she shook her head. The clothes were hanging on her. "Kitten, look at your broke-ass mommy. I'm gonna get drummed out of the Jew Corps. I say shopping is overdue."

"Meow-ah."

"Sure. I'll get you something nice. What are your colors?"

"Meow-ah."

"Jewel tones it is."

She grabbed a brown leather backpack, kissed Kitten on the head and was ready to face the world feeling 40% excited to shop, 40% worried she'd be arrested for double homicide, and 20% resigned to being killed by a vampire before either of the first two things could happen.

26

A DAY OF PAMPERING

On her way through the park, a voice called out, "Hey Morgan, come meet Bucky." For a moment, Sugar ignored it. Then, she suddenly remembered she was Morgan. Lili was setting up a mountain bike next to a tall, fit man. They were in front of what Sugar assumed was their RV. Another Sprinter. This one was tricked out and lifted for off-road fun. Bucky had his head down, inspecting something on the chain ring of his bike. The man looked up with an easy smile, then put out a hand. "Hey Morgan. Bucky."

"Nice to meet you. I think you're my first Bucky."

"How 'bout that. You're my seventh Morgan."

"Really?"

"Probably not." He smiled.

"Nice rig."

"Thanks. We're getting about twelve and a half to the gallon. We go as light as possible, but toys. You know. You have a bike? We're gonna ride Kokopelli. You're totally welcome to join."

Sugar thought, *This is the way of the West. Wanna ski? Wanna mountain bike? Wanna bench press boulders?* She liked Bucky as much as she liked Lili and was oddly glad that the two had found each other. "Thanks for the invite, but my sport today is clothes shopping."

Lili cringed. "Ooh. You're not gonna like the prices in town. It's all gotten so spendy."

"Way of the world. But my clothes look like I chased down a plus-sized model and ripped them off her."

Holding her tummy, Lili said, "Good for you. I can't get rid of this little belly."

Bucky bent down and kissed Lily's stomach. "I love that belly."

Lili giggled ticklishly. "Thank God." She looked at Sugar. "Right?"

"You have a man who appreciates the finer things."

Lili struck a half a pose. "How 'bout that. I'm a finer thing."

"Well, you two have a great ride."

"Will do. Will we see you tonight? There's a decent band at The Blu Pig."

"Maybe."

Bucky smiled. "Right. Never commit."

Sugar smiled back then raised a goodbye hand as she turned to leave. Behind her she heard, "Bye, Morgan."

Wandering out onto Moab's Main Street, Sugar saw the place was jumpin'. Lots of little joints offering a "homemade" bite to eat which, of course, was not made in a home. Stores with "authentic western" cowboy hats likely made in China. "Hand-sewn," floor-length floral sun dresses on a rack with too many others just like it to be hand-sewn. On the main drag, multiple loud, off-road side-by-sides with big tires and roll cages were rumbling past hoppin' hotels and bustling bars. She wondered if it would be worth fake-drinking to sit and listen to one of the local bands with Lili and Bucky. *No. I can't linger.*

The people passing on the sidewalk took no interest in her and she liked that. But she was interested in them. Not as individuals, but as types. She'd always been a people evaluator. It was one of the things that had made her good at her job. Sizing people up. Reading them. Understanding what motivated different individuals to take certain actions. As she walked, Sugar started putting people in categories. Locals were the folks with a bit of a hippie vibe. Not a sixties hippie, but someone who enjoyed some hemp in their clothing and some color in their hair. The Sportys looked like they just got off a mountain bike. Hair slightly matted from a recently worn helmet, at least one scab and a piece of gear attached somewhere to their person. Then there were the Camping Families. Disheveled parents and dirty kids, all happy to be out of their tent and getting a "home cooked" meal. Lastly, there were the Glampers. The people who enjoyed being in a camping, hiking, biking, paddling town, but preferred to experience it after waking between Egyptian cotton sheets on a bed someone else had made. As she played this game, she found she could describe everyone possessing combined percentages of the four categories. She thought back and decided that Lili was a 75% Sporty, 25% Local.

The game helped take Sugar's mind off other *things*. Feeling part of the flow of town, she was ready to select a store and refresh her wardrobe. *I can meet my demise in a new outfit. That would be nice.* She slipped into a boutique that seemed 25% Sporty, 25% Local, 50% Glamp. *Hey, it's not just for the living any more.*

The boutique was small, yet held a surprising amount of product. Her father would be impressed. Sugar flipped her way through the tightly packed racks thinking, *If I get this shirt, what will I get rid of? Easy. Everything. Maybe I should break down, engage in major shopping therapy, and buy a goddamn trailer to haul it all?* Shaking her head, she refocused on the rack. She eyed a top with a bit of interest on the sleeve and a pair of pants that made sense with it. Holding the pants up to herself, she wondered if she should get it in multiple colors. The 80% Local/20% Sporty gal at the register called to her. "Dressing room is right over there."

Looking in the direction that the fifty-something woman was pointing, Sugar spotted a dressing room hidden behind clothes racks. Her father, Henry, would not have been okay with that. "Thanks."

The tight room barely had enough space for Sugar to stand and not be stabbed in the eye by the clothes hook. Once she got the garments on, she checked the mirror. While her facial features were blurry per usual, the clothes were crystal clear. *Do I like them? I do.* They fit her new frame well and it was nice to have on something she hadn't been wearing for weeks. Or months. The first thing they'd replace would be her togs from last night's event. Or, as she now called it, Mommy's Moment of Murder Madness. She was about to change back into her old clothes when she heard arguing in the store. With the door to the dressing room being just a curtain, Sugar didn't need enhanced hearing to listen in on the domestic spat.

The man was saying, "Look. You dragged me in here. Get whatever you want."

The woman responded, "But do you like it?"

"How the hell should I know?"

"Come on Phil, give me a hint. I want you to like how I look."

"It's a dress on a goddamn hanger. How the fuck do I know how you'll look?"

Sugar thought, *Rough language, but fair point. Still, I hate you already.*

"Well, someone's in the dressing room."

Phil called out, presumably to Sugar. "Hey, you in there. You gonna be all day?"

"Phil, you're ruining Moab!"

Sugar made the snap decision to grab her old clothes and wear her new clothes out. When she emerged, the 90% Glamp/10% Sporty woman gave her an apologetic look and whispered, "He hasn't eaten yet today."

"I get it."

At the register, Sugar asked the woman, "Cool if I wear these out?"

"Sure. You look cute."

"Thanks." Sugar handed the woman a hundred.

"Let me see." The woman informed Sugar, "I need another twenty-two fifty."

"Oh." Sugar pulled more bills from her old pants pocket. Lili had been correct. This place was spendy.

From the back of the store, Phil bellowed at his wife. "Hey, you in there. You gonna be all day?"

The woman at the register shook her head. Quietly, just for herself and Sugar she winked saying, "Phil can't ruin Moab."

Back on the street with her new ensemble on and her old clothes in a bag, Sugar considered her options. More shopping? And then she saw it: What she'd been craving. Set back from the road was a small day spa. A chalkboard advertised yoga classes at 9 am, 11 am, 4 pm, and a 15% off special on mani-pedis.

"Mama's home."

Cautiously entering the spa, Sugar hoped the space wouldn't be full of mirrors. She was in luck. The interior was a warm blue green with a few ferns and the scent of minted lavender. There were three pedi stations, four mani desks and two doors to massage rooms at the back. A Russian-accented woman's voice said, "Greetings. How can we help you today?" Sugar hadn't noticed the muscular woman standing there. Perhaps because her leggings and crop top matched the color of the walls. Sticking out of a blond bun atop her head were colored pencils.

"Oh. Hi. I'd love a mani-pedi."

"Do you have appointment?'

"No. I don't. Can you fit me in?"

The woman walked to a receptionist station which had an open book resting on top. She pulled a pencil from her hair to guide her way as she scanned the page. "I see yes. You're lucky. No one wakes up early in this town except to ride bikes. Their hands and feet are disgusting. Come. Pick out color from wall and sit in pedi station number three. Boris will do you." Sugar thought, *You should really rephrase that last line.*

Scanning the racks of polish, she wondered if blood red would be too on-the-nose. Too "Alex." *How about a burgundy?* She selected a deep red that bordered on chocolate, then went to what she assumed was chair three. There was a woman getting worked on in the first chair and no one in the second. So, her money was on the far chair. She slid onto the seat and took her shoes off. *Crap, I'm in closed-toe shoes. So out of practice.* She hoped they'd have some throw-away thongs for her to walk out in.

A short, slight man took a seat on the stool in front of her pedi station. Sugar thought, *This is a Boris? That's a lot of name for a little man to carry.*

"You like water hot?"

"I do."

"Good. You have thick nails. Very strong. Hands same color?"

"Yes, thank you."

Boris reached for Sugar's left hand and inspected what would be the second half of his assignment. "You have blood under nail."

"Oh. Uh, shaving." *Shaving? What did that even mean?* Boris didn't seem to care. *Maybe he'd taken out a few people in his day.* Sugar made a mental note to tip him well, then sat back in the chair and let Boris work his magic. After all, the best part of the pedi had nothing to do with nail color. It was the extended foot and leg massage. In the right hands, Sugar had been known to fall asleep in the chair. It didn't take long to know that Boris had such hands.

Allowing him to place her feet here and there as required, her mind drifted back to a mani-pedi session in a posh New York salon with Amy and two of Sugar's girlfriends. With her eyes closed, the scene unfolded in front of her as if it is was happening all over again.

Amy was up from New Jersey for a lady's weekend in New York. Sugar reflected on how she'd liked Amy from the moment she'd met her. She was easy company. Serious, but always happy to laugh. And a heck of a good sport. Sugar and D. had their inside jokes and rhythms and when they were together, Amy could catch more than her share of the ribbing. And she took it with grace most of the time. On this visit to New York, few if any jokes were aimed at her. It was Amy's birthday weekend and she was to be pampered and celebrated. Sugar's friends Tess and Terri were happy to oblige.

Sugar had arranged to have a bottle of Veuve and four champagne flutes waiting for them at the salon. They all partook. Sugar raised a glass, "To Amy. Thanks for the excuse to cut class."

They all raised their glasses. "To Amy!"

"To me. Thanks for having me up. And for sharing your friends."

"You bet. Thanks for marrying my brother. He dated a few *gems* before you saved him. And me."

"You're very welcome."

Tess took a drink and, in her British accent with a hint of cockney, noted, "Sugar showed me a picture of your David. You did quite well."

"I think so."

Sugar joked, "He did better."

Terri lifted her glass, "To doing better!"

They all followed her lead. "To doing better!"

Sugar looked at her feet. "Don't you wish we could get every guy to get pedis?"

Tess shook her head. "O.M.G., I was goin' through JFK last week. Horrible place. And all these guys, these huge-hair blokes wearin' Tevas with their big meaty toes out. Flapping their toe meat everywhere. And the grody nails. Just, no."

Sugar laughed. "I know. Seriously. Do not put your feet on display unless you clean that shit up first. I don't want to see heel calluses, I don't want to see crap from the last month of your life under your nails, and I sure as hell don't want to have to look at anything yellow."

The women all bristled. Amy added, "Oh, I do David's feet. He thinks I love giving him a foot massage. Let me be clear. I don't. But after a little rubbing, he lets me file and do whatever maintenance has to happen. That I do for me."

They all nodded approvingly, leading to another round of glass raising. Sugar added, "If I as much as touch Curtis' feet, he passes out. Gets me out of a lot of jams." The women all laughed again.

On the heels of that, Terri added, "Oh my God, Dennis is the same. And I totally use it." She did a sweet-girlfriend impersonation of herself, "Sure, baby. We can watch that Viking documentary. Rub, rub. Snoring. I turn on *The Great British Baking Show*. Sure baby. I'll go with you to the woodworking museum. Rub, rub. Snoring. *Great British Baking Show*. Sure baby. I'll give you a blow job. Rub, rub. Snoring. *Great British Baking Show*."

By now, the group was laughing hard. Tears were rolling down Tess's cheeks. "I'm totally stealing that...the second I get a man." More laughing, even louder than before.

Amy started, "Well, David—"

"No, no, no." Sugar was waving her arms at Amy. "Don't wanna know 'bout my bro in the bedroom."

Amy snickered. "How about in the back of an Uber?"

Tess squealed, then leaned over, looking as if ready to hear the latest celebrity gossip. "Oh, I want to know. Is it juicy?"

Again, Sugar started to protest. Tess shushed her. "Shush up, Sugar. I need a good bit of nasty talk to keep me going 'til I get some nasty of my own. Please God."

A woman in the chair across from the group, snarled from behind her magazine, "Yes, Sugar. Shut the fuck up. Let's get nasty."

When Sugar looked over to this kill-joy, the woman's magazine lowered and Sugar almost jumped out of her chair. All by itself, her mouth was speaking the word "Alex."

"In the flesh, almost."

Sitting up straight, not able to tell if she was still in New York or back in Moab, Sugar saw her surroundings become fluid, containing elements of both places. She pulled her foot away from Boris. But it wasn't Boris. It was one of Alex's thugs from the ski slope. The one who'd invaded her dream. The man leered at her.

Alexandria got up, stepped closer and put her hand on the thug's shoulder. "Oh, C.J., I don't think the little princess is happy to see us." C.J.'s expression didn't change as he stood, stepping out of Alexandria's way.

Standing before her, Sugar was reminded just how piercingly stunning this *woman* was. Her reddish-black hair was a dramatic frame to her pale skin. Her hollow cheeks and angular nose directed focus to her oddly large, dark eyes. Eyes that had their own gravity. They sucked Sugar in as if they were black holes. It was hypnotic. Knowing she had to break the spell, Sugar made a snap decision. *This is your moment. Now!* Leaping from her chair, Sugar flew for Alex. With an easy sidestep and a whip-fast right hand, Alexandria sent Sugar crashing to the tile floor. Stunned by this woman's speed and strength, Sugar had no doubt she was in a match with absolutely no hope for a win. Still, she wasn't about to go down without a fight. *Fuck that. And fuck her!*

Trying to not telegraph her next move, Sugar didn't look up before she rose and spun, whirling a high kick towards Alex's head. This attempt was as easily diverted as the first. Alex caught Sugar's leg and used it to send her flying. Sugar found herself draped over the now broken armrest of one of the massage chairs. Blood was running down from above her eyebrow where her face had caught the back of the chair. She knew any further attempts at offense would meet the same fate.

"Get up, princess."

Sugar pushed herself up and slowly got to her feet. Trying to sound strong but failing, she said, "What do you want?"

"I want the same thing you want." When Sugar remained silent, Alexandria continued in her but-of-course tone: "A battle to the death."

Sugar's mind was racing and she tried to get control of it. *Be steely.* She prepared herself to look the inevitable in the face, showing as little fear as possible. She'd be as dead as Curtis and Werner soon. It was only right. "Then why don't you just kill me now?"

Alex laughed. "You know nothing. Look at me. I am not here."

Taking a closer look at Alex, Sugar realized that the figure standing before her was ever-so-slightly transparent. The shelf on the wall behind her was visible through her form.

"I'm in New York. You come to me, and we'll end this face to face."

"New York?"

With a wry smile, Alex said, "It never sleeps."

"Why wasn't New York in your little note? Why didn't you write, 'Meet me in New York' in your stupid red ink?"

"Because I apparently gave you too much credit. And now you're getting upset. Come to me. I'll be in our special place. You remember. Or do I need to put that in stupid red ink, too?" Alex leaned forward and whispered in Sugar's ear, "Come to me, and maybe I'll leave the rest of your friends to their little trailer slums."

In a flash, Alex and C.J. were gone. The New York salon with Amy and friends was gone as well. Sugar stood in the silence, trying to make sense of what just happened. She was glad New York had been just a memory and none of them had been drawn into this dark world and witnessed the fight. *If you could call it that.* The Moab spa was now empty except for Boris, one other nail tech, and the receptionist. They'd all backed themselves into the corner behind the receptionist stand. *What did they see? What actually happened? Not important. Just get out of here.*

Collecting herself, Sugar headed to the front door. But stepping out onto the side walk she realized she was in her bare feet. Her boots were still inside next to the massage chair. "Crap."

When she reentered to the spa, the three salon workers all took a step back. "Forgot my shoes." As she carefully slipped on her socks, she could feel them pulling against the still-tacky nail polish. Knowing that the pedicure was ruined, she put her boots on and, for a second time, headed to the exit.

As she passed, Boris said, "You have a bit of blood on shirt."

Sugar stepped back out into the gray flannel day. "So much for new clothes."

27

RETREAT!

Sugar was ready to get the heck out of Moab, but Moab had other plans. Walking through the entrance of the RV park, she spotted a small group of women, all in sport skorts, gathered around the cab of her Sprinter. *Shit. What are they doing?* Then she saw. Kitten was strutting and posing on the dashboard like it was New York Fashion Week. The cat must have pulled down the windshield cover.

One woman, speaking in a baby-talk voice, squeaked, "Look how cute you are. Look how cute!"

Another woman sounded cartoon-like as she attempted speaking cat-speak. "Meow, meow? Meow, meow, meow?"

A third woman was literally speaking for the cat. "I'm so beautiful. Yes, I am. I'd love to come out and play with you nice ladies. Yes, I would."

Sugar wondered if she could slip in through the sliding door, start the engine and just drive away without engaging with any of the cat lovers or running them over and adding to her body count. *Probably not.* But after her spectacle at the spa, she was low on patience. She needed to eliminate this annoyance as quickly as possible. Stepping closer, Sugar said, "She's a cutie and she knows it."

The women turned. Ms. Cartoon Voice Speaker raised her eyebrows so high they almost went over the top of her head. "Oh, my God. Is she yours?"

"She is."

Ms. Child Voice asked, "What's her name?"

"Spot." *If I can use an alias, why shouldn't Kitten?*

The woman all cooed, "Spot!" "So perfect." "Who's such a cute little Spot?" "Look at you, Spotty-spot!" "I look like a wittle mountain wion. Yes, I do." "Can I hold her?"

"Sorry. We have to hit the road. We're late already."

Over-talking, they whined their objections. "Nooooo!" "Oh, no." "Just for a second."

"Not this time, ladies. But I know she loved all the attention."

Mrs. Child-Voice put her hands on her hips and stomped one foot. "You're a meanie."

Sugar pointed directly at the woman. "You have no idea."

Mrs. Child-Voice stepped back. Leaving the women to pout, Sugar went around the van to enter through the side. Once inside, she re-stowed the few things she'd had time to move from their assigned seating then, after three quick turns around to triple check the space, deemed it safe to hit the road. Now in the cab, Sugar reached Kitten, aka Spot, off the dash. "Take a bow before the paparazzi show up."

"Meow-ah. Meow-ah."

The women outside stepped aside, waving goodbye to the cat as Sugar let the van roll forward, careful to not run over any of the 30% Sporty/20% Camper/50% Annoying women. Their voices, muffled by the windshield, whined and cooed. "Goodbye Spot." "Bye Spot." "Bye-bye, kitten cat and your meanie mom!"

Driving away, Sugar realized none of the women had bothered to ask what her name was. *Should I feel slighted? No. I didn't ask for their names either. And Kitten is clearly the cute one.*

"Who's so cute?"

"Meow-ah."

"Look how you already knew the answer."

Driving out of town the way she drove in, Sugar made it about forty-five minutes before spotting the tight knot of strobing lights in the distance.

"DUI checkpoint? Way out here? Kitten this makes zero sense."

Sugar pulled her sunglasses from the visor. *Best to be safe.* As she got closer, more of the scene revealed itself. The police were stopping cars in only one direction. The direction she was going. Sugar tried to calm herself. "What the hell are they looking for? Could be anything. Shit must happen out here all the time. It's not all about you, Shug."

Laughing at herself, albeit nervously, she wondered if putting on show tunes would make her seem less conspicuous. "What do you think, Kitten? Will Broadway make it better?"

"Meeeeeeeeow-ah!

"I'm calling that a big, furry yes."

Sugar tapped on the music system. She was greeted by Elaine Stritch blasting Stephen Sondheim's dry, wry ode to petty and meaningless middle-aged life and post-marital female decline, "The Ladies Who Lunch."

"Well, that's incongruous."

Sugar absently mumbled along as several songs had time to play through. She knew the words well enough to not have to give it any actual thought. The music was like a fidget spinner. Just a way of staying calm.

There were two cars ahead of her now, a Subaru and a Tesla. Sugar could see the tall, male officer on the driver's side asking questions, and she strained to listen. But even after rolling down the window, all she could hear were murmurs. "Kitten, can you hear them?"

"Meow-ah."

Sugar threw her hands up. "I'm an idiot." She turned off the music. Now she could distinctly make out the driver's voice. It was a woman. "...for about, I don't know, four days? No, wait, five. We were a little overserved at Woody's last night."

Another female laughed nervously. "Don't say that."

The first woman continued, "What? It's the truth. People drink. People sleep it off. Can't drink and drive, am I right officer?"

A tall trooper whose voice had deep resin in it spoke next. "Everything okay back there?"

Yet another woman answered, sounding more official than the two passengers. "All in order."

Trooper Resin said, "You ladies can go."

One of them said, "Thank you, officer. You can stay." They giggled as they drove away.

The Tesla driver, a man, was up next. "What's going on here, officer?"

Trooper Resin was all business. "I'll ask the questions. You in town for business or pleasure?"

"Pleasure." Mr. Tesla sounded mildly amused by Trooper Resin.

"I don't see any camping or cycling equipment. No paddles."

"Maybe I was hiking."

"Were you, or weren't you?"

"Why don't you tell me what this is all about?"

"Did you do any off-roading?"

"Does this vehicle look like it can go off-roading?"

"I'll ask the questions. You wanna pop the trunk?"

"No, but I will."

Sugar could hear the trunk release.

"How long were you here?"

"Got here today, leaving today."

"Short trip."

"Maybe if you folks were more fun."

Trooper Resin called out, "Anything?"

The female trooper called back, "He's clean."

"You can go."

"Hey, how did you know I'm not a local."

"You're not."

With that, Mr. Tesla drove away giving what was presumably a

V-Life

sarcastic wave as he left. Sugar was up next. She rolled the Sprinter up to the trooper, the window still down. "Good afternoon."

"New York. You're a long way from home."

"Road trip."

"How long were you in town?"

"Just an overnight."

"You didn't like it?"

"Oh, no. It's beautiful. But I need to be somewhere."

"Mind taking off those sunglasses?"

Sugar removed her glasses and Officer Resin gave her a hard look. *Does he know anything about vampire eyes? He clearly doesn't like my look. Do you know why, Trooper Resin? I bet you don't.*

"Where'd you stay."

"Paradise RV Park in town."

"Any off-roading?"

"Not this trip."

"You sure? Van looks awful dusty."

Sugar shrugged. "It's the desert." He aimed his flashlight around her cab. Kitten jumped from the passenger seat and ran to the back of the van.

"I'd like to take a look inside. You wanna open this thing up?"

"Well, I don't want my cat to run out."

"Lady, I don't give a shit about your cat. We had two dead guys in the desert. Now we have one. Know anything about it?"

"What? That's crazy." Genuinely surprised at the news, she suddenly remembered that Runt and Silent Jim's wallets were still in her center console, and Runt's knife was in the ashtray. *I'm a fucking idiot. Why didn't I throw them out in town?* She tried to not look towards the knife and flag her screw up.

Trooper Resin looked at Sugar. "Mm-hm." He called out, "O.G., wanna give me a hand with this one?" A short female trooper looked into Sugar's passenger window.

"Trooper Goldberg."

"Sugar. Knew it had to be you."

"You know this woman?"

Trooper Goldberg was now leaning against the door. Sugar chanted to herself, *Focus on her face. Don't look at the wallets. Focus on her face.*

"Oh yeah. We go way back. She's okay." To Sugar she asked, "You bring me a corned beef sandwich?"

Sugar choked out a laugh. "Not even a Reuben."

"You suck."

"It's a New York thing."

Trooper Resin was clearly over the girl talk. "You can go."

Suddenly Trooper Goldberg put her hands up. "No. Wait. Wait." *Fuck! What?*

The ex-New Yorker rushed away, leaving Trooper Resin and Sugar to wonder what was up. A knot was forming in Sugar's throat. *Something will happen.*

When Trooper Goldberg returned, she had something in her hand. "Check it out. After I saw you, I couldn't stop thinkin' deli, deli. So, I fuckin' did it. I made black and white cookies. Here."

Sugar reached over, accepting the freshly baked gift. The thick disk of soft cookie was graphically iced, half white and half black. "Damn. Look at you."

"Look at fuckin' me. Try it."

"I sure will."

As Sugar put the cookie on the dash, Officer Goldberg looked hurt. She opened door and hopped up onto the passenger seat. "No. Now. I wanna see if you think I nailed it."

Trooper Goldberg spotted Runt's knife and before Sugar could do anything, the woman used it to slice the cookie in two, evenly dividing the icing. "One for me. One for you."

Seeing the look of puppy-like anticipation, Sugar knew she'd have to ingest. Putting on her best, "This isn't gonna suck" smile she said, "You're too good to me." Then the two women each took a bite. For a brief moment, it tasted like the past. Quick flashes of Sunday brunches with the family swirled with the smells of her aunt's cooking and a flood of family over-talking. Then, the swelling of nausea hit. She commanded herself, *Be steely!* Through gritted teeth, she managed to smile, "Oh my God! It's perfect!"

Crumbs dropping from her mouth onto her uniform, Goldberg said, "You think? No. It is. I nailed it, right? I mean the icing's a little wonky but..."

Trooper Resin was now beyond over it. "Think we can end this cupcake party and get back to work?"

Goldberg winked at Sugar and got out of the van. "What are you, a moron? It's a fuckin' cookie."

As the troopers argued, Sugar could feel different fluids in her body scrambling for an exit. She wondered what might happen first. *Will I throw up, shit myself, or bleed through my eyes. How long can I hold it? Mother of God!* Her head was swimming.

Through her daze, she heard Officer Goldberg say, "You're all good, Sugar. Oh wait. This is yours. I steal pens, too." She handed Sugar Runt's knife.

"Thanks."

Trooper Resin squinted at Sugar as if he smelled what was bubbling up in her throat before giving a reluctant, "You can go."

As she started rolling away, she heard Trooper Goldberg call out. "Don't drive like shit and don't pick up any assholes."

With the cookie starting to settle a bit, Sugar called back, "Don't follow any more schmucks across the country."

"Bitch!"

Driving away, Sugar thought, *I just dodged a silver bullet.* Then she puked on the dash.

28

GO EAST, YOUNG LADY

It was a brisk evening back in Colorado as Sugar stepped out of the van. Colder than it had been the last few evenings. She'd spent part of the day parked in the middle of nowhere, hidden behind a boulder, hoping no one would notice her. No one did. The sky looked and smelled like it might have some weather in store for her. *Crap.* She hated driving in the rain, and snow was worse. She'd hoped she was done with that. *Fuck the Mountain West.* Only a week ago, she'd loved it out here. But that was before Alex darkened her door, killed Werner, and crashed her mani-pedi. Now she was retracing her steps and heading back to New York. Standing alone, she waved her arms and ranted to a nemesis who was nowhere near: "You could have just killed me in New York. Why didn't you kill me there? I was right fucking there! But no. You let me sell my apartment, buy *this* fucking thing, stress out about driving across the universe, and now, now I have to stress out over driving ALL the fucking way back while dodging texting drivers and truckers watching porn, and there's a shit ton of them both, and wasting ALL that fuel just to serve myself up on a fucking platter. You're fucking vindictive, you know that? And environmentally irresponsible!"

But Sugar knew if she didn't return, She-vil wouldn't stop making her existence, and maybe that of her friends, an undead hell on Earth. *Can you make a vampire's life more of a hell? Sure, you can.* She whispered, "I'm sorry, Werner."

Walking away from the boulder towards a tree to take care of her business, she wondered if there was anything she hadn't thought of to get some kind of advantage. All of her reading wasn't getting her anywhere. She'd tried taking another stab at Varney, but again was bogged down by melodrama. *Maybe I'm reading the wrong things. Maybe there's some hidden social media group. A Facebook group. What would it be called?* "Tramps, Scamps, & Vamps?" "Suck on this?" "Eat Pray Kill?" She'd have to check. But first things first. Assuming the position, Sugar wondered, *How is this still part of my life? I barely eat.* But she had eaten. She'd feasted on Runt and it was frighteningly good, even with his bad dietary habits. Thinking of Runt made her wonder about Trooper Resin's words. *"Lost a body." I killed two. I left two. Is there a necrophiliac roaming the desert?* Her mind searched for answers. The only thought that surfaced was, *Ditch the wallets and the knife, you fucking idiot.*

Back on the road eastbound, Sugar was putting miles between herself and her murder trophies, which now resided in a hollow tree. When she'd dropped them inside, she thought, *My gift to the Keebler elves.* Everything was making her tired. She stretched her neck. "At least we're not driving to Florida. Am I right, Kitten?"

"Meow-ah."

"What? You like the Dolphins? You would."

Surrounded by nothing, the night stretched out uninterrupted. Sugar had plenty to keep her mind occupied. Knowing now that she couldn't even hope to best Alex physically, she was playing out conversations in her head. Different attempts at reasoning with the killer. But none of them ended with the desired result. They all played out with Sugar finishing her carefully crafted speech and Alex cutting her down where she stood.

The phone broke the silence. "Oh my God, Kitten. I totally

forgot D. Shit." She reached to the phone on the dash and hit speaker. "D., I'm so sorry."

Her brother's voice sounded relieved. "There you are."

"Here I am."

"Are you okay?"

She detected no sarcasm in his voice and gave none back. "Yeah. I'm okay. I ran into a few challenges. I'm so sorry."

"You already said that."

"I meant it both times."

"Shug, you can't do that to me. I was about to declare you missing."

"Don't do that!" As soon as the words flew out of her mouth, she knew they sounded slightly panicked.

"Okay, now I'm worried. What's going on? Are you still in Colorado?"

She was, but driving through in the other direction and wasn't about to share that intel with him. "I'm driving."

"Where?"

Sugar looked for any landmark that would give her something to tell D., without revealing anything. But as she watched things pass, she noticed she was slowing down. *What's happening? The cruise control was set at 73.*

"Are you there?"

"I'm here. It's just. Shit, I'm slowing down and I don't know why."

"Something wrong with the van?"

"Or me. But I think it's the van."

"Need me to call back later?"

She was about to say yes, then, "No. Can you Google something for me?"

"Sure."

"Google, 'Why is my Sprinter van slowing down?'"

"Hold on." He muttered as he typed, "'Why is my Sprinter van slowing down?' Okay, wait. Video. Video. Video. Come on. Just give me something to read. Video. Wait. Here." He read, "Knowing how to troubleshoot these ten common problems with your Sprinter van will help you better speak to your Mercedes Dealer."

"Seriously?"

"Hold on. I'm looking. Okay. It could be a leak in your inner coolant hose."

"I have an inner coolant hose?"

"It could be a faulty EFR valve."

"Jersey Jew says, 'What?'"

"A faulty turbo actuator."

"This isn't helping me."

"I think you might need a mechanic, Shug."

"No. Keep looking."

"OK. You may have gone too long without replacing your DEF. Or you might have..."

"The DEF! That's it! I mean, I hope that's it." Looking at her dash, she saw the little light that indicated low DEF. "I'm an idiot. My head's been...I haven't refilled the DEF."

"Is that something you can do?"

"All I need is a Walmart and a Jackson. DEF is diesel exhaust fluid. It goes into a reservoir and it gets injected into the exhaust system."

"Look at you, getting all auto shop."

"And don't ask me what it does in the exhaust system. I have no damn idea. I'm just hopeful."

"Didn't know you were that, either."

"Comes and it goes." Sugar checked Google Maps for Walmarts on her route. There was one in twelve miles. "You think you could stay on the phone with me for a slow twelve?"

Speaking very formally, D. said, "I'd be happy to be your escort."

She laughed slightly. "Again."

"Come on. I thought we had the best dates at junior prom."

"I know *I* did."

"I thank you. Oh, God. Remember the next morning."

"Oh, yeah. Dad let me drive us all to breakfast in his brand-new Lexus."

"And you didn't tell him you were still drunk."

"He was on a need-to-know basis."

"If we crashed, he'd know."

"Exactly. And, we did not crash."

"You were an animal."

"I sure got sick like one. Oh, hey. Here's one for the crazy coincidence book. I met a cop in Utah who had Aunt Mirrah for Hebrew school."

"No shit."

"Too weird to make up."

D. laughed. "That has to be one of the worst voices ever to grace a synagogue choir."

"Word was, she was having a thing with the cantor."

"Noooo! Eew."

"I don't know for sure, but Mom caught them playing footsy under the *seder* table at Passover."

"Wow. Way to kill Judaism."

Sugar saw an Eclipse RV going the other direction and yelled, "Anal Eclipse!"

"What?"

"Oh. It's a stupid game some RVers play. You put the word "anal" in front of the model name of the RVs you pass on the road. I just passed an Anal Eclipse."

"You know how to party."

"Oh, yeah. But wait, there's more. Advertising pro that I am, I always try to add a tagline like, 'Anal Eclipse. Welcome to the black hole.'"

"Okay. Wait. Okay. 'Anal Eclipse. It's lights out.'"

"Nice. Wait. Wait. 'Anal Eclipse. Goodnight moon.'"

D. laughed. "Damn you."

"Too late."

"What?"

"Nothing."

"Oh, speaking of Anal Eclipse..."

"Really?"

"No. But I needed a segue. Barry got into a fight with Uncle Lou and Uncle Sal over how much their kids are getting for barely working in the store. I think the words he used were, 'Do the time or you don't get a dime.' Kind of a '70s flashback, but it worked."

"I love it! Dad was never going to say anything."

"No. Dad feels too responsible for everybody to tell them no. But he didn't stop Barry, so that's a step, right? To smooth the waters, Dad bought coffee and Danish for everyone. But then Sal got in a bunch because the apple ring didn't have enough apple. He was all..." David slipped into an impersonation of his Uncle Sal, "'Apple ring? How is that an apple ring? It's just a ring. What did some guy run through the room waving an apple? Where's the apple? It's all ring. Just say it's a ring. Why tease the apple if you're not gonna cough up any apple?'"

Sugar had to laugh at how accurately D. nailed their uncle. Having witnessed enough of these exchanges, she could picture the scene. "Perfect."

"Oh, and Mom is telling people you're working in a village in Africa."

"What?!"

"She thinks helping underprivileged people dig a well is less self-indulgent than driving around the country feeling sorry for yourself."

"Seriously? She said that?"

"Once a psychologist..."

"Is that what you think? I'm feeling sorry for myself?"

"Do you?"

"Spoken like the son of a psychologist."

"It's honest work."

She wanted to blurt out, *I'm trying to outmaneuver a fucking vampire who I wanted to kill, but who apparently wants to kill me and my friends even more. Oh, and I'm keeping it to myself so my family doesn't get sucked into the dark abyss that is now my life. You should be thanking me for sparing you from evil. But I'm not getting a thank you, am I? I'm getting fucking judgment. Where's the appreciation? Where's the, "Atta girl, Sugar. Good job unhooking your own sewer-line, Sugar. Way to live on rodents, Sugar. Nice double homicide, Sugar."* When she finished her mental rant, she wondered if she sounded too much like Uncle Sal. In the distance, the blue and yellow Walmart sign lit up a small corner of the night. It was time to deal with her immediate problem. "I see my destination."

"The Mart of Wal."

"Yeah. Can't thank you enough for talking me in."

"Well, you can. You can answer my calls, or at least get back to me within twenty-four hours."

"Done."

"And every once in a while, you can actually call me."

"You got it."

"And you can say an *aliyah* at Sarah's *bat mitzvah*."

How did I not see that one coming? She was silent.

"I don't hear a 'Will do.' Come on. Let's hear a 'Sure thing.'"

"D."

"I'm calling that a 'Yep.' Drive safe." The line went dead.

Sugar shook her head. It was a problem she'd deal with later. Probably by dying. Right now, she had to get into the parking lot and hope to someone besides God that she was right about the DEF.

The van limped into the lot, and Sugar found one of her preferred spots on the periphery, away from everyone. She had plenty to pick from and opted for away from a lamp post. Her night vision was stellar and she'd be able to clearly see what she was doing when she came back without being in a spotlight.

In the harsh Walmart lighting, on the way to the automotive section, she passed women's clothing and had a quick thought. *Should I pick up a shirt to replace the new one with blood on it that was replacing the old one with Runt on it? No. If I shop here, I'll never be allowed back in the family store. Maybe that would be a good thing. Their apple rings don't have enough apple.*

She found the gallon jugs of DEF against the back wall. Tons of it. *How many RV and truck drivers shop here? This place could exist on DEF alone.* She wondered if she could make money white-labeling it and changing the branding so it would be sexier for young, hip RVers. *Charge a bit more. I could be a DEF mogul. I'd need support. Human interaction. Damn. Mark the date. I just thought of myself as non-human.* She wasn't sure what to do with this realization, but she knew she wasn't about to unpack it right here and now in the lonely, stark white glow of night shopping. Instead, she grabbed a jug of DEF and decided to save her epiphany and business idea for consideration at a later date.

Before leaving the store, she also grabbed an air filter, just to be safe. Then, remembering that back in Moab she'd promised Kitten something new, she snagged a blood-red cat collar. *Kitten won't mind where her wardrobe came from. She's likely not as much of a snob as her mother. Give her time.*

Sugar had thought self-checkout would be optimal, but it was temporarily down. Her options were a fifty-something woman or a twenty-something guy with tattoos. *Fool me once.* Hoping to not be chided for another wrong pet-department purchase, she went for the woman. Robotically, the pleasant looking woman with overly large eyeglasses rang up the DEF and the air filter, but things changed dramatically when she saw the red, suede-like cat collar. In a cutesy baby voice, like the ones used by the women who stood around her van, she cooed, "Oh, someone's getting a present. Look how pretty. Thank you, Mommy."

Sugar wasn't sure how to respond. "You're welcome?"

Still in the cutesy voice, "How old is your little fur baby?"

"She's still a kitten."

"A kitten? How many weeks is little Whiskers?"

"I'm not sure."

This lack of information did not seem to please the woman but her cute talk was undaunted. "Oh, Mommy, you need to know all about your baby to be able to give her the very best care. Yes, you do. What's kitty's name?"

"Kitten."

"Hmm. Well. I suppose she's just lucky to have a home. And what do you feed her?"

Enough of this. "The cheapest damn shit I can find."

With that, the conversation and the cutesy voice were done. "That's 53-97."

The abrupt change in the woman was pretty much what Sugar was aiming for. She'd had enough of being judged by people who had no idea the burden she'd been hauling across the country. Staring directly into the checker's eyes to a place deep within the woman, Sugar said, "Free? Thank you so much. You're too kind. Have a great night."

The woman smiled and robotically said, "Thank you. Come again."

Celebrating her minor triumph, Sugar left the store wondering how she knew how to manipulate the cashier. It was just instinctive. Like Matt had said, you can't force it. What else could she do that she didn't know she could do? *I'm so in the weeds. And now I feel guilty for stiffing the cashier. Will she have to cover it? Should I go back? And say what? Sorry I Jedi mind-tricked you? Ugh! Just move forward. You have bigger transgressions to atone for.*

29

DOWN TIME

Back in the parking lot, Sugar filled the DEF reservoir from the jug of fluid. *People have no idea how much goes into RV living.* She remembered how foolishly romantic she and Curtis had been about the concept. It was never about the logistics of life on the road. They'd muse about all the places they'd go. How relaxing it would be to park by a lake. They were romantic about a lot of things. *Why did we have to fight? One fight. One epically shitty fight where I walked away angry.* Sugar tried to imagine herself not storming out. She pictured herself giving him a chance to explain. But at the time, the bomb of him being intimate with someone else seemed like a transgression there was no coming back from. *Vampire, judge thyself. I was a fool.*

After too much time spent trying to change the past, Sugar climbed into the cab of the van. She turned on the engine and a moment later turned it off. The exhaustion of the last few days had taken a toll. Yes, she had to get to New York, but Alex didn't give a deadline. *Deadlines are important. In business, if you wanted something on a certain date, you put it in writing. Send an email. Make it official. You didn't do that, did you Alex? Your bad.* Sugar switched to the passenger side, reached for the handle beneath the seat and swiveled around so she was facing into the living space. "I don't feel like driving anymore tonight. Kitten, mind if we stay here?"

A "Meow-ah" came from the back of the van.

"Thank you for understanding."

Grabbing her phone, Sugar got up and went to the bunk. Kitten jumped down from a shelf and joined her. Stretching her feet out, she felt something in her back pocket. "Oh, Kitten, I got you a present." She pulled the collar out and removed the hang tag with her teeth. "Hmm. Sharp." Holding the red collar in front of the cat, she asked, "What do you think?"

Kitten batted playfully at the long object, and Sugar was happy for the light moment. They continued until one of Kitten's claws snagged Sugar's finger. A drop of blood rose to surface and Sugar licked it off.

"Damn, that's good. Kitten wanna try on your new collar? Give me a fashion show?"

The cat didn't object and Sugar placed the collar around Kitten's neck, making sure it wasn't too tight. Kitten did her best to investigate her new bling, but ended up rolling butt over brain around the bunk.

"You may be the cutest klutz of all time."

When Kitten finally gave in to wearing the collar, she curled up next to Sugar and closed her eyes. Petting her ward, Sugar felt compelled to count Kitten's spots. *Why have I never counted before? Eleven on this side. I could just assume there is the same amount on the other side, call it twenty-two and be done.* But it nagged at Sugar. She turned Kitten over, disturbing the cat's peace. *I have to know. Twelve on this side for a total of twenty-three. Good thing I checked.* Kitten yawned and closed her eyes for a second time. In a cutesy voice, Sugar whispered "Who's the cutest kitten with the crappiest mommy?"

It was now the middle of the night. And while Sugar wasn't up for driving, she wasn't ready for sleep either. *Maybe I should get back to research. Try for more intel before it's too late.* This time, she started her search on social media. But digging through the vampire-themed groups just got her a mix of people who loved reading vampire books, people who liked dressing up as vampires, and people selling vampire or Goth paraphernalia. Then she found the people using vampire searches to try to sell their fetish wear. "Crap. Please don't follow me around the internet." She wondered if there was a code vampires were using that she didn't know of. Perhaps that was a question she should text to Lance or Maddie. She missed them all. *No. Keep working. This is life or death. Or re-death.*

Forcing herself to focus on the grim confrontation ahead, she reached to the narrow shelf above the bed for a notebook labeled, "Myths & Folklore." Thumbing through her earlier research, she found the section on regions. She'd made notes on lore from around the globe. Greece, India, Africa, but Sugar ignored those and went straight to Eastern Europe. That's where the more notable vampires came from. Russia, Romania, Ukraine, and Poland. Most of these groups could walk during the day. *That's not me.* A group called Upior had a barbed tongue. *Also, not me. Thank God.* Some craved the blood of children. *Not it.* The ways to kill these vampires varied from cutting the head off, burning to ash, dousing with holy water, and, that old chestnut, a stake through the heart. The side note on that one was you could only stab once. A second stabbing would bring the vampire back to life. She thought, *Loopholes are good. Should I be traveling with a stake, a sword, and holy water? Am I about to bust into a church and ask to borrow a cup of baptismal juice?*

Many cultures believed that those who were unbaptized and living outside the Christian faith were the most susceptible to becoming one of the undead. *Is that discrimination? Or is it just church propaganda to get followers? Probably that second one.*

She wanted to find a better match to her skills and traits. Thinking about her own Romanian and Austrian heritage, she figured, *Why not?* Grabbing her laptop, she started looking for intel on Romania and vampires. What she found was two groups. The Moroi and the Strigoi. Of the two, the Strigoi were the more dangerous. They were mentally twisted. Evil for the sake of being evil. Most had lost any connection to guilt. *Well, I am clearly not Strigoi.* The traits unique to them were the ability to shape shift to an animal and the ability to become invisible. Sugar thought, *Invisibility would be handy, but how the hell do you pull it off? Click your heels three times and say cheese? Great. Now I want a nice goat gouda.*

Kitten yawned. Sugar whispered, "What do you think? Want Mommy to turn herself into a kitten so you could have a playmate?"

Kitten purred.

"Seems like a pretty good life to me."

Back to reading. The Moroi, from Romania, required blood to live but they didn't have to be evil. *That's good news.* They were strong, fast, and seemed to have some abilities that could be described as magical. They also didn't live forever and could die from all sorts of human afflictions. *That seems fair.* Sugar liked the idea of a kind vampire. *Is that what I am and Alex was that evil brand? A Strigoi?* But, then she read that Moroi were born that way. She was made, not born. Sugar felt sifting out the truth in all this folklore was like trying to untangle a mass of necklaces that had just been thrown into a jewelry box together.

When she started digging into information about vampire folklore in Judaism, she was led to Central Europe and Lilith and flying and more shape-shifting and Kabbalah and she thought her brain was going to explode inside her skull.

"*Oy gevalt*, Kitten. Too much information." And she didn't know any more now than when she started. *Why am I fighting it? Do I want to keep living a V-Life? To what end? Everyone I loved is gone or off limits.* Frustrated, she closed her notebook, tossing it over to the desk. But her toss was halfhearted. The book caught the back of her chair, breaking its spine and then landed hard on the floor, pages spilling out in a fan.

"Fuck it. Just fuck it."

Flopping back on the bunk, she stared at the ceiling. After half an hour of listening to the sounds of random trucks pulling in for the night, she finally decided to be proactive about being mindless and started scrolling YouTube. Watching a mix of singers and comedians, she finally got to Adele and sang along with "Someone Like You." It was cathartic. Adele's emotions ran deep. Perhaps a touch melodramatic, but it made for a good outlet.

With her phone still in her hand, she thought, Screw it. I need a little social. She found Maddie's number, texted, *Tweedle-tweet!* and waited.

It didn't take long. *Tweedle-tweet!*

Just that small connection made Sugar feel less on her own. Less doomed. She texted, *How's the man?*

A pain in my ass. [laughing emoji]

You love it.

I do. Where are you?

Out and about.

Hey, wanna video chat? I miss your face.

Why not? Sugar sat up in her bunk and checked her hair with her fingers. She figured, good enough and pressed the video icon.

"Hey, Powdered Sugar!" It was Maddie. She was in the ambulance and waving at her friend on the phone.

"Hey, you."

Maddie called into the RV, "Matt, come here. Guess who I'm talking to."

Matt called back, "Your mother?"

"Still not funny."

Matt's head popped into Maddie's frame from the side making him look like a sideways Kilroy. He waved too, just not as furiously.

"Hey Matt."

"Hi Sugar. Where are you?"

Deflect. "Where are you?"

"Montana. Decided to catch the last of the snow. Colorado was getting pretty thin. And we just got dumped on here. A new foot overnight."

"Nice. Have you two heard from Lance and Willie?"

Maddie chimed in. "Nope. I bet they're in South Carolina by

now. Hey, let's get them too." Sugar could see Maddie's fingers punching buttons on her cell. Then excitedly, "Wait for it. Wait for it!" Then, less excitedly, "Ugh. I hate waiting for it."

Then, there they were. Lance and Willie soaking in what looked like a galvanized steel hot tub. Both of them were shirtless. Both were holding dark red umbrella drinks. In unison they said, "*Salud.*"

Sugar couldn't help herself, "Why Willie, what a hairy chest you have."

"I know. So manly, yes?"

Lance ran his fingers through Willie's fur. "Oh, so very."

"To what do we owe this honors?"

Sugar gave a small smile and tried to sound upbeat. "I was just missing my friends."

Maddie chimed in, "She left us to fend for herself."

Willie pouted, "Noooo. V-Life is no fun alone."

"Let's not make this about me. What have you all been up to?"

Willie started with a hand flourish. "Well, we are taking the long way around and slumming it up in the Lone Star State. We are presently drinking what we are calling John Doe cocktails."

Lance added, "A very recent vintage."

"Yes. And we are lounging in this very lovely pool that is made from a cow's water bowl."

Lance corrected him. "It is a watering trough, and it's all ze rage."

"My bad. It's a troooough." He turned to Lance. "Is that better?"

"Perfect." She hated to tell them that it wasn't a watering trough, either, but a stock tank. She'd been seeing them all over Pinterest.

Willie beamed. "*Dígame.* What is new with you people?"

Maddie raised her hand to answer, as if she was in grade school. Although she didn't wait to be selected. "Us next. We have a big surprise and Sugar, it's all because of you."

"Me? Really?"

"Yep. Wanna guess?"

Lance shrugged and took a stab at the useable target. "You got frostbites on your lady parts?"

Maddie laughed. "No. Sugar, you try."

"Hmm. You got a cat."

Maddie immediately deflated. "Nooo. You spoiled it."

"Really? You got a cat?"

"Matt, get Jinxy."

Matt left the frame. From somewhere out of sight he could be heard saying, "Come on. Here kitty, kitty. Come on. Here kitty. Cat, give it up! Fuckin'...Gotcha!" The next thing they all heard was a very annoyed cat yowling. When Matt returned to frame, he was holding the world's mangiest-looking Maine coon. The creature was huge and had its claws dug into Matt's chest. After a bit of struggle, Matt detached the beast from his flesh and held him to the phone. "Meet Jinx."

Willie gasped. "Is he dying?"

"What? He's handsome. We have a cat. Surprise!" Maddie's hands shot up over her head in full ta-da mode.

Making several attempts at the same question, Lance asked, "Oh, my. And does our Jinx here have, is he suffering from a, uh, some kind of...disease?"

Matt looked at the cat and shrugged. "No."

Sugar tried where Lance had failed. As delicately as possible, but without using a cutesy voice, she said, "Hello Jinxy. Did you just get a haircut?"

Maddie laughed. "Oh, that. We had to shave him."

Sugar couldn't help it and let out a laugh. "You shaved your cat?!" But then, she wondered why she was even surprised. *This is par for the course on the Matt & Maddie Show.*

Maddie went into fast-talk mode. "Yeah. Okay. So, when I found him behind a dumpster, he was totally alone. He looked up at me with these big, sad, lonely eyes. Then he ran away. But I could tell he wanted to come with us."

Willie cupped his hand by his mouth and said in a mocking stage whisper, "Oh, he wanted to come with *jou*."

"He did."

Lance asked, "And you were behind a dumpster because...?"

"Just because. Anyway, he ran and ran, but he kept looking back, you know, to see if I was still coming." Maddie was undaunted by the snickering of her friends. "Oh. He had really long fur. But it was all kinda' matted, you know. Then he ran away into these bramble bushes. So, of course, I had to chase him into the bushes and he got tangled up and the brambles got caught in his fur." She laughed, holding up a handful of her blond curls. "Mine, too. So, I snatched him up and brought him home. But there was all this other stuff in his fur and it was smelly and he needed our help so bad. So, we had to shave him."

Shaking his head, Matt rolled his eyes as the others laughed at the Maddieness of it all.

She explained, "We couldn't just take him to some vet that he didn't know."

Sugar shook her head. "Right. So much better with a vampire he didn't know."

Willie snorted and waved in pain. "Ay. Stop. I think I just got vintage John Doe up my nose."

"It was better with us because he knows we love him. Matt held him down with a towel and I shaved him. It was a good plan, but Jinxy was pretty upset and kept biting at us and scratching and we kept bleeding and so we had to get undressed so we didn't get blood all over our clothes—"

The group was now enthralled, listening to the crazy tale playing out.

Matt took over. "So, fur's flying everywhere in the ambulance. Everywhere. We're on the floor in our underwear, holding down this angry beast. Clumps of fur are sticking to our bloody arms and necks and legs and we finish, and Jinx looks like he just went through chemo and we look like we're touring in some shit-show road show of *Cats!*"

By the time Matt finished recounting the mania, everyone was laughing as hard as people can laugh. Matt reached off camera and produced a tuft of cat fur from somewhere. "Oh, look. More fur. It's fucking everywhere." He smiled as he held it to different parts of his face. "I can make a mustache. Or a soul patch. Or one bushy eyebrow."

Maddie took the fur, stood and held it in front of her, just below her waist. "Or a merkin."

Willie raised his hand. Through his laughter, he was able to ask, "What is a merkin?"

It was Sugar's turn to raise her hand. "I'll field this one. It's like a wig but for your more private areas. They use them a lot in making movies when there are nude scenes. For modesty."

Willie shook it off. "Pass. My natural fur is much nicer than *that*."

Maddie clapped, "Hey, get Kitten. She needs to meet Jinxy."

Sugar was happy to oblige. Kitten was a bit less so, but she let herself be lifted to the phone.

"Look how big you got. Look at you, Kitten! Say hello to my Jinxy."

Neither cat said anything, but Jinxy rumbled with a deep low growl. Kitten went with the standard hiss and spit.

In a mock coo, Lance said, "Aw, look. It's love."

Sugar put Kitten down and tried to be as nice to her friend as possible. "He's a very sweet cat. Enjoy him in good health."

"We will. Oh, hey. Did you like my present?"

Lance and Willie looked at each other. "Did you give us a present?"

"No. Just Sugar."

Lance acted put out. "Well, if you don't have enough for ze whole class…"

"Thank you for the weed…and the stone?"

"You're welcome. One for you. One for me." Maddie held up a stone that matched Sugar's. "Now we're connected. B-T-W, Angél was pretty pissed when she noticed the stones were gone."

"You stole from Angél?" Lance shook a finger at his phone, which made Sugar feel like she was being reprimanded as well. "Zat's a powerful one. Don't mess with her."

Willie agreed. "No. Not that one. Jou know she had a confrontation with the She-vil one and I heard Alexandria told her ruffians to give Angél a big berth."

Lance corrected him. "A wide berth."

"Potato, potato salad."

Sugar had to know. "What did Angél do? Do you know how she got Alex—er, She-vil to back off?"

Lance started. "Well, this is all secondhand, of course."

"That's fine."

"Ze way Vicki told it, Angél found out where She-vil has her—" he made his air quotes, "—vault. Her wealth. And Angél told She-vil if anything happened to her, she'd given someone instructions to release ze vault's whereabouts to ze entire V community. That would make her too big a target. Alone she's powerful. But with every vampire against her, perhaps not so much."

Sugar now chided herself for not pressing Angél to tell her what she knew. *Stupid.*

Matt mused, "Can you imagine how much money she's got? How many old families has she taken down?"

Lance answered, "Too many. We should have never let her spree continue. Now it's virtually too late."

Ever the optimist, Willie said, "It's never too late."

"*Peut-être.*"

They were all silent for a moment. Sugar guessed her friends were thinking about the evil in their community. But she was thinking of how this new information might help her. Could it? Was it a weakness? In that moment, she realized that she'd been researching the wrong thing. It wasn't about folklore or legends, or her or anything else. It was only about Alexandria. She needed to know more about her nemesis. What did she already know? They'd met in New York. Taking a stab, she asked, "Where does she live? New York?"

Lance shook his head. "No. No. She lives somewhere outside of New Orleans. I believe zat's where she was made. Zat is ze story. But she does like big cities."

Matt quipped, "Another reason to be on the road."

"Indeed."

Sugar pressed on. "Is Alexandria her born name?"

"Oui. Alexandria Cromier."

Boom. Alexandria Cromier from New Orleans. Sugar had a starting point. "Anything else?"

Lance did have more. "She keeps herself surrounded by her pack of V Boys. She made each one of zem and zey are devoted to her."

Sugar asked, "Are they?"

"How can you know what is in a man's heart? But she keeps zem in high style and on a short leash. Trés smart. Trés deadly." Even on the video chat, Sugar could tell Lance was looking directly into her eyes. "Be careful."

The gravity of his warning was palpable. They all felt it. Suddenly there was a crash. Everyone winced, but Sugar winced the most. Jumping up, Matt yelled, "Goddamn it, Jinx!" He stepped away, then poked his head back into frame. "The fucking beast just pulled down our space heater. I gotta go deal." And he was gone.

After cat growling and more crashing, Maddie frowned. "I better go help before Matt throws Jinxy out, or Jinxy gets rid of Matt."

She gave a big wave and everyone started voicing their goodbyes.

Sugar added, "I hope we get to meet up again."

Maddie smiled, "Why wouldn't we? We have nothing but time."

Sugar felt a tightness in her chest. It was the grip of impending doom lurking just a few days down the road. But she played along. "To having nothing but time."

Lance and Willie raised their glasses. "Nothing but time."

Thinking of Werner staring out from the sink, Sugar had her doubts. Maybe they all did.

30

ANY QUESTIONS

After the call, Sugar was left playing emotional ping-pong. It was great seeing her friends, who were worth fighting for. But so far, she'd been unable to envision a scenario that had her besting Alex. So, something to dread. But she wanted Alex to pay for utterly ruining her life. Something to fight for. But how could Sugar possibly win out over Alex's centuries of strength? Something to cower from. Yet, she now had a thread of information to pull at, albeit a thin one. Something to fight with.

Her first move was to Google "Alexandria Cromier New Orleans." Nothing. Search after search lead nowhere. She wondered how people readied to march into war against a vastly superior enemy. *Do I know anyone who marched to war?* Henry hadn't. D. hadn't. *Most of my friends don't even like marching into the boss's office to share that numbers aren't meeting projections.*

Although she needed sleep, too much was spinning in her brain. Reaching to the drawer below her bunk, Sugar pulled out the pouch with Maddie's weed and Angél's stone. *Why not? But how to smoke it? I have no paraphernalia. Hello Mrs. YouTube.* Somewhere along her travels, Sugar had decided to change the sex of YouTube's surname. Her search took her to pipes made out of things like apples or zucchini. That was no help. She kept no food. But then she found she could roll a joint from any book with very thin pages. The video suggested something like a Bible.

"That's just tempting fate."

But the wrongness of it made her think of new taglines for *The Holy Bible*. "'Save your soul. Smoke a bowl.' No. How 'bout, 'What would Jesus roll?'"

"Meow-ah."

"Yeah. I knew before I even said it."

Then she remembered the how-to pamphlet from putting up her TV mounting bracket. "Where is that, Kitten? Kitchen drawer?"

Sure enough, it was there. Choosing a page with the Spanish-language instructions and feeling confident she'd never need to install the same TV bracket in Mexico, Sugar made her rolling paper. After spilling a few of the dried leaves on her bunk, she rolled a decent joint, lit it with her extra-long, multi-purpose butane lighter, took a long drag, then sat back.

Quietly waiting for the cannabis to kick in, Sugar turned Angél's stone over in her fingers. *Is it anything?* With the phone conversation swinging to Alex, she didn't get to ask Maddie about the stone. Looking more closely at the mostly green jewel, Sugar noted that its blue vein almost shimmered. Maybe *Maddie thought just having something they shared would give me strength while I'm alone. Like two halves of a heart. Hard to know with Maddie.*

She texted, *Madds, any intel on the green stone would be appreciated.*

No response.

Sugar hadn't noticed Kitten licking up fallen pot leaves. Now, she looked up at Sugar as if to say, "What, no more?" Then the cat climbed onto Sugar's chest and together, they waited to be transported to a more relaxed state of being. They didn't have to wait all that long.

Sugar could feel herself drift away. The next thing she knew she was back in her old bedroom in her parent's house. The walls of the room swirled past. She was spinning. This was her childhood ploy for getting out of school. Spin and spin until she couldn't take it anymore. It made her pale and clammy, and she'd literally feel sick to her stomach. Sugar heard her ten-year-old voice moaning to her mother. "Mom. Mom!"

Faye called back from somewhere outside the room. "What? I'm making cereal." That's what her mother called putting cereal in a bowl and the milk carton on the table. Making cereal. As if she had puffed the corn and extruded the shapes herself. "Are you getting ready for school?"

"I don't feel good."

"You feel fine."

"I don't."

Faye came to the bedroom door. She took one look at Sugar, still dizzy on the bed, and seemed concerned. Her mother laid a hand on Sugar's forehead. "I don't think you have a fever. Maybe. But you're sweating." She sat back and assessed her daughter. "Put on fresh PJs and get back in bed. You're staying home today."

Sugar tried to look crestfallen at the news. She moaned an, "Okay."

As she left the room, Faye said, "I'll make you some tea."

Sugar hated tea, but it seemed a small price to pay for a day off. She felt clever for getting away with her tiny scheme. She'd thought, *Keep it simple. Don't say too much. Nothing to get caught on.* Then the guilt started creeping in. *Does this make me a bad person?* She loved her mother, yet she tricked her to get what she wanted. Young Sugar stared at her ceiling and wondered where this bad behavior would lead her.

She closed her eyes. When she reopened them, she was at work. Her PJs had turned into a pencil skirt and blouse. This was the presentation for Happy Cat Kitty Litter. Nine people, herself included, were seated around a glass table in a glass-walled conference room. She joked to herself, *Don't throw stones.* Sugar felt

V-Life

relaxed as she floated through the experience knowing how it had gone. *Even with a pencil skirt of PJ fabric patterned with flamingos, it should be fine.*

Two campaigns were going to be shown. Hers and the one from Jeff and Casey. Sugar'd happily let Jeff and Casey go first. Their campaign was all about smell. Getting rid of bad smells and replacing them with no smells. A now-you-smell-it-now-you-don't approach. There was a brief tee-up as they talked about the glorious history of cat litter before getting to their commercial. Their ad went into great detail as to why Happy Cat Kitty Litter was technically superior and could be trusted to do the job. The three representatives from the client nodded as they heard all the wonderful facts of their product played back to them. It ended with the advent of Happy Cat exploding onto the scene. Jeff and Casey looked pleased with their presentation. Then came an impromptu Q and A session. The clients asked about rewording a few things to be even more emphatic about their exclusive combination of odor-eliminating, cat-elevating compounds. Jeff worked like a negotiator, deciding on the fly what points he'd acquiesce to and where he'd dig his heels into the litter. He was a man in control. And Casey backed him up on every point.

When the Q and A was done, the agency's Happy Cat account executive, Lenora, a woman who always found a way to make flat shoes work with any outfit asked, "Any more questions?"

The clients had none. Jeff and Casey took their seats and Lenora continued, sounding a bit like a talk show host. "Okay then. As you know, we have two campaigns to present today. So, without any further ado, Sugar…"

Sugar stood and smiled at the group. "I'll keep this short, clean, and sweet." She clicked down the room lights and clicked on the huge TV monitor. Up came a video montage of cats and kittens rolling, jumping, and pawing through litter and just being cats. Sugar noticed Jeff rolling his eyes. Then, as the felines romped, Sugar clicked on the music. It was a cover of the Tom Jones song, "What's New, Pussycat." But the word "pussycat" was replaced with the name "Happy Cat."

The room was filled with a woman's voice singing, "What's new, Happy Cat!" The song was catchy and infectious. Towards the end, an announcer said, "Happy Cat Kitty Litter smells like...nothing. Happy cat. Happy you. What's new with your happy cat?" The clients were applauding even before the lights came back on.

"Oh, my God, I love it. Do you love it?"

"I love it."

"I can't believe we never thought of that."

"How much for the song?"

"We have to do it, right?"

Sugar was enjoying the confirmation that her hunch had been right. It was so much more about the feeling than the facts.

A hand went up across the table. When the chair turned to face the room, it was Alex. She was in tabby-toned fur from neck to toe. "I have a question. What makes you think I'm going to wait forever?"

Sugar's eyes widened at the one question she hadn't prepared for. "I had to...I was so tired."

As Alexandria stood, she thrust aside the glass table, pinning Jeff, Casey, and one of the clients against the wall. The three slumped forward and blood ran out of Jeff's mouth. Sugar was stunned. *Are they dead? Can you kill someone in the past?* Alex ran a finger through Jeff's blood and licked it.

"He tastes like stress."

Sugar tried to regather her composure and act cool. "Comes with the job."

Alex walked behind Casey and bit her on the neck. "Ah. We have a vegetarian. No. Vegan. Yum, yum."

Knowing, or at least thinking she was in a dream, Sugar tried to wake up, but couldn't. "Are you really here? How much of this is happening?"

"You think you're a very clever girl, don't you?"

Alex walked slowly to Sugar and stared deep into her eyes as if she was trying to break into her soul. Suddenly, Sugar felt a wave of cold racing through her veins.

Sugar no longer felt clever. Quietly she asked, "Why Werner?"

"You picked him. Not me. Though, I have always wanted to own a winery."

The relentless taunting was taking its toll. Sugar broke. "Get out of my dreams!"

Leaning forward, Alex whispered into Sugar's ear, "Oh. Don't you know? I like to play with my food." Alex bit hard on Sugar's ear.

The pain caused Sugar to scream herself awake. Her yell bounced off the close walls of the RV until there was silence. Something warm and wet was running down her neck. Her fingers found the spot and brought the blood into her view.

"What the fuck just happened?"

A text came in from David. *You OK?*

To no one she answered, No.

31

OUTTA HERE

As soon as the sun went down, Sugar hit the road. But not before grabbing Maddie's gift weed and heaving it the fuck out the window.

Her goal was to get to the far side of Iowa before needing to call it quits for the day. She'd make one last stop in Ohio and then put an end to this whole fucked up thing. No more vampire research. None of it held the key. She had to learn as much as possible about Alex. Her story. Find out what mattered to her. Something to exploit. If she didn't, all she could hope for would be to die as quickly as possible and somehow meet Curtis again. But years of not believing in an afterlife made that hope seem threadbare.

At least I won't have to worry about making money. I have more than enough for a few days. She drove, letting her mind wander to the ridiculous splurges she could make in the short time she feared she had left. A couple hundred thousand a day is baller territory. But nothing she used to dream about owning mattered anymore. *A huge house makes zero sense. I'll be gone before I get the furniture in. A trip to Paris? Why? To choke down a baguette and bring it right back up? A shiny new G-Wagen or Jag to drive for, like, a day? Hell, I could snag one, take it for a joyride, and leave it on the roadside. Fuck jail.*

Uttering Maddie's sage words, "Something will happen," Sugar started feeling a strange new level of freedom. Knowing an end was near made it all black and white. Kill or be killed. Either way, it would be over.

Kitten came from the back of the van and jumped up onto the passenger seat, still uncoordinated from her dip into Maddie's weed bag.

"Shit, Kitten. I'm going to have to make a plan for you. In case."

That was the saddest thought of all. And just like that, Sugar's newfound freedom was gone. "What am I going to do about you, Kitten?" She wondered, *Maddie? Maddie clearly loves Kitten. But she has Jinx now.* "Kitten? Kitten, wanna go live with Jinx?"

"Meow! Meow! Meow! Meow!"

"OK. Fine."

"Meow!"

"I got it. You made your point."

Maybe I could give Kitten to D. A bat-mitzvah present for Sarah. That's a good idea. Two birds with one cat. The next hurdle was logistics. How to get Kitten to D. She decided on sending D. a text that she needed him to come to New York. Tell him where the Sprinter was parked and leave a note with Kitten. She was positive her brother would be there as fast as humanly possible. *There's no way he'll leave Kitten behind. D.'s a good guy and a soft touch.*

"And let's face it, you are the cutest cat ever. Kitten, wanna live with a sweet girl with a big back yard?"

"Meow-ah."

"Okay, my little Jersey girl. We have a plan."

Sugar started to relax again. Saddened, but relaxed. To take her mind off parting with Kitten, she began assessing the billboards she was passing using an advertising pro's eye. Most of them had way too much information. Bunches of words no one would ever have time to read. And pat phrases that meant nothing. "One call. That's all." "For all your heating, air conditioning, plumbing, and gutter cleaning needs." "Just particle board, and more." She could feel herself shaking her head as she passed one ineffective billboard after another, each representing a colossal waste of money.

The next billboard was for Danny's Donut Express. Wondering just how fast someone actually needs their donuts, she began imagining the scene at the counter in Danny's. She broke into a donut rant. "Hey mister, mister! I need a Boston Cream. Now! Hurry! HURRY!"

Kitten looked up at the outburst. Sugar looked back at Kitten. "Personally, I would have ordered a plain donut, but Boston cream is funnier. Cruller would have been good too, but I don't think everyone knows cruller? Do you?"

"Meow-ah."

"See?"

Kitten leapt over to Sugar's lap, spun in circles, then settled into a comfy ball, and closed her eyes. Taking one hand from the wheel, Sugar stroked the feline's silky fur. The experience always felt indulgent. *How much do I care about this cat? So much.* It seemed mutual. *Kitten will just be one more thing to miss. But maybe I wouldn't have to. But I probably will.*

Apologizing to her brother who wasn't there, she whispered, "D. I'm sorry to dump this on you. It won't happen again."

32

BY THE LIGHT OF THE MOONGLOW

The familiar glow of the green and yellow Moonglow RV Park sign was arcing a flickering patch of bright against the thick, dark sky.

"What do you think, Kitten? Bad wiring?"

Kitten had no idea. Neither did Sugar. At her last fuel stop, she'd found the icon of her Moonglow app flashing. When she tapped it, it showed the nearest park location was only a few miles away. It currently had twenty-one RVs in gen-pop parking and five in the V section. Room for one more. *Why not spend a night with my kind?* She knew why not and went anyway. *I won't get too close.*

Pulling into the park, she found the entire layout bizarrely similar to the one in Colorado. Not just the sign. It had the same main office building with the same wrap-around porch. Same parking layout. Same landscaping. Same everything. Driving up to the office, she saw there was even the same kind of gathering of people in folding chairs listening to a small, acoustic band. *So odd.* When she stepped out and approached the building, she saw...

"Mary Helen?"

"In all my glory. Hey, Shug."

"Don't you work at the Moonglow in Colorado?"

"Baby, I own Moonglow. I go where I'm needed."

Happy for this familiar and welcoming face, Sugar asked, "Is it okay? Have room for me?"

Mary Helen made no mention of the *incident*. "I always have room for you. How 'bout lucky number seven around the back?"

"Perfect."

"Go get settled and come back and listen to some music with me."

"I don't know if I..."

Mary Helen cut her off with a wink. "You're so cute. Acting like I asked you a question. I don't think I did."

What could she say? "Right. See you in a bit."

It didn't take Sugar long to set up. There just wasn't much to do for an overnight stay. Just the city water and shore power, both of which she now managed deftly. Crouching by the side of the van, she wiped her hands and thought, *Just when I'm getting good at this shit. Oh well.* Wanting to get back and continue researching Alex, Sugar told herself, *Make this a shallow dive.* She stood and headed towards the music—and turned right into someone. "Oh, shit!"

"Sorry, lass. Thought ya harrrd me."

Sugar took a step back looking at the stranger who'd been hovering behind her. Slightly annoyed, she asked, "Can I help you?"

He had a Scottish accent and an easy manner. He was a trim, Black man, several inches taller than her, crisply dressed in jeans and a blazer. Not fancy, but everything was right. He was handsome, disarming, and definitely from the V section. "No. I'm fine. You're new, aye?"

"Less so by the minute."

He put out a hand. "Mackenzie. Me friends call me Mac."

Sugar hesitated, but only a moment. "Sugar."

"Sugar? I quite like that."

"I didn't invent it."

He smiled. "I was about to go listen to bad music and complaints about water pressure. Care to join?"

"It's a hard offer to turn down."

"Brilliant."

From his air, Sugar wondered if Mac would offer her his arm. He didn't. The two strolled casually towards the office.

"That's a fine rig you have. What kind of mileage does she get?"

Sugar shook her head. She was hoping for something more interesting from this well-packaged man. "That's like the standard RV-park opening line, isn't it?"

"Sorry to be redundant."

"No, I'm sorry. I didn't mean to act rude."

"Aye. It just comes naturally then?"

Sugar looked at Mac. "As a matter of fact, yes."

With that bit of banter under their belts, they continued to the main office and Mac guided her to where several residents of the V lot were sitting. Mary Helen was with them. Mac made a quiet, abbreviated intro. "Everyone, this is Sugar. Sugar, everyone."

She felt them sizing her up. Sugar did her best to act nonchalant, offering a simple nod. "Pleasure."

Looking toward the band, Sugar thought, *Just face the music.* Then she laughed to herself at the poignancy of the metaphor. But her head was elsewhere. She wanted to be polite to Mary Helen, then return to the van, and see what she could learn about Alexandria Cromier from New Orleans. *How long has the set been going already? How many more songs will they play?* Sugar sat anxiously through three numbers, when the players finally got up for a break. *Thank God.*

She was about to address Mary Helen, but Mary Helen got there first. Gesturing to a sporty looking man with long hair and green eyes, Mary Helen said, "So Shug, before the last set, Braden here was tellin' us about his big idea. What do you call it, baby? Add a strip?"

Shaking his head, Braden corrected her, his voice dripping with earnest. "No. Add a stripe. It's add a stripe. It's time. We need vampire inclusion. I was saying, why not add a stripe to the rainbow flag. It's LGBTQ plus, am I right?" He didn't wait for confirmation. "We're the plus. LGBTQV. It just makes sense. Am I right?"

"You're a child." Sugar looked at the trim man with thin, white-blond hair and well-manicured hands resting on his crossed legs as he asked, "How many times? How *many* times? You really believe we're beyond villagers with torches, do you? Child."

Braden snapped, "Shut up, Thomas."

Thomas had the look of a man who'd seen too much. He probably had. Without raising his voice, he asked, "That's your retort? 'Shut up, Thomas?' I can see this crusade will go far with that level of debating skill at your grasp. Now, if you don't mind," Thomas extended a hand to Sugar, "Sugar, I'm Thomas. I'm old, irrelevant, and very pleased to make your acquaintance."

Taking his hand, Sugar smiled. "Charmed." And she was. Thomas had an intelligent, mannered way that was easy to like.

"Will you be staying with us long?"

"Just tonight. I have somewhere I have to be."

Mac smiled ever so slightly and raised his chin. "Aye, does the lady have a hot date?"

"More of a pressing matter. But thanks for asking, Dad." Mac smiled. Sugar could feel the others trying to read her, knowing that some in the group might actually be able to.

Fortunately, the topic was changed by an Italian-looking woman with her hair in long braids. *Or is she Hispanic? So hard to tell with all this pale skin.* The woman said, "Well, I have a hot date." The woman's eyes danced and Sugar got a flash of a man with a broad chest and shoulder length hair, loosely pulled back. She had to stop herself from calling out, *Shit, woman. I just read your mind!* But the woman winked at her and gave a small friendly wave. "By the way, I'm Daisy. Not really. I was born Donatella Diafania DiGregorio. But I prefer 'Daisy.'"

"I do, too."

"What is Sugar short for?"

V-Life

She wanted to respond, *This world*, but went with the other truth, "Nothing. Just Sugar."

Braden leaned forward, "Where do you stand on V rights, Sugar?"

"I believe I have the right to remain silent." That got her a small round of applause from Thomas.

Braden abruptly stood and pointed an accusing finger at the group. "You all mark my words. If we don't fight for inclusion now, we'll slowly wither and die. We are just as worthy as gays and lesbians."

A woman in a lavender flannel shirt took the hand of the similarly dressed woman sitting next to her, raising it up. "Half of us are gays and lesbians, asshole. Don't try to suffer-draft off of us."

Throwing his hands up, Brandon quipped, "Well, don't you just check every box." With that, he stormed off.

The woman put a hand by her mouth and called after him. "We don't check the box. We lick it." Without looking back, Braden raised a middle finger and the woman and her partner enjoyed a good laugh at his expense. The woman then turned to Sugar with a playfully seductive look. "I like to be direct. Who do you prefer, me or baby boy Brandon?"

Sugar chose option C, self-deprecation. "I'm from New Jersey. We don't get to judge."

The woman looked at her deadpan, then laughed. "Fuck. I'm from Detroit. It's Jersey with a higher body count."

Sugar said, "You win."

The woman cocked her chin and added, "Mavis. No shit. My name is Mavis. And I'm not about to Daisy it up and change it to Marigold or some shit. Oh, and this is Sandra." Sandra gave a nod the same way Mavis had.

"Pleasure."

There was handshaking as the band members o' the night were taking their places back on the deck. As much as Sugar had wanted to connect with Mary Helen, she was feeling the pull of her research.

Once the music started and everyone was back to focusing on the not-so-entertaining entertainment, Sugar employed the Dutch goodbye and ducked out quietly, hoping they'd not think her rude. And even if they did, she'd likely never see them again.

Walking past the expensive RVs in the gen pop section, Sugar thought about what Braden had said. *Is he right? Could we petition for acceptance and understanding from the world at large? No more hiding. Would be nice. Or is Thomas right and they'd just be chased with torches?* She feared the answer was obvious. *Shame.*

Feeling an arm slip under hers, Sugar turned. Mac smiled, "I thought I'd escort ya home. Ya should always leave with the one who brought ya."

Smiling easily at him as they walked, she shared, "My father says that. But I do have some work to get to."

"Sounds official."

"Only to me." He smiled back at her and she tried to not let him see into her eyes.

"Anything I can help ya with?"

"Probably not."

"I'm a great one for research."

"I don't like having my mind read."

"Sorry. Nasty habit, that. I come from a long line of stiff-upper-lippers. One has to become good at reading what goes unsaid."

"I come from a long line of nothing-goes-unsaid-ers."

He laughed. "Really. And what's that like?"

It was her turn to laugh. "Loud."

"Sounds like fun."

"It can be. And sometimes not. A goodbye in my house can easily take two hours of 'Just one more story.' But that's Jews. We like to talk, and smother."

"Jewish. Interesting. We don't get many of your lot. Not sure why. But then, I'm a bit of a minority m'self."

"Maybe Braden can petition to get us a stripe."

"Braden, aye. He means well, but he's young. Or, should I say,

'New.'"

"I bet I'm newer."

"I know y'are." Mac stopped walking. "Sorry. Old habits again."

"You're forgiven. This time. Warning, I'm about to be abrupt."

Taking a fists-up stance like he might receive a punch, Mac said, "I'm ready."

"To what do I really owe this honor? Or do you escort all the *new blood*?"

Mac dropped his hands. "Wow. Hmm. I'm not sure and no. To be honest, there's something about your face. I hope that doesn't make me sound shallow. But I look at ya and it seems like a million thoughts are happening at once. It's truly fascinating."

Is that a line? Does Mac think every V girl has a truly fascinating face? Her read on him said, no. *But how sharply am I thinking?*

"Ya have nothing to say to that?"

"I was busy having one of my million thoughts."

He smiled. "Fair enough."

"Well, this is me."

"Care to give me a tour?"

Remembering what RV *tours* can lead to, Sugar shook her head. "Can I take a rain check?"

His face changed from gentleman caller to inquisitor. But he didn't say what was on his mind. "Ya may. May I hug you goodnight?"

Assessing this handsome man, Sugar knew that under other circumstances, she'd be thrilled with his attention. She nodded. Gently pulling her close, Mac hugged her. The feeling was so safe and Sugar found herself hoping his embrace would last for several days. But she didn't have several days. And if she let him get too close, he might not either.

He whispered, "Ya take care of yourself, Sugar Bernstein. And if ya have need of anything, I'm not far."

But everyone seemed far. *Did I ever say my last name? How much does this charming man already know?*

33

SHOW YOURSELF

Sitting at her desk, Sugar dove into Alex's past. But after about ten minutes, she gathered her things and spread out on her bunk. It gave her more space and she preferred the feeling of being in the middle of it all. With her laptop sitting where its name suggested it belonged, her tablet just to her side, and phone in hand she looked like a one-woman newsroom. A notepad was also out, but Kitten was perched on top, rendering it unusable. Working at her laptop, she wondered why her pen was in her mouth. To Kitten she explained, "It helps me think." Kitten seemed fine with the reasoning.

What can I learn about Alex that I can leverage against her? It has to be a mental game. She settled into the task. Knowing she had to be smarter about this than in her previous attempts, she decided her first hurdle was narrowing in on a date for Alexandria Cromier's birth. All she remembered was Lance indicating Alex had been around for about two hundred years. *Fine. It's a place to start.* Sugar Googled, "Life in New Orleans, early 1800s." As she read, she tried imagining the masses of people, the grime, and the stench described in the port city. It was oppressive. In short order, she was thrown into tales of the slave trade. Due to its location, New Orleans had turned into the largest slave trade market in the United States. A staggering 135,000 people had been bought and sold there. Even after Congress ended the legal importation of people from outside the country in 1808, it did nothing to stop the sale of people already here. So, the slave trade in New Orleans continued. Sugar caught herself shaking her head as she read. It's not that she didn't know her country had a slaving history. Of course, she did. How could you not? And she'd seen all the movies like *Harriet* and *Ten Years a Slave*. But those were movies. So, in addition to feeling pain for those enslaved, she also thought about the great acting, good editing, and excellent art direction. Art and artifice made it too easy to lose sight of the gravity. The agony of losing your freedom. The horror of being seen as less than human. Now, being confronted with not just the numbers but reading specific personal stories without the veneer of cinema made it so much more real. She found she could see people's faces as she read. Actually feel them.

Growing up, Sugar had been surrounded by stories of the horrors from the Holocaust. The friends and family killed and the ones who got out. The hate. Someone was always relating something happening in current day to the Jews' history of being an oppressed minority. There were repeated attempts to wipe Jews off the face of the Earth, yet they were still here. When friends told her she needed to see the movie *Schindler's List* so she wouldn't forget, she laughed saying, "Forget? Try growing up in my house." She assumed growing up in a Black home could be similar.

But the flood of information and stories had pulled Sugar away from her actual task. Finding Alex. After an immersion into New Orleans' history and failings, she needed to get back on point. Again, Alexandria Cromier 1800 got her nowhere. Just a long list of Cromiers. Too long and mostly men. *Come on. Where are you?*

"Think. Think. Think."

"Meow-ah."

"Not helpful."

"Meow-ah. Meow-ah."

Looking at Kitten, Sugar asked, "What? Did Timmy fall into a well again?"

"Meow-ah."

She reached over and picked up Kitten. "Am I not giving you enough attention? I'm sorry. But Mommy's trying to not die." Holding Kitten against her face, she got lost in her soft fur. "So soft."

The words echoed in her head. "So soft." But she wasn't the one saying them. It was Alex. It was the memory Sugar had been trying to block out of her brain. The aftermath of her big fight with Curtis. *Why did I pick that bar? Why did I sit next to that stranger? Why the attraction? Why any of it?* But there she was again. Alex was in the booth across from her, running her fingers through Sugar's hair, musing "So soft."

Sugar was about to block the memory out for the hundredth time, but something told her not to. Not this time. And she felt herself traveling back to the moment. She heard the soft murmur of conversations from people seated in the ripped Naugahyde booths flanking theirs. She could feel the bass from trance music thudding in the background. Wondering why she wasn't stopping this stunning stranger, Sugar took a nervous sip of her Old Fashioned. The woman was like a magnet, pulling her from within.

"Do you want to kiss me?"

She did. "I have a—I'm in a relationship."

"But you said he cheated on you, so you're free to do what you want."

"Still."

"Pity." Staring into Sugar's eyes, Alex put her glass to her mouth, sipped, lowered the glass, and licked her lips. "I think freedom is like banking. If you don't take ownership of your accounts, they will be stripped from you. At least that's what my father said."

"I don't understand."

"Would you like to?"

It was as if Sugar had no power over the attraction. She wanted to kiss this woman so badly. Why? Finally, she stopped fighting.

Leaning forward ever so slightly, Alex did the rest. Slipping her hand back into Sugar's hair, she pulled her close. The kiss was long and sweet. Sugar could feel her entire body awaken. It needed Alex.

"Come with me."

She did. Instantly, they were in the alley behind the bar. It was dark. No one around. As Alex licked her face, Sugar could feel the woman's fingers sliding under her shirt and bra. Her touch was sensational. There was the sound of people partying down the street. Young men having fun. Being almost in public was thrilling. She couldn't believe she was with this stranger. This woman she'd just encountered. Alex's hands were gliding down Sugar's torso. Her skilled fingers probing towards Sugar's most private places created an anticipation that was almost unbearable. As her body grasped for pleasure, she became aware of the woman biting down on her neck. Her head swam in hedonistic pleasure and pain.

Then, pain started to overtake pleasure. Sugar whispered, "Stop." But Alex didn't stop. *What's happening?* "Stop!" She struggled but couldn't break free. "Help! Help!"

The next thing Sugar knew, she was sitting against the wall in the alley. Alex was gone and half a dozen college guys stood looking down at her.

"You okay?"

"Lady, you want us to call the cops?"

"Who was that bitch?"

"Fucking nut."

"Need an Uber?"

Sugar opened her eyes, safe in her van, one hand holding Kitten and the other hand holding her own throat. She felt the full shame of her transgression. She'd needed more than an Uber. *Could I have stopped it? What should I have done differently?* She knew the answer. *Never leave Curtis. Let him explain and forgive him.* She wanted to yell, "I forgive you!" But who would hear? Still, there was a kind of relief in finally looking her failings in the face.

"Shit, Kitten."

Sugar kissed Kitten's head and put her back down on the notepad. Then a thought came. *Alex had said something about freedom and banking. Banking? Her father's words. Had her father been a banker?*

Sugar typed in, "Cromier 1800s New Orleans Banker." She waited just a moment, and...

"Holy bingo, Batman! Stéphane Cromier, founder of *Banque de Ville de Croissant* in New Orleans. Kitten, Kitten, Kitten. We are on the trail!" Trying to keep herself calm, Sugar talked as she searched. "Let's see. Stéphane, you were born, you were born, you were born? Here. Born 1772. And you died? Unknown. That's strange. Maybe not. What else? Nothing else. You were born, you banked, and you disappeared?"

She looked up from the screen at Kitten. "Don't you think that's weird? I mean a banker is a prominent person, right? How does he just disappear?"

She tried searching for the bank, but it was long defunct. She did find that a Francis Xavier had taken over as bank president in 1818. "Forty-six would be young for a man to retire. Did he die? No. There would be a record. Did he...what? Skip town?" She remembered that Lance said Alex came from nothing. "This doesn't make sense. Maybe Stéphane isn't our man. Just a dumb coincidence. Come on Kitten. Help me think."

She closed her laptop. "I thought we had her, Kitten. Shit, shit, shit." She wondered how long she'd been at this. "I gotta get some air."

Grabbing a light jacket, she pocketed her phone, and stepped into what was left of the night. She could hear animals scurrying in the distance. Farther away, in a rig to her right, a couple was having pre-dawn relations. To her left, someone was speaking quietly, trying to get their child back to bed. None of these people had any idea what Sugar was battling. Out here it was like it wasn't happening at all. She wandered through the back of the RV park and into the woods beyond. Passing into a clearing, she headed directly across the open space towards a large stand of trees on the other side. Stopping several yards in, she considered the beauty of the shadowy black branches. Behind the dark and crooked tree limbs, orange and pink patches of morning color were beginning to bleed into the sky. In the light breeze, the easy sway of the trees made it all look like living stained glass. Her breathing matched the air. It was peaceful.

Then suddenly, she said to herself, "Family tree?"

She immediately remembered the genealogy website account her ad agency had pitched. Sugar pulled out her phone and thumb-typed Strong Family Tree dot com. *Do I remember my password? Fuck it. Create a new account.* It didn't take long. She typed in what little she knew about Stéphane Cromier and waited. Boom. There he was. Stéphane Cromier, born 1772, died 1819. Wife Angela, born 1779, died 1819. Daughter, Alexandria, born 1798, died 1819. There was also a brother, Clayton born 1800, died 1871.

"What happened?" She wondered if a vampire had killed father and mother, made the daughter a vampire and somehow the son got away. *Did Lance get his information about Alex being poor wrong? Maybe. How can I use any of this to my advantage? It's all so far above my pay grade.*

When she returned to the RV, Sugar declared to Kitten, "I need help."

"Meow-ah"

"Don't worry. I didn't mean you. Just keep doing what you do." Kitten jumped down from the bunk and hunkered in the litter box. "Also, not what I meant."

In her head, she tried crafting the right email to Brooke, from work. Clear without sounding crazy. Brooke was like a bloodhound. She could track down anything. Her other notable skill was she could hold her liquor better than most truck drivers. And not those foofy drinks for people who don't like alcohol. Brooke drank all straight, all the time. Yet, she never seemed to go too far. Restraint and skill. Brooke was her gal.

After Sugar drafted a first pass at the email, she tweaked it five times before finally deeming it ready. "What do you think cat. Good?" Kitten was too busy stalking a rubber band to answer, so Sugar flew solo and hit send.

    Suddenly exhausted, she pushed all her work and devices to one side of the bunk, stretched out next to them, and hoped to not dream.

34

SO DAMN CLOSE

The first thing Sugar did when she woke was check to see if there was anything from Brooke. There was. The email read, 'Brooke Whiting will be out of the office until the 13th. If you need immediate help, please contact Jules Fleck.' And it gave Jules' email. Sugar tried picturing seventy-something Jules, with her thick-soled shoes and thicker-lensed glasses, offering immediate help against one or more vampires. *Not the right tool for the job.*

"Damn it. Kitten what day is it?"

It was the 10th. The 13th was not gonna cut it. Once again, she was on her own. What small triumph she'd felt before falling asleep was gone. Again, she replayed that fateful night. Having let the dark encounter fully materialize, her guilt was like a crevasse with a bottom she just kept falling towards but never reached. *It may be time to pay for my transgression. But aren't Alex's offenses worse, and more? Alex is a goddamn transgression factory. She could bottle transgression and sell it.* Again, Sugar thought, *I shouldn't go down without a fight.* Realizing that thought was self-defeating, she chided herself. "Way to assume the loss."

Time to go. As Sugar stowed her computers and notepads,

someone called from outside the van. "Hey, baby!" Hey, Shug. Can I barge in?"

Sugar slid open the door. "You could never barge."

Mary Helen giggled. "Oh, I bet I could if I tried."

Mary Helen entered the small space. Sugar suddenly felt like a bad hostess. "Sorry I don't have anything to offer you."

"Pish tosh. I know who I'm dealin' with. But I will trouble you for a seat and a sec."

After offering her guest the desk chair, Sugar stood, leaning against the kitchen counter. "Sorry we didn't get to visit last night."

"I'm here two seconds and I made you sorry twice. That was so not my goal. I just thought you might want to chat before you go, you know, take care of business."

"Business? Is that what we're calling it?" Again, Mary Helen giggled which now felt incongruous, but also seemed to open a door. With little to lose, Sugar said, "I gotta ask. You seem to know everything that's going on in the entire V world. What am I missing? Who are you?"

Mary Helen's smile made her feel like that wonderful aunt you always wanted. "Baby, all you had to do was ask."

"Really? Like Dorothy finding out she had the power all along, but first she had to go through an Oz-ian gauntlet of horrors?"

Kitten started sniffing around Mary Helen's ankle. Mary Helen bent and picked up the cat, petting her softly as she spoke. "Maybe not quite the same as Dorothy."

"But kind of the same?"

"Kinda'. You asked who I am. But I think the question you really wanted to ask is what I am. Am I right?" Sugar didn't answer. She didn't have to. As Mary Helen talked, she settled deeper into her Southern accent. "I'll tell you what I'm not. I'm not a vampire. But, my daddy was. Or, the man I consider my daddy. Momma was an empath. That I got from her. I'm gonna tell you a story, if that's okay."

"Go for it."

"The man I call Daddy, his name was Forrest. He fell for

Momma when I was, oh, seven. My birth daddy was, well he was a mean and worthless man named Trace." She smiled a wry smile. "It took me a lot of years to be able to say that. Trace was a mean and worthless man." Mary Helen seemed to enjoy the freedom of repeating the line. "He ran this mangy campground on the edge of town. One night, Trace was beatin' on Momma, which was nothin' new. But this night, he was doin' it in the little corner store in town. In public. I was used to seein' it, but for the cashier, well. And there's this man watchin'. This handsome man with big broad shoulders. Well, he doesn't watch long. He grabs Trace by the collar." She looked down at Kitten. "Just like he was grabbin' a housecat who'd jumped onto the table and into the potato salad. He pulls Trace out the front door. We could see the scuffle till they drifted around the building. Didn't last long. Trace was no match for Forrest. We heard some trash cans gettin' knocked around, and that was it. Momma and I never saw Trace again. And let me tell you, we did not mind. Funny thing was, no one else liked the man enough to mind, either. Good riddance to bad rubbish. But Forrest, that's my V daddy, Forrest starts takin' up with my momma. It was nice for a long while. Calm, you know. He told us right off what he was, and Momma didn't care 'cause he treated her real good. I mean, we knew he killed Trace. You didn't have to be an empath for that. But on we went. Forrest'd sleep while I was at school and we played at night. I loved him. And he turned the campground into a nice spot. Then, after a bunch of years, Momma told him he best go. Cause she was getting' older and he wasn't and she knew his mind. She knew he was gettin' restless. He didn't argue. But before he left, he set us up with Moonglow. And Momma told him there would always be a place for him and his kind there. She ran it till she'd had enough. Now it's mine. I modernized it. Branched out. The app is my latest update."

"Nice touch."

"Thank you. Gotta keep up with the times."

Sugar felt more connected to Mary Helen. "That's a hell of a story."

"It's mine and I'm keepin' it."

"Do you ever see Forrest?"

"No. I can tell he thinks it would be too hard on me. And him. But I can usually feel where he is if I try."

"Can I ask another question?"

Mary Helen pulled a piece of string from her pocket and started swinging it over Kitten. Kitten batted at it as she spoke. "You sure can."

"How much do you know about me?"

"I know you're a nice Jewish girl with a nasty *shiksa* enemy."

"*Shiksa?* Look at you, breaking out the Yiddish. Impressive."

"Know your audience."

"Do you know why Alex and I are enemies?"

"Some. I know she made you and I get the feelin' she hadn't planned on that. Happens sometimes. Usually vampires make other vampires 'cuz they wanna be with that person for a long time. Like Lance and Willie. Or with She-vil, all her disciples. But you were never gonna be one a' those."

"Not likely."

"I'm guessing she wants to finish the job. Tie up loose ends. I can't say for sure. She's hard for me to read 'cuz we never met. I mostly read from people she's been connected to. She's a troubled one. A dark empath. She gets in people's heads and uses their worst fears against them. V-Life can twist folks but I think that one got twisted up way before she was ever bit. But Shug, you're a good one. I feel it."

"Am I?"

"I know you are."

"You're not a very good empath." Sugar wanted to spill her purse out on the table. But the words were too painful. "I did a terrible thing." In her head, Sugar screamed her darkest secret and Mary Helen suddenly sat back as if she'd been shoved.

Looking like she was trying to mask her surprise she whispered, "Oh, Shug."

Sugar wished she could cry. Instead, her chest rose and fell with the pain of her past. "We were so stupid."

"People in love do stupid things. You can't let your emotions run away with you. It makes you vulnerable. That's what she'll exploit."

"I hate myself."

"I know. But let me ask you a question. Who do you hate more, yourself or Alexandria?"

Sugar genuinely had to think about that. Sorting through her feelings, she said, "I'm more *mad* at me. I should have been stronger. I let myself down and I let Curtis down. Does that make sense? But to answer your question, her. I hate her more."

"Then fuck her up. Take her down." Mary Helen smiled a devilish smile.

Sugar couldn't help but let out a small laugh. "Please, tell me. How am I supposed to do that?"

"You gotta stab at a weakness. Everybody has one."

Thinking back to her research, Sugar said, "New question. Do you know if she came from money? Lance said she'd been poor, and that her one goal was wealth. But I did some digging and it looks like her father was a banker."

"He was."

Learning that she'd been on the right trail, Sugar felt a glimmer of hope. *Maybe Mary Helen holds the key.* "So, did he leave her money? It looked like her parents died young."

"He didn't leave her anything."

"Why?"

"He didn't have anything. The man died poor."

"How do you go from banker to poor?"

"I know he got kicked out of the bank and lost everything. The whole family became sharecroppers. Sugarcane."

"Why did he get kicked out of his own bank? It had to be something major."

"I'm not sure."

"You must know something." Mary Helen sat silent. "What aren't you telling me?"

Mary Helen said nothing.

"Well, what about Angél? What's her story? That woman knows more than she said. I could feel it." Again, Mary Helen offered nothing. Sugar could sense the woman trying to shut down her thoughts.

Mary Helen stopped playing with Kitten. "Angél's very private."

"I don't care."

"Shug, there's some things I'm not at liberty to talk about."

"What?" Sugar could feel frustration building up inside her. "Some things that could save my life? Those are really important things, Mary Helen."

"I'm sorry Shug. I am. But Moonglow depends on me bein' able to keep my mouth shut about certain things. If I don't, your kind won't trust me. I'd lose my reputation and the whole thing would fall apart. I gotta put the V community first."

Sugar couldn't believe this nice woman, this woman she'd just quietly spilled her guts out to, was now potentially the biggest barrier to being able to stop Alex. She was suddenly aware of her eye teeth itching as her frustration mounted.

Clearly, Mary Helen could feel it too. "Well, I best skedaddle. Lots to do."

"Yeah."

Mary Helen got up and headed for the door. "I am sorry, Shug."

"Me, too." And she genuinely was. Sorry for all of it.

35

ONE DAY MORE

This time, as the billboards passed, Sugar was disinclined to try rewriting them. *If I can't save myself, why worry about saving some stranger's advertising?* She mulled over what little information she'd gotten from Mary Helen. *Does the fact that Alex had gone from wealth to poverty help in any way?* She thought again about crafting a speech to appeal to Alex's...what? *Her heart? No. That was long gone, if it was ever there to begin with.*

Think. If Alex was a client, what would my pitch be? How can I take what I know about the person and weave a story that will resonate? What's her true objective and how best to appeal to it? Was Mary Helen right? Does Alex just not like loose ends? It doesn't seem like enough of a motive. Avarice? Killing me wouldn't change her fortune in any way. What does she want? Something I don't know. Still, Sugar did know something more about Alex's beginnings. *What would it feel like to go from being a pampered child to a life in disgrace as a working hand? No idea. And it doesn't even make sense. I'm missing a piece of the story. What? Mary Helen, you're killin' me. Can I relate to Alex in any way? I know what it was like to work alongside my father. Is there anything in that? It doesn't feel like much. We both* like New York. I wonder if she likes musicals. We could sing show tunes and...

Her phone rang.

Shit. I should talk to D. Shit, this could be the last time. Damn. How am I going to make it through this call? Don't think. Just do. Trying to sound as upbeat as possible, she answered, "Hey D."

"Hey Shug. I just want to say in advance, I'm sorry."

"For what?"

The next voice she heard was her mother's. "Remember me? Your mother?" *How could I forget the person who kept me fed and clothed and paid for my college?*

Faye continued, "...The person who kept you fed and clothed and paid for your college?"

Sugar could hear her father calling from the background. "I paid half and the clothes came from my store."

As she drove, Sugar closed her eyes, but not for too long. *Why die at the wheel when you can die by evil vampire? Way more dramatic. This is so not what I need right now.* "Hey, Mom."

"So, you *do* remember."

"You're a hard act to forget."

"Did we raise you to be like this? To drive around God knows where, not talking to anyone? Not your friends. Your work people. Certainly, not your parents. For all we knew you could have been in a ditch somewhere."

There it was: the ever-present existential ditch. "Well, you'll be glad to know, I've avoided all of the ditches in North America. So far."

"I don't appreciate this attitude. Are you okay? Are you eating?"

Hmm. How to answer that? "I'm fine, mom. I just need time. It's hard to explain."

"What explain? I'm a doctor. I've seen this before. C. S., no names, when her Edward died—"

"What happened to no names?"

"Edward wasn't my patient. Anyway, when Edward died, C.S.

laid in bed for weeks. Utterly inconsolable. You know what I told her? I said, Que sera, sera."

"Ma, you're quoting the movie *Private Benjamin*."

"And they got it from Doris Day. Good advice is good advice. Look baby, what will be, will be. You can't change what happened by driving around the country like some hippie. Curtis died. There. I said it. Come be with your family. Your father and I love you." Faye switched to a whisper, "You're actually our favorite."

In the background, D sounded put out. "Jesus. Really?"

Speaking away from the phone, Faye said, "Shh. You sister needs to feel loved." Back on the line she continued, "We love you, but you're not so special. You're not the first person to shed a tear."

"Wow. So, we're going tough love now?"

"Well, think about this: Tough love is a two-word phrase that ends in 'love.'"

Sugar did think about it. She knew her parents loved her. A lot. Hurting them was not on her to-do list. "I love you too, Mom."

Henry called out, "And your father?"

Faye reacted to her husband, "Henry! Crumbs! If you're gonna eat that, could you get a plate?"

"Fine. I'm getting a plate."

Sugar had heard this act a million times. But this time she loved it more. "Dad, don't tell Mom, but you're my favorite."

Faye returned to the call. "So, you'll come home? When will we see you?"

"When you hear my key in the door."

"Ugh. That's not an answer."

"It's what I've got."

Faye took a deep breath. "Listen to me. I want you to call, and drive safe, and eat, and wash your hands after you touch anything."

"You got it."

"We love you."

Henry called out, a bit too loud. "We love you, baby!"

Stiff upper lip. "I love you, too."

After a long moment of dead air, the line clicked off. Sugar wondered how many tears she would have shed in the before-times. Did she love her family even more now, with so much evil on the horizon? No. But she appreciated them more. Looking at Kitten she said, "Well, that's done."

A moment later she got a text from D. *Sorry.*

She voice-texted back. *Forgiven.*

36

GOOD NIGHT MOON

For her last free night, Sugar chose to camp in a small clearing she found in western Pennsylvania. Her original plan was to stay in the Moonglow in Ohio, but the closer she could get to New York, the shorter her drive would be the next day. Which might leave her less tired for the big event. So, she'd pushed on. Now, having no idle conversation left in her, being away from everyone felt right. Parking under a large tree by a pond was like the calm before the storm. She cut the engine and sat for a long while, watching moonlight dancing on the water's surface. It was beautiful.

"This is nice, don't you think, Kitten?"

She felt the weight of Kitten landing in her lap. "Meow-ah."

"Me too. I've got a whole night planned for us. We have music. Treats. A new mouse toy..." Kitten purred as she rubbed her head against Sugar's belly. "I know. So exciting."

She got up and carried Kitten into the kitchen. "What do you want first, treats or toys?"

"Meow-ah. Meow-ah."

"Fine. Have both." Sugar grabbed a foil pouch and a small stuffed mouse toy from a cabinet above the sink. From the freezer, she grabbed a blood pop for herself.

Up on the bunk, the roommates enjoyed their treats while taking turns batting at the cat toy in silence. It was like a live-action game of Pong. Mindless and perfect. When Kitten finally tired of that game, she started a new one which involved rolling around with the mouse. But it was a game for one. Not feeling slighted, Sugar turned on some music and pulled out her laptop. Cole Porter provided the soundtrack for her last shot at learning more about Alex.

Thinking about what shreds of intel she'd gotten from Mary Helen, she searched for "Stéphane Cromier sharecropper." But it took her right back to what she'd already found about Stéphane Cromier, Bank Founder. She guessed there'd been little interest in sharecroppers back in the day. And the path from banker to sharecropper felt so unlikely. *Is it even right?* Trying Mrs. Cromier got her nowhere at all. Seems there was even less interest in female sharecroppers.

"Kitten, what was the brother's name?" As she tried to check her notes, Kitten started grabbing at the pages of the writing pad. Sugar let her play for a moment before taking the pad away. There it was. "Clayton. Thank you, Kitten. Okay Clayton, what do you have to say for yourself?" She typed, "Clayton Cromier born 1800." Nothing.

Asking the universe, she mused, "Really? Nothing? That can't be right." *What else?* She tried again, typing "Clayton Cromier born 1800 New Orleans." But this time, she added the year he died, 1878. Nothing for Clayton, but what she did get were ads for sites that helped find obituaries. She threw her hands up, wondering if she could possibly feel more obtuse. *Obits. Not born. Died.* Picking one of the sites and entering her information, Sugar found a short death notice for Clayton Cromier. It was from the *Weekly Democrat* and read, "Clayton Cromier, blacksmith, born 1800 died September 9th, 1878. Mr. Cromier was survived by sons Clayton Cromier, Jr. and Trevor Cromier."

The information was like a triumph and a dead end at the same time. *A blacksmith with two sons. What about that was telling? Nothing, yet. Press on.*

"Okay Trevor, what have you got?"

What he had was a wife and five children. He'd been an accountant for the New Orleans Cotton Exchange. By the few accounts she found, he lived an upstanding life.

"Fine. Be that way. How about you, Junior?"

All she found for Clayton Cromier, Jr. was a death notice. He'd died at the ripe old age of 19 years. No cause of death was listed. *Why do so many Cromiers die so young? Was it merely the darkness of the times?*

The word "dark" hung with Sugar. *Why?* Remembering that Mary Helen had called Alex a dark empath she wondered, *What does that mean, exactly?*

"OK, Google me this."

Typing "dark empath" got her an article from a psychology magazine explaining that dark empaths are intelligent and highly attuned to the feelings and circumstances of others, but feel no emotional attachment to them. In fact, they're prone to using their insights against others. They have a need for attention and lean towards grandiosity. They're vindictive, manipulative, and physically aggressive. They can be narcissistic, psychopathic, and/or Machiavellian. "Fantastic."

It was all in line with her experience with Alex. All of it. But knowing how evil Alex was didn't allow her to forgive herself. She starting thinking about skilled con men and scammers. *Should their victims feel guilty for falling prey? If they're Jewish, then yes. Jews feel guilty about everything.* In her head, Sugar wrote a Tinder ad for Alex. *Stunningly attractive single female. Mid 200s (age, not weight). Good listener. Late sleeper. Enjoys nightlife, invading dreams, killing for financial gain, and the deep pain of others. My nickname is "Shevil." My pronouns are she/her and fuck you till you're dead.*

Curious as to how someone actually becomes a dark empath, Sugar continued reading.

Seems being a dark empath is a lucky combination of nature and nurture. Being born with the proclivity is possible. But it more likely results from a traumatic event or events, coaxing the tendency for dark empathy to the forefront.

Thinking back, Sugar considered Mary Helen saying that Alex was dark before her V-life began. She wondered if being thrown out of a comfortable upper-class home and into the fields of a sugar plantation was trauma enough.

Thinking about the darker elements of life in 1800s New Orleans, Sugar felt her own sympathy rising, then fought it back. She had no desire to feel bad for the plight of her nemesis. *Fuck her...No. Isn't that the point of this whole exercise? Understanding my client? Using it? But, fuck her.* Letting her inner battle continue, she sensed something. Someone. She sat up tall. *Who do I smell?* Questioning Kitten, she asked, "Mac?"

A knock on the side of her van which was followed by a Scottish accented, "Hello? Sugar, are ya home?" confirmed her instinct.

"Kitten, we have a visitor." Wondering how and why he was here, Sugar went to the door. There he stood, looking as together as the other night, wearing jeans, a blazer over a T and a warm grin. "Mac?"

"At the risk of overstepping, I thought ya might like company tonight."

"How did you find me? Oh. Mary Helen."

"She asked me to apologize for her. But she thought I might be of some comfort to ya."

"She did? So how much do you know?"

"She-vil, tomorrow, dress to kill."

As much as she wanted to continue her search, her upbringing kicked in. "You, wanna come in? Can I get you something?"

"Something? What do you have?"

Sounding rather hostessy, she offered, "Care for a blood-sicle? I have fox and rabbit."

"Really?"

"I can't take credit. A friend showed me how to make them."

V-Life

"That's a fine friend. But it's a nice night. Why don't we walk?"

Sugar looked at the sky and breathed in the air. It was a nice night. But... "I appreciate the effort. Really, I do. And tell Mary Helen I'm not mad. But I should get back to my research."

"How about this? What say ya grab us each one of your...'sicles, is it? And we'll take a short stroll. Perhaps it will do your *situation* some good." Mac held out a hand. There was something about him that made the offer hard to resist. So, she stopped trying.

Walking along in the light of the half-moon, Sugar felt as if she was partying the night before a big exam. A feeling she was all too familiar with. Making short order of his treat, Mac pocketed the stick and smiled. "Mustn't litter."

"God forbid."

"Here, I'll take yours."

Sugar finished her treat and handed him her stick. "Thank you."

"Oh, no. Thank you." They continued their stroll in silence. Then Mac asked, "What are ya thinking?"

"Isn't that typically the woman's question?"

"I'm in touch with me female side."

Sugar attempted a Scottish accent, "Are ya, now?" then went back to Jersey. "Well, thank you for asking and not just trying to read my mind."

"Honestly, I did try. But ya have so many thoughts racing around in there, it's like tryin' to catch a hundred Super Balls all at once."

Sugar laughed. "I feel the same way."

"Fine. Pick a ball."

"Is that an offer?" They both laughed.

"It would be, in other circumstances. But ya're preparing for battle, aren't ya? You'll need your energy."

"No sex before The Big Game?"

"Something like that."

Sugar smiled. She liked this man. "I'm thinking about the family Cromier and wondering why they all died young. Or, most of them."

"Did they die?"

"Yeah, the father, the mother, the nephew and Alex—or, as everyone likes to call her, She-vil."

Mac stopped walking and Sugar looked at him. Suddenly, she read his mind. "I'm an idiot, aren't I? They're not dead. Not 'dead' dead."

"Look how smart y'are."

"If this is what smart feels like, Mensa's overrated. What am I supposed to do with this information?"

"Mary Helen thought it might help."

"But she told me that she couldn't betray secrets."

"Aye, she can't. It would be ruinous for her. Once the V community loses trust in someone, especially a human, well...That's why she sent me. For the record, I came as a willing participant. I find ya interesting, and rather handsome."

"Handsome? I don't know how to take that."

"Take it the way it was meant: as a high compliment."

Sugar decided to take the compliment. *Why not? I may not be getting many more.*

Mac took her hand. "Come climb a tree with me."

"Now?"

"Sure."

She could tell he had something in mind. That this wasn't just a whim. So, she went along with it. Together they half scaled, half flew up the tree. Finding a strong branch nearly two-thirds of the way up the large oak, they sat and surveyed the land and the sky. The light from the waning moon was rimming the tops of the trees. *If this is my last night on earth, it's a beautiful one.* Sugar wanted to feel at peace, but wishing didn't make it so.

Mac whispered. "Tell me a secret?"

"A secret?"

"Sure. Secrets are bonding."

"I'd rather not."

"Come on."

"Mac, I don't think getting close to me is a good idea. It could be, dangerous."

"I'll be fine. I won't get too close." After a beat that promised he understood the gravity, he began. "Here. I'll go first. So, I was eleven..."

"Wait. If we're going to do this, I don't want your standard secret. I want something really embarrassing. Something you've never told anyone." Folding her arms, she waited for him to take the dare.

"Aren't you the cheeky one. Okay." She could feel him honestly scanning his memories. He had a lot of them. "Okay. Fine. I've got one. Are ya sure you can take it, now?"

"I'll hold on." Sugar made a show of grasping one of the smaller branches. "Ready."

"Don't say I didn't warn ya. I was on a crossing from London. I should say, I was born into the V-Life and I had decided to try my fortune in the new country, as it were. I'd been told that the captain, a striking fellow with a large mustache, long sideburns, and a regal comportment, he had invited me to dine at his table. Quite an honor. But a' course, I couldn't dine with him, could I? But I also didn't want to offend the man. We still had days at sea. So, I accepted. My cover was going to be..." Trying to sound mysterious, "...a rare food allergy. I even came up with a name for my affliction. *Solidum cibum infirmum.*"

"Catchy."

"Thank ya. I thought so. It's Latin for 'solid food infirmity.' I delicately explained that the side effects are horrible wrenching and that it's worse at sea. I thought it was genius. I could politely sit and enjoy what promised to be lively conversation, perhaps get in a few witticisms of me own. No one would be the wiser."

"I feel a snag coming."

"A snag, indeed. They'd seated me next to a young doctor. Very sure of himself. He'd never heard of *solidum cibum infirmum* and insisted I was inventing the entire thing. It was all in me mind and that I was offending the chef and the captain. The man wouldn't let it go."

"What did you do?"

"What could I do? I proved my point. After several bites of coq au vin with an onion compote, I emptied my stomach into the good doctor's lap."

Sugar couldn't help laughing. *But that was Mac's intention, wasn't it?* "That's fantastic."

"Sadly, I didn't make it to the cherries jubilee. That would have made quite a show. And I was never invited back to the captain's table. It was the last poultry I ever ate. To this day, I don't like feeding on birds."

Maddie came to mind. "I have a friend I think you'd like."

"Friends are good."

"Especially if they're O negative."

"Aye, I haven't heard a good universal donor joke in some time."

"You're welcome."

"Okay. Your turn. But now ya have to tell me something embarrassing as well. It can't just be a secret."

"Oh, so much to choose from."

"I'll help ya narrow down. What is the most recent thing ya wish you never did? What would ya take back if you could?"

Before Sugar could stop herself, she said, "I killed my boyfriend." *That's it. It's out in the air and there's no reeling it back in. Why did I say it?*

Staring into the night, Sugar continued. "We were so stupid. Curtis said if I made him into a vampire, we could go through time together. Happy. Like some long fucking vacation. A never-ending world tour. At first, I said no. It was too crazy. But he kept pushing and pushing. Why did I agree to do it? I guess I wanted to believe so badly that everything could be okay. Almost normal. I was so afraid of being alone this way. So, I finally gave in. We talked about what Alex had done to me. Or what I thought she did. Every detail, so we'd get it right. But we didn't take into account that I hadn't tasted blood yet. It was so...addictive. I couldn't stop."

She pictured Curtis lying across her arms. The scent of his cologne filled her head. She remembered holding him until he was no longer warm.

"That's my big secret. My confession." *Do I feel better having said it? Do I deserve to feel better?* Answering the second question was easy.

"You're forgiven."

"You're not a priest and I'm Jewish. It doesn't work that way."

"We're vampires. It does."

Finally able to look at Mac's face, he didn't seem to be judging her harshly. "Why are you here?"

"I thought ya could use a friend. That ya deserved one."

With that, Sugar allowed herself to fall against Mac's side. He put his arm around her and she let him. *Deserved or not, it's comforting.*

"I want to do something for ya."

"You've done plenty."

He took off his blazer and laid it over the tree limb. Pulling back a shirt sleeve, he said, "I want you to drink." Sugar sat up, confused. "You need more energy. I don't want to scare ya, but that little ice pop isn't enough to fortify ya for battle." Looking deep into her eyes he added, "Vampire blood is the most powerful there is. It's okay. I'll stop you when the time comes. This isn't me first rodeo." With a slight smile he added, "I've always wanted to say that. I sound almost American, don't I?"

"Like a true cowboy."

"Giddy-up, cowgirl."

Sugar kissed Mac's cheek, then gently sank her teeth into his wrist. He was right. The feeling of energy racing through her body was like nothing she'd ever felt. *Vampire blood is the best.* Would it be enough?

37

GOOD MORNING. OR NOT

Waking to chicken-scented cat breath, Sugar was wondering if that was going to set the tone for the day. *Perfect.* Lying there, not wanting to open her eyes and break the seal, she thought about what parting words she'd say to Mac. Considering his kindness was a much better way to start her day. *He'd been a gentleman. Or a...what? Is there a word for polite vampire behavior? If so, I'd use it now.* But when she opened her eyes, he wasn't beside her. *Did he leave?* She sat up and looked around the space.

Kitten sat down by Sugar's pillow and purred.

"He left us."

"Meow-ah."

"Fine. He left me."

As Kitten shifted her weight, she made a crinkling sound. For the first time, Sugar saw there was a sheet of paper between Kitten and the pillow. "Cat, I think you're sitting on my Dear John."

Quickly, she whipped the paper from beneath Kitten like an old-time magician whisking away a tablecloth without disturbing the place setting. The cat was unfazed. Looking at the letter, Sugar noted that even Mac's handwriting was well-mannered.

Dearest Sugar...

"Dearest? My, we are formal."

Hope you slept well.

Thinking about her night, she had slept well. Better than she'd slept since this entire dark odyssey began. There were no dreams to remember, just deep, peaceful sleep. *Was that because of Mac's blood?* She knew it was, although she didn't know why it was. He had given her a tremendous gift. She read on...

I thought it best to leave you to your task and avoid an awkward goodbye. But I want to share a thought. Perhaps it will help. She-vil has grand ideas of her own importance. That's the world of a dark empath. She'll try to use your feelings against you. As much as possible, in the moment, focus on her, not you. Make all of your thoughts about her what's in her head. I have one other thought for you, but I'm choosing to save that for the next time we meet.

Yours, Mackenzie.

Sugar inhaled the scent of the note. A mix of outdoors and man products. She knew that scent. Folding the paper, she wondered what this man—this vampire meant to her. Whatever the answer, it had been a nice last night.

"Final leg. Kitten, we ready to do this?"

Kitten climbed on her lap and leaned against her.

Feeling a tightness in her chest, she kissed Kitten's head. "Shit, cat." She stopped herself from thinking about their impending goodbye. This was a good time to start testing Mac's strategy and not focus on her own feelings. She got up and readied herself, Kitten, and the van for the road, wondering if she could ever be ready enough.

38

WELCOME TO NEW JERSEY

The speech now running through Sugar's brain had to do with Shevil's brother Clayton. If Mac was right (and she had to assume he was, since Mary Helen sent him with the information), Clayton was the only member of Alex's immediate family who wasn't a vampire. But he was allowed to live a quiet life. *Was it as hard for you to leave him behind as it was for me to leave D.?* That would be an actual connection. Not like she was looking to make a BFFV—best friend for vampire life. But it was something.

Crossing the line into the Garden State, the nice man in the phone said in his Australian accent, "Welcome to New Jersey!" She laughed to herself. *Why does that welcome seem so incongruously funny? What is it about New Jersey that makes it the butt of so many jokes? Is it the hair?*

She wondered if Faye could sense that the daughter she'd clothed and fed and sent to college had just crossed the line into her home state. *Is Faye suddenly feeling an inexplicable urge to be disappointed?*

"Kitten, you're gonna be a Jersey girl."

Kitten popped up and peeked over the dash, then looked away just as quickly.

"Don't knock it kid. You're in good company. Meryl Streep, Queen Latifah, Brooke Shields, Kirstin Dunst. Mary J. Blige used to live here. Hey, what say we get some Jersey girl accompaniment?" Sugar said to her phone, "Search Queen Latifah, *Ladies First*."

The song came up, pumping, positive, and strong. As a young Queen Latifah sang about ladies who kick, Sugar let the words and rhythm embolden her. Sitting up taller, she started bobbing her head to the beat. She sang along with the chorus and thought, *Am I smiling? Maybe.*

Suddenly, BANG! CLUNK!

"Fuck!"

Deep into her song of empowerment, Sugar hadn't noticed the pothole to the right of her lane. It was huge enough to swallow a Lincoln Town Car. She also hadn't noticed the bumper lying deep down in it. *Is the rest of the car in there too?* Feeling her steering suddenly acting wonky, she swerved and heard something clanking beneath the van.

"This isn't happening."

But, of course, it was. *How does one person have van and vampire trouble all in the same day?* She pulled the wounded vehicle over to the side of the road as Queen Latifah continued singing about being just fine. "Queen, you're on your own."

With cars speeding past, Sugar walked around the van as if she had the ability to spot a problem and the understanding to fix it. She had neither. The next step was to pull out her phone and search, 'Why is my Sprinter making a clunking sound?' Up came three likely culprits. Tie rods, sway bar, and ball joints. None of them could be fixed by her. But her short reading made it seem that whichever of these it was, she could probably limp into New York being extra careful on turns. *What's my choice?* "Something will happen."

As she pocketed her phone, something happened. A shiny, deep-blue Mercedes cabriolet drove up and stopped on the shoulder, a few yards behind her. *Crap. Company. I don't need the time suck.*

A swarthy, barrel-chested 60-something man climbed out of the car. He was wearing a sportscoat, driving shoes, and dark denim jeans that looked like this was their first outing. He called to her, "Can I help you?"

Speaking loudly to be heard over the passing cars, Sugar answered, "Thanks. I'm good."

"If you were good, you wouldn't be on the side of the road in New Jersey." He pointed a finger at her and winked as if he'd just gotten the answer right on a game show.

She pointed back at him. "Nice one. But really, I'm fine. Thanks."

"The Sprinter okay? From one Mercedes owner to another, I know a few things."

"I bet you do."

Why is this guy trying so hard? Then, she remembered she wasn't as "fluffy" as she used to be and that, like her V friends, she was probably more attractive now. *Well, that sucks.*

"How far you headed? I could follow along. Make sure you get home safe."

She thought, *I could kill you. Make sure you get home dead.* But it was a busy road and she wasn't that kinda gal. Not yet, anyway. "I'm safe. And I really have to—"

BWOOP-BWOOP!

A state police cruiser pulled up behind the cabriolet, lights flashing. Sugar threw her hands in the air. "Happy now?"

The trooper, a large man wearing a cap with a highly-polished brim, climbed out of the cruiser and walked towards them, pecs first. "What seems to be the problem here?"

Sugar took the lead. "No problem. I just pulled over to make a quick call."

"On the side of the road? You just passed an exit. If you had to make a call, why didn't you get off and make your call where it was safe?"

Sugar thought, *Great, I have Sherlock Holmes here.*

Mr. Cabriolet added, "I'm just helping her."

The Trooper asked, "Miss, do you need help using your phone?"

"No. I'm fine. I told this man—"

"Bernard. I'm Bernard."

"I told *this man* I'm fine. You're right. It was a stupid place to pull over. I apologize. Won't happen again. I'll just hop in and get back on the road."

Trooper Holmes wasn't done. "May I ask where you're on the road to?"

Bernard jumped in, "I asked the lady the same thing."

Not seeming up for dude-bonding with Bernard, the trooper said, "Mr. Bernard, is it? Sir, I need you to please take a step back."

Bernard did not step back. "Hey, I was just trying to help a damsel in distress here."

Sugar could feel the clock ticking, her stress level rising and her fangs growing. The trooper took an authoritative step towards Bernard. "Sir, you're not helping. Please step back."

"Hey. I don't think you know who I am."

Maintaining a measured tone, the trooper responded, "You're Bernard. And you haven't stepped back yet. If you don't follow my request, I will have to detain you. Now please..."

Bernard released his inner-Jersey. "Detain? You mean arrest me? You're gonna arrest me for not taking a step back? I'm pretty sure not taking a step back isn't a criminal offence."

"I'm giving you one more warning, *Bernard.*"

Bernard puffed up his already large chest. "I don't think I care for how you say my name, Officer—" Bernard leaned in to read the trooper's name tag, "D'Berry? *Really*. Might that "D" stand for 'Dingle'? Go ahead, Officer Dingle Berry. Arrest me. Make my fucking day."

Just then, another Mercedes cabriolet drove past, then quickly pulled over several yards in front of Sugar's van. Out jumped two thick, twenty-ish men who rushed past Sugar to Bernard. "Dad, what's goin' on? You okay?"

Trooper D'Berry again tried to take charge. "You gentlemen will have to take a step back."

"You like that 'step back' line, don't ya, Dingle? Boys, this clown's tryin' to arrest me for not playin' mother-fuckin'-may-I."

"I promise you sir, you don't want to make me call for back up."

Bernard leaned forward with his arms out. "It would be the Dingle Berry thing to do."

The young men stepped up to their father and a moment later, the shoving began.

Feeling she was now the least interesting person in this scenario, Sugar followed Officer Dingle Berry's advice, quietly taking one step back. Then another and another until she was back in the van and rolling away. With Miss Latifah providing her anthem of independence, Sugar checked her rearview mirror. Fists were flying. No one seemed to notice her exit. The van disappeared around a bend, clunking as it went.

"Welcome to New Jersey, Kitten."

39

THE DROP

The traffic going through the Holland Tunnel was surprisingly civilized. *Is it a weeknight? Probably. Anyone driving at this hour on a weeknight would be leaving the city, not coming in.* Among all the daunting thoughts Sugar had about this night, driving a twenty-foot camper van through New York City was currently at the top of her list. She'd enter lower Manhattan and park the van in a lot in the Village. One with the high clearances her vehicle required.

God, it's weird to be back. Passing businesses she knew and streets she'd walked, she asked herself if it was feeling like home or just familiar. The sensation reminded her of being a kid and walking through the school gymnasium in street clothes. Equal parts familiar and awkward.

Arriving at the lot, she turned in over the curb, causing the van to make a final loud CLUNK. She stopped at the attendant's booth and lowered her window. A skinny kid who couldn't be older than seventeen was manning the post. Under a gray puffy jacket, he wore a t-shirt that used to be white. His teenage 'stache was thin, but trying. Without looking away from his phone, he said, "How long?"

Leaning out her window, she answered, "Overnight."

"Fifty bucks. Pull down to the left and bring me the keys."

"I'm not the one picking it up. A Mr. David Bernstein will come get it." The teen's eye didn't leave his device. She asked, "Are you gonna write it down?"

Still not looking up, he pointed to his head. "It's all in here. Hundred and fifty I.Q. I don't forget shit."

"Thank you, Mr. Hawking."

The kid's mouth gave the slightest hint of a smile. Feeling that young Master Hawking indeed had the info locked in, Sugar did as instructed and pulled the van into a spot in back on the left. She cut the engine, looking at the small cars around her, then rubbed her eyes. She could almost hear her aunt say, "Never rub your eyes. The world is a filthy place. Pink eye lurks around every corner." Sugar decided to take her chances. Between the drive, the fear, Bernard, the trooper and the clunking, she was spent. *Will I even be able to rest before heading into the night? It's worth a try.*

After she'd covered the front windshield, she headed to the back. Really wanting to sneak in just a little more precious cat time, she scooped Kitten out of the sink and the two curled up on the bunk. Kitten put up no fight with the arrangement. Lying still, Sugar buried her face in Kitten's fur, noting that her cat was getting bigger. *My girl is growing up.* "What good company you've been."

Kitten merely purred her response. Sugar tried to read Kitten's mind. While she couldn't be sure, she felt as if the cat's affection for her went beyond just Sugar being the provider of meals. If she was wrong, she was willing to live with the lie. "I love you, too." The two laid there, breathing in unison.

After relaxing somewhat, Sugar pulled out her phone to craft a text to D. She thought, *I won't send it until the last minute, but I can't compose it on the fly. It's too important. But less is better. Say how much I love him and he'll worry. Damn. It'll have to go unsaid.* She kissed Kitten's head and wrote the text in one pass.

D., I need you to come get the van ASAP. It's in a lot north of Houston. All paid for. There's a surprise for Sarah inside. Hint: It's a cat. Thanks. I'm mostly fine. Most-ly. She included the address and a winky, smiley emoji.

"How'd I do?"

"Meow-ah."

"You are nothing if not supportive. Okay. That's done. Next. What to wear?"

Again, she felt athleisure wear was her friend, but she wanted to make a statement. *Alex will most certainly dress for the event. What can I do to jazz up my look?* Not having a lot of options, she decided to go simple but dramatic. Slipping into her black, flair-legged yoga pants she said, "What else? What else?" She looked in the closet and...

Inspiration.

She slipped off her shirt and bra. Then, pulling the thick, leather strap-belt from a jacket, she wrapped it around her chest twice like an armored tube top. Tying the belt closed in the back, she wondered, *What would Faye say?* Laughing, Sugar wrote the monologue in her head: *You look like M.G. No names. You remember her. The one with the pills and the booze. You know, she could have been a dentist. Such a shame.* "Shame."

Next, Sugar dug out her violet puffy convertible jacket, unzipping and removing the sleeves. She put the resulting violet puffy vest over the black-leather armored bra.

Looking at her silhouette in the bathroom mirror, she felt it needed one more thing. "What else, Kitten?" Then she knew. "Disco hair." She pulled out hair product and a blow-dryer, and went for volume. Big hair. Parting it in the middle, she strategically added two long, sparkling barrettes at the front of her scalp. The effect looked crazed—flat hair at the center part, and puffing up at the sides like brilliant, dark-chocolate cotton candy. Looking at it, Sugar said to Kitten, "Maddie would be proud." Just thinking about Maddie made her feel oddly supported.

Next, Sugar gave herself the smokiest eyes of her life. Either life.

In the before-times, Sugar would often wear a piece of jewelry from one of her grandmothers, or something given to her by a friend, or by Curtis as a way of bringing the person with her. If she went to the ballet, she'd bring her grandmother Esther. A party, well that could be Esther, too. *She loves a party.*

From the drawer under her bunk, Sugar dug out the green jewel Maddie had stuffed into her pocket. *Such an odd blue vein.* Slipping it into the waistband of her pants, she felt she now had the strength of a good friend on her way to war. Battle juju.

After grabbing a knife, she looked in the mirror for a final inspection and decided to dub her look, "21st-Century Glam-Vamp on a Mission to Hell by Way of the Disco." *Snappy.*

"Well, that's it."

Kitten was still on the bunk, staring at her. "Meow-ah."

"Don't make this any harder."

Sugar went to a kitchen cabinet and pulled out a can of wet cat food. Kitten leapt from the bed and started clambering around Sugar's feet. With each turn of the can opener, Kitten became more excited. For a second, Sugar thought the cat might climb up her pant leg. When the food was in the bowl, Sugar lowered it to the floor. Kitten was in cat heaven. Touching her cat's head one last time, she knew Kitten was now food obsessed and ignoring her mother. That was the idea.

Sugar turned the music back on, low. "This Is Me," the anthem of self-acceptance from the Hugh Jackman musical, *The Greatest Showman* filled the van.

"Bye, my Kitten. Love you."

As Sugar stepped outside, the night air hit her face. She wiped a phantom tear from her dry cheek. Old habits.

40

WALK OF SHAME

Sugar's plan was to take Houston Street all the way East across lower Manhattan past Estela, a great Italian eatery, then Emilio's Ballato, another great Italian restaurant, then past Katz's Deli and make a left on Avenue A. She walked thinking, *That's right, I can't eat shit, but I still give directions by dining establishments.*

With the intense boost of Mac's blood pulsing through her veins, her strides were long and purposeful, matching the defiant show tune still playing in her head. *Sure, walking more slowly would buy me time. But time for what?* She planned on entering this confrontation strong, shoulders back, head high, heart in throat. The night was both quiet and loud. The sounds of subway cars passing beneath the sidewalk rumbled in her ears. Car horns honking blocks away wove their way into the audio tapestry. But there weren't many people out and about. It was too late for diners, and the downtown clubs weren't along this strip. Another reason she'd picked it: Less chance for an encounter with someone for whom she had no time.

The few people she did pass gave sideways looks to Sugar and her Mission to Hell by Disco ensemble. One older couple heading in the opposite direction, smiled politely. Their eight-dollar haircuts and their double-knit, fashionless fashion-wear made them a strangely middle-American pair to be out strolling the dirty city this late. After they passed, Sugar could hear the man joke, "Oh sweetheart, why don't you wear that?"

The woman answered, "I do. Just not when you're around."

And right there is why Sugar had always loved this city: The little gifts from strangers every day. There were no boxes into which you could neatly put these people. She missed that.

Passing Katz's Deli, she remembered a lunch with Faye and Henry. They'd come to visit their daughter in the big city. The argument o' the meal was over the kugel. Was it better than Grandmom Bitsy's? Henry said yes. Faye said no.

"Henry, you just like it because you're eating it right now."

"Can't that be part of what makes something good?"

"No."

"I say you're wrong."

"I'm right."

The right/wrong argument went back and forth like an old-Jews' tennis match until Henry said, "I think you're just arguing to argue."

Faye had let a sly smile grow on her face. Henry turned to Sugar, "She gets me with that every time. Every damn time."

The three laughed and Faye ended up taking home two pieces of kugel and a quarter pound of whitefish salad for later.

But Katz's was closed for the night and Sugar needed to get her head back in the game. She began replaying what Mac had told her. His parting thought. To the rhythm of her stride, she chanted to herself, "Focus on Alex. It's about her. Focus on Alex. It's about her." She tried packing away all thoughts of family and New York, and of her new friends and of Curtis. It was time to harden her heart to anything she cared about. Trying to mentally review what she'd learned about her nemesis, she said, "Make it about her, damn it."

A block onto Avenue A, the small, alternative nightclubs started popping up. Sugar was now walking through late-night life, where the young and the hip and the in-the-know go to party. Music and chatter from the nightspots spilled onto the street. A bouncer called out, "Hey, the party's in here." She didn't see him. A trio of twenty-somethings wearing their fashionable disinterest passed Sugar, giving her a wide berth. Swimming in the background of her conscious mind, she heard one say, "Lady, the seventies called. They want their hair back." Then there was laughing. Sugar thought, *I'm making a statement. Good.* Instead of worrying it might be the wrong statement, she let the attention embolden her.

After another block, across the street, she saw her destination just ahead. The black, metallic lettering of the signage was tall and narrow and backlit in purple. Its neon glow was barely visible in the East Village night: Club 13. It was dark and radiating sinister intent. But Sugar didn't need to read it, and the fewer people who did, the better. Old habits would normally have her trying to mentally change the past. Nagging at her as to why she ever stumbled into this bar in the first place. She was avoiding playing the what-if game. *What if I'd walked into any of those bars instead of this one. Or gone for ice cream and drowned my sorrows in sugar and butterfat. Or stayed home and heard Curtis out. Done something, anything differently.* She'd still be leading a normal life with the man she loved. But she didn't let herself fall into that familiar trap.

Trying to not give it much thought, she pulled out her phone, brought up the text to D., and hit send. *Okay, from here on, this isn't about me. Focus on Alex. It's about her.*

Picturing the family Cromier of 1800s New Orleans, Sugar crossed the street, stepped up on the concrete stoop, and reached for the ace-of-spades door handle.

To no one but herself she whispered, "Something will happen."

41

LADIES' NIGHT

Dark. Nothing special. Just as she remembered it. The club was a long, narrow room with a bar running down the entire length of one wall, and tight, worn booths running down the other. Trance music was pumping. Most of the light in the room was ambient, courtesy of the underlit liquor bottles along the wall of shelves behind the bar. Scanning the space, Sugar didn't see her date. *Is this not where Alex wanted me to be?* Choosing to not question herself further, she went to the bar and took a seat. *Alex can come find me.*

From the darkness, one of the two bartenders appeared in front of Sugar. The illuminated manuscript inscribed upon the young woman's bare arms left no room for more ink. "What's your poison?"

"Everything. But I'll have a bourbon rocks."

"Preference?"

"Basil Hayden's" It had been her favorite drink before. *If I'm going to pretend to nurse something, why not that?*

The bartender seemed to approve the order. "You bet."

Sugar didn't look around, not wanting to seem like a deer in the headlights waiting for impact. Her drink came. The feeling of the cold wet glass in her hand was nostalgic and appealing.

"You wanna start a tab?"

At that moment, a man sat on the stool next to hers, his familiar face half-turned her way. It was C.J., one of Alex's henchman. The one who'd invaded her dream and her pedicure.

"She's waiting out back."

Turning to her inky bartender, Sugar said, "He's got this."

C.J. half sneered at Sugar, pulled a roll of bills from his coat pocket, and begrudgingly pressed a twenty onto the bar. The powerful young man rose and started walking to the back of the space. Following him, Sugar felt his outfit was at least as ridiculous as her own: a long, dark green Edwardian coat, black leather pants, no shirt, and a few strategically placed chains.

He didn't look back at her as he sneered, "Cute."

"Ladies unescorted don't pay."

With each stride, she wondered how long she could keep up the bold front. *It's about Alex.* Digging her nails into her fists, she hoped the pain would make her more alert. But she felt nothing. When the back door opened, fingers of soft light from the alley crept into the space. Her large escort stepped outside, Sugar following in his wake.

And just outside the door, there she was.

Alex. Alexandria Cromier.

In the dimly lit alley, Alex posed with legs astride and arms akimbo. *Was she always that radiant?* She was wearing a catsuit of electric orange and a matching, hooded cape. Thigh-high red boots rounded out the costume.

Behind Alex were three of her V Boys. They were all wearing outfits identical to C.J.'s. Like a Goth boy band gone horribly wrong.

C.J. took his place behind Alex, becoming the fourth member of Alex's backup singers.

"It certainly took you long enough."

Sugar shrugged, offering "Jersey," as if that answered it all.

"Don't get me started." Alexandria's look turned skeptical. "I see you dressed for me. Or is that for Halloween?"

Trying to think only of Alex, Sugar didn't answer.

"Mmm. Not feeling chatty? That's fine. Oh, I brought an old friend of yours to join us." Calling towards a nearby dumpster, Alex said, "Please, Nolan, step out. I'm sure Sugar is just dying to see you again."

From behind the dumpster emerged a short man with a familiar face.

"Miss me?"

Is that..."Runt?"

Except now, he wasn't dressed like a Moab redneck in a heavy metal T-shirt. He looked like the other V Boys. Runt cocked his head and spread his arms. "Can't keep a good man down!"

Sugar tried to understand what she was seeing. *How was this possible? This is the man I killed in the desert, cleaned up and looking like the world's shortest runway model.*

Alex must have been reading her thoughts and answered them. "You're very bad at this Sugar. That's two kills gone wrong. You left enough life in our friend Nolan here..."

Nolan interjected. "Please. Runt."

"Mmm. Runt. Yes. Well, you didn't finish the job. So, I did. He's one of us now. And a very loyal pet." Sugar thought of her cat back in the van and Alex continued, "Like Kitten. Yes?"

Sugar knew she had to refocus, not think about her world, but the surprise of seeing Runt had thrown her off what game she had.

"I thought you might be a fun toy for our Nolan—I'm sorry, for *Runt* to play with. Would you like to play with this little toy, Runt?"

"Fuck yeah, I would." Runt bared his fangs.

Alex commanded, "Now!"

With that, Runt dove for Sugar, knocking her backwards onto the ground. The battle was on. But with the wrong vampire. Alex and her boys watched as Runt scrambled on top of Sugar, trying to bite her throat. Sugar's first reactions were automatic. *Hold him off. Don't die before getting a chance at Alex. He's surprisingly strong for a little man. But aren't I strong too?* Rolling him to the side, she got on top of him. Although she could feel her fangs out, she went for the head butt. Runt's head took the impact, then slammed back onto the concrete. Using the moment of surprise, Sugar pulled a blade from her jacket. She stabbed at Runt's heart, but he turned and she missed, cutting deeply into his side.

"Fucking bitch!"

Fueled by anger, Runt grabbed for Sugar's knife. Sugar sliced open his hand. Blood flew as he again tried grabbing the knife away from Sugar.

They struggled, seeming evenly matched. Sugar tried to focus. *What's in your head, Runt? What are you thinking?*

Then she knew.

Still struggling with him, she toyed, "I'm sorry. Are you missing your friend Silent Jim? He's really silent now, isn't he?"

Runt became a wild man. But his fury made him sloppy. Sugar freed her blade hand and stabbed him in the chest multiple times, her final slice opening his throat. He wasn't dead, but the fight was draining from him along with his blood. Getting to her feet, Sugar watched Runt on the ground, holding his bloody neck with his bloody hand.

Alex stepped forward. "Oh, Runt. Are you hurt?"

He reached a hand to Alex, and she pulled Runt to his feet. His other hand was still around his neck wound, blood seeping through his fingers. He stood staring at Sugar, like an angry, wounded animal. He gurgled, "I'm gonna fucking kill you, bitch."

Laying a calming hand on his shoulder, Alex spoke evenly. "Oh, Runt. I think we've had enough bitch talking for one night. Yes?" Then she commanded, "Oscar?"

Without any more prompting than that, one of the V-boys produced a long sword from under his coat and handed it to Alex. "You see, Sugar. You really are quite bad at this." Staring into Sugar's eyes, Alex wielded the blade. In one fluid motion, she sliced Runt's head clean off. As his body dropped to the ground, his head rolled towards Sugar's feet. Runt's short time as a vampire was over.

"Gentleman, would you be so kind as to put Nolan—I'm sorry,

Runt into the dumpster?" The henchman did as told. One grabbed for the body, but as another reached for the head, Alex called out, "Wait. Sugar, did you want that as a keepsake?" Sugar said nothing. "I don't think she wants it." Runt's head followed his body into the trash.

Laughing, Alex said, "I miss him already."

"I don't."

"Well, I lied."

Sugar's jaw stiffened. "You're good at that."

"Oh, no. Are you mad at me?"

"Why would I be mad at you?"

Alex taunted, "Exactly. You should be mad at yourself. Cheating on your man with a creature of the night. Then killing the love of your life. So horrible. And, of course, that outfit. It's all quite inexcusable."

She's baiting me. Get in her head. Turn the tables. "I suppose you never made a mistake. Are you so very perfect?"

"I made you. And I'm willing to admit, that was a mistake. But it can be corrected."

"No other mistakes? Maybe not bringing Clayton with you into this life. Or did he reject you? Was it hard to leave Clayton behind?"

With a long maniacal laugh Alex said, "I didn't leave Clayton behind." Without turning, she called behind her. "Clayton. I don't think you two have been formally introduced." C.J. stepped forward and put his hands on his hips. "Clayton, Sugar. Sugar, Clayton."

This makes no sense. Alex's brother died in his seventies. The man is young. Maybe twenty.

"You're right. He's not my brother. He's my nephew. Clayton Senior gave him to me. Wasn't that nice? Now, I don't think that was an act of rejection, do you?" Alex, Oscar, Clayton and the two other V Boys were now all leering at Sugar, fangs out. Each took a menacing step forward.

Sugar didn't know what to say. She was out of cards. *It's going to come down to a battle, isn't it?*

Flipping back her hood, Alex scoffed, "Did you really think you could get in my head as easily as you got into the head of someone who would call himself Runt? You got in my way. That was your real crime." Stepping even closer, so her face was less than an inch from Sugar's, Alex whispered, "A kiss for luck?"

Before Sugar could say anything, Alex made two swift, almost invisible moves. One backwards, one forwards.

Sugar felt the blade piercing her heart.

For a moment, the shock masked the pain.

Is that it? No battle? No chance to prove my skills? No blaze of glory as I fight to defend Curtis' memory? This can't be it.

But it was. She had failed, utterly.

As she felt herself sliding back from the blade towards the ground, the world darkened. Sugar's last thought was *Be steely.*

42

THERE'S NO PLACE LIKE HOME

Quiet voices were swirling around her. *Who is that? What are they saying? Am I dead? Is this the other side?* Her head was filled with fog. *Is this heaven? No. That can't be possible. Hell? Jews don't have hell.* It was the semi-comforting thought she'd clung to for months. *Can I open my eyes? Do I remember how?* Her lids were so heavy. It was easier to keep them closed. Finally and slowly, Sugar opened her eyes. *Where am I? Alive or dead, again?*

A hushed voice said, "There she is."

Then a familiar accent said, "Hey, Sleeping Beauty. I knew the Sugar Lady missed her Willie too much to stay dead."

Sugar tried to focus. Yes, it was Willie. He was leaning over her. *Where is this?* It felt like a very small room. *I've been here before.* Sugar closed her eyes again in an attempt to reset her brain. This time, when she opened them, she knew she was in Matt and Maddie's ambulance. Five familiar pairs of eyes were all focused on her. It was like the final scene from the *Wizard of Oz* and she'd just woken from a nightmare in Manhattan. *Lance is surely the scarecrow. Strange how that movie keeps coming up.*

Matt clapped and laughed triumphantly. "Ha-Ha! We got you! I knew we'd get you." He high-fived Lance. "Yes! In your face, She-vil!"

Maddie held up something large and half covered in fur. "Jinxy never left your side."

Standing in the farthest corner, which wasn't very far, was Mac, his arms folded and giving a friendly nod. Sugar's head was still in fog. *Am I going to be sick?* Scenes from the previous night flashed in her mind. The boy in the parking attendant's booth. The people on the sidewalk. The tattooed bartender. Runt's head rolling to her feet. Angry V Boys stepping towards her. Alex, a breath away as she plunged a knife into Sugar's heart. *Do I remember how it felt?* All she could recall was shock, then inevitability. *Can I form words?* "How?"

Still jubilant, Matt declared, "She speaks!"

Maddie's hand flew straight up in the air. Looking like she'd have been jumping if she had the overhead space, she blurted, "It was me. It was all me." Pulling a stool to Sugar's side, she sat and folded her hands in her lap. Then Maddie leaned forward to share something. "Let me show you."

As she reached into her bra, Lance put his hands up. "Not ze time."

"You wish." She retrieved a green stone from her garment. One that matched Sugar's. "You know the stone I gave you, right?" Sugar nodded. "I told you it would keep us connected. Maddie don't lie." She reached for Sugar's stone, which was on a small side table, and held it up with her own. The thin blue veins in both stones were now effervescent. They seemed to be moving. "See. They're connected. Don't ask me how it works. I'm just a stupid ski bum, right?" She winked at Sugar.

"You so are not."

"Shh. Don't tell anyone." Clearly knowing the answer, she looked at Matt and asked, "How pissed was Angél when she realized I snagged them?"

"Soooo pissed."

Maddie seemed to delight in her theft. "Permission is for chumps. I have a lifetime to ask for forgiveness, right? Anyway, Mary Helen told Lance it was gonna hit the fan, and he told us."

Lance put his hand on Maddie's shoulders. "She is ze tie zat binds."

"Me or Mary Helen?"

Sarcastically, Lance said, "Oh, definitely you."

"Ignoring. Anyway, wanna hear something funny?"

Sugar whispered, "A Jew, a vampire and a busload of regret go into a bar."

When Sugar didn't continue, Willie asked, "Then what? What happened in this bar?"

"I don't remember."

Willie shook his head. "That's so sad. It had such a good start."

"Sorry. I'm tired. Sure. Tell me something funny."

Maddie launched into fast talking. "Matt and I are flying like bats out of hell across the country to save you, right? Hey, wouldn't it be so cool if we could really turn into bats? They're protected, you know. Really. Did you know you can't kill a bat in your house? You have to release it into the wild?"

Matt tried refocusing his wife. "Off topic, baby."

She laughed at herself. "Right. Sorry. Anyway, we're watching the stone as we go. Turn right, getting warmer. Turn left, colder. Warmer, colder. Warmer, warmer. The blue vein is getting brighter and moving faster. We're doing crazy shit. Driving over curbs, mentally trying to turn red lights to green. Not pulling it off in time. Driving through red lights anyway."

Willie sarcastically rolled his eyes. "Madness."

"Shush. We get to New York. By the way, hate it. Loud, smelly. We pull up to Club 13. Then just as we're about to park, a fucking rat took our space. A literal fucking rat the size of a Subaru. Seriously. Never driving there again. So, Matt said, 'Fuck it' and parks on the sidewalk. Anyway, we get inside and a very nice bartender tells us

V-Life

you went out back. She looked fun. I tried to tip her but she wouldn't take it. So, we get out back and, surprise! Mac here is already there, dumpster diving for Sugar."

Mac nodded. "Guilty."

Lance made a head gesture towards Mac. "Sugar, you have quite ze fancy hero in our Mackenzie."

Waving him off, Mac said, "No fancier than you, sir."

"Don't believe it. His people go back to ze court of James ze Fourth."

"How did you find me?"

In an official tone, Mac explained, "I employed highly secretive V tactics...I tailed ya."

Maddie whispered, "You had bite marks all over you. They drained you dry, girl. We left the headless guy in the dumpster."

Sugar whispered, "Runt."

Confused, Lance asked, "Runt?"

"Just some guy who tried to rape me in the desert."

"So, no loss zere?"

"None."

Willie did his patented move of putting a hand by his mouth and loud-whispering. "No offence Sugar Lady, but jou looked like a little disco queen who lost her crown."

Sugar said, "I will survive."

Maddie added, "Hey, hey."

Deciding to take the next step, Sugar slowly sat up. Her head was still swimming, but she was pretty sure she wasn't going to throw up.

Matt suddenly produced a bucket. "Here. Buckets are your friend."

"You're very thoughtful."

"I'm not. It's a small space. Puke stinks it up pretty quickly."

"Got it. How long was I out?"

Lance sat by her feet. "About three weeks, my love."

It didn't seem possible. *Didn't I just battle and lose to Alex last*

night? Correction. Didn't I just stand there, doing nothing and lose?
"Three weeks?"

"We had to wait for ze full moon, didn't we? So, we put you in deep freeze. Mary Helen let us take over one of her ice machines. Couldn't have you starting to rot. What fun would zat be? To come back looking like Claudette LaCroix."

"Who?"

"Sorry. Just a leper I used to know."

It was all so much to take in. Remembering her reading, she thought of the passage she'd found about dragging a dead vampire into the light of a full moon to bring them back to life. *Note to self. Reanimation of vampires by full moonlight. True. Way to go, Varney.*

Placing a small bag on her lap Mac said, "Here. Your things. Phone. Cash. The clothes you were wearing."

Willie shook his head. "Oh, Sugar. We should have burned them for jou."

For the first time, Sugar realized she was dressed in a T-shirt that looked like the British flag with the words "Bloody Hell."

"I don't know what to say. Thank you doesn't come close, does it?" No one answered. She wondered, *What do you get someone for bringing you back from the undead? Nordstrom should get a registry for that.*

Lance patted her legs. "No need. It's all part of ze life." He turned to his friends, "Come people. Let's give ze lady some room, shall we?"

As they filed out, Sugar felt lucky to have each and every one of them. Before Maddie left, she plopped Jinx down onto Sugar's legs. "Here. Jinxy, sit with Aunt Sugar. Help her relax." To Sugar, she proclaimed, "He's a good nurse."

Willie whispered to Lance. "That nurse would give me nightmares."

Now outside the ambulance, Maddie said, "I heard that."

With everyone else gone, Mac pointed to Sugar's phone. "You've got a lot of texts and calls from a D." Sugar reflexively reached for her cell. "He has your van. And he wants to know if you're okay. Oh, and something about a ditch."

Sugar smiled. "It's a family thing." Her next thought was troubling. "Alex. She-vil. Does she know? Does she know I'm back?"

"No. We don't think so."

"But she can get in my head."

"Aye, but if she thinks ya're dead, she has no reason to try. Though ya'd be wise to not think about her."

Sugar wondered if that was true. It made sense. *Surely Alex must have scads of other people to terrorize. Other lives to ruin.* Sugar let her body relax.

Jinx stretched, then leaned his entire mass on Sugar's face. Wiping the fur from her mouth, Sugar tried to push the beast away. Not an easy task. *This is a lot of cat.* Once he settled on her lap, she put her hands on him to keep him from rising back up. A wave of longing hit as she wondered if Kitten was okay. She looked at her phone.

Mac asked, "Should I leave?"

"If you don't mind, I'd rather not be alone."

"I don't mind."

Mac took a seat as Sugar scrolled through the messages from D.

I tried to call. What's up with the van? You OK?

Don't leave me hanging. I need to hear from you.

You're scaring me.

Damn it, Sugar!!!

I have the van. And the cat. What the fuck, Sugar!

Call me!

Are you in a ditch?

I'm checking hospitals.

Fuck Sugar. Fucking call me!!!

The next few dozen messages read about the same. Concern, anger, and speculation as to what might have happened to her. *What are the chances he'll guess correctly?* She switched to her voice messages and read the transcriptions. It was all the same things she'd read in the texts. Plus, one from Faye. That one, she chose to listen to.

"This is your mother. Are you trying to punish us? If you are, it's working. Your father and I are beside ourselves. I've lost nine pounds. Me. My angina is in my neck. I can barely swallow. And your father's pacing the house, snapping his fingers. Snapping and pacing. If we don't hear from you soon, I'm going to lose my mind and my hair. Call us. Love, your mother."

When Sugar looked up, Mac's eyes were opened wide. "Well then."

"I know. It's a lot to unpack. My family practices loud love."

"Your mother sounds like she doesn't need practice."

Sugar laughed the first laugh of her third life. It was small, but still. Then she remembered, "You said you were saving a thought for me."

Mac smiled, put his hands behind his head and rocked his chair back onto two legs. "Aye. I did, didn't I?"

"Well?"

"It's nothing, really. Just, ya remind me of someone."

"Please don't say it's your mother."

"I promise I won't. Though I think she'd like ya. No. Someone I cared about, a lot. And I think I could care about you."

"I think you already do."

"Is that a problem?"

"A bit of a surprise. You know my worst secret."

"All of us have a worst secret."

Assessing the man sitting in front of her, Sugar thought, *He is nice, isn't he? That's a good face. I could get used to that face. And that accent. But why me? Why is he moving so fast? He has his own dark secrets. That's good. Although I don't want to know them.* Yet, the fact that he knew hers made her feel slightly less horrible about herself. *Not that I could ever let that go. I need to not let it go. Letting the guilt go would be like saying Curtis didn't matter, and he did matter. So much. But I like Mac. Maybe too much.* Her next thought was even more unsettling. The last two men she'd been intimate with were now dead. She was poison. *I can't. It's part of my penance.* The word penance made one of the super balls in her mind bounce to religion. Suddenly she asked, "What day is it?"

"Do ya have some place ya have to be?"

"Maybe."

43

MAZEL TOV!

Why did I pick a roadster? So low to the ground. After months of driving the Sprinter van, Sugar had gotten used to the higher vantage point and the ample legroom. *Still, the sports suspension on this thing is confident on the turns, and the connection to the road is pretty damn exhilarating. Okay, that's why.* After getting her strength back from her re-rebirth, Sugar felt she'd experienced a transformation. She was less naïve. Steadier. More in control of her new V-Life skills. As for her J-life skills, well... *Let's not ask for the moon.*

Closing in on her destination, she considered if she was being bribed. In truth, she was. Her friends had all advised her against going to the *bat mitzvah*. Matt said, "Just go steal back the van. Simple. And it's not really stealing 'cause it's yours anyway." Lance felt any mingling with people you'd been close to could only lead to trouble. "Don't put yourself and zem in zat situation. A clean break is what is called for." Sugar remembered all too clearly; it's what Mary Helen advised her months ago. Willie had invited her to join him and Lance at the beach. "The moon over the ocean is too beautiful. And the tourists are so delicious." She was pretty sure he was kidding about that last part. Mac had simply said, "Do what ya need to do." *Mac. I'll think about him another time.*

Turning into the parking lot of Temple Beth Shalom, Sugar immediately felt evil. Just being here was wrong and she knew it. There are places her kind shouldn't go and this sure as shit was one of them. *My kind? Yes. I am "this kind."* In that moment, she knew she'd accepted her lot in V-Life. *This is my path. I can't change it.*

The sun was starting to rise over New Jersey as she parked next to her blue-gray German luxury van. Being reunited with her home was comforting. She reached into the back seat of the car and grabbed a garment bag. The van keys were sitting inside the rear bumper right where D. promised they'd be. He'd assured her the synagogue had security cameras on the lot and not to worry. She hadn't.

Even before Sugar opened the sliding van door, she could hear the familiar cry and allowed herself to get excited. Carefully opening the door just wide enough for her to get through, she announced, "Momma's home."

Like a swimmer coming off the blocks, Kitten leapt to her. Sugar caught the cat in the air. "I guess you're happy to see me too."

"Meow. Meow. Meow. Meow."

Sugar closed the door and took Kitten to her bunk. She nuzzled the cat and said with affection, "Look how big you got while I was dead!"

Sugar just watched as Kitten traveled the bunk, jumping and rolling and rubbing against her and jumping and rolling some more. "I let myself get played for a cat."

"Meow-ah."

"It's okay. I accept my weakness."

D. had told Sugar he'd return the van with the cat if and only if she made an appearance at Sarah's Bat-mitzvah. That was after he gave her a raft of shit lasting over twenty minutes and ending with, "I really hate you." Which of course meant, "I love you too much." She'd said the only thing she could: "I really hate you, too."

Looking around the van, she could feel that D. hadn't touched much. He'd respected her privacy. At first glance, her desk seemed just as she'd left it, but then it didn't. She sensed things had been gone through and put back. Considering how worried D. must have been, she had to give him a pass on the invasion of privacy. *What did he think of my wealth of vampire research? Does it matter?* She let her hand drift down the side of the mattress and reached for the photo. There he was. Curtis. Once again, she brought the photo to her nose and sniffed. All she got was the heavy scent of the air freshener D. had left in the van. She'd have to get rid of it. Too many chemicals in his 'ocean mist' fragrance. First things first. She put Curtis back in his place, drove the van around to the back of the synagogue, and parked as close to the back door as possible. When the time came, she wanted to be able to get from the vehicle to the building with minimal exposure to daylight. *The caterers will just have to work around me. A few extra steps wouldn't kill them, but they could kill me. I've been killed too many times already.*

Back in her happy place, she rejoined her cat on the bunk. Kitten jumped and played a bit more, then finally calmed down. Walking up the length of Sugar's body, Kitten finally sat on her chest with her face at Sugar's mouth. "Cat breath. So much better than ocean mist. Should we develop a line of cat-breath scented air fresheners? Feline Fresh? Dead Tuna Mist? Is that where our big fortune will come from?"

"Meow-ah."

"You started it. Fine. Wake me in three hours."

Kitten gave her three and a half. Since being brought back to life, Sugar's dreams had changed. They were now a mix of guided tours through her past, some flashes of wildlife in the area, and fleeting glimpses of her friends. She wondered if those glimpses reflected their current realities or if they were just random visions. Either way, it was nice to see them.

The "tink-tink" sound of Kitten pawing at her food bowl was what finally roused Sugar. "OK. Give me a sec. Yes. I get it. She who must be fed."

Sugar got up and poured a meal of twenty-seven kibble nuggets into Kitten's bowl. "Live it up. I'm sure I'm about to be treated to a lovely meal of rubber chicken breast nesting on a bed of limp spinach with an amusing cream-of-mushroom-soup gravy." Digging into her food, Kitten displayed no sign of sympathy.

"Time to put on the dog." After rubbing in a layer of sunscreen, Sugar slipped into her new outfit and shoes. Checking herself in the mirror, she approved the shape of the light lavender suit with its chocolate pinstripes and belted waist. She'd always loved the look, but never felt her waist was trim enough to carry it. "I think this is appropriate wear for committing high sacrilege, Kitten. Wait, let's finish the affront." Sugar opened the drawer under her bed and pulled out Grandmom Bitsy's gold broach. "Come on, Bitsy. You and me."

She could hear the intermittent, low-level rumble of car engines and groaning automotive suspensions as people began pulling into the lot and people talking as they filed into the synagogue. Sugar asked "Kitten, what time is it?" No answer. "Be that way. I'll check." It was twenty-five of. Wanting to wait until the last possible moment for her entrance, Sugar chose to give it a little longer.

Turning the passenger seat so it faced the living space, she sat and looked at her phone. Not in the mood to see old friends clinking cocktails she couldn't drink or showing off a four-star meal she couldn't eat, she went to email. Something she hadn't done since her return. Looking at her inbox, she saw that an email from Brooke had come in weeks earlier. Almost too low for her own ears to hear it, she uttered one word. "Shit."

The email opened with, "Hey Sugar. So great to hear from you. Hope you're good and I'm not too late getting back to you." *Well, a little.* She read on:

This was a fascinating dig. Interesting stuff. Your Mr. Cromier was quite a man. But he wasn't a sharecropper. Not really. Get this.

While he was running the bank, he was also working the underground railroad. Hard to tell exactly how many slaves he helped gain freedom, but it looks like somewhere around a half dozen and all from one sugar plantation owner in Lafourche Parish named Thornton Jackson. Yay, Mr. Cromier, right? But he got caught. The bank did a good job of covering it up. Didn't want the press, I guess. Instead of jail, and this is crazy, Cromier and family were indentured to Mr. Jackson as restitution.

Side Note: By all accounts, Mr. Jackson was a mean son of a bitch.

I thought indentured servitude was illegal by the early 1800s, so I did some more digging. So worth it. The judge, the "honorable" (but totally not) Baxter Hamilton, a staunch anti-abolitionist, already had a beef with Mr. Cromier. Seems Judge Hamilton's son was turned down for a loan by Cromier's bank. The son owed money everywhere. The guy finally killed himself. Yikes! Guessing the Judge saw an opportunity for payback. Some nice vigilante justice from the bench.

Like you suggested, all but Clayton died young. First dad. Seems he was beaten for stealing a tea service from the main house. He may or may not have done it. Stealing was a convenient excuse in the day. What plantation worker needs a china tea service and where's he going to fence it? Anyway, he didn't survive the beating. No reason was given for mom and daughter's deaths, which isn't super surprising for back then. Who cares about us women, right? But this is the crazy strange part. Mom and daughter died on the same day. Which is noteworthy. If an illness was sweeping through, wouldn't others have died then, too? None did. If they'd tried to run off and been shot, that would have been recorded. Nothing. Then in 1865, the brother was released from indenture when the slaves were emancipated and lived out his life as a blacksmith two parishes over.

What's all this for? A book? Super fascinating. If you need me do to any more digging, let me know. Happy to help.

Oh, I didn't tell anyone you reached out. And I'm not taking your stupid money. We're friends. Take care of you.

Brooke

It was a lot to take in. Sugar could picture Alex and her family working their hands to the point of bleeding. Hands that had never been exposed to the rigors of farming. A total gut punch. *How could a child understand this punishment?* She envisioned Mr. Cromier lashed to a tree, being bull-whipped with his family watching him die. *Devastating. Was that the incident that hardened Alex's heart for good? Sealed her fate as a dark empath?* Lost in the past, she sat thinking and envisioning.

SLAM!

Outside, a heavy vehicle door slammed shut. Next came the sound of a van door sliding open. Sugar heard a man bitching. "Fucking bougie van in our spot. These people. This is why I try to stick to Protestants and Catholics."

Another voice said, "My family's Catholic."

"And?"

"They'd cut you for a parking spot."

Looking at the time, Sugar saw it was the top of the hour. She'd dawdled too long over Brooke's email. *Damn it.* But knowing no *bat mitzvah* in recorded history had ever gone off on time, she was sure she had a small cushion.

"Okay Kitten, this is me dressed and ready to get in trouble. How do I look?" She gave a few turns so Kitten could see her from all angles.

"Meow-ah."

"Thanks. You look good, too." Sliding her large sunglasses on, she said, "Reentry shields in place. I can't believe I'm doing this. D., you owe me so big." But she knew she was the one who owed him. Isn't that why she was here?

Sugar took a steadying breath. "Get ready for a face full of family." Then, like ripping off the world's biggest Band-Aid, she pulled back the door to the van, hoping her sunscreen would get her under the overhang above the synagogue's back door before she turned to a pillar of ash.

Running past the caterers, one called to her. "Hey, lady, how 'bout you pull this around front with the rest of the guests? This area's for..."

"How 'bout no?"

It would have to be a sunny day. The warmth was familiar and deeply concerning. *Hurry!* She made it to the overhang in under three seconds. Safe. But when she opened the door and tried to go in, she couldn't. It was like there was a force keeping her out. She tried again, but instead of moving forward, she was pulled back.

"Bad enough you park in our spot. You wanna not block the door, too?" A big, round man in a white catering jacket stood behind her holding a heaping serving tray of lox. Despite it being covered, Sugar was hit by the stench of dead salmon. A younger but similarly shaped man stood behind him with a tray of bagels. Stepping aside into the sunlight, she let them pass. The two men had no trouble walking through the door. Back under the overhang, she quickly realized the problem was her. She was a vampire and this place of worship wanted none of her. *Crap, crap, crap.* It had never occurred to her that a building would reject her.

The two men re-emerged empty handed. "You still here? Out or in, lady?"

Again, she stepped into the heat and let them pass. Her mind racing, she tried to devise a way to get in, but she came up empty. How was she going to explain ditching Sarah's big day to D.? Maybe something like, *Hey, you saw my research. Well, there's a really funny story about that. Side note. Never deep kiss a narcissistic vampire just because you're pissed at your man.*

"Can I help you?" Ready to catch more shit from the unhappy caterers, Sugar turned and saw a new face. It was a kind looking young man wearing round-lens glasses, a *yarmulke* and *tallis*, holding open the door.

"I'm sorry."

"No, no. I didn't mean to sneak up on you. I'm Rabbi Glass." He offered a welcoming hand.

She took it. "I'm Sugar."

"Ah, the aunt. I've heard good things. Come in, join us."

"Oh, I um, I think I left something in my van. I have to..."

He smiled, "It's okay. Come on."

Ready for another round of not-in-my-synagogue, Sugar braced for rejection. But the nice young rabbi guided her over the threshold and into the building. *How? Is he acting as the resident of this house of worship? Does he know what he's doing or is it just happenstance? No, he can't. It has to be dumb luck that he showed up at the right time.* "Thank you."

Rabbi Glass started walking and she followed. "Did David tell you, we're in the same softball league?"

"No."

"He's very good. I'm one hundred percent left field. And only because they needed a warm body. But I love the game."

"D., David was always a sports guy. Oh, uh, he wanted me to do an *aliyah*."

Rabbi Glass turned, giving Sugar another of his easy smiles. "I don't think that would be wise. Do you?"

Who is this guy? She made no argument. "No."

Continuing farther into the synagogue, he said, "I'm so glad you could make it. I know Sarah's excited to see you. Oh, I am very sorry to hear about Curtis. May he rest in peace." They arrived at the back of the main sanctuary. Most of people were already seated and the large wood doors were closed. "Well, it's time to play ball." He gave her hand a slight squeeze, then walked away. Standing alone, Sugar watched Rabbi Glass head towards the *bema*, shaking hands as he went. A man and woman scooted in the door and rushed to join friends seated halfway up the aisle. Sugar took a seat in the last row by people she didn't recognize, wondering about the strange, gentle religious figure who seemed to know more than he said.

From his place on the *bema*, Rabbi Glass raised his hands and offered a friendly, "Shabbat shalom."

The congregation responded in unison, "*Shabbat shalom*," marking the beginning of the service.

Sitting there, Sugar was experiencing the most enormous feeling of incongruity of her natural or unnatural life. The service started with a song. As people sang, she scanned the room. There they were. In the front row. David, Amy, and Sarah. Seated right behind them were Faye and Henry with Barry, his wife Carol, their three kids and her grandmother, Esther. Sugar wondered if the woman had gotten even smaller. Faye had her hand on D.'s shoulder. Even from the back of the room, her mother's kvelling was palpable. *They're all so near. But we can't be close. Not like before. This is going to be a hard day.*

Rabbi Glass asked everyone to turn to page twenty-four in their prayer books. Reflexively, Sugar reached for the book sitting in the back of the pew in front of her, but at the last moment pulled her hand back. *Bad idea.* She could feel the eyes of the woman next to her and thought, *Lady, mind your own Torah.* The woman immediately looked away. *Nice to have a skill.*

As the service went on, Sugar continued playing Spot the Relatives. A row behind Faye and Henry were Uncle Lou and Aunt Selma and their kids. And just behind them were Sal and Barbara with their crew. The Rabbi called Sarah to the *bema* and the young girl rose to join him. As much as her grandmother had shrunk, Sarah had grown. She was long and slightly awkward, as if she was not yet used to her latest growth spurt. Seeing her niece evolving to maturity made Sugar smile. Suddenly, being here felt right. Like a gift. And then, the gift was snatched away.

"So, you're hiding from us?"

"Hi, Mom."

"Hi, Mom," said Faye, mimicking her daughter. Then her tone

V-Life

changed to something halfway between caring and put out. In a hushed voice she said, "Do I at least get a hug?"

No more prompting was required. Sugar hugged her mother.

"My God, you're a bag of bones. I knew you weren't eating. You know, I almost didn't recognize you."

Taking in the scent of her mother's Jean Naté Bath Splash, Sugar whispered, "I'm fine. Now."

Faye sat back. "Look at you. You're too skinny."

"I'm not."

"Take off those sunglasses. This isn't a funeral. I want to see my only daughter's eyes."

In truth, Sugar had forgotten she was still wearing them. She slid the protection from her face. "Here are my eyes."

"You look different."

"So do you."

"I don't. Now come up front. We saved you a space. One of Sarah's little friends tried to take it and your father told the kid to piss off."

"Go, Dad."

As the two women quietly walked to the front of the room, Sugar felt like all eyes were on her. She tried to move as quickly as possible, not wanting to steal Sarah's thunder. Faye and Sugar slid into place next to Henry. He reached for her hand, whispering, "There's my girl."

D. turned around. "I knew you couldn't deny the bestest brother ever."

She was about to offer a smart-ass response, then went with "Never." Putting her hand on his shoulder, the connection was strong. He covered her hand with his own.

While no one else in the room would know it, the Rabbi's sermon seemed aimed directly at Sugar and her *condition*. It was about life and death. What does it meant to be alive? What does it mean to be dead and what are our obligations to those left behind? She wondered what her obligations were. How might she be an honorable dead person? The rabbi was vague in his conclusion. "It's a simple quest. We must all do our best." *A bit like the Special Olympics' motto, "Be brave in the attempt."*

The sermon was having a different effect on Sugar's family. She could hear the low conversation her Aunt Barbara was having with her Aunt Selma. "Would you look at these gorgeous floral arrangements. Have you ever seen anything so stunning? Just stunning. Such a shame. They die."

"Such a shame."

Sugar laughed to herself thinking, *You know ladies, the flowers are already dead. They're just freshly dead. Wait till you're freshly dead. Let's see how good you look. Shame.*

The rest of the service was pretty standard stuff. Sarah did a fine job of her Torah reading, D. didn't make any indication he noticed Sugar wasn't called up for an *aliyah,* and Barbara and Selma discussed all things dead and dying. Before it was over, the synagogue president got up and said a few words about upcoming events, then introduced the treasurer to discuss the fund drive. A woman in an expensive cream-colored suit and wearing a helmet of dyed blond hair stepped up to the pulpit.

D. turned to Sugar and mouthed, "That's her."

Sugar mouthed back, "Irma La Douche?"

"Yes."

The woman began in an overly sincere tone coupled with over enunciation, "Thank you Seth. You all may know me. I'm Meryl Green. And my son's in Sarah's *bar mitzvah* class. Sarah, you did a lovely job. Everett certainly has a high bar. I'm here today to remind you all to donate items and services to our yearly sisterhood auction. We need to raise a lot more money if we want to enjoy all these nice things like new prayer books, trips to New York, and our wonderful line-up of guest speakers. We can't do it without you. And I'm going to throw a special challenge out to the Bernstein family. I bet there's something in that great big department store of yours you could put up for auction."

Sugar leaned to D. and whispered, "O.M.G. So douchey!"

"Told you."

"I hate her."

"Me, too."

Amy leaned back. "Me, three."

When the douchey woman left the *bema*, Rabbi Glass announced there would be light refreshments after the service in the foyer, followed by a lovely luncheon in the entertainment room. He then asked everyone to stand for the benediction. Sugar stood with her family and bowed her head. It felt like a lie. Like maybe she'd just burst into flames. *Let's see little Everett Green top that.*

But she didn't burst into flames. Instead, when it was over, she was engulfed in D.'s embrace. "I missed you so much. God, you're effing skinny. And pale."

"I missed you, too."

"At the risk of getting all Mom on you, take some bagels for the road."

"Really? You're going there?"

He smiled. "If you don't leave with bagels you'll leave with guilt."

They laughed at the shared joke that referred to a time after college when Sugar brought friends home from New York, and Faye forced bags of leftover bagels on everyone. She missed sharing this shorthand humor with her twin. It was nice to revisit it. Even briefly.

And then it began. Family members and friends filed up to congratulate the *bat mitzvah* girl and, as feared, tell Sugar how glad they were to see her but she was so pale. And how sorry they were for her loss. And how a single woman driving a van all across the world was completely *meshugganah*. And how great she looked, not that she looked bad when she was "fuller-figured." And how they had a friend or nephew she should meet. And how they didn't want to be pushy, but... None of it was a surprise.

After what seemed an eternity, she was able to break free and congratulate Sarah. "Hey kiddo."

"Hey, Aunt Sugar. You look great."

"So do you. More importantly, you were perfect up there. Fantastic job. Poised, confident. You should be proud." At the compliment, Sarah looked down. With a gentle hand, Sugar raised the girl's chin. "And you should always look a compliment in the eye."

From across the room a group of young girls called, "Sarah, come on." In a playful taunt, one added, "You can't keep Everett waiting."

Confiding to her aunt, Sarah said, "I'm so bad at this."

Turning Sarah in the direction of her friends, Sugar said, "Be steely." And sent the girl on her way.

Knowing she now had to brave the reception, with more suggestions for her romantic future, and multiple questions slash judgments about her plans stay on the road, and of course requests to see pictures from "that trip to Africa Faye told us so much about," all while dining on a meal of fake eating, Sugar told herself, *You, too. Be steely.*

44

THE RECEPTION'S THE BEST PART

The huge, square room was a swarm of family and friends talking and complaining about the food between bites. People milling and sitting and eating and visiting around the ten round banquet tables. Others were over-filling their plates from the two long buffet tables covered with heaping serving trays. Several teens were hovering by the large, lavish layer cake with white and lavender icing. The cake was presented on its own round table which was covered in flowers petals for an extra ta-da effect. It was just like every *bat mitzvah* she'd ever been to. Loud. Overwhelming. A wonderful cliché. *What did this cost my brother?* On the far side of the room, a D.J. was spinning music for a demographic that didn't exist: Teens who love the hit music of their parents' high-school years. Sarah was talking to a gangly young man while pre-teen girls watched and whispered. Sugar hoped that the young man was Everett, but tried to not listen in. All the sounds of the celebration were becoming a bit much. Sugar walked towards the back of the room, holding a glass of wine as a prop while she tried to ignore every low talker and loud eater.

The confrontations about the novelty of her new look had died down, and she was glad for that. Although she could spot the less-than-stealth pointing and hear the private speculations.

"Her mother said she went to help out in Africa when the boyfriend died. Something about a well."

"Well, schmell. I heard she had a breakdown and took off in a camper."

"I think she was in rehab."

"I heard the boyfriend was killed by some vagrant. Horrible."

"I thought it was a gang."

"She found a hell of a weight loss plan. Maybe someone should kill you so I could drop a few pounds."

"You'd have to kill me and every boyfriend you ever had to look like that."

"Ass."

The classic pop hit that had been playing ended, and was suddenly replaced by the familiar strains of "Hava Nagila." The response in the room was almost Pavlovian. Everyone stopped what they were doing and made a beeline for the dance floor. A circle of people holding hands quickly formed and began dancing to the left. Then a larger circle formed around the first one. This one moved to the right. Dancing the hora was an ingrained exercise for the jubilant hive. People broke from their circle just long enough to grab someone still sitting and pull them into the celebration. Spotting Aunt Selma pulling her Aunt Mirrah into the circle, Sugar thought back to Officer Goldberg, then got nostalgic. *How much do I miss being a part of this craziness?* Eventually, most of the inner circle joined the outer circle, leaving just the immediate family inside. Then, in the very center, the individual dancing began. Henry went first. Henry always went first. Folding his arms, he crouched down, then popped up onto his heels. The crowd cheered. After five such impressive moves, Amy's father joined Henry and did his best to impress. Then the two men hugged and spun. Faye and Amy's mother were up next. Hooking their arms, they reeled around rhythmically to more cheers. Next, two twenty-something cousins jumped in, adding some pop & lock to the mix. As more people took their moment in the spotlight, Sugar was approached by 70-year-old Uncle Lou. With a hand out, he said, "Get in here, Slim."

She put up her hands. "I'm just gonna watch."

"Life's too short to watch." She barely had time to put down her prop wine before being pulled into the circle of joy. And there she was, wondering if she was the first vampire in history to dance the hora. *I hope so.* The next thing she knew, D. was grabbing her hands and pulling her into the very middle. Sugar didn't fight it. *This will likely never happen again.* She and her twin hooked arms and reeled. Then crossing arms, they grabbed each other's hands and spun. They danced a dance that was pure delight and Sugar reveled in the moment. Then Sarah was pulled into the center by Faye, and Sugar and David retreated into the crowd. That was enough dancing for her. She backed out of the circle and watched her family, clapping to the music from the sidelines.

"You're not eating."

Sugar turned and looked down into her Grandmother Esther's tough but warm face. "I ate."

"Don't bullshit your grandmother. You pushed it around on your plate. What are you, six?"

"I'm not much of a bagels and lox gal."

"More bullshit. You love it."

"Wow. This is a tough room."

"Come on. Sit with me." They took seats at an empty table. "Now, talk to your old grandmother. Is it the boyfriend still?"

Sugar smiled at the sturdy little woman. "No. I just don't have an appetite, Grandmom."

"Tell me. Are you happy out there, alone, driving?"

"I'm working on it."

"Good. Because this life's too hard if you have no happiness." Esther got a hopeful twinkle in her eyes. "Do you have someone new, maybe?"

"No."

"Well don't wait too long. Look at me. When your grandfather died, I thought I should wait a respectable amount of time before, you know. But I waited too long. Now I'm too old for someone to give a tumble."

Trying to not laugh too hard, Sugar asked, "You're looking for a tumble?"

"Don't act so surprised. I wouldn't mind a little action. Ech. Maybe it's better this way. I'd probably break a hip. Still, alone sucks."

"Agreed."

Esther patted Sugar's knee and Sugar returned the favor. Then the two women sat quietly and watched their world dance in circles.

Then, a hand touched Sugar's shoulder. "Mind if I steal her from you?" She turned to see Rabbi Glass standing over her.

With a lifetime of sarcasm under her belt, Esther answered, "Do I mind? Of course, I do. But who am I to refuse a rabbi?"

Sugar got up and kissed the tough little woman she loved so much on the forehead. "Thanks for the advice. I love you."

Esther smiled. "You should."

Sugar looked over at her brother dancing with his wife and daughter. They were happy. After a moment, Rabbi Glass asked, "Ready?"

Nodding, she let the rabbi take her arm. They said nothing as he walked her to his study. *What does he want?* The room was small and filled to the ceiling with books, yet it didn't feel messy. Just close. He offered her a seat, and instead of sitting behind his desk, turned the seat next to hers so they'd be facing each other.

"I want to be clear." There was now the addition of gravity to the man's kind look.

"Okay."

"You shouldn't come back here."

"Okay."

"And by here, I don't mean this synagogue. It's too dangerous. I know how much David loves you. And I know how important it was to him that you came today, but this must be it. Do you understand?"

"I do." And she did. Sugar lowered her sunglasses and stood to leave.

"Can I...*may* I ask you a question before you go?"

"Sure."

"Are they all like you?"

She assumed he meant nice. "No."

"I thought not. May I ask another question?"

"First, I want a turn."

"Okay."

"How did you know?"

"Oh. Well, I wasn't sure. I studied mysticism in rabbinical school in Israel. Fascinating stuff. I guess I'm a bit of a geek. Or maybe just obsessive. When David told me what he'd found in your van, I wondered. I hope you don't mind. He shared your notes with me. He also told me about some of your new habits. I got suspicious, but then I felt silly. I'm a man of God. I love God. And, of course, we're all of us taught to think that it would be crazy. Stuff of movies, right? But then I saw you and I just knew."

"And you invited me in."

"I'm a sucker for a nice Jewish face."

"What's your other question?"

Rabbi Glass looked her straight in the eyes. "Have you ever killed anyone?"

In that moment, Sugar decided the truth was overrated. "No." He seemed willing to believe her. She said, "I suppose a Dutch goodbye is in order."

"May I walk you out?"

"You may."

Again, he offered her his arm. They walked silently down the hall. Sugar could feel what a good man this was. Just being in his presence was calming. Rabbi Glass gave her one last smile before opening the back door of the synagogue. The sun hadn't yet set, but the day had turned gray and overcast. Standing just outside the door was a familiar face.

"Hello, Sugar."

"You've got to be fucking kidding me."

45

PARTY IN THE BACK

There she was. Alexandria stood in a short black swing dress and cropped jacket with long, fur sleeves. Her face was slightly fuller taking away a bit of its hard edge and leaving her completely stunning. Behind her were the V Boys, looking as menacing as ever. Alex moved forward. Sugar and the rabbi stepped back as Alex stepped to the threshold. "I hope I'm not overdressed."

A wave of dread washed over Sugar. Dread and guilt. Always guilt. She'd brought this evil to her family's doorstep. Whatever happened next would be her fault.

"You couldn't be a good girl and stay dead."

The nice, young rabbi clearly realized that darkness was at his door. With as much grace as possible, he said, "Would you ladies mind taking this outside?"

Sugar looked at him with contrition. "I'm so sorry." She stepped into the parking lot and heard the synagogue door close behind her. Its hollow, metallic echo and click seemed to add a note of finality.

Now she was standing directly in front of Alex. "Why?"

Alex smirked. "I just can't quit you."

Fuck. Did she feel me say that to D.? "Try."

"You know, we thought we'd finished you back in the alley, didn't we boys?" The only move the six vampires made was to flex in place causing their furry sleeves to bristle. "We tucked you into that dumpster. Clayton even put Runt's greasy little head in your lap for company."

"Thank you, Clayton."

Without turning to her henchman, Alex said, "Clayton, the nice skank thanked you. Tell her she's welcome."

Clayton smirked and said, "You're welcome, skank."

"I guess you were thinking of me today. That was so sweet of you. So, here where are."

Realizing the email from Brooke had triggered all her memories of Alex and woke up their connection, she thought, *Well that's some shit timing*. She needed to think fast. That, or accept her fate. "At the risk of sounding unappreciative, why me? Why do you care so damn much about me?"

Alex stepped up, putting her arm around Sugar, then started walking her across the parking lot as if they were the dearest of friends strolling through the park. Then she laughed, "It was never about you."

Doing her best to maintain composure Sugar said, "That's interesting. Because from my point of view, it's been a lot about me. The stalking, the luring, the killing. That's a lot about me."

With no warning, Alex whipped Sugar through the air, sending her flying back towards the synagogue. She slammed into the side of the catering van and landed hard on her ass. With the wind knocked out of her, she looked up to see Alex flying towards her. Before she could get up on her own, Alex reached for her, lifting Sugar by the lapels. The sky grew darker. Menacing clouds started rolling in. "Don't contradict me." Again, Alex threw Sugar. This time she landed hard against a light pole. She felt her shoulder dislocate, then pop back into place. Looking at her arm, she saw the sleeve of her jacket was ripped at the elbow and thought, *V-Life is a fucking bitch on clothing*. In the brief moment it took her to mourn her new wardrobe, Alex bounded up. Once again, the force of She-vil's anger sent Sugar into the air and she came crashing down on the hood of a car. Dazed, she looked through the cracked windshield and saw a thick folder labeled "Everett's Bar Mitzvah." *This car must be Meryl Green's, aka Lady Douche. One for our side.*

The sky was now completely blanketed by storm clouds. The sound and feeling of thunder began rumbling through Sugar's body. She could hear Alex saying, "Gil, Vincent, bring her to me. I'm tired of picking up my own trash." Seeing two V-boys bound towards her fangs out, Sugar ripped the hood off Meryl's car and hurled it at them. Gil ducked but Vincent was a half tick too slow. The corner of the car hood caught his forehead as he leapt for her. But Sugar flew straight up and he missed. She landed on the roof of a sedan and Gil came running. Sugar stood her ground as he lunged for her. In a flash, she sidestepped, spun, and kicked, sending him crashing to the blacktop. She jumped down to get away but Vincent was suddenly right in front of her and wrapped his massive arms around her body. She couldn't move. *Fuck!* Gil got up and the V-boys each grabbed her by an arm. Although she knew it was futile, she kept struggling as they delivered her to Alex. It just seemed the thing to do.

"Fighting back. So cute."

Rain started falling as thunder rang out. Blood trickled from Sugar's forehead and cheek. Alex leaned in and licked it off. "What is that? Clayton, taste this."

Clayton obliged, sinking his teeth into Sugar's wrist. "I think it's weasel."

Alex took another lick then cocked her head. "I think you're right. Sugar, you can't sustain yourself on rodents."

Sugar felt her shoulder setting. "At the risk of coming off as contradictory, weasels aren't rodents. They're mustelids."

Alex laughed. "You are feisty. Is that what Curtis liked about you? I can't imagine what else it would be with your blah, blah pudgy little life." Hearing Alex say his name felt at least as bad as being thrown. "He never did tell me what the attraction was."

What is she saying? As much as Sugar tried to control her mind, she knew her face registered confusion. With a clap of thunder, the rain came down hard. "You *talked* to Curtis?"

Alex smirked. "There wasn't much talking. I did like that thing he did with his tongue. The cleavage licking thing. Did you like that, too? I was so looking forward to enjoying that little move for a few hundred years."

What the fuck? Is this more baiting or is Alex the one Curtis cheated with? Was she who he wanted to confess about that night? Her world spun as rain came down in sheets. If Gil and Vincent hadn't been holding her up, she might have fallen down.

"I see you finally caught up to the rest of the class. Good for you. See, it was never about you. You were just going to be a snack before the main course. But I had to dash off and, completely inept little fool that you are, you went and killed Curtis. I know it's not healthy, but I do hold a grudge." With that, Alex thrust her sharp nails into Sugar's torso. Blood ran out as her fingers dug into Sugar's gut. Shock led the way for intense pain. A bolt of lightning lit Alex's face, making her features a mask of pure hate. "You broke up my new family and I hated you for it. But I'm done hating you." She barked, "C.J., sword!"

Clayton produced a long blade from behind his back and handed it to Alex.

"This time, you're going to stay dead. You dim, stupid little thing."

Sugar knew this was it. She was about to have her head cut clean off. Picturing Runt's severed head rolling at her feet, Sugar suddenly thought, *No. I'm not dying like that. Not like that.* Did she have anything left? *Think. Be steely. It's not about you. It's about her. Use Alex's words. Use them now.* Sugar spoke through clenched teeth. "You're being redundant."

"Dying vampire says what?"

"You called me "dim" and "stupid." You should pick one. Dim *or* stupid. Saying both is redundant. It just reflects poorly on you. I know you had an education. Well, I guess that ended when your father was arrested and you were all forced to work for that nice Mr. Thornton. I am so sorry about that. I understand how painful that must have been."

It was Alex's turn to look like she'd taken a gut punch. She spoke loudly over the sound of the rain and thunder. "You understand nothing."

Trying to control her face, Sugar summoned as much sincerity as possible. "Maybe not. But my people were slaves long before you."

"Don't try to trauma bond with me."

But she did try. Looking into Alex's eyes, Sugar mentally traveled back to everything she'd learned about the dark side of New Orleans in the 1800s. Of the slave trade, and the living conditions. Of Stéphane Cromier lashed to a tree. Suddenly, she was seeing past Alex's eyes and into her thoughts. Seeing events through her young eyes. She could smell summer in the deep south. Behind tears, she saw Stéphane Cromier's body being untied from a tree and left in the mud. Her mother being held back. A gruff voice barking, "Leave him there!" She felt the love Alex had for her father. The man in the mud. It was agony.

Then she flashed to Thornton Jackson, the plantation owner, struggling with Alex's mother in a one-room shack. Him forcing himself on her. The sound of her mother yelling at Alex to leave, echoed over the scene. "Go, Alexandria! Just go. I'm fine." Sugar saw Alex's bare feet running over grass, even felt her trip, get up, and keep running. Sugar experienced Alex's deep self-hate for abandoning her mother.

She flashed to Alex's wrist being pulled behind the barn. Saw a large man with a wide-brimmed hat. Smelled his scent of old tobacco and sweat. Sugar heard Alex begging him to stop as she struggled. "Please, no." Another ragged man joined the first. Young Clayton ran up, but was slapped down. Then the second brute held Clayton to watch events play out. Sugar saw tears stream down Clayton's face. Heard him whimper as he tried to save his sister. But he was a scrawny boy. No match for the large man. In the end, both he and his sister lost their battles in shame.

Every scene on the Jackson plantation was more brutal and devastating than the last. Sugar's empathy for Alex's pain was profound. She felt it all, the fear, hate, shame, loss. Her heart ached for the entire Cromier family. All being punished for Stéphane daring to take the moral high road.

Then came a loud cry. "Stop!"

Sugar felt herself drop to the ground as Alex's piercing yell broke her visions.

Again, with her hands over her ears, as if to block out the sounds of her past, Alex screamed, "Stooooop!"

Sugar could feel that Alex knew she'd seen her. All of her. Not with hate but with empathy.

Suddenly, a bolt of lightning that seemed yards wide exploded into the ground directly between Sugar and Alex, throwing Sugar backwards. Multiple blinding flashes were followed by thunder claps, then chunks of asphalt flying through the air like shrapnel. Sugar put her face down and covered her head with her arms as fiery pieces, large and small, rained down around her.

Finally, the sounds of the lightning's fallout slowed and then stopped. Sugar lifted her head and opened her eyes. She was alone on the ground under the boiling gray-black sky, her blood on the asphalt, mixing with the pouring rain.

46

ON THE ROAD, AGAIN

The gritty, slow pulsing hip-hop strength of "No More Drama" was playing over the speakers as Sugar drove her van through the darkness. Mary J. Blige's declaration of independence was Sugar's anthem of the moment. She spoke the words to herself as Mary J. sang them.

"No more drama, right Kitten?"

Kitten was draped over Sugar's shoulder like a sports rag, enjoying a neck scratch from Sugar's free hand. "Meow-ah."

"That's right."

As the physical and metaphorical miles clicked off between herself and her brief return to the Land of Bernstein, Sugar tried making sense of it all. The realization that Curtis had been taken in by Alex only left her feeling more guilty. *He hadn't cheated, had he? He'd been powerless. Like I was. Seduced and manipulated.* She wanted to tell him that she understood and that she forgave him if he'd forgive her. *Hell, even if he didn't.*

The lights from a gas station made Sugar look at her fuel gauge. "We should top off."

Spotting the diesel pump, she rolled the van alongside and cut the engine.

As she stood filling the tank, a big pickup with fat tires and a rugged-looking camper in its bed pulled to the opposite pump. A woman climbed out. She was wearing a flat-brim trucker hat. On her arm was a tattoo of a man's face. Below it were two dates and the words, "Forever means forever."

Standing by her own pump, the woman asked, "What kinda' mileage you get on that thing?"

"Bout twelve. Thirteen on the flats."

"Figured. How hard is it on batteries?"

"Not too bad. I have a DieHard Platinum 900 for the cab, and a pair of AGM Intimidators in back for the house."

"Nice."

"In a pinch, I could power an electric chair."

The woman looked up at the sky. She seemed to be assessing nothing and everything. "You out here alone?"

"Yep."

"Me, too. Well, I'm bringin' Duke along for the ride." She pointed to her arm.

Sugar nodded her understanding. She thought, *I'm carrying Curtis, but in a different way. No tattoos for Jews.* Funny how that was still a rule for her, while feeding on a cast of Disney characters and kicking ass on the un-dead in synagogue parking lots was A-Okay.

As the woman headed towards the minimart, she called back, "You stay safe."

"You, too."

With the tank full and fuel paid for, Sugar climbed back into the cab and eased the van back onto the road. How much longer would she drive tonight? She was still pretty awake. *Why not just roll with it and see where it takes us?*

"Kitten, where'd you go?"

Kitten had no destination in mind either.

"Fine. Thoughts on music?"

She was ready for something upbeat. As she was making her selection, her phone rang in its new mount on the dash. *Shit.* Since the *bat mitzvah*, she'd gotten a flood of texts from D. and returned exactly none of them. Sugar let the phone ring until it went to voicemail. A moment later, it rang again. Again, she let it go to voice mail. When it rang the third time, she reached to turn off the volume. But her hand passed over the answer button and she heard D.'s voice.

"Thank you for not completely ghosting me."

"It was an accident."

"The ghosting or the not ghosting?"

She didn't answer.

"What happened to you? You disappeared, and that crazy storm. Power lines down. Lightning literally hit the parking lot. There was a huge chunk taken out of it. Just gone. And you were gone. We had no idea if you were okay. God, Shug. It's not fair."

"What's not fair?"

"The way you just take off. People care about you. We were having such a great day. I don't understand."

"I don't expect you to."

"You're not going to try?"

"No."

"Rabbi Glass said he spoke to you and that I should give you space. What did you tell him that you can't tell me?"

"We just talked about life and death."

D. took a long breath. "Sarah loved the new kitten you got her."

"I'm glad." She truly was. Sarah had given Kitten back to her. That was a classy move for a thirteen-year-old and it deserved to be rewarded. "What did she name her?"

"You'll love this. She's calling her Cat Head."

"I do love it."

"And in other news, after the reception, Meryl La Douche turned an ankle on the broken asphalt. She was running out to see what happened to her car. The lovely woman fell and cracked her two front teeth."

"Ouch!"

"She threatened to sue the synagogue. But being the treasurer, someone pointed out that she'd kind of be suing herself."

Sugar laughed at the irony.

"Shug, don't cut me out."

She didn't know what to say to him. To this person she'd loved since birth. *Mary Helen and Rabbi Glass were right. It was wrong to drag him through this.* Then she considered how strange it was, putting those two completely divergent people in the same thought. *What an utterly bizarre existence I'm leading.*

"Listen D., I need some time."

"You've had time."

"I need more."

"Promise you won't totally shut me out?"

She said nothing.

"Promise me."

After a long silence all she could think to say was, "I promise."

"We love you."

"I know."

He sighed. "What should I tell the folks?"

I have no damn idea. Then, looking at her pale hands on the steering wheel, she smiled. "Tell them, I'm going to Boca to work on my tan."

THANK YOU

Thank you so much for reading *V- Life*. If you enjoyed your travels with Sugar and her friends, please take a moment to leave a review on Amazon, Goodreads, or Bookbub. Reviews like yours are the best way to help new readers discover books by authors you like. Those reviews also help authors you like to continue writing.

To learn more about Honey Parker, and find out about other books she's written, visit www.HoneyParkerBooks.com

ACKNOWLEDGMENTS

To Kim & Dave for being the individuals that you are. And for every time a new *Careful-ish* book came out, for saying, "Yeah, but when is that vampire book coming out?"

To Matt for being the bestest brother and sharing a relationship with me that I now get to share with the world, mostly.

To Gwynne for a cat name that was equal parts obvious and perfect.

And to Blaine (AKA Mr. Parker) for being my guy, teammate, editor and foxhole buddy. There's no one else I'd drive across the country in an RV with. Let's not do it again soon. ;-)

Made in the USA
Columbia, SC
16 June 2024

36743568R00176